Rae leaned on the rust-stained sink—

/ NEVER KNOW WHAT HIT HER /

—to get a closer look. And suddenly a blast shook the floor beneath her feet. Something hard struck the back of Rae's head. She fell to her knees, white dots exploding in front of her eyes.

Something warm was dripping down her neck. *Blood,* she realized slowly. From her head. She had to get up. Had to get help.

She grabbed the sink with both hands—

/ THEY'LL THINK ANTHONY DID IT / DEFINITELY KILL RAE / GET OUT OF HERE /

—and pulled herself to her feet. She gripped the sink harder so she wouldn't fall again.

/ HOW DOES THIS THING / SHOULD HAVE BROUGHT / DEFINITELY KILL RAE /

That thought again. Why did she get that thought again? *Definitely kill Rae.* Had someone just tried to kill her?

MELINDA METZ

Echoes

Haunted

Trust

HARPER TEEN
An Imprint of HarperCollinsPublishers

HarperTeen is an imprint of HarperCollinsPublishers.

Echoes

alloyentertainment
Produced by Alloy Entertainment
151 West 26th Street, New York, NY 10001

Library of Congress catalog card number: 2010926758
ISBN: 978-0-06-196878-5

Typography by Andrea Vandergrift
10 11 12 13 14   LP/RRDH   10 9 8 7 6 5 4 3 2 1
❖
First HarperTeen paperback edition, 2010
Previously published as *Fingerprints #1: Gifted Touch*,
Fingerprints #2: Haunted, and *Fingerprints #3: Trust Me*.

For Jane Cooper, who helped me become a writer.
For Liesa Abrams—editor and inspiration.
For my cousin Amanda Lee Hafner.

CONTENTS

Echoes

$\mathcal{P}rologue$

R ae Voight studied her palette, only dimly aware of the sound of the bell ringing and everyone else in her art class bolting for the door.

"I have to head over to the cafeteria. I'm on guard duty today," Ms. O'Banyon told Rae as she paused by Rae's easel. "But stay and work if you want. I love what you're doing here."

Rae dipped her brush in the deep purple paint, not bothering to glance up. She was in the zone, that place where it felt like electricity was running through her veins instead of blood. Nobody should expect her to talk right now. Nobody should expect her to do anything but paint. She jammed the brush onto the palette again, really globbing on the pigment, its pungent scent filling her nose. And then her hand was slashing the brush across the canvas. Faster. Faster.

Done. Rae let out a long, shuddering breath as she took a step back from the easel and studied her work. She'd been intending to paint the words in the style of an old-fashioned storybook—ornate capital letters, with maybe even some gold around the edges. But when she was in the zone, her hand had a will of its own, and the words had come off the brush in a psycho-killer scrawl. *Once upon a time, when we all lived in the forest and no one lived anywhere else . . .*

At least the writing matches the rest of the painting, she thought. When Ms. O'Banyon had assigned the class to do a landscape, Rae had planned to do a kind of fairy-tale forest, with beautiful flowers of improbable sizes.

The flowers were still there, but something was off about them, as if when they had grown so large and lush, they had also mutated in other ways, becoming sentient and greedy for even more size and power. One of the flowers had a dove trapped deep in the hollow of its dewy petals. Another's roots were wrapped around what appeared to be the slender leg of a fawn.

"Hey, Rae, do you really think it's a good idea to leave Marcus alone in the cafeteria?" a familiar voice called from the open door of the art room. "I mean, it *is* Marcus Salkow we're talking about."

Rae quickly threw a sheet over her canvas and turned to face Leah Dessin. Leah was her best friend, but Rae didn't especially want her to see the painting. Leah would just think it was weird, and weird was something Leah had a low tolerance for.

Rae just shrugged. She dunked her paint-smeared brush into a coffee can filled with water, then started unbuttoning the big white shirt she'd snagged from her dad—that she always wore when she was painting.

"Oh, right. Now that you've grown breasts—unlike me— no guy can resist you. I forgot," Leah teased.

4

"There's nothing wrong with your breasts," Rae said, hoping to distract Leah, who had the capacity to discuss her breasts and other parts of herself—the frustrating straightness of her black hair, the unattractiveness of the line that ran from her waist to her hips—for multiple hours at a stretch. Which was pretty annoying sometimes, considering that for all Leah's complaints, she was gorgeous. Her face was all angles—high cheekbones, pointy chin, perfectly straight nose.

Leah didn't take the bait this time. Instead, she whipped off the sheet from the easel and studied Rae's painting. Rae felt her stomach shrivel into the size of an aspirin. Paintings like this . . . They made Rae feel like there was another person living inside her. A person who was really and truly her mother's daughter.

Rae grabbed the sheet back from Leah and covered the canvas again. "Come on. I'm starving." She steered Leah out of the art room, taking half a second to jam her painting shirt on one of the hooks by the door, then led the way down the hall.

"What is Kayla Carr wearing?" Leah said, her voice low. She jerked her chin toward Kayla as she disappeared into the girls' bathroom. Kayla must have been going for the bohemian look, but somehow she'd ended up as grandma instead.

Rae giggled, then felt a little spurt of guilt. *But come on,* she told herself. Rae hardly lived for fashion. She'd be just as happy—happier, actually—in paint-stained sweats with her wildly curly auburn hair in a ponytail. But she was smart enough to know that that wouldn't cut it. In the critical summer between public school sixth grade and private school seventh grade, she'd done the makeover thing. First the basics—the clothes, the hair, the makeup. Then the name—she'd started out the seventh grade as Rae, not Rachel, because Rae was more distinctive and because there was just something cool about a girl whose name sounds like a guy's.

She and Leah had become friends pretty much on day one of being Rae. Leah was a new girl that year. Rae liked that Leah didn't even have a flicker of memory of the somewhat dorky Rachel, the girl who'd drawn unicorns on the top of every single assignment she'd turned in. Unicorns with *names* printed under them—names like Flirtalina and Fabulousa.

"So tell me about last night," Leah said as they started past the mural that ran from the main office to the cafeteria. "You and Marcus disappeared from the party for quite some time, young lady." Leah nudged Rae with her elbow.

"Leah, there's this thing called privacy," Rae answered.

Leah flipped her chin-length, sleek black hair away from her face. "Just tell me one thing—did all your clothes remain on?"

"Yes. And that's all I'm saying," Rae responded, her mind flooding with memories of last night with Marcus. He had slid his hand under her shirt, and she'd felt like—

"Was there something you wanted to get out of there? Or did you just want to admire the form and line of your locker?" Leah asked, pulling Rae out of her thoughts.

A hot flush shot up the back of Rae's neck. She reached for her lock, and her binder fell to the floor. When she bent down to snag the binder, her knees, which had become all quivery during her little mental visit with Marcus, didn't feel

6

like they'd support her, so she pressed one hand against Amy Shapiro's locker for balance.

/Please, please, please, let me pass the physics test/

Rae jerked backward. Why had she thought that? She didn't even take physics.

"Are you okay?" Leah asked, a hint of impatience in her voice.

"Yeah. Fine." Rae grabbed the binder, shoved herself to her feet, and dialed in her locker's combination. "I just have to get Jackie's French book. I borrowed it ... ." She grabbed the textbook off the little shelf near the top.

/Rae thinks she's so special/

"What?" Rae demanded.

"What, what?" Leah asked, arching one of her perfectly plucked eyebrows.

"Nothing. I just . . ." Rae let her words trail off. What was she going to say—*I just thought I heard someone saying something très snotty about me, then realized it was me thinking something très snotty about myself?* She slammed her locker shut and snapped the lock closed. "Never mind. Let's go." Rae strode toward the cafeteria. She used both hands to push her way through the heavy double doors.

/If Andreas says even one thing/*can see that zit from*/hope it's pepperoni/at four-thirty I have to/

A whirlpool of emotion ripped through her—anger, anxiety, anticipation—and Rae's heart fluttered in her chest. She was a vegetarian. There's no way she'd be hoping for

7

pepperoni. And the Andreas thing . . . Rae didn't even know anyone named Andreas. Where were these bizarre thoughts—thoughts and *feelings*—coming from?

She tried to stop the answer from forming, but it slammed into her brain so hard, she could feel the impact all the way through her body.

Was this how it had started for her mom? With thoughts and emotions that didn't feel like her own? Was Rae going to end up in a mental institution, too? Was she going to die there the way her mother—

"Are you waiting for a round of applause from the masses or what?" Leah asked, giving Rae a little push.

Rae realized she had frozen in place, with one hand pressed against her chest, as if that would slow down her heart. Trying to make it look casual, she dropped her arm back to her side. "Well, I did think everyone needed a chance to admire my new boots," Rae answered, relieved when her voice came out sounding steady.

She stuck out her foot and turned her ankle back and forth, showing off the softly worn leather. *See, you're fine,* she told herself. *If you're going crazy, you can't cover up that you're going crazy. So you're not going crazy.*

Rae led the way across the cafeteria to the frozen yogurt machine and grabbed one of the jumbo cups. She pulled down on the silver handle.

/ It'll be okay if I skip dinner and get on the Elliptical the second /

Little dots of light exploded in front of her eyes. Rae

8

squeezed them shut. "Okay, stop it, just stop it. I've never even been on an Elliptical machine."

"What?" Leah asked as she reached for one of the cheap plastic spoons.

Rae kept her eyes shut a second longer, then forced them open. She took in all the ordinary sights of the cafeteria: the tall windows overlooking the manicured lawns; the banners made by the cheerleading squad; the same groups of people sitting at the same polished wooden tables, chewing, talking, laughing, harassing, studying, flirting. *Everything is normal,* Rae told herself. *You're normal.*

"I didn't hear you," Leah said, shooting a sharp look at Rae.

"I was . . . um, just talking to myself," Rae answered.

"You're losing it," Leah told her, carefully turning her cup in a circle as she made a swirling mountain of fro-yo.

"I *am* losing it," Rae agreed quickly, forcing her lips into a smile. Leah wasn't trying to be sadistic. She didn't know about Rae's mom. Rae didn't plan to let anybody have that kind of ammunition against her. Ever.

Leah grabbed a handful of napkins and headed toward their usual table. Rae plucked a plastic spoon out of the metal container and followed her, bracing for the next moment of . . . She didn't allow herself to name the phenomenon she'd been experiencing.

But whatever it was, it didn't come. As she followed Leah over to the usual table, all her brain murmurings felt . . . organic. Just regular Rae stuff.

It's over, she told herself. She focused her gaze on Marcus, already sitting at the table with the rest of their friends. She always liked watching him when he didn't know she was looking. It made her want to grab a brush and try and capture the sprawl of his long legs, all the shades—from wheat to cream—of his close-cut blond hair, the perfect shape of his mouth, everything.

As if he could feel her staring at him, Marcus looked up, his green eyes locking on to her immediately. He snagged her by the waist and pulled her down on the bench next to him. Rae gave him a fast kiss. Their lips touched for only a second, but it brought back every sensation she'd felt lying on that bed at the party last night, giving her a full-body blush.

"My parents have this cocktail thing after work, so the house is all ours tonight," Marcus murmured in her ear. His breath was hot against her earlobe as he waited for her response.

Rae wanted more of what she'd felt last night. But *more* and *everything* weren't the same.

"Actually my dad needs me home tonight," Rae lied. "Some kind of faculty get-together at our house, and he wants me to play hostess. You know, an end-of-spring-semester thing."

Marcus nodded, but his smile faded and he glanced away, turning his attention back to his lunch. He was probably wondering how he'd gotten stuck with the immature girlfriend who couldn't just relax and—

"Hey, Do Rae Mi, did you remember my French book?" Jackie asked from across the table.

"Got it right here." Rae dug around in her fringed hobo until her fingers found the spine.

/Rae thinks she's so special/

The thought brought a bitter taste into her mouth. A bile and fro-yo blend. That was *not* her own thought about herself. This time she was sure. It had come from someplace else. But—

"Well?" Jackie prompted, her palm outstretched.

"Oh, yeah." Rae realized she'd been in some kind of suspended animation, staring down at the book. Jackie snatched it from her hands, her dark green nail polish glistening under the fluorescent lights.

Just hang on, Rae coached herself. *Ride it out.*

Rae forced herself to eat a little yogurt. That's what normal people did at lunch. They ate.

"Pass the salt, Rae?" Vince Deitz asked from the other side of Leah. He smiled at her, exposing his chipped front tooth.

"Not a problem," Rae answered. She could spoon yogurt into her mouth. She could pass the salt. No problem at all. She grabbed the yellow plastic shaker and—

/Know I got a D on that Spanish quiz, maybe even an F/

—shoved it into Vince's hand. Her eyelid began to twitch. She rubbed her eye fiercely until it started to water. She could feel her mascara beginning to streak. But the lid kept on twitching. And a tiny nerve on one side of her nose was twitching, too. And one in her lower lip.

Take a few more spoonfuls of the yogurt, Rae told herself, *then calmly stand up and go to the bathroom. You can go home if you have to, but for now, just hang on.*

"Are you crying?" Jackie asked, her caramel-colored eyes wide.

"Of course not," Rae snapped, even though she probably had mascara down to her chin by now. "I have something in my eye." Something like her own stupid fingers. Why had she rubbed so hard? Rae reached out and grabbed the metal napkin holder.

/My mother knows that I/

"My mother doesn't know anything!" Rae blurted out. "My mother's dead!"

The table went silent.

Rae's heart was pounding so hard, the sound filled her ears. The little twitches in her eyelid, nose, and lip began jerking in time to its thundering. "Sorry. Um, I just . . . Sorry." What else could she say?

"That's okay," Leah reassured her. "Not a problem."

Rae yanked a napkin free and started dabbing her weeping eye. But that didn't stop her from seeing that everyone at her table—everyone who mattered at school—was still staring. And Leah, for all her "not a problem," looked faintly repulsed. Is this how people had looked at her mother when she'd started acting strange?

Her breath started to come in short pants, as if her lungs were shrinking, as if her whole chest were shrinking.

Rae shoved herself to her feet. The napkin holder clattered to the floor. Automatically she climbed over the bench, bent down, and picked it up.

/My mother's going to kill me if/

"Why do you keep talking about my mother?" Rae shrieked. Now everyone in the cafeteria was staring. Whispering.

A nerve in the back of her hand began to twitch in time with the others. Rae gave a howl of frustration and hurled the napkin holder away from her. It bounced twice on the linoleum floor. No one glanced at it. They kept staring at her.

Marcus sprang up and started toward her. "No!" Rae screamed. "Stay back. I don't know what I'll do if you come closer." She tried to pull in a breath, but her ribs felt like they'd wrapped her lungs in a tight, tiny cage. And her heart—how could it beat so hard without exploding?

"Rae, it's just me. It's Marcus," he said. He took one hesitant step closer.

"Get back!" Rae screeched. She saw Ms. O'Banyon running toward her. "I don't want to hurt anyone."

The way her mother had.

Marcus obediently backed up. Ms. O'Banyon stopped where she was, one hand stretched out toward Rae. Everyone else just stared. Because they could see it. They could see the truth.

They knew Rae had gone insane.

Chapter 1

"Is there anything you need for school tomorrow?" Rae's father asked as they drove down the freeway at precisely fifty-five miles an hour. "We could swing by the mall after your, uh, meeting. I'd be willing to hand over my AmEx for, say, twelve or thirteen minutes." He took his eyes off the road long enough to give her something that she knew was supposed to be a smile, although it came out more like a grimace. Too many teeth.

Rae knew that was her cue to launch into a long and elaborate whine-protest that would convince him just how key the right clothes and accessories were to having the kind of school year she'd want to look back on fondly when she was his age.

"What do you say?" her father prodded. He rubbed the little mole on his right cheek, the way he always did when he was stressed.

"I'm good," Rae answered. She was sure there were some things she *should* want for the start of her junior year. A new shirt or a tote bag or something. But she had no idea what the things she should want were. It seemed safer to stick to the stuff she already had. She could trust that Rae, the pre-freak-out

Rae. But the only-days-out-of-the-hospital Rae—that was not someone who could be trusted with something as delicate as picking out appropriate clothes.

Her father's smile-grimace faded. "Well, if you change your mind . . ." He let his words trail off and studied the freeway stretching out in front of them with unnecessary intensity. Rae stared through the windshield, too, letting the waves of heat rising off the asphalt and the white lines flying past mesmerize her. Ever since the freak-out, her happiest times were moments like this—when she could blank out, her mind quiet. Which was pretty pathetic. She could just imagine her first day of school.

Hey, Rae, what did you do this summer?

Oh, I had a nice, long rest in a kind of . . . resort. I took a lot of baths, which was great because in the tub, my mind actually seems to work fairly non-psychotically. What about you?

And that was *if* anybody was even willing to talk to her at all after her meltdown in the cafeteria last spring. She'd seen Marcus only once since that day—he hated hospitals—although he'd sent a couple of sweet cards. Leah had actually shown up at the hospital a couple of times—with a few other friends in tow—but she'd been better about sending an endless stream of little gifts. Not that Rae could blame her. A day at the hospital wasn't exactly the definition of summer fun.

"Pass me my sunglasses?" Rae's dad asked.

"Sure. You should always wear them when you're driving. It's dangerous when it's this bright," Rae answered, doing her look-how-normal-I-am routine. She opened the glove box.

/What am I supposed to say to her?/

The thought was followed by a vicious wrench in the muscles between Rae's shoulder blades. A tiny gasp of pain escaped her lips.

"Are you all right?" her father demanded, his voice filled with needles of anxiety.

"Yeah, fine. Just banged my elbow on the door handle," Rae answered quickly. She'd managed to convince her dad and her doctor that the strange thoughts that had started slamming into her brain without warning were gone. And she wasn't going to give either of them any reason to suspect that she'd been lying; otherwise she'd be on the express train back to squirrel city.

"Sunglasses?" her father reminded her, sounding a little more normal. Neither of them sounded completely normal anymore.

Rae snatched up her dad's dorky, geek-professor-attempting-coolness mirrored shades—

/a bald spot/

—and handed them to him, absentmindedly stroking the top of her head. She didn't try to figure out where the thought about a bald spot had come from. She'd given up on searching for explanations months ago and accepted the fact that this was her life now. All she could do was deal—and try not to foam unattractively at the mouth.

Rae focused her attention back on the heat waves and the white lines. But just as she was starting to reenter the blank

16

zone, her dad changed lanes and moved onto the off-ramp. Three turns later the sign for the Oakvale Institute came into view. It was more low security than the hospital. No fences or anything. But it probably still had that smell, that bargain-brand-disinfectant smell.

"I don't know why I even have to do this. I'm fine. Dr. Warriner said I was fine," Rae said.

"And you *are* fine," her father answered, his voice a little too loud. "You're doing great. The group sessions are just to help you keep on track, especially with school starting tomorrow." He pulled into the institute's parking lot and maneuvered the old Chevette into a spot in front of the main doors. "I'll be right here when you're done," he said, giving her arm an awkward pat.

Rae noticed he'd been touching her more since she got out of the hospital. She wondered if that was something Dr. Warriner had encouraged him to do in one of their private sessions. Rae wished her dad wouldn't bother. They'd never been touchy with each other, and now it just felt weird.

"See you in a bit," Rae answered. She climbed out of the car—

/What's the point?/

—and started to shut the door. Her father reached over and held it open.

"I was thinking . . . or wondering . . ." His blue eyes looked hopefully up at her. "Maybe afterward we could stop off at Best Buy and pick up a DVR." He sounded like he was offering a five-year-old an ice-cream cone after a trip to the doctor.

But this was big. Her father had resisted all her previous attempts to get a DVR. Since he never watched TV, he had no favorite shows to record. And now . . . Rae felt a lump form in her throat.

"TV is the opiate of the masses," Rae said, quoting him. "If I had it my way, we wouldn't have a TV in this house at all." She turned and headed for the main doors before he could answer. Six months ago she'd have been ecstatic over the chance to instantly watch, say, the Blair and Chuck limo kiss, again and again. But now . . . It would just be another sign of how much things had changed.

She hesitated when she reached the doors. *Going to group will show that you're committed to your mental health.* Rae snorted. Maybe *committed* wasn't exactly the word to use. She shoved open the doors—

/WHAT A WASTE/*sweater too tight*/ Project Runway on tonight/

—and stepped inside, letting the hum in her head die out. Sometimes her bizarro thoughts came with this staticky hum. It was like having an electronic beehive in her brain or something. Other times the bizarro thoughts were loud and clear—no bees. Rae wasn't sure which was worse.

The middle-aged woman behind the reception desk smiled. Rae smiled back, since that was what normal people did, and she wanted to look ultranormal. "I'm here for Ms. Abramson's group," she said.

"Down the hall, take the first left, then second room on

18

the right," the woman answered.

Rae nodded, then checked the clock over the woman's head. She had ten minutes, and she did *not* want to spend them sitting around with the losers. She spotted a bathroom as she started down the hall. She stepped inside just as a girl with extremely short brown hair stepped out. Fashion choice? Or a grown-out hack job? Rae wondered. A couple of girls at the hospital had taken scissors to their heads as part of the meltdowns that landed them there.

She wandered over to the closest sink and stared into the mirror over it. This place was definitely lower security than the hospital. No way would they have allowed a patient in the same room with anything as potentially dangerous as a mirror, which could be broken to create knife-sharp blades.

"Looking good. Looking normal," she told herself. "Except for the talking-to-yourself thing." She washed her hands and dried them carefully with one of the rough brown paper towels.

Rae strolled over to the bathroom door and opened it.

/**HATE THIS PLACE**/

She snorted at the staticky thought. It wasn't hers, but it might as well have been. This was definitely a place that was easy to hate. And it did have that cheap disinfectant smell. She headed down the hall, trying to ignore the way her stomach was folding itself into some kind of origami creature. Way too quickly she reached the door of the room where her group

19

therapy was going to be held. She walked through the open door without hesitation, head up, making eye contact with anyone she noticed looking at her, smiling back at the losers who bothered to smile.

Possibly I shouldn't call them losers, considering, Rae thought. *Maybe they're just like me, coming here because somebody said they had to, trying to get back to some semblance of regular life.*

She sat down in the closest empty chair—gray metal folding, of course—in the ragged circle, shooting a glance at the guy next to her. *Now, I'm sorry, but he is a loser,* she thought. *A Jonas Brothers T-shirt, and he has to be, like, sixteen or seventeen. Please.*

"Looks like the gang's all here," a thirtyish woman with black hair in dozens of tiny braids said as she strode into the room and shut the door behind her. "Except Jesse Beven. Know where he is?" she asked the Jo Bros fan.

The guy, helpfully, shrugged.

The woman shook her head as she turned to Rae. "I'm Ms. Abramson. And you're Rachel Voight."

"Rae," she corrected automatically.

"Okay, Rae," Ms. Abramson answered. "You'll get a chance to meet everyone in a little while when we go around the circle. But I want to start with an exercise."

There were a few muffled groans. Ms. Abramson ignored them. She turned her attention to the door, which was opening very slowly. "Glad you could make it," she said as a gawky redheaded kid who looked about thirteen sidled through the door, clearly hoping not to be noticed. Rae assumed he was the missing Jesse. He muttered an apology in Ms. Abramson's direction and took the seat on the other side of the Jonas Brothers guy.

"I want you to pair up," Ms. Abramson said as she headed toward the other side of the room. "And not the usual pairs, please. Anthony, you and Rae work together. Jesse, you team up with Matt. Nobody with anybody you've paired up with in the last three sessions. Are you listening, David and Cynda?" she asked a guy and girl across the circle from Rae. The two practically had *we're-a-couple* tattooed across their foreheads.

Ms. Abramson paused by the cupboards under the row of windows that lined one side of the room. She pulled out drawing pads and crayons, then began handing them out to everyone in the circle to more groans, not so muffled this time.

Jo Bro—Anthony, Rae supposed she should start calling him—reluctantly hauled his chair around to face her. She scooted hers toward him, then shoved it back a little so their knees wouldn't touch.

"What I want you to do is draw a family portrait," Ms. Abramson continued. She reached Rae and Anthony, handed them supplies, and kept working her way from pair to pair. "And then draw a significant object in each person's hand— something important to that person. And no, Rebecca, I won't give you an example," she said to the hack-head girl

21

Rae'd seen earlier. "There are no rights or wrongs. Just go with your gut instinct."

Cake assignment, Rae thought. She selected a couple of crayons—

/***LIKE BLUE***/blister driving me nuts/call Dan/

—ignoring the flicker of random thoughts and the buzz underneath them, then handed the box to Anthony. He clearly had no interest in talking to her, which was a bonus. Rae decided to do her father first. High forehead. Nose with a bump. Bad posture. Thinning blond hair. She'd drawn him lots of times, and the sketch came out fast and easy. Choosing his significant object was a no-brainer—a book for the English prof.

Now me, she thought. That was harder. She wasn't into self-portraits. *You're not doing this for Ms. O'Banyon,* she reminded herself. *Just get something down on paper, be the good little group therapy girl so you'll be able to stop coming sometime this century.*

Rae started to draw. Curly, reddish brown hair—lots and lots of it. Nose with a bump, like her dad's. Stubby eyelashes. Blue eyes.

Anthony reached over and took the brown crayon out of her fingers without asking. Rae ignored him, switched to another crayon, and kept drawing, so caught up, she hardly registered the alien thoughts. Mouth like Angelina Jolie's. *Like Mom*—the unwelcome thought flashed through her brain uninvited. Basic bod. And she was done. Now all she needed was her significant object, which was as much of a no-brainer as her dad's—a paintbrush.

"Can I get that brown crayon back, please?" she asked Anthony. "Just when you're done. Take your time," she said with pointed politeness. He immediately thrust the crayon at her.

/AM I LIKE HIM?/

A wave of yearning swept through Rae, and she felt the sting of tears in her eyes. She blinked rapidly. No way was she going to have a crying jag in her first day in group. *It's just one of your brain hiccups,* she told herself. *That feeling has nothing to do with you.* She forced herself to return to her drawing. The handle of the paintbrush came out too long. It ended up as a root wrapped around Rae's ankle in the sketch.

"Just two or three more minutes, gang," Ms. Abramson called.

Damn. She didn't have time to start over. "Can I have the red?" she asked Anthony, then grabbed it without waiting for an answer.

/NICE HAIR/

Somehow that thought felt a little like the am-I-like-him thought. They felt like they could almost be from the same person. *They're not from anyone,* she reminded herself. The thoughts were in her own head.

Rae drew a big red flower in the hand of the sketch Rae so the root would be coming from somewhere.

"Okay, time's up," Ms. Abramson announced. "Now, I want you to really study your drawings while you show them to your partner. Who are you standing next to? How close are you? Is one person in the drawing much smaller or larger than the others? What about the significant objects—what do they say about each person?" She gave two sharp claps. "So, talk among yourselves. Partners, don't be afraid to ask questions and make observations. But as always, no personal attacks."

Oh, great, Rae thought. *Why don't I just install a zipper from my throat to my belly button?* She shot an annoyed glance at Anthony. "You first, Jo Bro."

A dark flush crept up Anthony's throat, but he obediently held up his drawing. "This is me. And this is my mommy. And this is my daddy," he began in a singsong voice, pointing to one stick figure after the other as he spoke. "This is my half brother Danny. This is my half brother Carl. This is my half sister, Anna. This is my stepbrother, Zack. This is my stepfather, Tom. This is my previous stepfather, Rob. There are a bunch of significant boyfriends who were briefly family, or at least who lived with us, but I ran out of room."

"That's . . . a lot of people," Rae said.

"I'm so glad Abramson made us partners," Anthony answered with mock enthusiasm. He shoved his hand through his sandy brown hair and shot a glance over his shoulder, probably to make sure that said Abramson wasn't in earshot. "I can see that with your help, I'm really going to learn a lot about myself. When I leave here, I'll probably cry a little and then go do some work in a soup kitchen because I'll have realized there are worse-off people than me. And it will all be thanks to you."

"What's your problem?" Rae demanded. "All I did was make a simple observation—That's. A. Lot. Of. People." A loser with attitude. Could there be a worse combination?

"Your turn," Anthony told her, his dark brown eyes expressionless.

Rae shook her head. "Uh-uh. Not so fast. I get to ask questions." She studied his drawing. Make that his sticks with big circle heads. They all looked almost alike. But she was asking something. No way was she letting him off the hook. She jabbed her finger at the tallest stick figure. "This one is about twice as tall as the other ones. Which one is that again?"

"My dad," Anthony answered.

"Is he actually that tall?" Rae asked. "I mean, I know he's not a mutant who's double the size of other people. But is he a lot taller than average?"

Anthony jerked his chin toward Rae's drawing. "Why is that flower so huge?" he countered. He pointed at the red blossom. "It's bigger than the girl's head."

Rae automatically glanced at the flower and wished she hadn't. It was like the ones she'd painted in her landscape for art class that time—somehow more predator than plant.

"When it's your turn, you can ask what you want," Rae told him, forcing her eyes back to Anthony's drawing. "Now, talk. Dad. How tall?"

Anthony didn't answer. The muscles in his jaw were all tight, like he was grinding his teeth.

"So I'm guessing height is a sensitive subject," Rae said. "Does it make you feel inadequate that Dad is tall while you're . . . not?" Because Anthony was definitely short, probably shorter than most guys in his class. He made up for it in muscle, though. Rae couldn't help noticing that.

"Rae, Anthony, how are we doing over here?" Ms. Abramson called before he could answer. She came over and put one hand on Rae's shoulder and one on Anthony's.

Anthony tightened his grip on his drawing until the edges got crumpled. Rae considered repeating her significance-of-the-size question in front of Ms. Abramson. That would force Anthony to cough up some kind of answer, possibly winning some good-observation-Rae brownie points for herself. But her eyes were drawn to Anthony's clenched fingers, the knuckles white with strain, and she decided to give the guy a break.

"It's going well," Rae answered. "Anthony was just telling me that there were more people—boyfriends of his mom— that he should have drawn."

Ms. Abramson nodded. "Good sharing, Anthony." She gave Rae's shoulder a squeeze, then wandered off.

Anthony loosened his grip on his drawing, and it fluttered to the floor. Rae picked it up—

/AM I LIKE HIM?/

—and handed it over. The reception on that thought was good, she thought absently. Sometimes the thoughts were blurry, barely even clear words. Sometimes they were practically static—like the noise that came through on an out-of-reach radio station. But this one came through distinctly.

26

"So, which of these guys do you think you might be like?" she blurted out.

Wait—what had she just done? Am-I-like-him was a head thing, not an out-loud thing. *You can't do that, Rae,* she lectured herself. *If you do, if anyone figures out you're still having your brain seizures, it's welcome back to the funny farm.*

Anthony shot a glance at Rae. Where the hell had she come up with that question? It's what he'd been thinking about his dad when he drew the picture. He'd never met the guy—well, not that he remembered, at least. He'd been less than a year old when his dad bolted. But he'd always wondered if they had stuff in common. Which might be cool since he definitely didn't want to be like anybody else in his family.

"I'm not like any of them," Anthony mumbled. He wished they weren't sitting so close together. Every breath smelled like oranges. No, grapefruit. Who wore grapefruit perfume? It made the back of his throat itch.

"What about your dad?" Rae leaned forward and studied the drawing. "Don't you ever wonder if you're like him? I mean, I'm always wondering if I'm like my mom." Rae suddenly grabbed a crayon and began adding more petals to her freaky flower.

"He was a sperm donor. That's it," Anthony answered. He definitely wasn't going to spill his guts about how much he wished he could meet him and then go live with him and— Anthony didn't allow himself to finish the thought. Way too pathetic. Besides, Rae wasn't even listening. She'd asked him a question, then started coloring away without even bothering to pretend she wanted to hear the answer.

"Okay. Flower. What's the deal?" he asked. He reached over and snatched the crayon out of her hand so she'd have to pay attention.

"I don't believe that you think of him as just a sperm donor," Rae said, finally meeting his gaze with her blue eyes.

"Good for you. Now I'm asking the questions," Anthony told her. "That flower is not normal. It's like out of a sci-fi movie. And is it attacking her—I mean you—or what?"

"It's just a flower," Rae answered. She folded her drawing in half so he couldn't see it.

"That's crap," Anthony shot back.

Rae leaned closer to Anthony, getting right in his face. The grapefruit scent filled his lungs, grapefruit mixed with shampoo, and a kind of warm-skin smell. "And sperm donor isn't?" she challenged.

He didn't answer. She didn't say another word. And neither of them blinked. *Fine,* he thought. *She wants to have a stare down. I can handle it.*

Before either of them won the battle of the eyeballs, Abramson gave a couple of claps. "Good work, everyone," she called from the center of the circle. "I want all of you to bring your drawings home. Take a little time before next group to study them. You may be surprised about what insights occur to you."

Rae jerked her chair back around so it was facing Abramson. Anthony hauled his around, too, the metal chair legs squealing on the floor, then folded up his drawing and jammed it into one of the front pockets of his jeans.

"It's time to go around the circle and hear how everyone's doing," Abramson announced. "Let's start with David today."

Anthony obediently looked across the circle at David, but his thoughts kept circling around to his dad, thanks to Rae and her stupid questions.

A couple of years ago he'd actually tried to find his father. At least he'd asked his mom some stuff. She'd started getting all teary, so he'd backed off and tried doing some Internet searches instead. But he didn't have enough info to track him down.

"Anthony, do you have some feedback for Julia?" Ms. Abramson asked, snapping him out of his thoughts.

She always knew when he wasn't paying attention. It was like she had radar or something.

"I think Julia needs to treat herself as well as she treats other people," Anthony answered, parroting what Abramson said to Julia practically every other session.

"I agree," Ms. Abramson said.

Anthony suppressed a smile. *Got away with it. Yeah.*

"Your turn, Rae," Ms. Abramson went on. "Just tell us how your life is going, what's coming up for you, anything you feel like sharing."

Anthony turned toward Rae. She sat up a little straighter

and folded her hands in her lap. He couldn't help snorting at the good-little-girl pose, which earned him a head shake from Abramson.

"Well, I've only been out of the hospital a few days," Rae said. "I start back to school tomorrow. I'm looking forward to it. I think it will really help me to get back in my old routine and see my friends and everything."

Anthony managed not to snort again.

"Any other feelings about going back?" Ms. Abramson asked.

She knows it's crap, too, Anthony thought.

Rae used both hands to push her curly hair away from her face. She raised her eyes to the ceiling, as if she were looking for an answer graffitied up there. "I'm a little nervous, I guess," she said finally. "But I know I'm ready."

Total bullshit. Anthony waited for Abramson to call her on it. But she didn't.

"We'll all be eager to hear how your first couple of days went at our next session," Ms. Abramson said. "That's it for today. I'm sorry we didn't get around the whole circle. We'll make sure we get to everybody we missed next time. And if anybody needs me, feel free to call." She handed Rae a card. "That has my home number on it and the number here. It's never too early or too late."

Anthony didn't even get the chance to stand up before Jesse was in front of him. "Got a new skateboard. It's by Element. Want to check it out? It's at reception. They wouldn't let me bring it in."

30

I have three little brothers. I really don't need another one, Anthony thought. But Jesse was okay.

"Sure," he said. "I've just got to take a leak. I'll meet you up there." He grabbed his jean jacket and headed for the door. When he stepped into the hall, he saw Rae up ahead of him.

"Hey, new meat," he called out, without exactly deciding to do it first.

She turned around but didn't take a step toward him. *I'm trying to do her a favor and she has to be all snotty,* he thought as he headed up to her. But she had been decent when Abramson came up to them during that drawing exercise, so he kind of owed her one.

"If you want to be able to stop coming to our little parties anytime soon, you're going to have to start giving it up in group," he told her.

"What are you talking about?" she asked.

"I'm talking about all that crap you gave back there. About how you're looking forward to going back to school and seeing all your friends. Didn't you see Abramson's face? She wasn't buying it," Anthony answered.

Rae pulled the straps of her purse higher on her shoulder. She opened her lips, like she was about to say something, then snapped them closed.

"If you want out, you're going to have to put on the show. Talk about your *feelings.* Crying a little wouldn't hurt."

Rae didn't say thanks. She didn't say anything. Okay, payback was over. If she didn't want to listen, forget it. He swung his backpack over one shoulder and started past her.

"It wasn't crap," she called out.

Anthony turned around to face her. "Oh, come on. We're talking about school. You've got to know everyone's going to be talking about you on the first day back, staring at you, wondering if you're going to go nuts again. Somebody'll probably ask if they gave you electric shock."

The muscles in Rae's throat started to work. *She knows it's true,* Anthony thought.

"That's not how it's going to be," Rae insisted, but her voice came out husky, and Anthony thought he saw a sheen of tears in her blue eyes.

Great, Anthony thought. *This is what I get for trying to help somebody out. In another minute she's going to be blubbering, and I'll have to deal with it.* He twisted his head to the side, trying to crack his neck. "Look, I'm not exactly jumping for joy at the thought of going back to school myself. In fact, knowing I'm going to have to be there tomorrow makes me want to puke. It'll suck for you. But you'll live."

Rae's chin came up. "I really don't need advice from a guy in a Jonas Brothers T-shirt," she lashed out. At least she didn't sound like she was about to bawl anymore.

"Fine. Stay in group therapy till you're eighty. I was just trying to help you out," Anthony told her. His arms were itching to cross themselves over his chest and block out as much of the T-shirt as possible, but he didn't want to give Rae the satisfaction. How could he have forgotten to turn it inside out when he left the house? He'd had to wear it—his little sister Anna would have gone into a fit if he hadn't. It was her birthday present to him. But he hadn't meant to actually be seen in it.

"Sorry," Rae muttered, surprising him. He would have bet she didn't even know the word. She met his gaze directly, and he realized that they were almost exactly the same height. At least she wasn't taller. "And thanks, I guess," she continued. "But you're wrong about school."

"Ten dollars," Anthony said.

"What?" Rae asked.

"Ten dollars says *you're* wrong," Anthony told her. "You can pay up next session."

Chapter 2

Somebody'll probably ask if they gave you electric shock. Rae shook her head as she rinsed the conditioner out of her hair. She twisted the hot water knob to the right until the shower was as hot as she could possibly stand it.

Loofah. She needed the loofah. She reached up and snagged it off the little ledge under the high bathroom window, then squirted on a line of her ginger grapefruit bath gel and started to scrub her shoulders.

Somebody'll probably ask if they gave you electric shock.

Rae scrubbed harder, straining to reach the center of her back. She'd already washed her hair three times and conditioned it twice.

Somebody'll probably ask if they gave you electric shock. She could feel the thick fibers of the loofah doing their job. *Use some muscle,* she ordered herself, grinding the loofah into her skin.

More gel. That's what she needed for truly flawless skin. She grabbed the tube and positioned the loofah underneath it. "Oh God," she whispered. "Oh my God." The loofah was streaked with blood. She could even see tiny pieces of skin caught in the fibers.

Rae's knees buckled, and she sat down hard on the tile floor of the shower. She rocked back and forth as the water turned from hot to ice cold. *How could I have done that to myself?* she thought. It was . . . insane. A new kind of insane. She'd really hurt herself. And if she could do that—Rae forced herself to complete the thought. If she could do that, she could do anything. What if next time she picked up a razor blade instead of a loofah?

"It would be better than what happened to Mom," Rae whispered. "I can't live the rest of my life in a hospital. I won't."

A knock came on the bathroom door. "I'll be out in a minute, Dad," she called, her voice cracking.

"It's Yana. Your dad let me in. And I have Krispy Kremes."

Yana Savari was a friend. Sort of. She'd been a volunteer at the hospital. And even though she and Yana were almost the same age and everything, volunteer-patient friendship wasn't exactly a friendship. If Yana saw her in crack-up mode, she'd probably report it to Rae's doctor. For Rae's own good.

Rae scrubbed her face with her hands. Then she used the slick, wet wall of the shower for balance as she struggled to her feet. "One sec, Yana," she called. She took a deep breath, then stepped out of the shower and dried off as quickly as she could, wincing when the towel touched her tender back. She slipped on her cotton robe, then opened the door.

Yana held up the box of doughnuts and grinned. "I remembered how you were always talking about them at the walnut farm."

Rae gave a semihysterical snort of laughter. "You dyed your hair," she blurted out.

"You like?" Yana asked, holding up a few of her newly pale blond strands.

"I like," Rae answered. "It makes your eyes look even bluer." She tightened the belt on her robe. "I can't believe you came all the way over here to bring me doughnuts."

"It's not that far," Yana answered. "And I figured we could both use a pre-first-day-of-school sugar rush. I'm on split session, so I don't have to be at my school until noon."

"Um, thanks," Rae said.

"You look shocked to see me," Yana commented.

It *was* pretty freaky to see Yana standing in Rae's hallway, underneath the fluffy white clouds Rae had painted on the blue walls when she was twelve. "I sort of thought when we did the number-and-address-exchange thing, you were just being nice to the psycho girl," Rae admitted.

"I'm not that nice. And you're not that psycho," Yana answered. She smiled, showing the little gap between her front teeth. "But you're late. Your dad let me in on the way out, and he made me swear I'd get your butt out the door within the hour. Do you already know what you're going to wear?"

"Yeah. I spent about a million hours last night deciding," Rae confessed. "And what did I choose? Jeans and a sweater, which was the first thing I tried on."

"A little boring for my taste," Yana said. She ran her hand down her Ramones T-shirt, the one she'd cropped to show off the DNA-strand tattoo that circled her belly button. "But perfectly acceptable."

"The kitchen's through the living room. You can hang there while I get ready. Have some coffee or whatever," Rae said as she started down the hallway toward her bedroom.

"Oh my God," Yana exclaimed. "Rae, what happened?"

Rae turned around. "What?"

"Your back." Yana's eyes were wide with alarm. "It's bleeding."

Rae froze. *I can't go back to the hospital. Can't, can't, can't.*

"I must have, um, cut myself on the edge of the shower door," she blurted out. "It's really sharp."

Yana hurried over to her. "Let me look at it." Before Rae could stop her, Yana circled behind Rae and pulled down the back of her robe. "Ouch," she said softly.

Silence stretched out between them. Rae's heart was pounding so hard, she wouldn't be surprised if Yana could hear it.

"This doesn't look like a cut," Yana finally said. "It looks like a layer of skin was . . . *scraped* off." She pulled Rae's robe back up. "What really happened?"

Rae turned to face her. Yana's serious expression made it clear that another lie wasn't going to cut it.

"I was really nervous, about going back to school, you know, post- . . . everything. I got obsessed with wanting to look perfect." Rae's voice started to tremble. "I was just . . . I wanted to get off a layer of dead skin. I really didn't mean to hurt myself. Really. You've got to believe me. I just—"

"Got a little overzealous with the exfoliator?" Yana supplied.

"Loofah," Rae said. She gave several quick blinks because her eyes were suddenly feeling wet. "It was an accident. You're not going to tell Dr. Warriner, are you? I can't go back to the hospital, Yana. Please—"

"God, do you think I'm here as some kind of spy?" Yana interrupted. "I finished my hours of community service. Which, by the way, I was assigned to do by the court. The doctors didn't think it would be good for the patients to know that little tidbit."

"The court?" Rae repeated, feeling kind of dazed.

"Frat party. Many cups of lethal punch. Much stupidity. Long story," Yana answered. "Do you have any Bactine? I want to put some on your back."

"Medicine cabinet," Rae answered.

"Go start getting ready." Yana waved her off, then headed back toward the bathroom. Rae stared after her for a long moment, then turned and walked down the hall to her room. On autopilot, she began to get dressed. Yana hurried into the room right as Rae was zipping up her pants.

"Just pretend you're at the gym," Yana said as Rae grabbed a towel to cover her chest. "Turn around."

Rae obeyed. She focused her eyes on the wall across from her. She'd painted it herself, going for a faux marble look in a deep green with black swirls.

"It's not really that bad," Yana told her as she sprayed the cool Bactine on Rae's back. "It's already stopped bleeding."

"But what kind of a nut bucket does that to herself?" Rae muttered. She patted her back with the towel to dab away any remaining blood and Bactine.

"I don't want to hear you call yourself that again," Yana said, her voice harsh. "They let you out of the hospital because you're okay. You're just stressed out this morning."

"You sound like my dad," Rae said as she put on her favorite La Perla bra and then gingerly shrugged on her sweater. "Except I actually half believe you," she added, turning to face Yana.

Yana opened the Krispy Kreme box and held it out to Rae. Rae picked a chocolate-glazed old-fashioned. Yana grabbed a cinnamon twist. "You don't believe your dad?" she asked. She plopped down on Rae's bed and ran her fingers over the green bedspread with the black diamonds.

"You've got to know my dad. He's an English professor— early stuff, like medieval; you know, Arthurian legends," Rae said. She pulled the black leather chair away from her desk, a couple of the strange thoughts flashing through her brain, and sat down on the edge of the seat. "He's just not all that well acquainted with reality. He hardly even watches TV, although he's finally mastered the concept of online banking. And you should hear him talk about my mother. He—"

Rae snapped her mouth shut. She'd almost told Yana the thing she'd spent her whole life trying to keep a secret.

"He what?" Yana asked.

Rae felt like her ribs were pushing together, digging into

39

her heart. "Nothing," she mumbled.

"Come on." Yana brushed some cinnamon off her chin. "You have to tell me now. You can't get that far and stop. It's against the friendship code."

Rae considered. Yana hadn't freaked when she'd seen Rae's back. And she knew Rae'd been at the walnut farm, and that didn't stop her from coming over with doughnuts.

"Come on, Rae," Yana urged.

Rae swallowed hard, her throat feeling as dry and scratchy as an emery board. "Okay. My mom, she did something really terrible to someone." She swallowed again, realizing that she couldn't do this—couldn't spill what she'd worked so hard to keep secret. Not yet.

"Trust me—it was awful," she continued. "So bad that she would have gone to prison, except she was found mentally unfit to stand trial. She died in a mental institution," Rae said in a rush. "And my dad . . . Anytime he talks about my mother, which isn't that often, he goes on and on about what a great person she was. He totally believes it. That's the sick part. He's not just trying to make me feel better."

"Wow," Yana said softly.

"Yeah." Rae turned her doughnut over and over. It left a sticky trail on her fingers. "So, anyway, you can see why I don't exactly believe everything he says."

Yana pointed at the doughnut. "Eat," she ordered. Rae obediently took a bite. She kept shooting little glances at Yana's face. Was she wondering if Rae was just like her mother? Was she repulsed to be sitting so close to her?

"I never believe anything my dad says, either," Yana commented, her tone matter-of-fact. "But that's probably because he's always telling me how stupid I am. And how lazy. And how unreliable. Isn't that just a pretty, pretty picture?"

"That's awful," Rae said.

Yana stood up. "Yeah, well, in a couple of years we'll both be father-free. Or at least we won't have to live in the same house with them anymore." She pointed at the boots positioned neatly next to Rae's closet. "Now, put those on. I'm driving you to school. I promised Daddy darling you wouldn't be late, remember?"

The bell rang. Rae knew she had to stand up. She knew she had to head down to the cafeteria. But she felt like all the bones had been surgically removed from her legs. How could she stand up when she had no leg bones? She busied herself putting her English book and her binder into her backpack, not her thoughts popping in her brain like carbonation in soda as the rest of the class hurried out, laughing, talking, and shooting fast little I'm-not-looking glances at her.

"Rae, would you mind doing us a favor?"

Rae jerked up her head and saw Mr. Jesperson, her English teacher, standing in front of her. Next to him was a guy she didn't recognize—which was probably why he was actually meeting her eye.

"This is Jeff Brunner," Mr. Jesperson continued. "He's new,

and he needs someone to show him to the cafeteria. Since it's my first day here, too, I don't think I should be playing tour guide just yet." He gave her a sympathetic smile, a smile that told her he'd already picked up the 411 on her in the teachers' lounge. He probably thought it would be easier for her to return to the scene of the "incident" if she had someone with her. Which was so not true.

"Um, sure. I'll show him," Rae answered because it would be too weird to say no. And without consciously deciding to stand, she was on her feet and leading the way to the door. She pulled it open.

I can't believe Rae came back / went psycho/

God, it was bad enough just getting random thoughts. But these ones were so personal. Having them rush through her brain, with all that static underneath, was like getting attacked from the inside. And they felt so *real*—like they were actually coming from the people around her.

"Thanks for doing this," Jeff said as they stepped into the hall.

"Actually, the cafeteria is incredibly easy to find," she answered. "You know where the main office is, right?" She forced herself to look up at him, and he nodded. "Well, you just follow the mural that starts by the office. It ends right in front of the caf."

"You're not coming?" Jeff asked, his gray eyes all puppy dog. He was cute and possibly trying to flirt, but she was far from flirt mode right now.

"No, I am. Just not right this second." The thought of

walking back into the cafeteria was making her dizzy with anxiety.

"Oh. Okay. So, I guess I'll see you around," Jeff said. And he actually blushed. His skin was so fair that the splotches of color looked almost painted on. He gave a half wave and started to stride away from her.

"Wait," she called. He immediately stopped and turned around. "Look. You're new. So you don't know. Although I'm sure you will soon enough." Jeff raised his eyebrows, clearly puzzled. Rae hurried on. "Anyway, last spring I had this kind of meltdown in front of pretty much everyone. Trust me, you don't want to go into the cafeteria with me. You'd be a freak by association." She made a little pushing motion with her hands. "Go on. I'll give you a head start."

Jeff smiled and took a step closer to her. "You're trying to protect me?" He combed his dark hair away from his face with his fingers. "I don't care what people think," he said. "Let's go together."

Rae raised an eyebrow, surprised. Every new kid knew that who you're seen with those first few days is crucial.

It would definitely be nice not to have to walk into the cafeteria alone. Those first few seconds, when everyone realized she was there and got all quiet—it wouldn't suck to have someone normal standing next to her.

"Fine," Rae said. She started down the hall without another word. Jeff stayed in step beside her. The hallway had less and less air the closer they got to the cafeteria. She felt like she had to gasp for each breath, though she knew she was breathing in a normal way. Which was her goal for the day—breathe normal, walk normal, talk normal, *be* normal.

"Well, here we are," Rae announced, feeling like she had to force the words out of her mouth. She straightened her shoulders, then pushed open the cafeteria's double doors with both hands—

/gross/ *see Rae*/gym next period/

—and stepped inside. Was it just her imagination or did the volume of noise drop to near silence? Her body felt hot all over from all the eyes that were focused on her.

"So this is the cafeteria," Jeff commented.

Rae scanned the room for her friends, spotting Marcus, paying for a slice of pizza. Her stomach clenched in fear at the same time that her heart rate zoomed. She'd spent so much time imagining this moment—seeing him again. But she had no idea what he'd been thinking, what he expected to happen between them now that she was back.

You're supposed to be acting normal, Rae reminded herself. And normal meant her and Marcus, together. It's not like they could just pick up right where they left off, but if she made sure he knew she was better now, that she still wanted to be with him . . .

"I'll be back in one sec," Rae told Jeff. She raced over to Marcus, wrapped one arm around his waist, and pressed her free hand over his eyes. "Guess who?"

"Could it be . . . Dori?" Marcus asked, his voice teasing.

Rae's hand slithered off Marcus's face. "That would be no," she answered, the words coming out a little choked.

What did you expect? she asked herself, her stomach churning with acid. *Did you expect Marcus Salkow to ignore the existence of all other girls for an entire summer?*

She *had* at least figured Leah would give her a heads up if he was seeing someone else.

Marcus turned around. Rae thought she caught a flicker of disgust in his expression, but then he gave her the Salkow smile, his teeth gleaming white against his tan.

"Sting Rae! You're back," he exclaimed, then wrapped her in a fast hug. Too fast. Like he didn't want to touch her for too long. Like she might be contagious. The acid in her stomach splashed up into the back of her throat.

"Come on," Marcus urged. "Everyone wants to see you."

Rae hadn't gotten the chance to buy food yet, but she followed Marcus toward the usual table. "Jeff, you want to come?" she called over her shoulder. He was standing where she'd left him, his hands shoved awkwardly in his jeans pockets.

"Sure," he answered. In about two seconds he'd caught up to her and Marcus. Rae put her hand lightly on Jeff's arm. "Marcus, this is Jeff. He's new this year."

"Hey," Marcus said. He grabbed Rae by the wrist and started walking faster, tugging her along with him. Jeff kept right up with them.

Good. It wouldn't hurt Marcus—and everyone else who was still staring at her—to see a guy look at her in that she's-hot way, not in the did-you-hear-she-spent-the-summer-in-a-nuthouse way.

"Leah, look who I found!" Marcus called when they

reached their usual table.

Leah let out a whoop the second she saw Rae. She sprang off the bench and gave Rae one of those long, rocking hugs, her smooth black hair pressing into Rae's cheek. "It's so great to see you," she said as she finally released Rae.

"Hey, I think you grew a little upstairs," Rae said softly.

"Yeah, I might actually start having to wear a bra," Leah answered. And for that moment it was as if Rae'd stepped back in time to B.C.: before crack-up.

"It's the Rae of sunshine!" Jackie called from the other side of the table. Her voice came out a little too loud and a little too high, but at least she was trying.

"It's the Rae man," Vince bellowed from his seat next to Jackie. "She's back!" Vince sounded like regular Vince. Rae knew he was totally glad to see her. The nice thing about Vince, which was also sometimes the annoying thing about Vince, was that he was a no-subtext kind of guy.

"Sit down," Leah urged, twisting the silver locket she wore around her neck.

"I actually didn't get food yet," Rae answered.

"I'll do it. I know everything you like." Leah turned toward the food counter.

"Wait," Rae said. "Take Jeff with you." Rae pointed to him and noticed he was starting to blush again. It was actually kind of sweet. "He's new, so be nice to him."

"Aren't I always nice to cute boys?" Leah asked with a wink. She grabbed Jeff by the arm and whisked him away. Rae sat down next to Marcus. Then wished she hadn't. She didn't want to look too eager or like she was assuming too much.

"So, Rae, what classes do you have this semester?" Jackie asked. She leaned across the table and patted Rae's hand. Actually *patted* her hand.

"I bet you're doing art again," Vince jumped in before Rae could answer. "You're really great at that." He grinned, and she noticed he'd gotten the chip in his tooth fixed. How many other things had changed while she'd been gone?

"Rae's an awesome artist," Marcus added. He glanced nervously over his shoulder.

Rae followed his gaze and saw Dori Hernandez heading toward them. Dori had completely done the caterpillar-to-butterfly thing over the summer. She'd always been cute, but now, she was *hot*. Her long, dark brown hair fell almost to her waist, and her formfitting top showed that she'd lost the few pounds of baby fat she'd been toting around. But what Rae really noticed was how often Dori's eyes darted to Marcus.

A lump the size of a plum formed in Rae's throat. She swallowed hard, then plastered a smile on her face. There was going to be no scene in the cafeteria today. "Hey, Dori. You look great," she said as Dori reached the table.

How long did it take you to make your move? Rae wondered. *A week? A month? Or did you go for it the second after I had my little fit? Did you comfort Marcus about his poor, sick girlfriend?*

"Um, thanks," Dori finally answered, a deer-in-the-head-lights expression on her face. She glanced from the empty seat by Rae to the empty seat on the other side of Marcus, shifting uneasily from foot to foot. Marcus finally put her out of her misery by patting the seat next to him.

"Rae was just going to tell us what classes she's taking," Marcus said.

"Oh, great!" Dori cried, sounding like she'd just won an all-expense-paid trip to Hawaii.

"It's just the usual. You know, English, history, bio, gym, trig, plus art, of course," Rae answered.

"Oh, great!" Dori cried again.

Oh, please, Rae thought.

"One Rae Voight special," Leah called as she hurried up to the table with Jeff trailing behind her. She slid a tray in front of Rae. It had one jumbo fro-yo and a salad.

"Thanks," Rae said.

"You're extremely welcome," Leah answered. "Oh, you need napkins," she added. She grabbed a handful out of the holder in the center of the table and thrust them on Rae's tray.

Oh God, Rae thought. *Is this how it's going to be forever? Is everyone going to keep being all fake and nice, like I'm some kind of severely challenged child visiting the school?*

She picked up her plastic spoon—

/can Rae tell I'm weirded/

—and scooped up some yogurt. *At least no one asked me if I've had electric shock,* she thought. *But I'm definitely going to owe Anthony ten bucks.*

Chapter 3

E *nglish first period,* Anthony thought as he slammed his locker shut, then headed out of the building. The perfect way to start the day. His class was over in the row of trailers behind the baseball diamond. Fillmore High had run out of space sometime in the seventies, and the trailers were supposed to be a short-term solution. Yeah, right.

"Yo, fat 'n' smelly," a voice called as he headed outside. Anthony didn't even have to look to know who it was. Brian Salerno was the only guy who still called Anthony by his grade-school nickname. Salerno was also the only guy who still actually thought the fact that Fascinelli, Anthony's last name, sounded sort of like "fat 'n' smelly" was freakin' HBO-comedy-special material.

"Hey," Anthony said. He didn't slow down as Salerno fell into step beside him. He wondered if there was a possibility that by the time they graduated, whatever millennium that might be, Salerno would figure out that not only weren't they friends, but that they had never *been* friends.

"So you in Goyer's class?" Salerno asked as they cut across the baseball field.

"Yeah." They reached the trailer, and Anthony climbed up the flimsy aluminum steps, pulling open the door. The metal was warm under his hand, and it wasn't even ten in the morning. He stepped inside and immediately spotted a lot of familiar faces. "Bluebirds," he muttered.

No one was called Bluebirds, Canaries, or Cardinals anymore, but they were still the Bluebirds all right. And everybody knew it. Just like back in the third grade no one had had a problem breaking their teacher's little reading-group code. Bluebirds equaled morons.

The second bell rang. Goyer stood up from behind her desk and wrote her name on the board. "I'm Ms. Goyer. Welcome back to school. I hope you all had a great summer." She smiled as she picked up a stack of paper, then handed sets of stapled-together sheets to the first kid in every row. "After I call roll, we're going to do a little reading aloud. Just to ease you back into the routine."

Just to see who are the biggest Bluebirds of them all, Anthony thought as the girl in front of him passed back his set of papers. He shifted in his hard wooden chair. Dots of sweat had popped out all the way down the groove in the center of his back, and they were itching like crazy. He checked the clock. Not even two minutes of class time had elapsed, and the second hand was moving in extreme slow motion.

Anthony stretched his legs out into the aisle. He clenched and unclenched his fingers. *Relax, okay?* he told himself. He gave a "yup" when Ms. Goyer called his name, not bothering to return her bright you're-so-special smile. Goyer was clearly one of those special-ed teachers who was sure a little love and attention would get all her Bluebirds in the air, flying like Cardinals. Which was slightly easier to take than the special-ed teachers who thought all a Bluebird needed was to have its feathers plucked so it would learn a little discipline. Slightly.

Mental porn. That's the only way he was going to get through. *Girl from the Gap ad,* he decided. *The redhead. Yeah.* She came so clear in his mind that he could see every freckle.

"Okay, you take it from there, Anthony," Goyer called in her all-they-need-is-a-little-encouragement voice. It took him a second to bring the sheet of paper on his desk back into focus.

Both armpits started pumping juice. The trickle of sweat down his back turned into a stream, gluing his T-shirt to his skin.

"Mike," Anthony read. That was an easy one. A picture of his friend Mike flashed into his head as soon as his eyes hit the letters, so he instantly recognized the word. *Ran.* As soon as Anthony had pictured himself running, the word had easily come out of his mouth. He moved his eyes to the next word— *to.* One of his heels started slapping up and down on the floor. "To," he said. He'd actually had to think about that one. Two letters and he'd had to think about it.

Anthony moved on to the next word—*the.* Another word that didn't bring up any kind of picture. *But you know it,* he told himself. *It's one of the easy ones. It's one of the ones kids still in diapers know.* He intensified his focus. "The," he said.

"Good. Keep going," Goyer urged.

Anthony didn't look up from the sheet. He couldn't lose his concentration. "Store," he said. That hadn't been a problem. He'd seen the word, and a picture of the grocery store near his house had popped into his head, but he got blank brain again on the next word—*and*. He focused until he felt like a steel belt was wrapped around his head, getting pulled tighter and tighter. "And," he read.

He wished whoever was chewing gum would stop it. The sweet grape smell was making him nauseous. And somebody else was gnawing on a pencil, which made his teeth want to crawl right out of his mouth.

"Try sounding it out," Ms. Goyer prompted.

Anthony jerked his eyes to the next word. The image of him handing money to his pot dealer appeared in his mind. "Bought," he said. He moved his eyes to the next word. No picture. "Some," he managed to get out.

The belt around his head cinched tighter. His foot tapped harder against the floor. The smell of grape gum felt like it was filling his nose and throat and lungs. And his teeth were practically jumping with each crunch of the pencil from the other side of the room.

"Why don't you start again at the beginning," Ms. Goyer suggested.

Anthony put his finger under the first word of the sentence. He knew it made him look like a goon, but it helped. An image of his friend Mike appeared in his mind. "Mike," he said. He moved his finger to the next word. An image of himself running appeared. "Ran." He moved his finger to the next word. His mind went blank again.

"Sound it out," Ms. Goyer said. "What is the sound of the first letter?"

Anthony dug his finger into the paper under the word. The little two-letter word. He pulled in a deep breath, a sweet, grape-scented breath that made him want to gag.

"Mike ran to the girl with the humongous melon breasts," Anthony said in a rush, half under his breath. He cut a glance at Goyer. She didn't look angry. She had an aw-poor-little-Bluebird-acting-out expression on her face.

"We'll go over some techniques for attacking unfamiliar words next class," she said. "Brian, continue, please."

Anthony checked the clock again. They'd just about hit the halfway mark. But he needed out of here *now*. He called the Gap redhead up in his mind again and made her unbutton her sweater. She slipped it from her shoulders and let it fall to her feet in a pink puddle. *Yeah.*

When he got tired of Red, he switched over to one of the blond chicks from the ad. Blondie kept him occupied until the bell rang. Then he was out of there. He broke into a run as he cut across the baseball diamond, loving the way his muscles obeyed his slightest command, the way his crammed-with-stupid brain never would. Man, he couldn't wait for gym. That was the one place *he* was the Cardinal. No, forget that. He was the Eagle.

But gym wasn't until last period. Next up was math. Blue-bird math. *At least it's not in the trailer park,* he thought. He headed into the main building and started toward his locker, then hesitated and pulled out his cell. He shouldn't have to do this . . . but he'd bet anything his mom had forgotten. He punched in a number.

"Sunny Days Day Care," a voice that sounded a lot like Ms. Goyer's answered.

"This is Anthony Fascinelli," he said. "Carl Doheney's brother. Carl's on antibiotics. He needs to take a pill at lunch with food, okay? The pills are in his backpack." He hung up without waiting for a reply and continued toward his locker. At least now he wouldn't have to listen to Carl screaming all night because his earache hurt so bad. Something you'd think the kid's own mother would care about.

"Mr. Fascinelli," a familiar voice called. Way too familiar.

He turned around. "Mr. Shapiro. Hi! I hope you had a fabulous summer," Anthony said with mock enthusiasm. He couldn't believe this. First Bluebird English *with* reading aloud. Now a chat with the principal. He bet that girl from group's first day at school was a walk in the park compared to this.

Shapiro didn't look amused. His muddy green eyes were all squinty, and his thin lips looked even thinner because he had them pressed together so tight.

"I got an update on you from your group therapy leader at Oakvale," Mr. Shapiro said. "It looks like you're making some progress in your anger management skills. I expect to see some evidence of that this year."

Anthony nodded. Clearly he wasn't expected to say anything here.

"I'm giving you fair warning," Mr. Shapiro continued.

"One step out of line this year and there's no second chance. You're out of here."

Anthony nodded again. It was a better anger management choice than slamming his fist into the closest wall. He'd learned that much. But what was the guy's problem? Anthony hadn't done anything. *Anything*. And Shapiro was already busting his butt. What a nice welcome to his junior year.

"You better head off," Shapiro said. "You don't want to be late to class your first day."

"I sure don't," Anthony answered, unable to keep the sarcasm out of his voice. He strode past Shapiro, getting in a little shoulder knock that could possibly have been an accident. Instead of going to his locker, he swung into the bathroom. He couldn't deal with another class right now.

Anthony ducked into the closest stall, opened his backpack, and pulled a plastic bag out of one of the zippered compartments. Just holding the bag in his hand made his heart rate go down and loosened the belt around his head.

He rolled himself a joint as quickly as he could. *Yeah,* he thought as he inhaled, holding the smoke in his lungs, *now this is the way to start the first day of school.* He heard the bathroom door swing open, and he checked the lock on his stall to make sure it was in place.

"Someone has been using that wacky tobaccy in here," a voice said.

"And *somebody* better be willing to share," another voice added. "That means you, Fascinelli."

A second later Gregg Borgenicht's head popped over the

left side of Anthony's stall, followed almost immediately by Mike Tarcher's on the right. "Gimme, gimme, gimme," Gregg begged. He sounded like a little kid. And with his round face he looked kind of like one, too. Even with the scruff.

Anthony took another pull before he handed Gregg the joint. Who knew when he'd get it back. But he was glad to see the guys. Smoking with them was definitely more fun than smoking alone. They always managed to crack him up.

"We have to ask Anthony our question," Mike told Gregg.

"Definitely," Gregg answered, speaking with his lips almost closed so he wouldn't lose any smoke. Although clearly he was already at least partially in his special happy place, judging by the red eyes, eyes with pupils so big, they almost blocked out the blue.

"So, okay. Say the world was made of cheese," Gregg said. He looped his elbows over the edge of Anthony's stall, probably to keep his balance on the lidless toilet seat he had to be standing on. "What do you think money would be? I say crackers. Because hey, with cheese you gotta have crackers. But to Mike money would be—" Gregg paused since it was his turn to suck, then continued, his voice thick. "He thinks money would be Dr. Pepper."

"Because Dr. Pepper is great with cheese," Mike cut in. "You just can't eat cheese without Dr. Pepper." He reached for the joint with his long, skinny fingers. Gregg started to hand it to him, but Anthony intercepted. It *was* his last one.

Anthony gave a bark of laughter. "Why wouldn't money

still be money, geniuses?" he asked. "Then people could buy Dr. Pepper or crackers or whatever they wanted to go with the cheese."

Gregg snorted. "You're not getting it, *genius*. The world . . . It's *made* of cheese. That changes everything. Everything! People wouldn't still be walking around with, like, quarters."

"Yeah, 'cause there would be no metal to make into quarters," Mike added, throwing a hand through his greasy hair. "There'd be, like, veins of Cheez Whiz that you could lap right up."

Anthony took another toke while he tried to imagine Cheese World. He'd bet anything Rae and her prep school friends didn't have conversations like this. They probably only talked about what college they were planning to go to—with Mommy and Daddy's money.

"So are the buildings made out of cheese, too?" Anthony asked, already starting to feel more at ease.

"Cheese would have to be the main construction material," Gregg answered authoritatively.

"Maybe peanut butter could be the mortar. Like in those crackers at the 7-Eleven," Mike suggested.

"I love those crackers," Anthony said. He smiled as he thought about them. So orange. So crunchy.

"But peanut butter is the mortar between *crackers* in those things. It's not the mortar between pieces of *cheese*," Gregg told Mike, sounding annoyed. "What are you thinking?"

"Would you keep it down?" Anthony said. "We don't want Shapiro joining the party."

"I really want some of those crackers," Mike murmured. "Time for a 7-Eleven run. You comin'?" he asked Anthony.

Anthony scrubbed his face with his fingers, almost burning one eyebrow with the joint. "I gotta go to my next class," he said. "I already missed one."

"We all already missed one." Mike snagged the joint. "But what we do is leave now, then come back at lunch, when we can blend."

And I could score another bag from Rick, Anthony thought. He was probably working today. And if he wasn't, he was probably hanging out in the 7-Eleven parking lot so all his regulars could find him.

"So are you comin' or what?" Gregg asked.

Anthony checked Gregg's watch. There was no way he could get back in time for Bluebird history. It's not like he wanted to sit through another hour of torture, but he did want to graduate so that someday the torture would end. If he hung out too much with Gregg and Mike, that wasn't going to happen. Gregg had already been held back a year.

"Can't do it," Anthony said. "But get me some of those peanut butter crackers. And don't eat them on the way back," Anthony ordered Mike, then handed him the money. Mike and Gregg each gave him a half salute and disappeared from sight. The door swung shut behind them before Anthony realized that Mike had made off with his last joint.

Just as well, Anthony told himself. *You don't want to become a walking baked potato like those guys.* He sat down on the edge of the toilet. *Or working at the 7-Eleven, selling munchies to Gregg and Mike.*

And I am outta here, Anthony thought as he headed through Fillmore's main doors. Just a couple dozen steps and he'd be off school property, at least until tomorrow. He started walking faster, then stopped short when he saw Rick Nunan leaning against one of the two oak trees that dominated the front of the school. Rick had already spotted him, so there was no point in Anthony pretending he hadn't seen the guy.

"Knew you had to be down to the seeds," Nunan said as Anthony approached. "Since you're one of my very special customers and all, I decided to make a delivery."

Translation: You needed some fast cash, Anthony thought. Nunan was an okay guy. They'd partied together. But he wasn't a doing-it-out-of-the-goodness-of-his-heart type. Not by a long shot.

"Gonna have to pass," Anthony answered.

"You broke? I can spot you for a few days." Nunan ran his fingers over his shaved head. When he was high, just the feel of the skin under his fingers could make him giggle for hours.

"Nah. I just . . ." Anthony shrugged. "Not in the mood." Which was total crap. But he'd ordered himself not to buy any more. He was going to graduate from this place without taking ten years to do it.

"Not in the mood?" Nunan repeated. "You smoke some, you get in the mood." He ran his hand over his head again.

"Just go find one of your other very special customers, okay?" Anthony asked. *And right now,* he added to himself. His fingers were already twitching, ready to go for his wallet.

Nunan took a step closer, and Anthony was blasted with the smell of smoke.

"It's totally primo stuff. Nunan tested, Nunan approved."

Anthony didn't think. He just reacted—by reaching out and shoving Nunan away with both hands. Nunan, the little weenie, ended up on his butt.

"Is there a problem, Mr. Fascinelli?" a voice called. Anthony glanced over his shoulder. Perfect. Mr. Shapiro *had* to have seen that little encounter. And his lips were clamped together so tight, they'd practically disappeared into his mouth.

"No problem." Anthony reached down, grabbed Nunan's hand, and pulled him up. "No problem, right, Rick?"

"Nonstudents aren't allowed on campus," Shapiro told Nunan. It took a second for Nunan to realize that meant he should leave, but he finally got it and wandered off.

"I have the feeling you weren't listening to me this morning, Anthony," Shapiro said, opening his mouth only enough to let the words squeak through.

"No, I was. I was," Anthony answered. He hated the way his voice came out, like a little kid's. *Don't be mad, Mommy. I'll never do it again.*

Shapiro nodded. "We'll see, won't we." He turned and walked away without another word.

Chapter 4

"So how was school?" Rae's father asked before she even had her butt all the way into the car.

Rae slammed the door.

/ *Milk, eggs, bread, chicken* /

"Day two was pretty much like day one," she answered. Stares. Extreme niceness. Extreme weirdness. Random not-her-own thoughts about how psycho she was. Plus some totally-her-own thoughts about how psycho she was, just for variety. "You know, just basic getting-organized stuff," she added as her dad pulled out of the driveway.

A sour taste filled Rae's mouth. She popped open the glove compartment—

/What am I supposed to say to her?/

—and rooted around for some gum. She didn't find any, so she slammed the glove compartment closed.

/ Rachel /

God, that thought, it *felt* like her dad. It wasn't in his voice or anything. But it had a Dad . . . *flavor.* Could she actually be picking up his thoughts?

She reminded herself what Dr. Warriner had said when

61

she'd admitted that sometimes the thoughts really seemed to come from other people, especially thoughts *about* her.

That's part of what paranoid delusions are, Rae. You're imagining that people must be thinking these things of you, and so you're projecting the thoughts onto them—in your own head.

Rae leaned back and rubbed her forehead. *Maybe some sort of exorcism would be useful,* she thought.

"Would you like to stop for a Slurpee on the way?" her father asked.

"No, thanks. Not unless you want one," Rae said. She turned her head toward the window so he couldn't see the film of tears coating her eyes. Would he ever stop *offering* her stuff in that hopeful, eager voice?

"I'm not really a Slurpee person. Although I like the word. *Slurpee. Slurrrpeee.* It's onomatopoetic, don't you think?" her dad asked. "The word *slurp* sounds like the sound that you make when you slurp."

Oh God. He's slipped into educational mode, Rae thought. She gave a couple of blinks, and her eyes cleared up.

They were still about fifteen minutes away from Oakvale. She was not going to be able to take this. "Dad, what was Mom like when you went to visit her in the hospital?"

Rae shot a glance at her dad. He didn't seem upset. He looked like he was giving her question careful consideration.

"She was very much herself," he finally answered. "Although sometimes the medication they had her on made her a little . . . dulled. Your mother, usually she sparkled." He reached out and briefly touched Rae's face. "You sparkle, too, sometimes."

How to sparkle. Step one—go insane, Rae thought. Not an article soon to appear in *Self* magazine.

"We had some wonderful conversations when I would visit," her father continued, his voice the slightest bit thick. "We talked about you a lot, of course. She wanted to know every single detail. Every burp. Every smile. But we'd talk about philosophical questions, too, the way we had when we were dating."

He loved her so much, Rae thought. That was clear every time he talked about her. Every time Rae *let* him talk about her. She knew he'd talk about her more if Rae didn't go into shark-attack mode when he did, reminding him what this goddess had done.

"Did you ever have any sense that something was wrong? Before what happened, I mean," Rae asked. She usually hated talking about her mom. But this was info she needed now.

"No," he answered immediately. "Not really," he added, his words coming slowly. "Except that near the . . . the time, she seemed agitated. She was ecstatic because you had just been born. But I knew she was worried about something. She wouldn't tell me what. She never did, not even afterward, when she was in the hospital."

He shot a glance at Rae, his blue eyes unusually intense. "I think she was protecting me from something. She was like that, always putting other people first."

Rae focused all her attention on adjusting the air-conditioner vent in front of her. If it helped Dad to be delusional, maybe she shouldn't burst his pretty bubble.

"I didn't want to push her. Not when she was in the hospital. I thought there would be plenty of time for her to tell me what was bothering her. But then, a few months after she was institutionalized, she got sick. Her body began to deteriorate. It happened so rapidly that her doctors weren't able to diagnose her before she died," he continued. "And I never got to . . . We never got to really talk again." Her father grabbed his sunglasses off the dashboard and put them on, but not before Rae saw the tears in his eyes. "They wanted to do an autopsy," he continued. "But I wouldn't give them permission. I just . . . I couldn't." Her father wiped his face with the sleeve of his white shirt. Then he pulled onto the exit leading to Oakvale.

"Thanks for telling me," Rae said softly.

"I'll always answer your questions," he said, shooting her a glance. "I *want* you to know about your mother. You would have liked her, Rae. You would have loved her."

Rae tucked her hair behind her ears. She and her father fell into a somewhat comfortable silence that lasted until he pulled into Oakvale's parking lot.

"See you in an hour," her dad said. Rae nodded and pulled open the door.

/ *Milk, eggs, bread, chicken* /

That thought again. She'd noticed that some of her not-her thoughts were on a loop or something. They'd come back now and then, but each time they were a little bit fuzzier. Which would be encouraging, except she got new not-her thoughts all the time, and they came in loud and clear.

Rae slammed the car door —

/why is this/

—and hesitated. There was something about that why-is-this one that was more comfortable than a lot of the others. Closer to one of her own thoughts, but not exactly. Why? She had no clue.

"So where's my ten bucks?" a voice called from behind her as she headed up to Oakvale's main doors. Rae turned around and saw Anthony striding up, his hand stuck out for his money.

At least he's not sugary nice to me, she thought, *like one wrong word and somebody's going to have to go running for a strait jacket.*

Rae didn't even bother to pretend that Anthony was wrong about school. She just reached into her bag, feeling for her wallet. Before she could find it, Anthony caught her by the wrist, his fingers light but firm.

"You don't have to pay," he told her.

Rae glanced down at her wrist, and Anthony instantly released her. She noticed he wasn't wearing his Jonas Brothers T-shirt today. Just a faded tan T-shirt that made his brown eyes look even darker. It fit a little better, too, showing off some nice definition in the chest and ab areas. Make that very nice.

"Were they completely, uh, hellish? Your first two days?" Anthony muttered, not quite looking Rae in the eye.

65

Rae snorted. "Well, let's see," she said sarcastically. "To people at school, I'm either this poor thing who can't even eat without someone to wipe her mouth for her. Or I'm this freak who should be avoided in case I might still be contagious with some kind of insanity disease. Even to my friends. Would you call that hellish?"

"That sucks," Anthony said. He managed to briefly look at her. Rae was surprised to see sympathy in his eyes. Not poor-little-Rae pity. Real sympathy.

"Yeah," Rae agreed. "It completely sucks. So what about you? Did you end up puking or anything?"

Anthony gave a harsh laugh. "No, but hanging around with the Bluebirds all day made me want to."

"Bluebirds?" Rae shook her head. "What are—"

A deep flush started to creep up Anthony's neck. "Slow learners," he muttered. "I have to go take a leak." And he bolted.

All righty, then, Rae thought. *That was a bizarre little exchange. One where I think we actually both told each other the truth—and didn't exactly plan to.* She pushed open half of the double door—

/WHAT A MORON/

—and stepped inside. A girl from group, around Rae's age, who looked like she bought all her clothes from an army surplus store, immediately rushed up to her. "I can't believe we're back here again. Can you believe group meets three times a week? It's ridiculous."

"Yeah," Rae agreed. She had the urge to back away a step

but didn't. *Is this how I look to people?* she wondered. *All nervous and jittery and about to go off?*

"Hey," the girl said, nervously tickling the side of her neck with the end of her braid. "Your mascara is sort of smudged. Do you know where the bathroom is? It's—"

"I know. Thanks, Cynda," Rae said, finally remembering the girl's name. *Thanks for giving me a great excuse to get away,* Rae added silently as she hurried down the hall. She pushed open the bathroom door—

/TOTAL MORON/

—and almost bumped into Anthony. "Guys' is flooded," he mumbled as he ducked past her.

Whatever, Rae thought. She headed over to the closest mirror and peered in. What was that Cynda girl talking about? Rae's mascara wasn't smudged at all. She leaned on the rust-stained sink—

/ NEVER KNOW WHAT HIT HER /

—to get a closer look. And suddenly a blast shook the floor beneath her feet. Something hard struck the back of Rae's head. She fell to her knees, white dots exploding in front of her eyes.

Dimly she could hear shouts from the hall. But the voices sounded much too far away. And something warm was dripping down her neck. *Blood,* she realized slowly. From her head. She had to get up. Had to get help.

She grabbed the sink with both hands—

/ THEY'LL THINK ANTHONY DID IT/ DEFINITELY KILL RAE / GET OUT OF HERE /

—and pulled herself to her feet. Her legs felt soft as marshmallows. She gripped the sink harder so she wouldn't fall again.

/ HOW DOES THIS THING / SHOULD HAVE BROUGHT /
DEFINITELY KILL RAE /

Had someone just tried to kill her?

Anthony jumped out of his metal chair so fast that it crashed to the floor. That explosion—it sounded like it came from the direction of the girls' bathroom. *Rae.* His body reacted instantly, and he was out the door and down the hall in seconds, then pushing through the bathroom door.

A dozen different pieces of data hit him as soon as he was inside. Stall door blown off. Smell of smoke. Smell of blood. Pieces of broken tile. Rae swaying on her feet in front of the cracked mirror.

Anthony reached her just as her knees buckled and caught her before she hit the floor. He scooped her up, one arm around her shoulders, one under her knees, and carried her out of the bathroom, using his back to open the door. Her face had lost all its color, and her eyes were only slitted open. "I'm taking her to the nurse," he announced as he strode past Ms. Abramson and most of the group.

"Everybody back to the room. And no one goes into that bathroom," Abramson called. A second later she caught up to Anthony. "Rae, can you hear me?" she asked loudly.

Anthony stared down at Rae's face. His stomach turned over as her eyelids fluttered open and she looked directly up at him. "I don't need to be carried," she said. "I'm fine."

"Yeah, right," Anthony answered, not even considering putting her down. What was it with this girl and being helped?

"I'll get the door." Abramson rushed on ahead and jerked open the door to the nurse's office. "Sheila, we need you," she cried, her voice shrill.

When he reached the door, Anthony turned sideways and carefully maneuvered himself and Rae through. The last thing she needed was another bump on the head. He could feel her blood soaking into his T-shirt.

"Put her over there," the nurse ordered, waving toward the closest of three empty cots along the back wall.

"I can walk," Rae protested again, giving a little squirm.

"You can fall on your butt," Anthony answered. He strode over to the narrow cot and carefully laid Rae down on the thin blue blanket. "Don't even think about trying to sit up," he warned her. He backed up to let the nurse move in next to the cot, but he didn't take his eyes off Rae, his gaze locked on the tiny scratch that ran along one side of her face from the top of her cheek to the corner of her mouth.

"Anthony, we've got it covered now," Abramson told him. "You can go back to the meeting room."

He nodded, but he didn't move. He kept thinking there was something he should be doing. Water. He bet Rae would like a drink of water. Anthony scanned the room and spotted a water cooler, then he hurried over to it. He rejected the wimpy paper cups and picked a big blue plastic one off the shelf over the coffeepot. He filled it almost to the top and rushed back over to the cot.

"Here. I'm leaving this for you." Anthony put the cup on the little table next to Rae. He hesitated a moment, but he couldn't think of anything else she might want, so he headed out.

He could hear the chaos in the meeting room before he was even halfway there.

"Is she okay?" Cynda asked as soon as he stepped back in the room. She gnawed on the end of her braid as she waited for him to answer.

"Yeah," Anthony said. He started toward the closest empty chair but was intercepted by Jesse.

"They're saying it was a pipe bomb," Jesse said, clearly eager to be the one to give Anthony the info.

"Sounds like bullshit. Who would put a pipe bomb in the girls' bathroom?" Anthony asked. His heart was still beating like crazy, and his body hadn't figured out that it was okay to stop pumping the adrenaline. Not to mention the sweat.

"I don't know. But that's what I heard Mr. Rocha saying," Jesse answered. He used his fingers to comb his red hair off his face. "You should have seen him. That little vein by his eye looked like it was about to explode. Rocha's totally out for blood on this one."

Yeah, and I bet I'm on the top of his list, Anthony thought. Mr. Rocha, the director of the institute, was exactly like Mr. Shapiro in that way.

But this time I'm totally clean, Anthony told himself. *Even if Rocha wants to, he's not going to be able to pin this on me.*

Except for the little fact that Rae saw Anthony coming out of the girls' bathroom. The sweat on his body turned cold. Rae could place him at the scene about two minutes before the bomb went off. If that.

Anthony gave the sleeve of his T-shirt a yank. Rae's blood was starting to glue itself to his arm.

Fascinelli, you are totally screwed.

Chapter 5

"Are you feeling okay sitting up?" Mr. Rocha asked Rae. "We can go back to the nurse's office and talk. That way you could keep lying down."

"I'm fine," Rae answered. She lightly touched the bandage on the back of her head—

/ good as new /

—and grimaced when she realized a little blood had soaked through.

"You're sure?" Mr. Rocha pressed.

Like you care, Rae thought. She didn't see any real concern in his hazel eyes. And even though it would feel good to lie down again, she did *not* want to have this little chat with Rocha with her in bed and him looming over her. Just too icky.

"I'm fine," Rae repeated.

"You're also very lucky," Mr. Rocha told her, adjusting the crystal paperweight so it was exactly in the center of the stack of papers on his desk. "If you'd been a few feet closer to the bomb when it went off, we wouldn't be talking about whether you're feeling well enough to sit. You'd be in the hospital. Or dead."

"Wait. Bomb? There was a bomb?" Rae demanded.

The not-her thought she'd gotten in the bathroom ripped through her mind. Was someone really trying to *kill* her?

"A pipe bomb," Mr. Rocha answered. "It was in the stall closest to the door." He leaned across his desk toward her. "What I need to know is, did you see anything unusual in the bathroom?"

Anthony, she thought, her stomach doing a slow-mo flip-flop. That was pretty unusual, seeing a guy coming out of the girls' bathroom.

"I mean *anything*," Rocha said, a few droplets of spittle flying out of his mouth.

The cut on the back of Rae's head began to throb in time to the beat of her heart. "I don't get it. What's the point of a pipe bomb in the girls' bathroom? Was someone trying to blow up the entire place or what?"

Because that sort of made sense. It's not like people came to Oakvale because they were *stable.* Maybe one of the squirrels decided that their mission was to send the place to heaven.

Rocha shook his head. "Not unless whoever is responsible severely miscalculated," he answered. "The bomb wasn't big enough to damage more than the bathroom. Now, try to remember everything. Even the smallest detail can help me find the person who did this."

Wonder what he'd think if I told him that I had one of my not-me thoughts in the bathroom? One that said, "Definitely kill Rae." She could just hear herself. *The bomb was set because someone wanted to murder me, Mr. Rocha. Something in my head told me so.* Yeah, that would get her back in the hospital nice and fast.

And probably for a lot longer than a summer vacation.

But I'd definitely have been dead if I went into that stall, Rae thought suddenly. A tremor snaked its way through her body. She reached out and grabbed her big cup of water off Rocha's desk.

/SHE'S OKAY/SO PALE/WHAT ELSE COULD I GET FOR HER/

There was something familiar about those thoughts. Like when you heard an announcer on TV and then later realized it was some washed-up celeb like Kirstie Alley shilling for Burger King.

"Anything at all, Rachel," Mr. Rocha pressed.

"All I did was walk in and go over to the closest sink," Rae told him. The not-her thoughts kept repeating in her mind, growing slightly fuzzier, not staticky, just softer and not quite as clear.

/SHE'S OKAY/SO PALE/WHAT ELSE COULD I GET FOR HER/

Anthony, she thought suddenly. *They remind me of Anthony.* He'd handed her the cup. Had he somehow transferred his thoughts to her? That made no sense. Except that when he was carrying her to the nurse's office, he'd looked so scared. Scared for her. The thoughts sort of fit with how he'd been acting.

"I checked my makeup in the mirror. Then—bam! I didn't even realize it was a bomb. I didn't have time to realize anything." Rae knew she should mention Anthony. Seeing him was a lot more than the smallest detail. But in those thoughts . . . It was like Anthony was really worried about her. Like he . . . like he . . . *cared* about her, wanted to help her somehow.

Uh, hello? Psycho girl? Remember Dr. Warriner? Those thoughts in your head didn't come from Anthony. And the ones that sounded like Dad, they didn't come from Dad. And the one about definitely killing Rae, that didn't come from anyone else, either. Believing they did is going to a whole new number on the nutso scale. But still, it was getting harder and harder *not* to feel like the thoughts were real.

"What about people?" Mr. Rocha asked, his flat hazel eyes intent on Rae's face. "Anyone near the bathroom when you went in?"

There were more not-me thoughts in the bathroom, she remembered. *What were they?* There was one about Anthony. Something like, *They'll think Anthony did it.* Did that mean Anthony was being framed? Because if he was, then she absolutely shouldn't say—

"Rachel, are you having trouble concentrating?" Mr. Rocha asked. "I'm starting to think that blow to your head was more serious—"

"I was just wondering about my dad," Rae said quickly. "Is someone checking the parking lot for him? I'm sure he went to get coffee or something. Usually he just sits in the car and reads until I'm through."

"Sheila—the nurse—is watching for him. She'll bring him in as soon as he gets here," Mr. Rocha answered. "Now, what about who you saw? Was there anyone?"

75

Rae shifted her plastic cup from one hand to the other.

/SHE'S OKAY/WHAT ELSE COULD I GET FOR HER/GONNA FIND OUT WHO DID THIS/

God, those thoughts really *did* feel like Anthony, even though they kept getting a little softer, a little *blurrier.*

"Rachel, if you saw someone, you have to tell me. We're talking about a serious crime here," Mr. Rocha said, impatience flaring in his voice.

"Rae. My name's Rae," she told him sharply.

"Fine. Rae. Now, Rae, did you see anyone around the bathroom?" Mr. Rocha asked again. "I'm sure the police will ask you the same question. But it would help me to hear the answer now."

This wasn't going away. She was going to be asked about what happened again and again. So should she lie or what?

Rae put the cup back down on the desk. She just couldn't picture Anthony setting a bomb.

Reality check, she thought. *The guy's not going to group therapy three times a week for nothing. You have no idea how he ended up here or what he would or wouldn't do. Yeah, he was somewhat nice to you, in his own perverse way, but you don't owe him anything.*

She picked up the cup again and—

/SO PALE/WHAT ELSE COULD I GET FOR HER/GONNA FIND OUT WHO DID THIS/

—took a sip, stalling. "I'm just trying to think. Everything is a little jumbled," Rae said. She wished hearing those psycho

Anthony-flavored thoughts didn't make her feel all warm inside.

"Take your time," Mr. Rocha said, although she noticed the vein next to his eye had started to pulse.

Rae squeezed her eyes shut for a moment. *You don't really have a choice here,* she thought. She opened her eyes again and met Mr. Rocha's gaze. "When I was going into the bathroom, Anthony was coming out."

"Anthony Fascinelli was in the girls' bathroom?" Mr. Rocha asked eagerly.

Rae nodded. And a spike of pain jammed itself into her head.

Anthony's head jerked to the door as it swung open. Rae walked through. Not quite so pale, he noted. Before, even her lips had been bloodless. Now they were back to their usual deep pink, and there was a little color in her cheeks, too. Anthony felt the muscles in the back of his neck relax a little.

Then he realized that Rocha was right behind Rae and that Rocha's little hazel eyes were locked on him. All Anthony's neck muscles tightened up again. So did the muscles in his shoulders. And the ones all the way down the length of his back. *Rae gave me up,* he thought with a sinking feeling.

"Anthony Fascinelli, please come with me," Rocha ordered, sounding so damn pleased with himself. Anthony shot a glance at Rae. She didn't even have the guts to look him in the eye. *Thanks for nothing,* he thought as he grabbed his backpack and headed for the door. He couldn't believe less than an hour ago he'd been having an actual conversation with that girl. Telling her about the stupid *Bluebirds* and everything.

"Now," Rocha added. Anthony stumbled to his feet and followed Rocha down the hall in silence, his mind racing.

Anthony could just see himself sitting in that hard chair across from Rocha and explaining what happened.

See, my pot dealer, my former pot dealer, is an idiot. Even though just yesterday I told him I didn't want to buy, I get this message that he decided to do me a favor and leave some for me taped under the toilet in the last stall of the girls' bathroom. I did mention he's an idiot, right? Anyway, I had to go get it because I was afraid the genius wrote my name on it or something. I'd show you the pot, you know, to back my story up. But I flushed it. You believe that, don't you, Mr. Rocha? It's written all over your files that Anthony Fascinelli is a pothead. But you believe I've changed, right?

They reached Rocha's office, and Rocha held open the door for him with exaggerated politeness.

Anthony knew the drill. He sat down in the wooden chair while Rocha circled around and plopped his butt down on the padded chair behind the desk.

"Rachel Voight told me she saw you coming out of the girls' bathroom. Want to tell me what you were doing in there?" Rocha demanded.

It's not like he wasn't completely expecting the question. But it still made his whole body stiffen.

"The guys' was really crowded, and I had to go," Anthony blurted out. "I drank one of those massive Big Gulps on my way over here. No one was in the girls', so, you know." He shrugged, feeling like a moron.

Rocha made a note on the yellow pad in front of him. Anthony tried not to wince. It wasn't going to be all that hard to check on the crowded-bathroom story, either, he realized. All Rocha would have to do was ask every guy in the place if they'd gone to take a leak around that time.

"I'm sure you've heard a pipe bomb was set off in the girls' bathroom," Rocha said. "Did you notice anything out of the ordinary when you were in there?" Anthony could see Rocha's tongue running around between his top front teeth and his upper lip, like he was trying to get rid of a piece of food or something.

Anthony forced his gaze off Rocha's gross dental hygiene action and went for some eye-to-eye contact, which was supposed to make you look truthful. "I didn't notice anything. Sorry. I wish I had. I would love to help you find whoever did it."

Shut up. Just shut up, Anthony ordered himself. Even though he *would* love to find whoever did it and beat them into a bag of squishy pulp. Not for Rae, like he owed her any favors, but for himself.

"Did you see anyone around?" Rocha asked. He made another pass across his teeth with his tongue. "Any other guys decide to use the girls' bathroom because, as you said, the boys' was so full?"

"No," Anthony answered, figuring one-word answers were probably safest.

"Would you mind if I took a look in your backpack?" Rocha

asked. "Just so I have something more solid to tell the police. Then we can all go on looking for the people who really did this."

Sadistic bastard, Anthony thought. *He's so sure I did it, and he just can't resist really rubbing it in.* Anthony tossed his backpack on the desk. He kept his eyes on Rocha's face, wanting to see the disappointment when he didn't find anything.

But Rocha smiled when he unzipped the backpack. "Pliers. A dowel. Tissue paper. Superglue. And gunpowder," he said. "All ingredients for a pipe bomb."

Anthony's body went cold. Like all he'd been eating for days was ice cubes.

Rae twirled the blue cup in her fingers—

/SO PALE/WHAT ELSE COULD I GET FOR HER /GONNA FIND OUT WHO DID THIS/SHE'S OKAY/

—trying to pay attention to the hack-head girl, who was talking about her feelings. Her feelings about *what,* Rae wasn't exactly sure. Her mind kept wandering to Anthony. And as she twirled the cup—

/SO PALE/WHAT ELSE COULD I GET FOR HER/GONNA FIND OUT WHO DID THIS/SHE'S OKAY/

—with the Anthony-flavored thoughts repeating in her head, getting fuzzier and fuzzier, she kept wishing she'd just kept her mouth shut.

But if she had, who knew what would have happened? Maybe Anthony did set the bomb. Maybe he would have set another one. She set the cup down at her feet. *Maybe, maybe,*

maybe, she thought. But maybe he'd just been in the wrong place at the wrong time. Or maybe someone did set him up. Although why the freak thought in her head would be true, she had no idea.

The door to the meeting room opened, and Mr. Rocha walked in. *Oh God, don't let him want to talk to me again,* Rae thought.

"I just wanted to reassure you that we have already discovered who was responsible for the pipe bomb," Mr. Rocha announced from the doorway. He adjusted his tie, looking sickeningly pleased with himself. "I'm sad to say it was Anthony Fascinelli. He will no longer be a member of your group."

"No way," Jesse burst out. "No way would Anthony do that!"

"Jesse, I know it's hard to—" Ms. Abramson began.

Jesse shoved himself to his feet and took a step toward Mr. Rocha. "What's going to happen to him?"

Rae felt like her heart stopped beating while she waited for the answer.

"The authorities are coming to pick him up," Mr. Rocha answered. "I assume that after the police talk to him, he'll be held in a juvenile detention center until he gets a trial date."

"I'm feeling dizzy," Rae said suddenly. And it was true. Her brain felt like it was spinning inside her skull. "I want to go lie down until my dad gets back."

"Fine," Ms. Abramson said. "Now, Jesse, I want you to—"

Rae didn't hear the rest. She pushed past Mr. Rocha and

rushed down the hall. She had to find Anthony. She had to tell him—she didn't know what she had to tell him. But something.

He's probably in Rocha's office, she thought as she broke into a run. Each step sent pain slamming into the back of her head, but she didn't slow down. There wasn't time.

As soon as she reached the office, she grabbed the door knob—

/knew Fascinelli was a bad one/

—and jerked on it. Locked. "Anthony, are you in there? It's Rae," she said, keeping her voice low.

There was no answer. But he had to be in there. She glanced down the hall, looking for Rocha. He wasn't coming back. Not yet.

"Anthony. I . . . What I did . . . I didn't know what would happen to you," Rae said.

There was no answer. But she could hear someone moving around in there.

"Could you just say something. Please?" Rae begged.

Silence.

Rae didn't know what else to say. There was probably nothing Anthony would want to hear from her right now. Or ever.

*C*hapter 6

Anthony slammed open the toilet seat, grabbed the scrub brush, and started scrubbing away. He was the new guy at the detention center, and the new meat always got the crap jobs.

Crap jobs, he thought. *I should be a comedian.*

"You better not be leaving any brown smears, Fascinelli," one of the guys called from the doorway. "If anyone in our dorm screws up, none of us gets TV privileges tonight."

Anthony gave a grunt and kept on scrubbing. *I should have cleaned the floor first,* he thought. What was wrong with these guys? They weren't five-year-olds. They should have mastered point and shoot by now.

He dunked the brush into the water, then started working on a particularly stubborn stain. It's not like he cared about watching some dumb TV show. But he knew if he made the other guys miss their *Family Guy* reruns, they'd find a way to make him pay. Probably sticking his head in the toilet or something. Then he'd end up throwing some punches, and— it would not be a happy situation.

"Clean enough to eat out of," Anthony muttered as he

studied the bowl. He slammed down the seat, sprayed it with the noxious bargain brand cleaner the center used, and started polishing away with a rag, like a good little boy. "You know who should be doing this?" he mumbled. "Rae Voight. I wouldn't have ended up here if it wasn't for her big, fat mouth."

An image of her big, fat mouth flashed into his head. Her lips were actually more juicy than fat, and—Anthony shook his head. He wasn't doing mental porn with Rae. The little snitch.

Anthony shoved down the toilet lid, then sprayed it and that grungy little place behind the lid, where the screws were.

Except Rae's not the one who set me up, Anthony thought. *She's not the one who put the pipe bomb stuff in my backpack.* That just made no sense. But anyway, even though she didn't set him up, if Rae hadn't blabbed to Rocha, no one would have been looking in his backpack, and—

"You have a visitor, Anthony," a voice called. "You can finish up in here when you're done." Anthony backed out of the stall and saw Bible Bob smiling at him. He was always quoting the "good book." At least he wasn't one of those jerks who took jobs like this because they got off on taking names and kicking butt.

"You know where the common room is, right?" Bob asked.

"Yeah." Anthony dumped his cleaning stuff in the corner and started washing his hands. "Do you know who it is?"

"Your mom," Bob answered.

Anthony dried his hands on the legs of his jeans. "She alone?"

"Yep. You can have as many visitors as you want—as long as you keep your act together. If there's someone else you want to see—" Bob said.

"There isn't," Anthony interrupted. He strode out of the bathroom past Bob, pasting a good-boy smile on his face, and headed down the hall. *So I don't have to deal with stepdad, the sequel,* he thought. Tom was a decent enough guy. But every once in a while he'd go all father on Anthony. Tom had lived in their house for, like, eight months. He knew nothing about Anthony. Nothing.

When Anthony reached the door to the common room, he hesitated, then pulled in a deep breath and opened the door. His eyes went immediately to his mother. Probably *anyone's* eyes would have gone immediately to his mother. She dressed more like a hooker than a mom most of the time because, as she always said, with what she'd paid for her body, she had to show it off. He bet she'd given several of the guys some new images for their mental porn. *Gee, thanks, Mom.*

"Anthony, over here," his mother cried.

I'm heading right toward you, so obviously I see you, he thought. But that was another thing about his mom. She was loud. He took one more step, and she was out of her chair and coming toward him, screeching his name. Then she had him wrapped in a tight, hard hug, the smell of her floral perfume almost choking him.

Anthony knew that the other guys in the room had to be looking, but he didn't let his mother go. For one long moment he closed his eyes and just held on, held on until she finally stepped away.

"Oh, baby, what were you thinking?" his mother asked.

Of course she just assumes I did it, Anthony thought. He opened his mouth to protest, then snapped it shut. He didn't want to have this little talk in the middle of the room. He stalked over to the table in the corner and sat down. At least it was empty, although there were people at the two tables surrounding it.

His mother took her time sliding onto the bench across from him. "What were you thinking?" she repeated, her voice twice as loud as anyone else's in the room. Anthony knew there was no point in trying to get her to keep it down. If he said something, the next few words would come out softer, then the volume would automatically go back up. It's like she couldn't help herself.

"You realize they called me at work. I had to tell my boss why I was leaving early," his mother continued. "Do you know how that made me feel?"

"I didn't do it," Anthony muttered. "And thanks for asking."

"Anthony, they found the stuff in your backpack." Tears welled up in his mother's eyes.

Oh, great. Just perfect, he thought. His mother cried even louder than she talked. In another few seconds she'd be giving everyone in the place a real show.

"Somebody set me up," Anthony told her.

"It's these boys you hang around with. If you had nice boys as friends, things like this wouldn't happen," his mother answered. The tears were hanging off her heavily mascaraed lashes now. "I tried to . . . to help you. Remember? I made . . . those parties? And . . . and . . ."

And we're off, Anthony thought as his mother started in with the big, gulping sobs. Maybe it would have been better if Tom had come with her. Even though he'd have been totally pissed at Anthony, he'd at least have tried to keep her somewhat in line.

His mother rooted through her purse, probably looking for Kleenex, her crying so loud, it was practically echoing. Anthony focused his eyes on a crack in the linoleum floor. He couldn't look at her right now.

There was no point in trying to say anything. When she got on a crying jag, it was like she went deaf. She wouldn't be able to listen to him until she was finished with her little fit.

"I don't know what I'm supposed to do. Tell me what I'm supposed to do," she said, snuffling. "I can't follow you around all day, making sure that you don't get into trouble. I would if I could. But I have to work. You know that."

Anthony heard a snicker. He gripped the edge of the bench with both hands. If he didn't, he'd have to punch someone.

Her crying got a little quieter. She was winding down. "There's nothing you're supposed to do," Anthony told her. "You do everything a mother's supposed to do."

He heard another snicker, but he ignored it. "Look, just don't worry," he continued. "At my trial everything will get straightened out. Everything will be fine." Because it's not like there was any *evidence* against him or anything. Just a backpack full of pipe bomb crap and an eyewitness who could place him in the bathroom.

"But what if—" his mother began.

Anthony couldn't let her get started again. He leaned across the table and kissed her cheek. "It won't," he answered. "Now, you should go. It's almost time for Carl to take his antibiotics again. Tom won't remember."

His mother stood up, patted her hair, then pulled out a lip gloss and added a fresh coat. "I'll come and see you tomorrow."

"Don't ask for more time off work, okay?" Anthony said. "I'm all right." He saw that her eyes were refilling with tears. He stood up fast, kissed her again, then hurried out of the room.

A few seconds later he heard footsteps in the hall behind him.

"Fascinelli's mom is hot," a voice said.

Anthony didn't turn around.

"Yeah, did you see her boobs? She's got to be a double D," another voice answered.

Anthony didn't turn around. Getting in a fight on his first day in this place would be a total Bluebird move.

"Hey, Anthony?" the first voice called. "When you gave your mommy those kisses, did it get you excited?"

If we weren't in here, you guys would already be bleeding,

Anthony thought. But they *were* in here. And who knew how long Anthony would have to stay?

Rae started slowly toward the cafeteria. She wasn't ready for another round of Who Wants to Be Sickeningly Nice to Rae? Being nice should be a good thing, she guessed. But her friends were sooo nice, it made Rae feel like a freak. Or like a charity project. Dori Hernandez was the worst. She'd stare at Rae with these big, sympathetic eyes—while practically sitting on Marcus's lap.

When she reached the double doors, she pushed through them—

I talked to me a lot / my perfect brother wouldn't / *will Rae go off again if /*

—without hesitation. *Attitude,* she reminded herself for the billionth time. She strode over to the food line and grabbed a tray.

I didn't have to act like I was / iced tea /

Rae had been noticing a trend with her not-me thoughts. They kind of matched her surroundings. She didn't get dad-flavored thoughts at school. Or Leah-ish thoughts at home. What was that about? She took a bean burrito even though she didn't feel hungry. *You're eating it all,* she told herself. She hadn't eaten anything last night or this morning. And she was *not* going to go anorexic. She had enough problems. She took a bottle of water, paid, and got change, a burst of static filling her head. Way underneath Rae thought there

89

were words, but she couldn't make them out. She'd gotten a bunch of the little static blasts since she was hospitalized. Just another little variation on her "specialness."

Rae turned toward her usual table. Leah was laughing at something Vincent had just said. *If I go over there, she'll stop laughing,* Rae thought. *She'll go into her overprotective mode— making sure I have napkins, making sure I got enough food, making sure that everyone is being nice to me, which of course everyone will be, at least to my face.*

Still, she had to keep trying, right? One of these days her friends would have to go back to normal around her. She took a deep breath and headed toward them.

"So it's okay if we don't invite Rae, right?" she heard Jackie's familiar voice say just as she neared the table. She stopped, her heart slamming against her chest. Invite Rae where?

Rae turned her back to them and rested her tray down on an empty table, holding her breath as she listened.

"It's better for her," she heard Leah answer, a note of defensiveness in her voice. "I don't think she'd really be up for a party yet."

"That's what I figured," Jackie said quickly. "So Dori, you and Marcus can—"

Rae jammed the water bottle and the burrito into her bag, letting the not-her thoughts flow through her mind as she spun back around and speed walked toward the exit. No food was supposed to be taken out of the cafeteria, but screw that. If she had to sit at the table with her quote-unquote friends, she wouldn't be able to swallow a bite. She hurried back out the doors—

/Carrie White/door—<u>puerta</u>/

—and started down the hall, blinking rapidly. It was one thing when they were all treating her like some little kid that practically needed to be spoon-fed. At least she still felt like they cared. But to hear them sitting there coming up with excuses to keep her out of their social life—that was too much.

Maybe she could eat in the art room. She could hang out there, do some work on her painting. Rae jerked to a stop. *Yeah, working on that painting would really help your appetite,* she thought.

She'd just started another one of those paintings where her hand did what it wanted. Big mistake. She'd ended up with the beginnings of a face that she absolutely knew would become Anthony Fascinelli. Anthony Fascinelli, looking at her like he wanted her dead.

God, how much did she wish she hadn't said anything to Mr. Rocha yesterday? All she could think about now was those not-her thoughts that felt like Anthony, the thoughts that kept trying to convince her that he was innocent. *If he is or if he isn't, there's nothing you can do about it now,* she told herself.

A couple of girls from her English class passed her, giving her semiweird looks. Rae headed toward the stairwell. She could eat there without anyone looking at her or being nice. No, not nice. *Fake* nice.

Pretty pathetic, she thought as she opened the door.

/will she be here?/

She pulled a notebook out of her backpack, letting the not-her thoughts roll on by, and put it on the top step so she'd have something to sit on. *I'm not going to walk around all day with a dirty butt,* she thought. *People are staring enough as it is.* Before she could even retrieve her burrito, the door swung open behind her.

She glanced over her shoulder and saw Jeff Brunner standing there.

"Hey," he said, looking a little embarrassed. "I saw you come in here and . . ." He let the sentence trail off.

Rae raised an eyebrow. "You just *happened* to see me come in here?"

"I was looking for you in the cafeteria," Jeff confessed, one of his adorable blushes coloring his face. He probably hated being a blusher. "I saw you leave," he continued. "Then I sort of followed you, and that's when I happened to see you come in here."

Oh my God. Is he actually interested *in me?* Rae searched his face, looking for any hint that he was doing his good deed for the day or getting his jollies by hanging out with the school nut job. But his smile was just a nice, normal, slightly shy smile.

Rae allowed herself a quick body scan on Jeff. He was tall and lean, with a swimmer kind of build versus the football-player type. Nice.

"So, um, what do you think of Sanderson so far?" Rae asked. She got her foil-wrapped burrito out of her backpack and unwrapped it, ignoring the blurry thought.

"I'm liking it more all the time," he answered, looking right at her.

Rae laughed in his face. His blush got a little deeper, but he laughed, too. "Smooth, huh?" he asked.

"Real smooth," she answered. She took a bite of her bur-rito, suddenly starving. "Aren't you going to eat?"

"Eat. Right," Jeff said. He sat down next to her and pulled a sandwich and a bag of pork rinds out of his backpack. "Want some?" He shook the bag in her direction.

"I'm a vegetarian," Rae answered, wrinkling her nose.

Jeff hurled the pork rinds down the stairs. "So am I. Those things disgust me."

Rae giggled. She was surprised she hadn't forgotten how.

"Some sicko put them in my backpack," Jeff told her. "You believe me, right?"

"Of course I believe you," Rae answered with mock sincerity.

She couldn't help thinking of Anthony. Who could have put the pipe bomb stuff in his backpack? Everyone had been talking about it after the meeting yesterday. She pushed the thought away. For once she had the chance to be . . . the girl she used to be. The girl who could flirt, knowing that the guy would like it.

"Really," Jeff insisted. "I never eat those things."

"You better not," Rae teased. "I could never sit this close to a guy with pork-rind breath."

Jeff moved a little closer, just the tiniest bit, but close enough that Rae could feel the heat of his body. "How do you feel about peanut butter?" he asked, holding up his sandwich.

"I'm totally for it," Rae answered.

He started to take a bite. "Strawberry jelly?"

"The best," Rae said. "You have my permission to eat it."

Jeff took a bite, then held the sandwich up to Rae's lips. She took a bite, too.

Let me spend the rest of my life right here, she thought. *It wouldn't take one other thing to make me happy if I could keep on feeling normal. Just normal.*

Chapter 7

Rae headed across her front lawn, eager to get inside the house. She had about two hours of total alone time. No school. No group. No Dad. And no housekeeper, thank God. Her dad had actually wanted to hire someone as a live-in housekeeper, aka baby-sitter, when Rae got out of the hospital, but she'd managed to convince him she could be trusted in the house by herself for the two or three minutes a day when she was there without him. And they still had Alice Shaffer come in twice a week to clean and freeze some meals for them.

She pulled out her key—

/just let me/

—and unlocked the door, then grabbed the knob. She gasped when her fingers touched it—

/that bitch, Rae/

—and she jerked them away. The thought had been like a scream in her mind, so full of hate that it made her nerves sizzle. It hadn't *felt* like anyone familiar, the way some of the thoughts had started to. But that almost made it worse. It was like there was a stranger in her head who wanted to hurt her.

Just go get in the tub with some of that Burt's Bees milk bath, put

your plastic cushion under your head, and veg until you're a prune,
Rae told herself. *You can even get in some fantasizing about that
guy Jeff. He'll make good mind candy.* She forced herself to open
the door—

/that bitch, Rae/

—then stepped inside and closed it behind her.

/if I get caught/

Rae's heart gave a kick in her chest and started beating
double time. That thought had been so full of anxiety that
it had affected her body. *You've got to let them rush through,* she
instructed herself. *They're mind elevator music, nothing more.
Annoying, but that's all.*

Her little self-lecture didn't slow down her heart. She
started for the kitchen to make herself some hot chocolate to
drink in the tub.

Why is the hall light on? she thought. Her dad had a fit about
anyone wasting electricity, so Rae was in the habit of turning
off the lights when she left the house. And he never forgot. She
veered over and flicked off the switch.

/Rae'll be sorry/

God, it was the same . . . the same *flavor* as the other not-
her thoughts she'd gotten—the ones off the door. That person
who hated her. Even with the static she could tell that. Who
could hate her so much?

"Not a who. Elevator music," she whispered. "That's all."
But the little hairs on her arms were standing up. So were the
ones on the back of her neck. Rae glanced behind her. No one
was there. But she didn't feel alone. She could swear there was

someone in the house with her. A shiver slithered through her, and she wrapped her arms around herself. But it didn't make her feel any warmer.

Okay, forget the bath, she thought. *This is way beyond bath comfort. Call Yana. Invite her over.* Rae rushed down the hall to her bedroom and yanked open the door.

/teach her /

"No," she whispered. "I don't—why?" Her brain felt like it was hardly functioning. She pulled in a deep breath and tried to take in what she was seeing.

Her comforter had been shredded. Clumps of the cotton batting were lying all over the floor, along with pieces of glass that Rae recognized as the remnants of her perfume bottles. Each breath burned Rae's throat and lungs, and it didn't feel like she was getting oxygen, just a mix of citrus and musk and flowers.

She couldn't stop staring around the room. The canvas of her newest painting had been slashed. Rufus, her very first stuffed animal, had been ripped almost in two. Rae knelt down, picked up the worn bunny—

/teach her /

—and cradled it in her arms. Was this some kind of hallucination? Was she becoming even more psycho? What if she called Yana and Yana said the room looked perfectly ordinary? Rae squeezed Rufus tighter.

/teach her /

She walked over to her dresser, the glass crunching under her feet, then leaned down and stared into her mirror, as if looking at herself would tell her whether she was becoming like her mother. Becoming totally, irretrievably insane.

Her blue eyes looked scared, but not crazy. *As if a crazy person would be able to make that call,* she thought. She started to straighten up, then froze. There were words reflected in the mirror. Words that had been painted on the wall behind her.

Slowly Rae turned around and read the message that had been left for her: *Keep your big mouth shut.* She walked over and ran her fingers over the words. They were still wet.

This would be a very good time to get out of here. A very, very good time. She took one step toward the door, then froze again. She'd heard something. A tiny sound coming from the bathroom.

Whoever had done this to her was still in the house.

Anthony locked his eyes on the screen, not that he cared which of the idiots on *Jerry Springer* had slept with which of the other idiots. He wanted to blend, and shutting up and watching TV was the easiest way to do it.

"Did you hear what happened to McGlynn?" one of the guys on the couch asked. Anthony knew the guy wasn't talking to him, so he didn't even glance over. This wasn't a place where you just joined in a conversation.

"What?" some other guy asked.

"Got sent to Ashton," the first guy answered.

Anthony tried to actually pay attention to the *Springer* freaks. The last thing he wanted to listen to was a bunch of crap about Ashton. If things went bad at his trial, he'd be at the youth prison soon enough, and then he'd see it all for himself.

"Fascinelli, your head is in the way," said Paul, a guy from Anthony's dorm. Anthony slid over a foot and crossed his legs, trying to get comfortable again on the floor's thin carpet.

"It's still in the way," Paul said.

Anthony didn't move. Clearly Paul was making a little power play. If Anthony moved again, he knew Paul would keep pushing him, trying to figure out exactly how much Anthony would take. He figured it was better to deal with Paul now instead of letting it escalate.

"Are you deaf?" Paul asked. He gave Anthony a kick in the back. Not too hard, but hard enough.

Anthony shot a glance over at Bible Bob. He was in the middle of an earnest conversation with one of the younger kids. Anthony turned back to the TV, then he reached over and grabbed Paul by the ankle. He gave a hard jerk, and Paul came out of the chair and landed on his butt on the floor. "Now can you see?"

A couple of guys laughed. Anthony didn't. He wasn't trying to score points. He was just trying to make it through his stretch here without getting the crap beat out of him. And if he had to be a badass to do it, so be it.

Some of the tension drained out of his body as he realized that Paul wasn't going to try taking things to the next level. At least not this time.

"If you tried that at Ashton, you'd be missing a limb right about now," one of the guys on the couch commented.

"I'm not going to Ashton," Anthony muttered. But even as he said the words, he didn't believe them.

Should she try to leave? Just run for it? Rae shifted her weight from foot to foot. What if she wasn't fast enough? What if whoever was in the bathroom caught her? Maybe she should just hide in the closet or something. Wait him out.

She hesitated. Neither solution felt right. *You have to do something,* she ordered herself. Then she heard the bathroom door swing open. If she ran, he would see her. If she darted to the closet, he would hear her.

Footsteps started down the hall toward her room. A figure started past the open door. Rae didn't think. She just let out a howl that was half terror and half fury and hurled herself at the guy. He hit the ground with a thud, and she heard his breath come out with a wheeze.

"Who are you?" she demanded, voice shaking. Then she realized the guy was smaller than she thought at first, just about her size. Rae roughly flipped him over onto his back. She recognized his face immediately from group therapy. It took a second longer to come up with his name. "Jesse," she cried. "Jesse Beven! You did this? Why would you do this?"

Jesse started to struggle to his knees, but Rae shoved him back down. His face was so white that she could see every freckle. *He's as scared as I was,* she thought. "Answer me," she barked.

"I don't have to tell you anything." He jerked his body to the left and managed to scramble up before Rae could grab him again. He took off down the hall.

"Hey, Mensa boy, I know your name, you know," Rae called after him as she shoved herself to her feet. He stopped. "Ms. Abramson knows where you live and your phone number," she continued. "By the time you get home, the police will be waiting for you."

Jesse turned around. "Fine. Get me sent to the detention center with Anthony. I'd rather be there."

"So that's what your little painting on my wall was about. Anthony," Rae said. She let Rufus fall to the ground.

"Duh," Jesse muttered. He jerked up his chin, and his red hair fell away from his face.

God, he was a baby. Barely thirteen.

"Look, my dad will be home in a few hours. Clean up my room before he gets here, and I might be able to forget this ever happened," Rae told him. "You can pay me back for the stuff you trashed. A little every week," she added.

Jesse stared at her for a long moment. Then he walked over, picked up Rufus from the ground, and handed him to her. He stepped past her into her room without a word. Rae followed him. She put Rufus on her bed, feeling overwhelmed by the amount of damage Jesse had managed to do. "I'll get some garbage bags," she said, hurrying to the kitchen without waiting for an answer.

She opened the polished doorknob of the little supply cupboard, a closet she and her dad rarely bothered going into since most of their cleaning involved paper towels and water, and pulled out a box of the jumbo lawn trash bags—

/need to pick up candles/

—then rushed back to her room. She didn't want to leave Jesse alone too long in case he thought about bolting again.

"Here." She lobbed the box of trash bags at Jesse, who was crouched on the floor, gathering up pieces of comforter stuffing.

He gave a grunt that she decided to take as a thank-you.

Might as well help, she thought. She grabbed some turpentine and some rags from a box in her closet, letting the not-her thoughts—although these were of the variety that felt *more* like her—buzz on through her brain, then started working on getting the paint off the wall. Her father would freak if he saw it. Forget about a live-in housekeeper; he'd probably hire an armed guard.

They worked in silence, without looking at each other. "Can I open a window?" Jesse finally asked.

"Yeah. It reeks in here," Rae answered. "And by the way, you're going to have to cough up some major bucks for the perfume."

"I will. It was stupid. It's just—you don't know Anthony," Jesse blurted out. "I do. He would never have set off that pipe bomb. There's no way."

He was saying what Rae had been thinking. Make that what she'd been hoping. *Are we both delusional?* Rae wondered. She turned to face him. "How long have you known Anthony?"

"Couple of years," Jesse answered. "And I know he wouldn't set off a pipe bomb. When Anthony gets pissed, he just starts throwing punches. He doesn't stop and plan, like you'd have to do to set a bomb."

"So you're saying he's violent. But too hot tempered to take the time to plant a bomb?" Rae asked sarcastically, even though a part of her, a big part of her, wanted to believe Anthony was innocent. She just didn't want to be an idiot about it.

"Forget it," Jesse mumbled. "You don't want to hear it." He tied one of the garbage bags closed with a tight knot.

Rae crossed the room and sat down next to him. She opened a fresh garbage bag and started picking up pieces of her perfume bottles, fragments of thoughts popping up in her head every few shards. "I do want to hear it," she finally said. "I just don't want to be played."

"I'm not playing you," Jesse answered as he gathered some pieces of glass in one cupped hand. "Anthony gets in fights when people piss him off." He dumped the glass into the bag. "Like when this guy at the 7-Eleven was busting on me, Anthony broke his nose. Blood geyser."

Jesse sounded way too impressed. Rae shook her head.

"He totally backed me up, with no questions. That's what you'd get if you knew him. You should see what he does for his little brothers and sister. He even wore a Jonas Brothers T-shirt one day so he wouldn't hurt his little sister's feelings."

So that was why he'd worn the stupid shirt. She picked up another piece of glass, and a tiny sliver jammed itself into her finger. She carefully began prying it out with one fingernail, trying not to get all gooey over the picture of Anthony being that sweet to his little sister.

"So if Anthony didn't do it, who did?" Rae asked, pulling the glass sliver free. She sucked lightly on the cut, which was barely bleeding—just a couple of drops. She was curious to see if Jesse had any theories. She'd love some hard info instead of her thoughts and feelings, which she'd be crazy—literally—to trust.

Jesse shrugged. "I just know it wasn't Anthony," he answered, without a hint of doubt or deceit in his voice.

"The stuff was in his backpack," Rae reminded him.

"Then somebody set him up," Jesse shot back.

Gonna find out who did this. She remembered how good it had made her feel when she'd held that blue cup and heard that thought the first time. That Anthony-flavored thought. It had made her feel kind of warm inside. Safe. Like someone was looking out for her. And from what Jesse said, Anthony *was* the kind of guy who did that—looked out for people.

You can't start believing your crazy person thoughts, she reminded herself. But she felt almost positive that Jesse was telling her the truth. And her own instincts, or whatever you wanted to call them, agreed.

"Maybe you're right," Rae said softly.

"What?" Jesse exclaimed.

"I said, maybe you're right about Anthony," Rae told him. "Now, keep cleaning."

Chapter 8

"Rae. Over here!" Yana called. Rae smiled as she spotted her in the school parking lot, leaning against her beat-up sunshine yellow VW Bug.

"Nice pants," Rae said as she hurried over.

"Just the pants? What, you don't like the shirt?" Yana asked. She adjusted the collar of her turquoise bowling shirt. Rae noticed that the name Betty was embroidered over the pocket.

"No, I like. But shredded black jeans, ankle boots, and a bowling shirt?" Rae shook her head. "One of these things is not like the other."

"That's me. Full of surprises," Yana answered. She opened the car door and slid behind the wheel. Rae took shotgun, some of her own special elevator music playing in her head.

"Thanks for taking me," Rae said. "I could have bused it, but—"

"Oh, shut up," Yana interrupted. "We're friends, remember?"

Rae could feel her smile widening into something that was

probably ridiculous looking. The casual way that Yana used the word *friend*—it made her feel all toasty inside. Which was pathetic but true.

Rae's BlackBerry buzzed, and she pulled it out of her purse and answered it, trying not to let the not-her thoughts popping up in her head distract her.

"Hi, Rae. It's Ms. Abramson. Your dad gave me this number. I hope that's okay with you," she said.

"Yeah. Fine," Rae answered, although she wished he hadn't. It was hard to feel normal when your group therapy leader could call you anywhere, anytime.

"I just wanted to let you know we'll miss you in group this afternoon," Ms. Abramson continued.

"Um, thanks," Rae said, not adding that she wouldn't miss Ms. Abramson or anyone else. Not having to sit around and emote with the other sickos was the one bonus of having to go to the police station and give a statement.

"I know it's probably a little scary for you to talk to the police. But all you have to do is tell them what you saw," Ms. Abramson said, her voice filled with concern. "Call me afterward if you want to talk things through."

"Okay. I will. I have to go, but thanks." Rae pressed END without waiting for Ms. Abramson to say good-bye, then stuck the phone back in her purse.

"Look at you with your fancy phone," Yana commented.

"More like a tracking device," Rae corrected her. "It was a present from my dad. I think he thinks if he can be in touch with me at any moment that somehow I won't have another psycho fit."

Yana shot Rae an irritated look, her green eyes narrowed, as she pulled to a stop in front of a red light. "Okay. Here's the deal. The next time you use the word *psycho* or *freak* about yourself, I'm going to slap you. And I'm talking hard."

"What about if I just say"—Rae leaned toward Yana and lowered her voice to a whisper—"that I'm not quite my old self." She returned her voice to a normal level. "I heard someone saying that about me when I was in the bathroom today. Doesn't anyone bother to check under the stall doors anymore?"

"Clearly whoever said that has no life," Yana answered. "If they did, they wouldn't be hanging around in the bathroom, talking about *you*." She gunned her engine at the Jag next to her. The guy behind the wheel grinned.

"Yana, that guy has to be thirty," Rae protested.

"But cute!" Yana answered as the light changed and they started across the intersection. "So what's going on with you and guys, anyway?"

In truth Rae had been thinking about Anthony nonstop. Actually, she still sort of was, with an underlayer of her brain. But at least part of her attention was on the conversation with Yana.

"From the look on your face, I'd say guywise you're doing okay," Yana teased.

"Oh, sure. Except for the little fact that my old boyfriend

dumped me. Not that he actually ever bothered to say so. He just appeared the first day of school with this girl Dori Hernandez surgically attached to him," Rae answered.

"Yowch," Yana said with a grimace.

"Yeah. But I met this other guy. Jeff," Rae added quickly, not wanting to seem like a total loser. "We've only hung out a few times. Just at lunch, you know. But—"

"But you looove him," Yana said. She made a right turn so fast, Rae's seat belt cut into her side.

"He has his good points," Rae admitted. "One of the big ones is that he's new. So even though he heard about me losing it last year, he didn't actually witness my psy—"

Yana held up one hand. "I'm warning you."

"He doesn't act all weird around me," Rae amended, avoiding the slap.

"So give me the deets," Yana said.

"Um, okay. Tall. Light brown hair. Nice hands, you know?" Rae began.

"Boring. What about his butt?" Yana asked.

"That's also nice," Rae answered. *This is exactly the kind of conversation I'd have been having with Leah last year,* Rae realized.

"We're almost there. Are you starting to get worried about talking to the cops?" Yana asked. "It's not going to be a big deal. You say what happened. They write it down. It's over."

"Except for Anthony," Rae said.

"Not your problem," Yana answered.

Yana pulled the Bug into the parking lot of the police station and found a space right in front of the building. "And anyway," she continued. "It's not like what you have to say matters that much. They found all that bomb junk in his backpack, right?"

"Right," Rae replied. "Right," she repeated.

But that was just circumstantial evidence. It didn't prove anything. It didn't make the accusations against Anthony true. What felt true was Jesse's belief that Anthony wasn't capable of the kind of cruelty it would take to set off the bomb. What felt true was Rae's own belief—based on pretty much nothing—that Anthony was innocent.

"I'll be waiting for you when you're done," Yana told her. "We'll get ice cream."

Rae nodded. "Thanks again, Ya—"

"Didn't I tell you to shut up about it?" Yana interrupted. She gave Rae's shoulder a shove.

"Okay, okay. See you in a little while." Rae climbed out of the car and slammed the door.

/need better ID/

Then she headed up to the glass front door and pushed it open—

/why did he/ can't be here again/ SO WASTED/

—and headed over to the cop at the front desk. "I'm Rae Voight. I have an appointment with Detective Sullivan."

The cop nodded, adjusting the clump of hair he'd combed over his bald spot. He picked up the phone and punched a couple of numbers. "The girl is here," he said.

Thanks for remembering my name, Rae thought.

"She'll be right out. You can sit over there." The cop jerked his head toward a long wooden bench against the wall. Rae obediently walked over and plopped down. Her stomach was already twisting itself into an extreme pretzel, and she hadn't even seen the detective yet.

Rae took her comb out of her purse—

/need a trim / Anthony wouldn't/

—and began pulling it through her hair. She was getting better and better at picking up on the flavors of the not-her thoughts. That first not-her one actually felt like her. Like it was a thought of hers, but not the thought she was actually having at that moment.

And the other one, it had given her a Jesse vibe. The mix of anger and fear and frustration just felt like him somehow. The kid was going nuts thinking that Anthony might get sent away. Talking to Jesse while they cleaned had given Rae the idea that Anthony was pretty much Jesse's surrogate big brother.

How am I even going to look at Jesse in group if I help nail Anthony? Rae thought. Before she could come up with an answer, a forty-something woman strode toward her, looking much more glam than Rae expected, with an ash blond bob and a petal-pink manicure. "Rae? I'm Laura Sullivan." She gave Rae's hand a quick, firm shake. "Come on back."

Detective Sullivan led Rae through a maze of desks and into a grungy office. She'd tried to make it a little nicer with some potted plants and a Picasso print on the wall. But nothing Ms. Sullivan had done could compensate for the ugly metal desk, the beat-up chairs, the stained carpet, and the worst shade of green paint Rae'd ever seen. "We'll make this short," Ms. Sullivan said. "I'm sure that you have other things you'd rather be doing."

"Pretty much anything," Rae admitted, sitting in the chair voted the most likely not to collapse.

"Just tell me what you saw." Ms. Sullivan positioned her hands on her computer keyboard.

Easy for you to say, Rae thought. If she told what she saw, she'd ruin Anthony's life.

Ms. Sullivan tapped her fingers on the keys impatiently. Rae took the hint. "Okay. Well. I stopped off in the ladies' room. I just wanted to check my makeup," she began. "I stepped toward the mirror. And then I was on the floor. I didn't even realize a bomb had gone off until they told me."

Gotta do something, she thought. *Gotta do something right now to stop this thing. But what?*

"I hit my head," Rae added quickly. "Things got a little fuzzy."

Now, that just might get you—you and Anthony—out of this, Rae told herself. *You hit your head. You don't remember too well what happened. Yeah.*

"I bet," Detective Sullivan said as she typed. "Then what happened?"

Rae brushed her hair off her face. "Then I . . . I was sort of dizzy. There were white dots in front of my eyes and everything, you know?" Ms. Sullivan nodded. "I grabbed the sink and pulled myself up. . . ."

Rae suddenly pictured herself blurting out what really happened next.

And that's when I got one of my not-me thoughts. One that said Anthony could have been set up. Oh, and by the way, I also got a thought saying somebody wanted to kill me. That helps, right? You know not to bother with Anthony. And you know the real bomb setter is someone who would like me dead. Oh, and probably I should tell you that I was recently released from a mental hospital. But that has nothing to do with the thoughts. They were real. That's how I know Anthony is innocent. Well, that, and that when I touched this blue cup, I could tell he was really worried about me, that he really cared. And that makes him a good person. And a good person wouldn't set off a pipe bomb. So you can call the juvenile detention center right now and tell them there's been a mistake.

"You pulled yourself up and then . . . ?" Ms. Sullivan prompted.

"It's kind of fuzzy," Rae said. "I know that someone helped me down to the nurse's office."

"Let's go back to when you first went into the bathroom," Ms. Sullivan said. "Did you notice anything unusual? See anyone?"

You know I did, Rae thought. *You already heard everything from Rocha.* "Like I said, it's blurry," Rae answered. She shifted in her chair, unable to find a comfortable position.

"It's blurry even before the bomb went off?" Ms. Sullivan asked.

"It's weird," Rae answered slowly, hoping for inspiration.

"When I think about going to Oakvale that day, it's all a little, you know, fuzzy. I *did* hit my head pretty hard. It was bleeding in back and *everything.*"

Ms. Sullivan looked up from her computer screen and studied Rae's face. Rae felt like she had the words *big, fat liar* written in lipstick on her forehead.

"Do you remember telling Mr. Rocha what happened?" Ms. Sullivan asked.

"Sort of," Rae admitted.

"You told him that someone was in the bathroom when you went in. Do you remember that?" Ms. Sullivan pressed, her eyes alert, the kind of eyes that noticed everything.

"Yeah. I remember," Rae answered.

"And who was it you saw?" Ms. Sullivan asked.

Rae met Ms. Sullivan's gaze straight on. Then she said the only thing she could say.

"It was Anthony Fascinelli."

Anthony headed to the common room. He prayed his mother would be wearing something that wouldn't get too much attention from the guys. He pushed open the door—and saw Jesse sitting at the table in the back corner. But he wasn't alone—Rae was sitting next to him.

No way. He had to take a lot of crap in this place. But he did not have to take this. Anthony strode over to the table and leaned down until he could look Rae directly in the eye. "Get out of here," he ordered. "Right now."

"She wants to help," Jesse said.

"That's crap," Anthony shot back without taking his eyes off Rae, careful to keep his voice low enough so that the counselor supervising the room wouldn't hear. "I wouldn't be here if it wasn't for her."

"Sit down, Mr. Fascinelli," the counselor called from across the room. Anthony sat, still locking eyes with Rae. Her gaze finally skittered away from his, and he felt a surge of satisfaction.

"That's not totally true, you know," Rae protested, her eyes lowered and her voice all whiny. "They found the stuff in your backpack, so—"

"They wouldn't have been looking in my backpack if you hadn't opened your fat mouth," Anthony shot back.

Rae's chin jerked up. "What were you doing in the girls' bathroom in the first place?" Her voice wasn't whiny now. It was sharp, accusing. And this time she was the one getting in *his* face, going practically nose to nose with him, her blue eyes bright with anger.

"I can't believe you're coming in here asking me questions," Anthony said. He shot a glance at Jesse. "I hope this wasn't your idea."

"It wasn't," Rae answered. "Look, let's back up, okay?" She reached out and touched his wrist for a fraction of a second, and he felt the heat of her fingers down to the bone. "I didn't come here—" She hesitated, started again. "I came here because I don't think you set off the bomb. And I don't want to be part of putting you into Ashton."

Ashton. The word was like a bullet to the gut.

"There's nothing either of you can do about it." He gave Rae a pointed look. "Unless you plan on lying to the cops."

"I already gave them my testimony," Rae admitted. She gave his wrist another fast finger brush. "I'd already told Rocha everything. I thought it would make things worse if I changed my story. I'm sorry."

"So you're here so I can say, 'Oh, that's okay. I know you feel bad, but it's not your fault.' Is that it?" Anthony's hands curled into fists.

"That's not why we came. We're going to figure out who did do it," Jesse said eagerly.

"Who are you? Nancy Drew and the Hardy Boys?" Anthony asked. He felt a twinge of guilt when he saw the hurt expression on Jesse's face. But really, what were they thinking?

"We're what you have," Rae said quietly. "And it's not like anything we do is going to make things worse." Jesse didn't say anything. He wouldn't even look Anthony in the face.

Anthony rubbed his face with his fingers. "You're right," he admitted. "So, what's the plan? Is there a plan?"

"Not yet," Rae said. "We thought if you could just tell us . . . something, we'd, uh, try and dig up some evidence."

Her face turned pink all the way to the roots of her hair, like she was embarrassed to be saying that crap. And she should be. This was hopeless.

"Why *were* you in the girls' bathroom?" Jesse asked, shoulders hunched like he was afraid to say the words. "They're definitely going to ask you that at your hearing."

"The guy I buy weed from said he left some for me in

there," Anthony said. He did a check on the counselor. The guy was still too far away to hear, hovering by a table where a girlfriend had brought her boyfriend some brownies, clearly hoping for a handout.

"In the girls' bathroom?" Rae asked.

"The guy's a moron," Anthony answered. "But even for Nunan this was a new low."

"So it's not the usual place for a pickup," Jesse said. And he actually pulled a little notebook and a pencil out of his pocket.

Anthony shook his head. "I usually just go over to the 7-Eleven and get it from him."

"So, okay," Rae said. "I'm no Nancy Drew, but I say the first thing we do is talk to this Nunan guy. See why he chose the girls' bathroom. And find out if he saw anything when he made the drop." She glanced at Jesse, and he gave a little nod, then started scribbling away. They were quite a pair.

"Couldn't hurt, I guess," Anthony said. He locked his hands behind his head and leaned back, trying to crack his spine. It felt like it was made of cement.

"Don't sound so grateful," Rae told him irritatedly.

"Is that why you're here? You want gratitude?" Anthony demanded.

"No," Rae answered. She ran her finger over one of her eyebrows, smoothing it down.

"Then what? Explain it to me. You don't know me at all. Why are you so sure I didn't set the bomb?" Anthony asked.

"Shut up. We know you didn't do it," Jesse said.

"I know *you* know I didn't do it," Anthony told Jesse. Then he turned back to Rae. "But I don't get why you're here. And I really don't like the idea of getting help from somebody when I don't know what's in it for them."

"I just . . . You don't seem like someone who—" She stopped and did the eyebrow-smoothing thing again.

"Bullshit," Anthony said. "Tell me the truth. Or get out. Jesse can talk to Nunan alone."

Rae didn't answer. She was quiet for so long, he started to think she was never going to. Then she let out a shaky breath. "Jesse, do you mind waiting outside for me?" she asked.

"Why?" Jesse asked, crossing his arms over his chest.

"I want to talk to Anthony alone for a minute, okay?"

Jesse looked over at Anthony, and Anthony nodded, then Jesse stood up reluctantly and headed for the door.

"This better be good," Anthony said.

Rae studied him for a moment, her blue eyes wary. "Oh, it's good." She shifted in her chair, then grabbed her purse and pulled out her lip gloss. She coated her mouth in a couple of quick moves.

"You need lip gloss to talk about it?" Anthony asked, trying not to fixate on her mouth, now that it was all slick and shiny.

"I'm nervous, okay?" she snapped. She dropped the lip gloss back in her purse, then cradled the purse on her lap. "You know I was in the hospital, right?"

"Yeah. You had some kind of breakdown," he answered. What did that have to do with him?

"Yeah. I totally lost it. What happened was, I started getting all these thoughts in my head. Thoughts that weren't mine," she said in a rush, pressing her purse even closer to her body.

"What's that supposed to mean—not yours?" Anthony asked. Was the girl a total fruitcake? She'd seemed okay at Oakvale, but this was not sounding good.

"I can't explain it. The thoughts . . . . I wasn't *thinking* them. They kind of just appear in my head. Sometimes clear. Sometimes fuzzy. Sometimes almost blocked out by static or something. And sometimes . . . sometimes they *feel* like other people. Like my dad. Or Jesse. Or . . . you." She gave a harsh laugh. "Don't think I don't know how this sounds. When you get out of here, you can organize a sanity hearing and testify against me."

Anthony kept his eyes on her face. He was good at telling when people were lying. Rae looked kind of freaked-out, but he didn't think she was making this up.

"What does all this have to do with why you've decided to take me on as a charity case?"

"When I was in the bathroom, after the bomb went off, I got some of the thoughts, the not-me thoughts. That's what I call them. I have them so much, I needed a name for them. Anyway, one of the . . . the thoughts . . ." Her eyelashes fluttered down, blocking him from looking into her eyes. "It was about you. It was something like, 'They'll think Anthony did it.' It's like someone was framing you."

She raised her eyes back to his, her gaze intense. Like she was trying to tell if he believed her. Anthony struggled to keep his face expressionless.

"And later, in the nurse's office, I was holding that blue cup of water you gave me. And this time the thoughts weren't about you. The thoughts *felt* like you. Like whatever you were thinking got transferred to the plastic." Rae continued, almost pleading with him to believe her.

"You got thoughts that felt like me," Anthony repeated. He leaned his chair back on two of the legs. "What were they?" He wasn't sure he wanted to know.

Rae pulled a tin of Altoids out of her purse. "Want one?" she asked.

"I want you to answer my question," he told her.

Rae popped one of the mints in her mouth and ground it between her teeth. "Basically it was just that you . . ." She stopped while she put the Altoids tin back in her purse. Anthony felt like screaming with frustration, but he waited for her to go on. "I got thoughts that made it sound like you really cared about what happened to me," she said so softly that he had to strain to hear her. "That you were worried about me. And that you wanted to find out who did it."

Anthony let the front chair legs fall to the floor. This was bizarre.

"And you think they were really my thoughts? I mean, are you supposed to be some kind of mind reader or something?"

Rae gave a helpless shrug. "I have no clue where the not-me thoughts come from. Maybe they are just more insanity." She shook her head. "But it doesn't feel that way, especially lately. I'm starting to wonder if—I don't know, if I'm *not* crazy. Not imagining things. Because these thoughts—they really *feel* like they're coming from other people."

"Look, I—" Anthony cleared his throat. She looked so scared, so vulnerable. Almost the way she did after the bomb. "I did have some thoughts like that. Seeing you all pale and everything, it freaked me out. I wanted to do something for you. But I didn't know what to do. That's why I gave you the water. It was lame, but it was *something*."

"It was a lot," she murmured, sounding a lot shyer than she usually did.

Anthony scooted his chair closer to the table. "If you really believe these *thoughts,* then why'd you tell Rocha you saw me? You could have stopped all this right then."

Rae pushed her hair away from her face. "God, I wish that's what I'd done. But it would be pretty psycho of me to actually believe these thoughts are true, right? I mean, what kind of person . . . I *still* don't know if I'm just losing it." She put her hands down on the table, sort of reaching out to him without quite getting close enough to touch.

"I get it," Anthony told her. A few strands of her curly hair were glued to her forehead. She was getting the sweats. He was, too. This was mind-blowing. "Are you getting any of the thought things now, while we're talking?"

It was kind of like watching a train wreck. He couldn't stop pushing her, needing to know exactly what he was dealing with here.

"Yeah," she admitted.

"Tell me," Anthony urged.

"It's full of static. But it's like, 'Can't stand another day.' 'Better than being at home.' 'Have to get Tom some Dos Equis,' " Rae muttered.

Anthony felt a trickle of cold sweat run down the back of his neck.

"I've completely freaked you out, haven't I?" Rae stood up. "I don't know what I was thinking. How could you believe me? Most of the time I don't even believe myself." She turned and started to walk away.

"Have to get Tom some Dos Equis," he repeated. "That's weird."

Rae turned back to face him, her purse held in front of her like a shield. "Why is that weirder than anything else?" she asked.

"Because Dos Equis is the beer my stepdad drinks. And his name is Tom," Anthony explained.

"That is kind of weird. But typical. Lately, anyway. Look, I've got to go." She hesitated. "So is it okay with you if I help out Jesse?"

"Yeah. If you want," Anthony answered, half his mind still on the Tom / Dos Equis thing. He didn't know what he was supposed to think about Rae's "not-me" thoughts. But whatever else was going on with her, now he was convinced she wanted to help him.

Rae took one step, then hesitated again. "There was another thought I got in the bathroom that day," she admitted. She dropped her eyes to the ground. "I got the one about you being set up. But I also got one about me."

"What was it?" Anthony asked when she didn't continue.

She raised her eyes to his. "The other one . . . It said, 'Definitely kill Rae.' So, if I'm not insane, which is a total possibility, that I am insane, I mean—" She stopped, taking in a quick, sharp breath. "If I'm *not*, then whoever set you up was planning to kill me with that bomb."

*C*hapter 9

R ae ducked into the bathroom—
I got my period I wonder if Vince/
—instead of heading right to the cafeteria. If she was going
to have a "spontaneous" Jeff encounter, which she was pretty
damn sure she was, she wanted to brush her hair and apply
some fresh lip gloss.

Rae headed over to the sinks. She started trying to squeeze
between two other girls so she could see a little patch of mirror. The girls immediately backed off, giving Rae a whole
mirror to herself.

One of the benefits of being an out-of-the-closet psycho, Rae
thought. But it bugged her that she'd never even seen the girls
before. They were clearly freshmen—the fact was practically
painted on with their overdone makeup—so there was no
way they'd witnessed The Incident in the cafeteria last year.
Still, they'd obviously heard all the gory details.

The freshies rushed through their primping and hurried
out of the bathroom. "It's not contagious, you know," Rae
muttered. One of the stall doors behind her swung open. *Oh,
great, now somebody's heard me talking to myself,* she thought. She

glanced over her shoulder and saw Leah heading toward her.

"What's not contagious?" Leah asked.

"You know. My insanity," Rae answered.

"Did someone say something to you?" Leah demanded. She looked ready to storm out into the halls and start kicking butt.

"No. Not really," Rae said. "It's just, you know, I can tell people aren't exactly *comfortable* when I'm around."

"Butt-head kind of people," Leah answered as she washed her hands. "Not your friends. Speaking of which. What's up with you being a no-show at lunch the last couple of days?"

Rae shrugged. So did Leah think it was in Rae's "best interest" to keep eating lunch with them, even if it wasn't good for her to show up at their parties? Rae had to bite back the comment.

"Let me guess. Marcus and Dori. I told them they shouldn't let you know that—" Leah stopped short.

"I don't need to be protected from stuff," Rae snapped. "I'm not going to lose it if everyone's not perfectly, sickeningly nice to me all the time." She noticed a faint blush on Leah's cheeks but rushed on. "You know what would have helped, though? If someone had given me a heads up. I would have liked a couple of minutes' warning."

Like from my supposed best friend, she added silently.

Leah nodded. "I should have said something. You're right. It's just that I told them to keep it a secret, at least for a little while. But Dori, the girl can't keep her hands off Marcus for a—" Leah stopped herself again. She took a step toward the door. "So are you coming?" she asked, her voice suddenly all cheery and peppy. "We can sit at a different table."

Rae flinched. "I brought my lunch," she said. "I think I'm going to eat in the art room. I'm right in the middle of this painting."

"Oh. Okay. I know how you get when you're in one of your creative modes," Leah answered, sounding the faintest bit relieved. "So I'll see you later," she added. She gave a little wave as she headed for the door.

Rae quickly brushed her hair and did some minor makeup repair, ignoring the not-her thoughts that buzzed through her brain. She hurried out of the bathroom and made straight for the stairwell. When she reached the door, she grabbed the knob—

/get lucky/

—then hesitated. Maybe she was being a little too eager. Nothing was less attractive. She'd figured that one out pretty fast when she'd first started playing the guy-girl game. It wouldn't kill Jeff to have to miss a day with her.

Although it might kill me, Rae thought. She'd been looking forward to her vacation to the land of normal all morning. Especially with all the Anthony stuff heating up, Rae needed a little bliss time. *Tomorrow,* she told herself. *Jeff doesn't need to know—*

Before she could finish the thought, the door swung open. And Jeff was grinning at her from the other side. He grabbed her by the wrist and pulled her into the stairwell, then shut the door behind them. "I made us a picnic," he told her.

"I can see that," Rae answered, staring down at the square of folded sheet loaded with food.

"And just in case you're wondering, no animals were harmed in the preparation of this lunch. Although I cut my finger when I was making the carrots." He showed her the Band-Aid on his pinkie.

"Poor baby," Rae said, smiling.

"You could kiss it and make it better," Jeff suggested.

Rae laughed. "I guess I could do that. Since you got the injury cooking for me." Then she took his hand and gave his finger a quick kiss.

The atmosphere in the stairwell became charged, like the air before a thunderstorm. Rae's eyes found Jeff's, and they stared at each other for a long, dizzying moment. Then Jeff leaned forward, just a little. Rae leaned a little toward him. And somehow they were kissing.

I've known this guy for—what?—four days, Rae thought as she slid her hands into his hair. *This is probably not the best idea.*

But it felt so good. Her whole world was his hands and her hands, and his mouth and her mouth. And that world was a wonderful place to be.

Rae spotted Jesse in the 7-Eleven parking lot as the bus pulled up across the street. *Show time,* she thought. The bus's doors wheezed open, and she climbed out, did a quick traffic check, then ran over to Jesse.

"So is that guy Nunan working today?" she asked when she reached him.

"Yeah," Jesse answered. "I could have just gone in and talked to him myself."

"Do you know him at all?" Rae asked, not bothering to lecture Jesse about why this wasn't something he should do alone.

Jesse shook his head. "Not really. I've seen him with Anthony a couple of times."

Rae peered through the window at the guy behind the counter. He was stroking his shaved head and giggling to himself. Unfortunately, he looked like the type who might have difficulty remembering a variety of things. "So you ready to do this?"

Jesse answered by moving toward the door. He held it open for Rae, and they headed to the counter side by side. "Nunan," Jesse said. "How's it goin'?"

Nunan ran his hand over his head one more time, then peered at Jesse. "Do I know you, little guy?"

Rae saw Jesse's shoulders stiffen at the little-guy crack, but he let it go. "I hang here with Fascinelli sometimes. This is his new girlfriend." Jesse jerked his thumb at Rae.

Is he saying that because he thinks that will make Nunan not worry about talking in front of me? she thought. *Or because he actually believes it?*

"Oh. I was hoping you were comin' in to meet me," Nunan told Rae. "Strange girls are always dropping by because they've heard the legend of the Nunan."

Rae managed not to snort as she took in his little potbelly pushing out his ancient Sublime T-shirt. "I can understand that," she answered, playing the flattery card. "But actually Jesse and I had something we wanted to ask you."

"Shoot." Rick grabbed a handful of sunflower seeds from a bag behind the counter and crammed them all into his mouth.

"When you left the, um, package for Anthony in the Oakvale bathroom, did you notice anything strange?" Rae asked. "Because somebody left a bomb in there. It almost killed me. I'm still freaking out, and I really need to find out who put it there just so I can feel safe again." She figured Nunan might like helping out a damsel in distress. Lots of guys did.

Rick's forehead furrowed. "Sorry—I didn't go to Oakvale," he answered. He spit out a couple of sunflower seed shells. "Not everyone can shell them in their mouths," he explained to Rae. "It's all in the tongue."

Oh. My. God, Rae thought. "Huh," she commented. "Anthony said you left some weed for him in the girls' bathroom."

"Wait." Rick spit out a couple more shells onto the counter, then swept them onto the floor with his hand. "Yeah. I remember now. I gave the stuff to this guy in Anthony's support group. He was buying some, and he told me he'd make the delivery to Anthony. I knew Fascinelli would be dying for some. Which, by the way, he owes me the cash for."

"What guy?" Jesse asked.

"Um, I can't remember his name. I was kind of wasted," Nunan admitted. He giggled, and a couple of wet sunflower seeds came flying out of his mouth.

It seems to be kind of your perpetual state, Rae thought, taking in Rick's bloodshot eyes. "Do you remember what he looked like, at least?" she asked, trying to keep the impatience out of her voice.

"He was . . . I don't know. He was some dude," Rick answered.

"White? Black? Asian? Brown hair? Blond hair? I'm looking for anything here," Rae urged.

Rick spit out a few more shells. "I think he might have been wearing a green shirt."

"A green shirt," Rae repeated.

Nunan nodded. "Absolutely. Green. Or possibly blue. Something watery."

"O-kay. Well, thanks," Rae said. *Thanks for nothing.*

"Then he goes, 'Something watery,'" Rae said.

"Classic Nunan," Anthony answered. He leaned back in his chair until it was balanced on two legs. The guy supervising the common room frowned at him, and Anthony let the chair drop back to the floor.

"Jesse's going to ask around a little at our next group meeting," Rae continued.

"No. You can't let him do that," Anthony said, an electric

jolt of fear running through his body. "There's a good chance the person who stashed the pot also set the bomb. If they were setting me up, they'd want me seen in the bathroom. Jesse asks the wrong person the wrong question, and he could get hurt."

Rae's eyes widened. "I can't believe I didn't think of that. You're right. I won't let him," she said quickly. "But I think I already told Nunan too much."

"Not a problem." Some of the tension eased out of Anthony's body. "He doesn't have enough brain cells left to remember much. But be careful. Not everyone's a Nunan." He studied her face, trying to make sure she was taking what he said seriously. "Maybe both of you should just leave it alone."

"I'm not going to leave it alone," Rae shot back. "You wouldn't be in this place if it wasn't for me."

"I wouldn't be in this place if someone hadn't framed me," he corrected her, finally accepting that that was the truth. Yeah, Rae played a part in getting him here. But she hadn't put the evidence in his backpack. He lowered his gaze to the table. "Listen, there's something else I want to talk to you about."

Anthony hesitated. He felt kind of like an idiot bringing this up. Maybe it was just encouraging her to be delusional. But he'd been awake most of the night, going over what she'd told him about her not-me thoughts. In the morning he'd done some research—a first for Anthony Fascinelli— and come up with a theory. And even though a Bluebird had no business coming up with a theory of any kind, Anthony thought maybe, just maybe, he was right.

"You know how you were telling me about those not-you thoughts?" he continued. He shot a quick glance at her. Her face had kind of tightened up.

"Uh-huh," she answered, doing her purse-as-shield thing again.

"I was reading this book." Well, actually he'd gotten one of the volunteers in the detention center library to read it to him. He'd been slick, he thought. He was pretty sure the woman hadn't realized that he was getting her to read it because it would take him a zillion years.

"A book," Rae repeated, her voice flat.

"Yeah, a book on psi abilities," Anthony answered, leaning close to her so no one would overhear and getting a whiff of that grapefruit stuff she wore. "It said there are people who can touch an object and know the history of it. I was thinking that your thing might be something like that. Not that you're getting history, exactly. But some kind of data. You said it was like my thoughts had been transferred to that cup I gave you."

"We should try to figure out what to do next," Rae said, ignoring him. "Maybe I could try Nunan again and manage to catch him when he's not wasted."

"He's pretty much always wasted," Anthony answered. He unzipped his backpack and pulled out a pencil. "Try touching this." He wasn't going to let her back away from this. It was too important. For both of them.

"It's not about touching. The thoughts come into my head,

okay? It's not psi; it's just psychotic."

Anthony shook his head. "If you were sure it was just insanity, you wouldn't have told me about it. And you wouldn't be doing all this stuff to help me. You believe the thoughts mean something. Why are you so afraid of trying to figure it out?"

"I'm not afraid," Rae insisted. "I just think it's stupid."

"You'd rather go on walking around feeling sorry for yourself, poor little crazy girl?" Anthony shot back. Rae looked like she wanted to slap him, but he didn't care. "Besides the thing with the cup, you had your hand on this table when you told me a thought that sounded exactly like one my mother would have had. When she came to visit me, she was sitting at this table, too. So it's not like it's totally impossible that you—"

"Have some kind of supergirl powers?" Rae asked sarcastically. But she snatched up the pencil.

Anthony watched her intently. Looking for what, he had no idea. "Are you getting anything?"

"Rot in hell," Rae said.

"Forget it. I was just trying to—" Anthony began.

"No. That's what I *got*. The not-me thought. 'Rot in hell,'" Rae answered.

Anthony's heart gave a slam against his ribs. "Okay, one of the guys stabbed another guy with that pencil the other day. So 'rot in hell'—that could be some kind of vibe or something from the fight."

"What else have you got?" Rae asked. She sounded bored, but Anthony could see the tension in her body. If she was feeling even half of what he was, she had a volcano going off in her right now. Fear and excitement and triumph were gushing through his veins.

Anthony tossed a deck of cards on the table. Rae snatched it up. "I'm right," she muttered.

"That's what you got? 'I'm right'?" Anthony asked. The lava inside him cooled. Maybe the rot-in-hell thing was a fluke. Maybe it was just how Rae was feeling about Anthony at that second. Because the guy he'd gotten the cards from was mega depressed. He spent all his free time sitting on his bed, playing solitaire. The guy didn't even go into the TV room or anything. Anthony doubted he ever thought he was right about anything.

"The weird thing is, the 'I'm right'—it felt like you." Rae flipped the deck of cards over in her hands. She gave a little jerk and dropped the cards.

"Did you get another one?" Anthony asked, leaning even closer.

Rae shoved her curly hair away from her face. "Yeah. I got another one, not an Anthony-flavored one this time. It was, 'I wish I was dead.'" Rae swallowed hard. "God, I could feel this *loathing,* this self-hating crap."

"That's exactly what I'd expect you to get," Anthony told her, his voice rising. He forced himself to keep it low. "But I don't get the 'I'm right' thing. The cards aren't mine." He frowned, thinking. Then he sat up straighter. "But I was holding them," he said, his excitement returning. "And I was thinking about how I was right! Because you picked up something from the pencil!"

"The thoughts do kind of match up with where I am," Rae admitted. "I guess that could be because of what I'm touching."

Anthony felt like a Cardinal. Rae was getting all the thoughts of the different people who'd touched an object. But how? He looked down at her hands, watching as she drummed her fingertips nervously on the desk. Her fingertips. Suddenly a vague idea began to come into focus in his mind.

"We've got to try something else. Come on." Anthony scrambled up from the table. "Got to show my friend where the bathroom is," he told the common-room supervisor. He got a like-I-care nod. He rushed across the room, glancing quickly over his shoulder to make sure Rae was following him. She was, but she didn't look happy.

He led the way to the kitchen and peered through the little glass window in the door. Perfect. It was empty.

Anthony headed straight over to the dishwasher and yanked it open. "Pick up one of those spoons and tell me what you get," he ordered. The spoons had been touched by tons of people, but they were freshly cleaned. If he was right, she wouldn't be able to get anything from them.

"Nothing." Rae looked thoughtful.

"Let's try something else." He tried to clear his mind, then he picked up one of the clean spoons, still warm from the final cycle. *I'm brilliant,* he thought.

"Now, you take it from me and touch it right where I'm

touching," Anthony told her. "But don't tell me what you get. *I'm* going to tell *you*." Rae eagerly took the spoon from Anthony. "You got it?" he asked, tripping over his words in his eagerness.

"Yep," Rae answered.

"Okay, here's what your not-you thought was—'I'm brilliant,'" Anthony said. "Am I right?"

"Yeah," she exclaimed. "And it felt like you again."

"Touch the spoon someplace else," he told her. Because he thought he had it nailed now. The whole thing. Not just that she was picking up people's thoughts. But *how* she was doing it.

He watched as Rae moved her fingers to a new spot on the spoon. She hesitated for a moment, then shook her head. "Nada. Try something else."

The dancing doughnuts won three flamingos, Anthony thought as he picked up another warm spoon.

Rae took it from him, putting her fingers at the bottom. "I'm not getting any—" she started to say, but he reached out and gently moved her hand to the part of the spoon he'd touched, ignoring the low-level sparks of electricity he felt as his fingers brushed against hers.

She looked at him in amazement, then slowly began to speak. "The dancing doughnuts—"

"Won three flamingos," Anthony said along with her. The spoon slipped from Rae's fingers and clattered to the floor. She stared at it for an instant, then bent to pick it up. About halfway down she seemed to change her mind and knelt next to the spoon.

Anthony crouched down beside her. "Are you okay?"

She didn't answer. She kept staring at the spoon.

"The doughnuts-and-flamingos thing—that's exactly what I was thinking when I touched the spoon," he explained. "But you had to touch the spoon exactly where I did to know the thoughts."

"It's like I'm getting thoughts from people's fingerprints," Rae said.

"Your brain's not screwed up. You aren't crazy," Anthony said.

Rae squeezed her eyes shut. Anthony watched her helplessly. Finally he reached out and stroked her hair. It felt soft under his fingers. "You okay?" he asked again.

She opened her eyes, and he could see a film of tears on them.

"I'm not crazy," Rae repeated, her voice trembling.

"No way. You're amazing," Anthony answered. "You're a . . . a fingerprint reader. No one's going to be able to keep a secret from you—not without wearing gloves all the time."

"Fingerprints," Rae whispered. "God, fingerprints."

She reached out and grabbed Anthony's hand. Then she matched her fingertips to his. He felt a sizzle, like a current had gone from her to him or him to her. His fingers began to burn with a cold fire as if his skin were pressed against dry ice instead of warm flesh.

Rae dropped his hand. "Did you get something?" Anthony asked.

"I . . . I have to go," Rae said, backing toward the door.

"What? Why?" Anthony asked. He could see that she was shaking. "What did you get? What's wrong?"

"Nothing. I just have to go." Rae turned and bolted.

Chapter 10

Rae slowly walked home from the bus stop, her hands jammed in the front pockets of her jeans. She didn't want her fingertips to accidentally brush up against anything. Not now. Her brain felt raw. Tender. When she'd touched Anthony, it was almost like she'd become him, like every thought she had was his thought. Like there was no Rae anymore for that one instant.

It had been overwhelming. She didn't just get a few clear thoughts and some static. She got hundreds of thoughts, layers and layers of them, but somehow she'd been able to take them all in, although most of them had faded now. All she had left were a few impressions and feelings. Longing for his father. Fear of what could happen to him at his trial. Triumph in figuring out what was really going on with Rae. Deep appreciation about what she was doing for him. Concern for her. It had been so intimate. So intense.

Rae shook her head as she turned onto her block, remembering back to the time when rolling around on a bed with Marcus had been the most powerful thing she'd ever experienced. It felt so long ago now.

She cut across her front lawn, the long blades of grass flicking around her ankles. At the front door, she hesitated. Then she slowly pulled her hands out of her pockets. "Not going to be able to get in the house without touching something," she muttered. Her fingers shook as she reached into her purse and pulled out her key.

/hope that guy Nunan/

It was one of the not-her thoughts that felt like her, with some of the static in the background. So if Anthony was right—which seemed pretty damn likely, freaky as it was—she'd just touched a fingerprint on the key and gotten a thought echo from the person who left the fingerprint. The thought they were having when they left a print.

Rae's heart gave a double-quick beat. That's why it felt like her. The key was hers. The fingerprint on the key was *hers*. So she was picking up the thought she had when she locked the door this morning.

Oh God. It was really true. It wasn't that she hadn't believed Anthony. The two of them had proven his theory. But it was like she'd only believed it with her mind, and now she was starting to accept it in her gut, in her bones.

She used the key to unlock the door, then reached for the doorknob. Her hand froze half an inch away from it. *Just do it,* she told herself, then she lightly ran her fingers over the metal.

/that bitch, Rae/she should be home /mmm . . . Jeff/

139

meeting at three/*back alive from the hell mouth/*
make her pay/bald spot

She felt tears sting her eyes, just like they had when she
was with Anthony. "I'm not insane," she whispered. "I. Am.
Not. Insane." Because it all made sense now. The "mmm . . .
Jeff" and "back alive from the hell mouth" thoughts felt like
her because they *were* her. And it wasn't hard to figure out
who had left the other fingerprint thoughts, even with the
static buzzing behind them. "That bitch, Rae" and "make
her pay"—those were from Jesse. Those were exactly the
kind of thoughts he'd be having when he was getting ready
to trash her room. And the other ones—dear old starting-to-
go-bald Dad.

Rae felt like letting out a whoop of pure relief and pleasure.
She felt like dancing down the street, telling everyone she saw
that she was *not* crazy. But that kind of behavior was much too
weird for Rae Voight, perfectly sane girl.

Instead Rae played the doorknob like a piano, touching the
fingerprints like keys.

/*that bitch, Rae*/make her pay/bald spot /bald spot/bald
spot/*mmm . . . Jeff/mmm . . . Jeff/*

She noticed that each thought got a little fuzzier every
time she accessed it. Which made sense. Every time she
touched a fingerprint, she probably smudged it a little. Rae
reached up as high as she could. *I'm not crazy,* she thought
as she touched the top of the door. She pulled her finger
away, then immediately pressed it back in the same spot.

140

The thought came right back at her—*I'm not crazy*—strong and clear with no static.

Rae added an I'm-not-crazy thought to the doorknob. She wanted them everywhere. That way every time she touched something, she could hear the amazing news. She pressed one finger onto the new fingerprint on the doorknob. It was clear, but there was static underneath it. *Maybe the static comes if there are a lot of old fingerprints already on,* Rae decided. *The doorknob has tons of fingerprints, but the top of the door probably only has that one.* She promised herself she'd check out the theory later. She'd probably figure out tons more stuff now that she knew what was going on.

Rae opened the door and rushed inside. She tossed her backpack—

/*Jeff*/

—on the sofa. Everything around her looked a little brighter somehow. She was okay. She was really okay. No, she was more than okay; she was, she was . . . *gifted.* That's what you called someone who was psychic . . . gifted.

Rae hurried down the hall to her dad's cramped little study. She wanted to play with her gift some more. *This is so amazing,* she thought as she sat down in her father's ergonomically correct chair and scanned the desk. What should she try first? Pencil, she decided. Her dad was a compulsive pencil tapper. Whenever he was thinking hard—tap, tap, tap. She picked up the closest one by the little pink eraser and ran the fingers of her free hand down the shiny yellow surface.

/ not sure Rae's better / Arthur as Christ / she's keeping something from me / Melissa /

He's so anxious when he thinks about me, Rae realized. The thoughts carried a little of the emotion with them, and the muscles of her shoulders had tightened painfully with her father's worries. And when he thought about her mother, Melissa, the grief was still so raw, it was as if she'd died last week instead of years and years ago.

How can he still care about her so much after what she did? Rae thought. *How can he still love her?* Rae dropped the pencil. She decided not to try another one. It was as if her dad decided to read her diary—not that she kept a diary. It didn't feel right to go rooting around in his head. And anyway, she'd probably just get more worries about her, more thoughts about his King Arthur junk, and—gag—more thoughts about how much he loved his perfect dead wife.

Rae stood up and wandered back into the living room. *I'll have to make sure that Dad knows I'm okay,* she thought. *I don't want him to have a stroke worrying about me.* But she definitely wasn't going to tell him the truth. A person who had been hospitalized for "paranoiac delusions" should not go around spouting off about how all she really had was this amazing ESP talent.

She flopped down on the couch and rested her head on the padded arm. Her thoughts kept returning to her dad, like a fly that kept landing on a doughnut no matter how many times you tried to shoo it away. The past months had clearly been almost as hellish for him as they had for her. And she hated that.

Back when she was a little girl—*Be honest,* Rae told herself. *It wasn't just back when you were a little girl. You did it until you were well into your twelfth year as a walking, talking example of the word* dork. Anyway, back then, whenever she and her dad had a fight or it was his birthday or Father's Day or whatever, she'd make these little drawings and leave them in the pocket of his robe. She had a sudden urge to do that now.

"So what if it's dorky," she muttered as she stood back up and headed to her room. "He'll like it. And maybe it will make him relax about me a little." She went over to her desk and grabbed her drawing pad and a handful of markers, letting her old thoughts and the static wash through her. She studied the sheet of blank white paper for a moment, then she smiled and started to work, the markers squeaking away.

A few minutes later she had a caricature of her dad done up as King Arthur. *Hi, Dad,* she scribbled at the bottom. Then she ripped the sheet off the pad, folded it into quarters, and made her way to her father's room before she freaked out about exactly how geeky she was being.

"I'm not going to make a habit of this or anything," she mumbled as she walked over to her father's closet and slid open the door. She jammed the drawing in the pocket of his old plaid bathrobe, then started to turn away.

But her eyes locked on the cardboard box on the shelf above the clothes rod. It had some of her mother's stuff in it.

Rae's dad had told her, well, actually he'd urged her, to look at it whenever she wanted to. She'd never even pulled the box off the shelf.

Fingerprints last a long time, Rae thought, a tickle of anticipation running down her spine, anticipation mixed with fear. *I might be able to get some of her thoughts. I could see for myself what she was really like. 'Cause I'm never going to get anything but the fairy tale from Dad.* She hesitated. Should she? Did she really want to know? Whatever she found out was going to stay in her memory forever.

But she couldn't remember her mother's touch or her voice or the way she smelled. This was her chance to know a thought, actually feel one of her mother's feelings. How could she pass that up? Rae snatched the box—

/ love you, Melissa / miss you / sweet /

—down and opened it before she could lose her nerve. She sat down cross-legged on the floor with the box in front of her and studied the contents. Gently she pulled out a shimmery perfume bottle made of blue and green glass.

Rae gasped as the first thought hit her.

/ going to be a mother /

Her body felt light. Her blood felt . . . fizzy. Joy. She'd gotten an infusion of absolute joy. Rae closed her eyes, the feeling so intense, she felt like the floor was spinning beneath her.

Tears filled her eyes as the mother-flavored emotion faded. *I was just a little speck, and she already loved me that much,* Rae thought.

But she was crazy. Remember that, Rae? She was crazy. And not just crazy in a nice I-see-leprechauns-and-unicorns way. Crazy in a horrible, vicious way.

Except what if she wasn't? What if she was just like Rae, but she never understood what was happening to her? The thought was like the blow of a hammer. It could be true. Rae'd been thinking she inherited some kind of mental disorder from her mom. But what if what she'd really gotten from her mother was her . . . psychic ability?

Poor Mom. Rae remembered how terrified she'd felt the first day she'd started getting the alien thoughts in her head. Of course people would have thought her mother was insane. Of course her *mother* would have thought the same thing.

Rae felt a burst of sympathy for her mother. Her heart actually ached. *I wish I could have told her,* Rae thought. *I wish I could have—*

And then it hit her. How could she have forgotten for even a few moments? Her mother—the woman who Rae's heart was getting all mushy and achy over—had done something too horrible to imagine. And even if she did have Rae's fingerprint power, that was no excuse. There *was* no excuse.

The pleasure—the *joy*—she'd felt when she'd touched her mother's fingerprint drained out of her, like dirty water going down the drain. She went all numb inside. Which was just as well. Because if she wasn't numb, she'd hurt so bad, she might never be able to stop crying.

Rae dropped the perfume bottle back in the box and closed the lid as quickly as she could. She jammed the box back onto its shelf and closed the closet door.

Rae didn't even consider going to the caf when the bell rang for lunch the next day. She went straight to the stairwell. She needed her Jeff fix—and right now.

Her *gift*, the gift she'd been so thrilled about yesterday, wasn't feeling quite so much like a gift today. Because now she knew for sure that there were people—people right here in her school—who thought of her as a complete freak or at least some kind of damaged girl interrupted. It had been bad when those thoughts were flying around in her head unexplained. But the explanation, well, it wasn't exactly comforting. *At least you're not insane,* Rae reminded herself. *But you're not normal, either,* she couldn't help adding.

The stairwell door swung open, and Jeff appeared. He looked at her. She looked at him. And it was like suddenly their bodies were magnetized. Rae wasn't sure who took the first step, but an instant later they were in each other's arms. An instant after that, they were kissing, a sweet, soft kiss that made her feel warm all over, as if she were wrapped in a big fluffy towel straight out of the dryer.

Somehow, they managed to lower themselves to the hard cement floor. They sat down on the top step without breaking the kiss.

Jeff flicked his tongue across her lips, and she eagerly parted them, allowing the kiss to deepen. She loved the taste of him. The feel. Warm and wet.

"Mmm, Jeff," she murmured into his mouth. He laughed, which made Rae start laughing, too. They struggled not to break the kiss, their mouths slipping and sliding across each other's but always keeping some kind of lip-to-lip contact.

Jeff slid one hand down her arm, then wrapped her hand in his. *Closer,* Rae thought, too delirious to form sentences anymore. *Want closer.*

She maneuvered her fingertips until they were resting on top of Jeff's. And a tidal wave of his thoughts rushed over her, overwhelming her.

/knew she'd be easy/loser girls are grateful for it/nice little setup/no demands/oh God/yes/

She jerked away, ripping her lips off Jeff's. "What's the problem?" he demanded.

Rae sprang to her feet, swallowing hard. "Let me ask you something," she said, forcing herself to sound calm, firm. *Normal.*

Jeff stood up and gave her a lazy smile. "Don't tell me you're suddenly worried about how I really feel about you."

Rae shook her head. "That's not what I was going to ask." Fury pumped through her veins, but she kept her voice even. "My question is—what kind of a guy would only want to fool around with a girl he thought was a loser?"

"What?" Jeff gave a rapid couple of blinks.

"I mean, I don't have a degree in psychology or anything, but don't you think a guy who thinks only a loser girl would want him—wouldn't you think that guy would have to be pretty much of a loser himself?"

"Um, I guess so," Jeff muttered.

"I guess so, too." Rae walked out of the stairwell without another word and headed down the hall toward the bathroom. She felt like taking a shower, a long, long shower, but she'd have to settle for washing her hands.

She ripped open the bathroom door, ignoring the thoughts and static, and rushed over to the sinks. Leah stood by the nearest one, drying her hands with one of the thick paper towels.

"We have to stop meeting like this," Leah said when she saw Rae. She tossed the paper towel in the big metal garbage can, gave a little wave, and headed for the door. "See you later," she called.

"Okay," Rae answered, glad Leah hadn't decided to stay for a little nicey-nicey chat. She couldn't deal with that right now. She turned on the cold water at the closest sink.

/ glad Rae didn't show at lunch/

Rae recognized the flavor of that thought immediately. It was Leah all the way. The hairs on the back of her neck stood up. And Rae realized the little frisson of fear she was feeling was Leah's fear.

Leah's fear of Rae.

Rae stared at herself in the mirror, taking in her big eyes and pale face. *I'm never going to be the same,* she realized. *I'm never going to be able to walk around feeling like people are basically decent. I'm always going to know what's going on underneath. I'm always going to see the fear and the hate and the . . . the slime.*

At that thought she felt something die inside her. The

little bit of Rachel she had left, the Rachel who drew unicorns and almost believed in them.

It's better to know the truth, Rae told herself. *About Leah. About Jeff. About everybody.*

Including whoever it was out there in the world who wanted her dead.

Chapter 11

R ae stood at the bus stop near the police station, peering down the street. She saw a bus coming toward her, shimmering in the heat. "You better be on that bus, Jesse," she muttered. She checked her watch. He was already five minutes late. Rae couldn't believe it. It felt more like five hours.

The bus groaned to a stop in front of her. Jesse was the first one out, pushing his way in front of a couple of old ladies, who did not look at all pleased with this example of a young southern gentleman. "Let's go, already," Jesse urged, as if he'd been the one waiting for *her*.

They did a speed walk—minus the geeky arms—to the police station. "First thing we have to do is find out where the evidence room is," Rae said. She followed Jesse through the door, grateful she didn't have to touch it herself. The cocktail of thoughts she'd get off that door would probably not be at all pleasant.

"I'll handle it," Jesse said. Without bothering to explain how, he started right for the main desk. Rae hung back. She didn't think the guy at the desk, the one with the bad combover, would remember her, but it seemed stupid to risk it. A few seconds later Jesse was back. "Second floor, a little ways down from the elevator on the right," he said.

"What? You just went up and said, 'Hi, what floor is the evidence stored on'?" Rae asked as they headed to the elevator.

"No," Jesse answered, sounding disgusted. "I told him my cousin is working the evidence room today and he told me to stop by so he could give me the ten bucks he owes for our grandmother's birthday present."

"Not bad," Rae told him. She let him push the elevator up button and then the button for the second floor. There were some things she just had no real desire to know. *Maybe I'll have to be like some of the old ladies who still wear white gloves,* Rae thought.

"My turn," she said as the elevator doors opened. She took a deep breath, then stepped out, Jesse right behind her. Without hesitation she strode down the hall. She saw something that looked kind of like a bank teller window. It had a short counter running in front of it, with a sign-in sheet and pen lying there. "Hi," Rae said to the guy behind the window. "Someone told us there was a soda machine up here."

The guy shook his head. "First floor," he answered.

Rae smiled at him, looking him straight in the eye. "Thanks," she said as she pulled out a stick of gum and managed to accidentally-on-purpose drop it on the guy's desk. "I got it," she said, before he could move. She leaned through the window and ran her fingers over as much of his desk as she could with her left hand—

/Alan fighting at school/friggin' paperwork/talk

—as she reached for the gum with her right. "Come on," she told Jesse as she started back to the elevator.

"Did you get anything?" he whispered when they were out of sight.

"Enough, I think," Rae answered. She couldn't believe how casually Jesse asked her that question, like he knew dozens of people who could pick thoughts off fingerprints. Or like it was something minor she'd revealed about herself—like that auburn wasn't her natural hair color.

He'd had questions, of course, when she'd told him the truth, figuring he needed to know if they were going to come up with the best possible plan. And he'd made her touch about a hundred of his fingerprints as proof. But then he'd been kind of like, "Okay, cool," as if she were one of the X-Men or something.

"So now what?" Jesse asked.

Rae thought for a minute, glad that the hallway was still empty. "Can you sound any older on the phone?"

"Definitely," Jesse answered, deepening his voice. And he actually did sound reasonably grown-up.

"Okay, here's what you do. Go downstairs and call up to the evidence room. The pay phone won't show any caller ID. Ask for Walter Child. That's the guy's name. I saw it on his desk. Anyway, tell him you're calling from the school and that his son Alan got in a fight. Tell him you need him to come over right away to pick Alan up and take him home because he's not going to be allowed to leave without a parent," Rae said. "That should get him out of the room for a few minutes—even if he just goes to find someone to cover for him. I'll sneak in and—"

"I know the plan, remember?" Jesse interrupted.

"Sorry. I'm just a little nervous," Rae said.

"I'll come back up as fast as I can," Jesse promised.

"No," Rae told him. "We can't both get caught. You have to be my backup. If something happens to me when I'm in there, I'll need you free to deal with it."

"All right," Jesse said, a little reluctantly. "I'm takin' the stairs. The elevators are too slow." He turned and rushed out the door leading to the staircase. Rae positioned herself near a drinking fountain that was out of the sight line of the evidence guy.

Now she just had to wait and see if Mr. Walter Child would take the bait. It didn't take long. About three minutes after Jesse hit the stairs, Rae heard a door open down the hall. She spun toward the drinking fountain and leaned over it, letting her long hair curtain her face. When footsteps neared her, she allowed herself one quick peek. *Yep. There goes Wally,* she thought.

As soon as he was through the door to the stairs, she bolted down to the evidence room and scrambled through the window. She landed on all fours on the desk, then half jumped, half fell to the ground.

Rae crouched in front of Walter's computer and managed to find the files that detailed each case. She typed in Anthony's name, ignoring the thought fragments she picked up, and seconds later she had the number of the bin where the evidence for his case was held. Staying low, she hurried across the little office and through the back door. Rows of long metal shelves filled the large storage area.

"Pretty much like using the library," Rae muttered as she spotted the cards at the end of each row that indicated the bin numbers. She trotted down the row that had Anthony's number, found the bin, which was just your basic box, and opened it. A bunch of junk that looked like it could make a bomb was inside. "Bingo," she said, slipping into geekspeak in her nervousness.

Rae ran her fingers across the handle of the pliers—

/ GET ME A MOTORCYCLE/WHY WANT TO KILL RAE/ HOPE IT DOESN'T EXPLODE IN MY FACE /

the tissue paper—

/ GOT TO BUY A DIAMOND NOSE RING/GONNA BE LOADED / FASCINELLI WOULD HAVE GOTTEN BUSTED FOR SOMETHING EVENTUALLY, ANYWAY/

and the wooden stick—

/ MAYBE TAKE OFF FOR MEXICO /THAT NEW GIRL, RAE / BUT I'M NOT REALLY THE MURDERER/

Rae heard the door that led from the office swing open. "It's me. Jesse," a voice called, low and anxious.

"I told you not to come in here," she answered.

"The guy . . . He's coming back. . . . " Jesse said, breathless. "We have to get out of here. Now."

Rae didn't need to be told twice. She slammed the top back on the box and ran. Jesse fell into step behind her. "You get enough?" he demanded.

"Hope so," she answered.

"So our guy is into motorcycles. He knows Rae's new in group. He probably has a girlfriend with a nose piercing. And likes Mexico." Anthony glanced at Jesse, who was in his usual chair at their usual table in the visitors' room.

We're regulars already, Rae thought.

"Sound like anyone we know?" Anthony asked Jesse.

"David Wyngard," Jesse answered. "All he ever talks about is motorcycles."

"And Cynda," Anthony added. "She has piercings everywhere."

"Wait. Cynda, which one is she?" Rae asked.

"She's in our group, too. You know. Dyed black hair. Wears those army camouflage pants a lot," Jesse answered.

Rae knew exactly who he was talking about. "That's who told me to go into the bathroom the day the bomb went off," she exclaimed. "She said I had to fix my makeup or something. God, she wanted to make sure I was in place at exactly the right time."

"So, it's gotta be David," Anthony said. "That jerk. I can't believe he framed me. We're supposed to be friends. Sort of."

"I did get a thought where he was telling himself you'd get

caught for something eventually, anyway," Rae offered.

"Yeah. I go around trying to kill people every couple of days," Anthony muttered.

"I still don't get why he—or Cynda—would want to off Rae," Jesse said.

"You mind keeping your voice down a little?" Anthony asked, with a glance toward the guy supervising the room. "I don't know why, but for some reason, they don't really like us to talk about offing people during visiting hours."

"Sorry," Jesse said, a faint blush creeping up the back of his neck. "But like I said, I don't get it."

"Me neither," Rae added. "I'd never even seen either of them before my first day at group, so it's not like they have something against me."

"But it was all about you; that's what you picked up," Anthony said.

"Yeah," Rae answered.

Anthony ran his fingers through his hair. It was a little greasy and a little long, and it definitely gave him that bad-boy look. "We shouldn't bother trying to figure it out until we're positive David's the right guy. It's not as if liking motorcycles is all that unusual."

"I'll bring him to the 7-Eleven after group tomorrow," Jesse volunteered. "Nunan can get a look at him."

"Sounds like a plan," Anthony agreed.

"What about Cynda?" Rae asked. "She could've been in on it."

"Probably not," Anthony answered. "Even though she

dresses like G.I. Jane, she's kind of a wuss. One time I saw her make David catch a spider and put it out the window. She didn't want it near her. But she didn't want him to kill it, either."

"If I get Nunan to ID David, then we can worry about the Cynda thing," Jesse said. "He might not even be our guy."

"I'll go with you tomorrow," Rae told Jesse.

"No," Anthony and Jesse said together.

"You don't even know David, and it's not like you and Jesse have been buds or anything. It'll be too suspicious if you try to tag along," Anthony explained. "Jesse's hung out with me and David a few times at the 7-Eleven. It won't be weird for him to maneuver David over there."

Rae nodded reluctantly. It made sense. But she wasn't all that happy with the idea of Jesse and the potential wanna-be killer drinking a Slurpee together.

"You guys should go. My mom might be stopping by, so . . ." Anthony let his words trail off. It was obvious he didn't want them meeting his mom.

What is he embarrassed about? she wondered. She couldn't imagine anyone whose mom wasn't a *murderer* like hers actually caring. She would give anything for a mom who just talked a little too loudly or gave her big hugs in front of her friends. But there was no way she'd let Anthony, Jesse—or anyone—know the real truth about *her* mom.

Rae sighed, standing up alongside Jesse.

"See you later," Jesse said.

"Bye," Rae mumbled. She started to say something else, some kind of thank-you, but everything she thought of sounded stupid, so she just followed Jesse out of the room. About halfway out of the detention center she decided she was being a total wimp.

"I, um, forgot my sunglasses," she blurted out to Jesse. "I'll be right back." Without waiting for an answer, she turned and ran back to the visitors' room. She wasn't sure if she was happy or not when she saw that Anthony was still at their table.

Get a grip, she told herself. She hurried over to the table and started speaking without bothering to sit down. "I just wanted to say thanks," she told him. "What you did for me— God. Do you even know?"

Anthony stared up at her, his expression unreadable.

Rae sat down and leaned toward him. "When I was having all those, you know, not-me thoughts, I figured I was going totally insane. I mean, they're why I ended up in the hospital. To know that I'm . . ." She swallowed hard and rushed on, her words crashing into each other. "To know that I'm okay, sane, it changes my whole life. And you did that for me." She stood up fast. "So, that's it. Thanks."

She bolted without waiting for Anthony's reaction.

Chapter 12

A nthony watched Jesse head across the visitors' room the next day. He could tell just by looking at the kid's face that the 7-Eleven plan had worked. Jesse looked like he'd swallowed a lightbulb or something.

"David's the guy Nunan gave the pot to," Jesse whispered as he swung himself into his usual chair. "We've got him."

This has nothing to do with him. But he's acting like he's the one something great happened to, Anthony thought. Jesse had been pretty amazing during this whole thing. He'd believed in Anthony 100 percent, which Anthony's own mother definitely couldn't manage.

"We've got *something*," Anthony agreed. He didn't want to make Jesse feel like a loser. But he didn't want Jesse to think everything was all fine, either. That would be treating him like a baby, and if Jesse was anything like Anthony—and he was, sort of—nothing would make him more pissed off.

Jesse's eyes darkened. "What do you mean? David's going down. And you're getting out of here."

Bible Bob strolled over to the table before Anthony could explain. "It's nice to see you getting so many visitors," he told

Anthony. "Not everyone does." He rested his hand on Jesse's shoulder. "Is this one of your brothers?"

"Nope," Anthony answered. "He's just a bud."

"Yeah," Jesse muttered, not sounding too happy.

"An honorary brother kind of bud," Anthony added. Jesse smiled, a smile so big, it hurt Anthony to look at.

"That's the best kind to have," B. B. said. He glanced at his watch. "You guys will need to wrap it up in about five minutes. Anthony's group is setting up the dining room tonight," he explained to Jesse. Then with a half salute he wandered off.

"So what'd you mean about us having *something?*" Jesse asked as soon as B. B. was out of earshot.

"It's not like we can just tell the cops that David set off the bomb," Anthony explained. "There's no way they'd believe it without proof."

"Is that it?" Jesse looked extremely pleased with himself. "Not a problem, bro. Rae's getting proof right now."

"Wait. Where is she?" Anthony demanded, adrenaline starting to slam through his body.

"She's at David's," Jesse answered. "I found out that David was going over to Cynda's after he left the 7-Eleven. I told Rae, and she said she was going to go search his place. I wanted to go in with her, but she said there would be less chance of getting caught with one person, so I just told her where it is. Then I came straight here."

"I can't believe her," Anthony muttered, fury and fear building inside him. "David tried to *kill* her. And she's just

160

going to go strolling into his house?" He felt his heart squeeze into a hard ball in his chest. "You have to go stop her," he ordered Jesse.

Jesse's eyes widened. "It's way too late."

"Oh, great," Rae muttered when she saw the car in David's driveway. She and Jesse had been so psyched at having a little stretch of time when they were sure David would be out that they hadn't even thought about anybody else in his family.

Rae shook her head. She wasn't turning back. There had to be a way. All she needed was someone to distract whoever was home at David's while she did her search. She snatched up her BlackBerry, tuning out her old thoughts, and punched in Jesse's number. No answer.

Who else? Who else? She realized she was standing right in front of David's house, staring. Not too bright. She turned and walked away at a casual stroll. *Just out on a little walk, everybody*, she thought. *No need to alert the neighborhood watch.*

Her fingers tightened around the cell. Who else? Not Marcus, that was for damn sure. And not Leah. Leah was already afraid of her. If Rae called her, babbling about needing backup on some secret mission, she'd flip out.

Who else? A name sprang into her mind. Yana. In a way they didn't know each other nearly well enough for Rae to be dragging her into this. But she was the only one, other than the not-home Jesse and the locked-away Anthony, who Rae trusted enough.

She didn't give herself time to debate. When she turned the

corner, moving out of sight of David's house, she just called. Yana picked up on the second ring. Rae gave her the rundown as quickly as she could—how she and Jesse had found out some stuff that convinced her Anthony really had been framed for that bomb, and now she just needed to get the evidence that could clear him. She didn't mention the fingerprints stuff. She was still weirded out that Anthony and Jesse knew. And she really, really wanted a friend, one friend, who she could just be normal with. Yana was cool about the hospital. But that didn't mean she was into the psychic friend thing.

"So what do you think?" Rae asked, wrapping up her story. "Are you up for it?"

"Are you kidding?" Yana exclaimed. "I always wanted to be a Charlie's Angel."

Rae knew better than to thank Yana. She'd already figured out Yana hated that. "I'm on the corner of Madison and Winchester. It's—"

"I know where it is. I'm there." Yana hung up without saying good-bye.

Rae kept the phone to her ear, trying to look like she was in the middle of an important call, just in case anyone was wondering what she was doing hanging around in the neighborhood without even a dog to walk or anything.

She didn't have to wait long. About ten minutes later Yana's yellow Bug came flying around the corner. Not exactly inconspicuous, but hey, at least Yana was there. That counted for a lot.

Yana parked and jumped out of the car. "I have a plan," she

announced before Rae could say anything. "Take me to the house."

"Do I get to hear this plan of yours?" Rae asked as she led the way back around the block.

"Nope. You have to trust me." Yana grinned.

Rae couldn't help but grin back. "It's hard not to trust someone in a Happy Burger uniform."

"I actually work there, if you can believe it," Yana answered, staring down with disgust at the big purple smiling face button pinned to her collar. "I put this on because I thought it would be a good disguise. Generic and all."

"Crafty," Rae said. "But really—the plan? What is it?"

"You gotta trust me. I told you. I just need to know if this guy David has a girlfriend," Yana said.

"Yeah. Her name's Cynda," Rae answered. Even without knowing the plan, she was starting to feel confident she and Yana were going to make this work somehow. It was that Yana vibe kicking in. The girl was nothing if not confident.

"That's all I need," Yana said.

"Good. 'Cause we're here." Rae jerked her chin toward a cozy little house with gingerbread trim. It looked too sweet for a wanna-be killer to live in.

"Just whatever I say, don't disagree with me," Yana instructed as she led the way up the flagstone path and gave a double knock on the door. A woman with yellow hair—*yellow*—opened the door. Rae figured she had to be David's mother. Yana's bottom lip started to tremble the second Mrs. Wyngard looked at her. "Where is he? Where's David?

You have to tell me," she pleaded.

A frown line appeared between Mrs. Wyngard's eyebrows. "He's not home," she answered. "Is there something I can do for you?" Mrs. Wyngard was clearly hoping Yana would say no. Instead Yana pushed her way into the house, dragging Rae behind her.

"Well, we're going to need a car seat. And some bottles and stuff. And Pampers," Yana rattled off.

"What?" Mrs. Wyngard cried. "Pampers? What?"

Yana put her hands on her hips. "He didn't tell you, did he? He promised me he would. And he promised he'd go shopping with me today to pick out a cradle. But he never showed up." She let out a wail that Rae was sure could be heard for blocks.

"Are you telling me—" Mrs. Wyngard began.

"I'm telling you you're going to be a grandma. In about seven months," Yana interrupted. "And that girl Cynda. She's history."

Rae choked back a burst of hysterical laughter. Yana was amazing.

"I'm sorry. What's your name?" Mrs. Wyngard asked, sounding dazed.

"It's—oh God. I think I have to puke again. Where's the bathroom?" Yana burst out.

"First door on the right," Mrs. Wyngard answered, pointing to the hall.

"Come with me," Yana told Rae. She grabbed Rae by the sleeve, and they flew down the avocado-colored carpet and into the bathroom. Rae shut the door behind them. "Do you think you could get me some soda crackers, Grandma Wyngard?" Yana called, plopping down on the fuzzy purple toilet seat.

There was a muffled sound from the hall that sounded like half a yes and half a moan. "I'll stay here and make puking sounds," Yana whispered. "You go search David's room. She'll think you're still with me."

Rae cracked open the door, checked the hall, then crept out. She tiptoed to the next door, feet silent on the carpet, and took a fast look into the room. It was a sty. *This has to be the place*, she thought. She ducked into David's room and closed the door—

/ CYNDA AND ME /

—behind her. God, where to start first. Under the bed, she decided. She grimaced as she stretched out on her stomach on David's carpet. There were dirty clothes everywhere, and they all had that funky overripe guy-who-badly-needs-a-shower smell. She jammed both hands under the bed and felt around.

/ GET CONDOMS / DOG FOOD / GROUP THERAPY /

Nothing useful. Rae shoved herself to her feet and took another look at all the crap. There was a Coke can on David's dresser that seemed out of place. Only because it was standing upright in the midst of a pile of junk. On impulse, she headed over to it. She'd seen a Coke can in Spencer's Gifts once that was fake—it twisted open in the middle. She could see David as the kind of guy who would think that was cool.

Using the very tips of her fingers, Rae twisted on the can. It opened. And there was a stash of gray powder inside. She took a sniff. Yes! Gunpowder. Rae closed the can. Lightly, very lightly so she wouldn't leave any fingerprints of her own, Rae stroked the can.

/ TONS O' CASH / GET OUT OF HERE / WON'T EVER GET CAUGHT /

That's what you think, Rae thought. She slipped the can into her big canvas bag, which she'd emptied out for evidence gathering.

"I have the crackers," she heard Mrs. Wyngard call from down the hall.

"Leave them outside the door, please," Yana answered. "And if you have some ginger ale, I think that would really help." Loud puking sounds followed. Then Rae heard footsteps heading away from the bathroom—and David's room. *Thank you, Yana,* she thought, *even though you don't want to be thanked.*

Rae did a quick dresser drawer search. They were almost empty, which was no surprise since it seemed like every article of clothing David owned was on the floor. She crouched down and checked under the dresser. There was half a dog bone and a partially chewed-up piece of wood. Wood that looked like the same size as the piece that had been with the pipe bomb stuff. With a sigh Rae got down on her stomach again. She slid her arm into the tight space under the dresser and snagged the wood with her fingertips.

/ HOPE I REALLY KNOW HOW TO DO THIS /

As she pulled her hand back out, it snagged on something rough. "Damn it," Rae muttered. "That took off a layer of skin." She let go of the piece of wood, curious what she'd gotten caught on. It looked like a ragged piece of floorboard. She gave it an experimental tug, and a thin piece of wood came away in her hand.

Rae's stomach felt like it had gotten onto a down elevator, one that was moving with superspeed. She twisted onto her side, then wriggled her fingers into the little hole that had been hidden by the wood. She felt something soft against her skin. *Maybe it's more of the tissue paper,* she thought. She managed to squeeze a clump of the paper between two of her fingers, then she pulled it out of the hole.

It wasn't tissue paper. It was money. A whole wad of hundred-dollar bills. Rae pulled the money free. Then she ran her fingers lightly across the metal of the heavy silver money clip.

An involuntary gasp escaped her throat. She hadn't been expecting this. None of them had.

Rae didn't get up from the park bench when she saw Anthony walking toward her. It was just a little too weird seeing him here. Not in the detention center. Not in the group. Just in your basic real life.

"Hey," he said.

"Hey," Rae said back. "You going to sit down or what?" The words came out kind of surly sounding, as if she didn't want him to get anywhere near her. Which wasn't true.

At least it mostly wasn't true. It was just that this guy knew way too much about her.

You know stuff about him, too, she reminded herself as he stiffly took a seat. *Like how he feels about his dad.*

"Jesse's not here yet?" Anthony asked, sounding equally uncomfortable.

"No. I mean, do you see him?" Rae asked. God, she was being a bitch. And Anthony definitely didn't deserve that. But besides being nervous around him, she was still creeped out by what she'd found at David's house.

"That stuff you sent to Ms. Sullivan worked fast," Anthony commented. He rested one arm along the back of the bench, then immediately lowered it back to his side.

"Yeah. Well, I'm sure the cops figured out that the wood and the gunpowder were the same," Rae answered. "Plus David's hands were all over the money and everything else. I told them to check the fingerprints in the note I put in the envelope."

"We have to figure out a way to prove that David was really trying to kill you," Anthony said. "He'll probably get put in juvie for the bomb. But he'll get out—and not all that long from now. You're not going to feel safe when that happens."

The discovery she'd made at David's hit her full force again. But she wasn't going to mention it to Anthony. It wasn't his problem. She'd helped put him in the detention center, and she'd helped get him out. They were all even now. And that's how she liked it.

"I'm not trying to freak you out or anything," Anthony added. "It's not like you'll have to worry about David right away. It's just something we should be thinking about."

"I'm not worried about it," she told him, shooing a bee away from her face. Why had she even agreed to meet up with him and Jesse for this little celebration? It was ridiculous. She had much more important things to do. Like figure out how to save her life.

"You're not worried about it," Anthony repeated.

"Look, I'll handle it when I have to handle it," Rae said sharply. "And I won't need any help to do it."

Anthony shoved his hands in his pockets. "Okay. I get it. You can run along now. You wouldn't want one of your prep school friends to see you with me and Jesse."

"Oh, please," Rae muttered. "Get dramatic, why don't you. Like you said, David's going to jail. So I don't have to worry about—"

"Come on," Anthony interrupted. "You have to be scared crazy at the thought that the guy who tried to kill you is going to be wandering free in Atlanta in a few months. But you hate the idea of spending one more second around a guy like me, so much that you're willing to risk getting killed instead of letting me help you." He picked her tote up off the ground and thrust it toward her. "Here. Don't bother waiting for Jesse. You don't have to do us any favors."

Rae didn't take the tote. She stared at Anthony until he reluctantly met her gaze. "Aren't you gone yet?" he asked.

"Don't do you any favors? Is that what you said?" Rae's

voice got louder with every word. "What have I been doing all this time except favors for *you?*"

"Just because you felt guilty," Anthony shot back. "Which you should have. Because if you hadn't opened your big mouth—"

"This again?" Rae sprang to her feet. "You know what? I think I will take your advice just this once. I'm outta here." She grabbed her tote.

/ WHAT A COMPLETE CARDINAL /

Rae spun back to face Anthony. "What's a Cardinal? Is that some kind of code or something?"

Anthony's head jerked slightly, like he'd been slapped. "Keep your fingers out of my head, you mutant," he barked.

Rae got only one step away from the bench before Anthony snagged her by one of the tote straps and hauled her back.

"You said you wanted me to leave. Now you won't let me," Rae muttered, turning toward him again.

"I don't think you're a mutant," he confessed. His voice was harsh, but his eyes searched her face as if he was actually worried he'd hurt her.

"You said it. You must have meant it," Rae answered.

"You going to believe what I said? Or you going to believe what I thought?" Anthony asked. He raked his hands through his hair. "A Cardinal is, you know, one of the elite." He used the toe of one sneaker to wipe a spot of mud off the other one. "You know, smart, pretty, classy. All that."

"Oh," Rae muttered. She knew he meant it. She just wasn't sure what to say in response.

Rae reached out and gave Anthony's sleeve a little tug as she searched for the words. "It's not that I'm embarrassed to hang out with you—or Jesse. But there's no reason for either of you to get all involved with my problem. You didn't have anything to do with—"

"You think I'm just going to walk away and let some maniac come after you because it's not my problem?" Anthony sounded outraged. "What the hell do you think I am? Anyone who would do that doesn't deserve to take up space." He sat back down and slapped the spot on the bench next to him. Rae hesitated, then sat back down, too. It would be so good not to have to go through this alone. And even though she'd known him only a couple of weeks, Anthony was definitely the guy she'd want to have her back.

"So are we going to come up with a way to prove David tried to kill you or what?" Anthony asked.

"It's not David we have to worry about," Rae admitted, relieved at the chance to let out her secret, to stop holding this terrifying thing inside her.

"Then who?" Anthony asked, his dark brown eyes intent.

Rae pulled a small paper bag out of her purse. With her fingertips she removed a silver money clip. "I found this at David's. It was holding together a wad of cash. When I touched it . . ." Rae heard her voice tremble a little. She pulled in a deep breath, trying to keep it together.

"When you touched it . . ." Anthony prompted.

"I got a thought from David," Rae admitted. "Anthony, somebody *paid* David to kill me. I don't know who. I'm pretty sure he doesn't even know himself. But whoever it is is out there somewhere. And—" She swiped viciously at her eyes. "And how am I even going to know when they'll try again? Or who they'll pay next time?"

Rae glanced over her shoulder, suddenly nervous. Even now, sitting in the park with Anthony, someone could be watching her, waiting for their chance to strike. She shivered in the warm September sun, realizing just how dangerous her world had become.

Epilogue

Rae Voight has . . . abilities. I know it. But I need time to discover exactly what they are. She's starting to trust me, but she isn't the kind of girl who trusts people easily. Maybe she was before the breakdown, but now she's got a wall around her. She won't be able to keep her secrets from me forever. Soon, she'll *want* to tell me all of them.

I want her dead. Now. But I have to wait. Watch. Smile at her as if there is nothing evil developing inside her, as if I don't want to destroy the bitch with my bare hands for what she did to me. When I finally learn her secrets, then it will be time to kill her. Not just for revenge—although it will feel really good. But because Rae can't be trusted. When she becomes confident in her abilities, whatever they are, she'll be dangerous to anyone she comes in contact with. And I will gladly kill her to stop her from harming an innocent. The way her mother did.

Haunted

Chapter 1

R ae Voight's alarm started blaring. Without lifting her head off the pillow, she reached over and jammed the snooze button.

/ I'M WATCHING YOU, RAE /

Rae scrambled out of bed, her heart scraping up against her ribs. Someone had been in her room. A stranger. The thought echo she'd picked up when she touched the snooze button didn't feel familiar. It wasn't from her dad. It wasn't from Alice, the woman who cleaned their house. It wasn't from anybody who had any reason to be there.

"Come on, you freak, tell me who you are," she muttered. She ran her fingers lightly over the alarm clock, then over her nightstand, including the little lamp.

/ I'm watching you, Rae / *I'm watching you, Rae* / I'M WATCHING YOU, RAE / I'm watching you, Rae / I'M WATCHING YOU, RAE /

The thoughts felt like they came from different people, and they were full of hatred—hatred and fury. She could feel the emotions rush through her body, starting the acid pumping in her stomach, making her knees shake, increasing the temperature of her blood.

This can't be happening, Rae thought, her heart ramming into her ribs. A whole . . . a whole *team* of people couldn't have been in here. It was impossible.

Impossible? Like someone planting a pipe bomb in a bathroom to kill you? Rae asked herself. It hadn't even been that long since it happened.

Slowly Rae backed away from the nightstand, her eyes locked on it as if it was going to jump up and attack her. She stumbled into her desk chair and grabbed its soft leather back to steady herself.

/ I'm watching you, Rae / ***I'm watching you, Rae*** / I'M WATCHING YOU, RAE /

She shoved the chair away from her—

/ I'm watching you, Rae / I'M WATCHING YOU, RAE /

—and bolted to the door, wrenching it open.

/ I'M WATCHING YOU, RAE / I'M WATCHING YOU, RAE /

The hallway was quiet except for the faint sound of Rae's father snoring. She stood perfectly still, trying not to even hear her own breathing. The intruder—no, the *intruders* were gone.

Shower, Rae thought, letting out her breath. Then she could think—really think—about what she should do.

Rae hurried to the bathroom and shoved open the door with her shoulder. She pulled the door closed with two fingers and locked it.

/ I'm watching you, Rae / I'M WATCHING YOU, RAE /

Shaking, she switched on the water. These people . . . they

178

had been here, too. Everywhere. What *hadn't* they touched in her home? She stood under the warm spray, the scent of her ginger grapefruit shower gel filling her nose. She turned away from the nozzle, then leaned back her head and let the water soak her long, curly hair. She'd wash it. Then she'd come up with some kind of—

Rae's eyes locked on the showerhead. There was something glittering behind the dozens of little holes. Every nerve in her body went on red alert. Had they done something to the shower? Was this the second attempt to kill her?

Rae jerked off the water, then pried at the showerhead with her fingernails. She had to get it off, had to see what was under there. One of her nails pulled away from the skin. The pain brought tears to Rae's eyes, but she kept jerking at the showerhead. Finally the part with the little holes came free from the base, and underneath—

"A camera," Rae whispered. She leaned out of the shower and grabbed her toothbrush from the sink.

/ WATCHING YOU /

Ignoring the thoughts from the brush, Rae used it to stab at the tiny camera lens until it cracked, then she scrambled out of the tub, banging her anklebone on the side and managing to step on one of the pieces of glass.

Damn. She grabbed one of the big bath sheets off the towel rack and wrapped it around herself. She needed to do a full-house search for more cameras. But she couldn't walk around leaving a blood trail. She balanced on one foot and pulled the piece of glass free, then opened the medicine cabinet—

—and screamed. A man was peering at her between the little shelves. He reached through and grabbed her by the shoulders. Shook her.

"Rae," the man exclaimed. He sounded like her father.

Rae's eyes flew open, and she saw her father standing over her, his blue eyes locked on her face. She sat up, pulling free of his grasp.

Oh God, it was a dream, she realized, glancing down at the blanket clutched in her hand.

"Sorry. I guess that scream was real, huh?" she asked, trying to sound normal.

"I'll say," her father answered. "It must have been quite a nightmare." He waited, and Rae knew he was expecting her to tell him what it was about. But she didn't want to think about it for even a few seconds more.

"Yeah," she answered. She glanced at her alarm clock. 4:01. "But I have time to get in a good dream before I have to get up." She hoped she didn't sound as freaked as she felt. She didn't want her dad to start worrying. For months that's all he'd done—worry about her.

"Let me get you a glass of water," he said.

"That's okay," Rae answered, but he was already out the door. Rae used both hands to shove her hair away from her face. The roots were damp with sweat.

It was just a dream, she told herself. But that didn't make her feel any better. Yeah, it was just a dream. But in real life, someone out there wanted her dead. And she had no idea who. Or when they might try again.

Rae's dad hurried back in with the water and pressed the glass into her hand.

I thought she was getting better?

"It was just a dream, Dad," she said, wanting him to believe it, even though it wasn't really true. She wanted him to believe that their lives were back to normal, that even though she'd spent the summer in a mental hospital, she was fine, fine, fine. "Just a dream," she repeated, then pulled the covers up as high as she could. But she still felt chilled, as if her spine had turned to ice.

Rae headed toward the cafeteria, trying to exude . . . just your basic normalcy. For years there'd been nothing she wanted more than to be noticed. And she'd done it. She'd been right there in the center, girlfriend of Marcus Salkow, Sanderson Prep's It boy. Then she'd had her little freak-out—make that humongous freak-out—in the cafeteria on the day she first started hearing echoes of other people's thoughts, and she'd been sent off to a mental hospital. Now her biggest ambition was to blend.

Which wasn't all that easy. People were still way too interested in whether or not she was going to have another meltdown to take their eyes off her for long. Rae's steps slowed down. Or did one of them have a different reason for staring? Could one of the people checking her out be the person who wanted her dead? Her eyes jumped from face to face. It seemed ridiculous to think that anyone who went to her school had tried to kill her. They spent all their time planning what to wear and how to get invited to the best parties, and how to get the SAT scores to make it into the college Mom and Dad had their hearts set on. But that was it. Right?

Rae did another quick face scan. When her eyes fell on Jeff Brunner, he blushed the color of an overripe tomato, then lowered his head so he wouldn't have to look at her.

Jeff wasn't acting all guilty because he'd tried to off her. No, all scum boy had done was decide Rae was such a loser that she'd be *grateful* to let him into her pants. Fortunately Rae'd gotten that piece of info from his fingerprints before Jeff had even gotten close to scoring, and she'd put him in his place. She watched him scurry into the guys' bathroom like the rodent he was.

It's gonna be a while before he decides to try his luck with another "loser" girl, Rae thought with satisfaction.

She continued down the hallway, almost bumping into a guy who stepped away from the drinking fountain without bothering to look where he was going. "Sorry," he said, turning to face her.

Marcus Salkow. Rae's heart gave a jerk and ended up somewhere in her throat. *The parade of the scum boys continues,* she thought, trying to get a grip.

"Um, how's it going, Rae?" he asked, looking somewhere near her face but not directly at it.

"Fine," she mumbled, heart still slamming around in her throat like a bird that wanted to get out. God, while Marcus couldn't look at her, she couldn't *stop* staring at him. Did he have to be so gorgeous? He was like a poster boy for prep school. A clean-cut, well-muscled, blond, green-eyed example of a young southern gentleman. "Fine," Rae muttered again. She continued down the hall, not wanting to drag out the encounter, afraid if she looked at him another second, she'd start drooling or something equally humiliating.

You let him off so easy, she thought. Rae hadn't allowed Jeff to treat her like dirt. Why should Marcus be any different?

Because I loved him, Rae answered herself. *Because I thought he loved me.* Which actually made what Marcus did to her a million times worse.

Without giving herself time to reconsider, Rae spun around and hurried back up to him, ignoring the way her heart now seemed to fill every inch of her body. Pounding, pounding, pounding. "When I said I was fine, it was true," Rae told him, her words coming out clipped and hard. "Except for the fact that I came back to school and found out that you're with Dori Hernandez, which no one bothered to tell me." She hauled in a deep, shuddering breath. "Including you."

Marcus didn't answer. He just continued to do that not-quite-looking-at-her thing. Rae took a quarter step to the side, putting herself directly into his line of vision. Her heart pounded harder.

"Look. I'm sorry," Marcus finally said. "You were in the hospital, and I didn't think it was a good idea to upset you by telling you . . . you know. I was worried about you." Marcus

183

gave a helpless shrug, then reached out and pushed a lock of her curly hair away from her face. "Really worried," he added softly.

Rae shrank back from his hand. She didn't want him touching her, especially because it still did something to her, started turning her all soft inside. "You were so worried, you never came to visit."

"I came—" he began to protest.

"Once," she interrupted. "People I've barely said hi to came once."

He clicked his teeth together nervously. She'd seen him do the same thing in class when he got called on and didn't know the answer. Rae's heart returned to its usual place in her chest, and the pounding eased up, leaving her feeling numb and hollowed out.

"Rae, it's just that . . ." Marcus's words trailed off.

Before he could start clicking again, Rae jumped in. "Whatever, Marcus. Go find Dori." She turned and walked away. When she reached the cafeteria's double doors, she used her shoulder to open the closest one and slipped inside. She didn't want to hear anyone else's thoughts right now. Her own were more than enough.

She felt a tap on her shoulder and nearly jumped, then spun around.

"Fro-yo?" Leah Dessin asked.

Rae's shoulders relaxed. It wasn't her would-be killer—just the best friend who'd totally abandoned her.

"Fro-yo," Rae agreed. She didn't have the energy to do anything else.

Leah led the way over to the frozen yogurt machines, her sleek black hair shining under the fluorescent lights. This felt so normal. But it wasn't. Not anymore. Because now Leah was afraid of Rae. She never said it, of course. And she didn't even really act like it. But Rae knew it was true. Fingerprints didn't lie.

"Do you want to sit?" Leah jerked her chin toward the usual table—correction, what used to be the usual table—as she made her fro-yo sculpture.

She's trying, Rae thought. *Even though she's scared of me, she's trying.*

"Could we maybe be adventurous and—"

"Sit someplace else?" Leah finished for her, still sounding just a little too peppy. *Clearly overcompensating,* Rae decided as Leah moved out of the way so Rae could get to the machine.

"Just for today," Rae answered, grabbing a cup and a spoon—new, no prints. She didn't want Leah to think she was going to have to spend all year baby-sitting her freaky used-to-be best friend. But for this one day it would be so nice just to sit with someone and look normal, a normal girl with a normal friend. No psychic ability. No streak of insanity. No one out to kill her.

Rae took a napkin out of the metal holder and used it to pull down the handle. "It's always sticky," she explained to Leah as the yogurt spiraled into the cup. God, she wouldn't want to see Leah's expression if she heard the truth.

See, if I touch the handle after you touched it, I'll know your thoughts. And really, I'd rather not. Because you deserve some privacy. And I deserve not to hear how creepy you think I am.

"There's a place over there." Leah nodded at a couple of empty seats that were about halfway across the room from the usual table.

"Looks good," Rae answered, leading the way. She took a seat, and Leah sat down across from her. *Now what?* Rae thought. *What am I supposed to say?* Something nonfrightening. Something normal. But what?

"So, how's your homework load this semester? I'm already screwed," Rae said. Pathetic. But at least it was words.

"Yeah, me too." Leah shot a glance over Rae's shoulder.

What is she looking at? Rae wondered. Then she got it. Leah was looking at *the* table, watching Jackie and Vince and Marcus and Dori. *She can't sit without them for one meal?*

Rae got an image in her head of a massive steel door swinging shut, separating her old life—her prehospital, prefingerprint power life—from her new life. Leah was on one side. Leah and Marcus and Vince and Jackie and all Rae's old friends. And Rae was on the other. All alone.

Don't get all soap opera, she told herself. *You're not alone. Dad's on your side of the door. And . . . and Anthony Fascinelli and Jesse Beven.* Both the guys from group therapy knew the truth about her psychic ability. Anthony was the one who'd helped her figure out where all the strange thoughts were coming from. And he and Jesse were both okay with it.

And don't forget Yana, Rae reminded herself. Yana Savari had been a volunteer at the hospital. When she'd asked Rae to exchange numbers, Rae'd thought Yana was just taking her on as a charity case. But Yana was turning into a real friend. A Leah kind of friend, before Leah got all weirded out by Rae.

So get over yourself, Rae thought. She had friends. Maybe not a lot of them—but enough.

"Um, I'm taking chemistry this year, and forget about it. Just the work from that class is killer," Leah said. She took a bite of her yogurt.

Rae took a spoonful of her own. When Leah snuck another glance at her usual table, Rae pretended not to notice. What was the point of making a big deal about it? She and Leah wouldn't be doing this again.

Where the hell is she? Anthony Fascinelli checked his watch. It was still ten minutes before their group therapy session started up. But Rae should be here.

What if whoever had hired David Wyngard to set that pipe bomb and off Rae had already tried again? Or hired someone else to do it? What if she was lying dead somewhere? His stomach did a slow roll. What if—

And then he saw her. Walking across the parking lot like one of those girls in a shampoo commercial, her curly reddish brown hair all bouncy, looking like she owned the world and everyone should just fall at her feet if she smiled at them.

She wasn't being careful. Pantene pro-V-perfect did not

equal observing everything that was going on around her. What was wrong with her?

"You're late," Anthony snapped as she approached. "And you're stupid."

She glanced at her slim silver watch. "I'm early," she corrected him. She didn't bother responding to the stupid part.

"What's been going on the last few days? Have you noticed anything unusual? Have you noticed *anything?*" He wanted to reach out, grab her by the shoulders, and shake her. Instead he jammed his hands in the pockets of his jeans. "Has there been a strange car in your neighborhood? Someone you don't really know trying to get all friendly at school? Someone—"

"A stranger in a van offering me candy if I get inside?" Rae interrupted, smirking.

"Is that supposed to be funny?" Anthony demanded. He took a step closer and lowered his voice. "Someone is trying to kill you, remember? I can't believe you're acting like it's all a big joke."

"What do you want me to do? Am I supposed to walk around being afraid of everybody?"

Her voice shook, and Anthony realized she was pretending to act casual. "I just want you to be safe," he muttered.

"Yeah, well, I want that, too. But it's not like I can be suspicious of the whole world. I'd end up back in the mental hospital," Rae answered.

"We'll figure something out," Anthony said. Although he had no idea how. He shifted from foot to foot, not knowing what to say next. "I guess we should go in," he finally added.

"We're not waiting for Jesse?" Rae asked.

"If we do, we'll all be late, and Abramson will be three times as pissed," Anthony said. He led the way inside and down to the group therapy room. Most of the metal chairs were already filled, but there were two together by the door. He sat down in one, and Rae slipped into the one next to him. He'd feel a lot better if he could keep her this close all the time.

Ms. Abramson hurried into the room. She shut the door behind her and strode to the center of the circle. She was wearing one of those sleeveless dresses again. Anthony figured she had to lift weights because her dark arms were all muscle, none of that jelly at the top like a lot of women her age had.

"I have a couple of announcements before we start," Abramson said. She flipped one of her many braids over her shoulder. "First, Anthony Fascinelli was not responsible for the pipe bomb. I'm sure you all heard that Mr. Rocha found materials for a bomb in Anthony's backpack, but they were put there by David Wyngard. Obviously David will no longer be a member of our group." She turned her gaze to Anthony, her eyes bright with emotion. "On behalf of Mr. Rocha and me, I want to apologize for making a judgment too quickly and to welcome Anthony back."

Yeah, right, Anthony thought. He could believe Abramson felt bad and wanted him back in group. But there was no way the director of the institute was at all happy Anthony was back at Oakvale. Rocha had been thrilled to have a reason to give Anthony the boot.

Abramson began to pace back and forth across the center of the circle. "My other announcement is a disturbing one. I got a call from Jesse Beven's mother."

Anthony sat up straight, the bones of his spine suddenly feeling sharp against his flesh.

"Mrs. Beven told me that Jesse has run away," Abramson continued. "I'm sure this news will bring up all kinds of feelings, and I wanted to take the first part of our session to talk about them."

Anthony leaned toward Rae, the bones of his back biting into his muscles. "This is crap," he whispered. "Jesse wouldn't take off. Not without saying something to me."

"So what do you think happened?" Rae whispered back.

"I don't know. But I'm going to find out," Anthony promised.

Chapter 2

Rae headed toward the exit leading to the school parking lot. She heard footsteps behind her, and her breathing started coming a little faster.

Calm down, she told herself. *Of course you hear footsteps behind you. There are people everywhere.* She sped up, anyway. The footsteps sped up, too. Someone was keeping pace with her. *Okay, when you get to the parking lot—*

"Rae, can I talk to you for a minute?"

Rae whirled around and saw Mr. Jesperson. Her breathing returned to normal. The expression on Mr. Jesperson's face told her exactly what he wanted to talk to her about. And it definitely wasn't what book she planned to write her English paper on. No, he wanted to see how she was *doing.*

"I just wanted to check in, see how you're doing," he said when he reached her.

God, this must have been on the agenda at the last teachers' meeting, Rae thought. *Item 1: Everyone make sure Rae Voight isn't about to have another public freak-out.*

She forced a smile. "I'm doing well. Still going to group therapy, which is helping." That wasn't really true, but it was what Mr. Jesperson wanted to hear—what they all wanted to hear.

He nodded, and Rae expected him to walk away, having done his good deed for the day. That was what usually happened. But Mr. Jesperson took a step closer, proving he had no clue about the meaning of personal space. "I know I wasn't around last year when you started, uh, having troubles. But I want you to know that you can talk to me. My classroom door is always open. Whenever."

Rae knew that a lot of girls thought Mr. Jesperson was a total hottie with his black hair and that trace of stubble he always had going. But he was kind of giving her the creeps. She wished he'd back up, even just half a step.

"I'm doing okay. Really. Thanks, though." She took a step away, hoping it looked casual and not scared.

Mr. Jesperson moved closer. "When I was in college, I went through a bad stretch," he confessed, his voice dropping lower. "I almost flunked out. I was pretty messed up there for a while. So don't think if you did decide to talk to me that I wouldn't understand."

"Thanks," Rae repeated. "I've gotta go. I'm meeting a friend."

"Good. That's good. Friends are really important," Mr. Jesperson said. "Go on. I'll see you in class."

"See you," Rae answered, moving quickly down the hall and out the exit. In the parking lot, she scanned the cars— lots of Beemers, a couple of Range Rovers, and a bunch of other SUVs—looking for Anthony's beat-up Hyundai. Well, actually, Anthony's mom's beat-up Hyundai. Not there yet. And he'd given *her* grief for being late yesterday. Although that was just because he was worried about her. Even without all her therapy, she wouldn't have had a problem making that diagnosis. Rae smiled. She wondered if Anthony knew he had marshmallows for guts.

A horn honked to her left, and she turned, expecting to see Anthony. Instead she saw Yana's yellow Bug zipping in her direction. Yana screeched to a stop next to Rae, then leaned her head out the window, her white blond hair almost covered by a baseball cap, and grinned. "You up for the Atrium? If I don't get to a mall in the next half hour, I'm going into withdrawal. Not that I have any money to shop with. But still."

Rae shook her head. "Sorry. I can't today. I'm meeting someone."

"*Someone*," Yana repeated with a sly smile, clearly having broken the code that *someone* equaled *guy*. "Can't you even remember his name? I mean, I know prep school boys are made from cookie cutters—all clean-cut and white teeth. But I thought you'd at least be able to tell them apart."

Rae wondered what Yana would think of Marcus. He *was* kind of cookie cutter: the cookie all the other guys wanted to be like.

"So can I meet him?" Yana asked. "I could stash the car on the street. I know that you probably don't want to be seen with someone who actually drives a decades-old car."

"It *is* pretty humiliating," Rae answered with a smile. "But don't stress about it. The guy I'm meeting drives a Hyundai." She didn't bother pretending the someone wasn't a guy. Clearly she was busted.

"You're blowing me off for a Hyundai driver?" Yana cried, her blue eyes narrowed in mock anger.

"It's Anthony," Rae explained. "The guy who got framed for that pipe bomb—the one you helped me clear. And we're not going to be having *fun* or anything. We're meeting with the mother of this kid from our group who supposedly ran away."

"Supposedly?" Yana asked.

Rae shrugged. "I don't know him that well. But Anthony does, and he doesn't think that's what happened. And he thought, um, it might help to have a girl be there when he talked to the mom, that it might make her more comfortable or something." She definitely wasn't telling Yana that she was going to do a fingerprint search. Yana might be totally cool about it, but Rae just didn't want to risk it, or put Yana in danger.

"I guess helping out a friend is a decent reason to pass on the shopping. But you have to promise to go with me later this week," Yana said.

"How about Saturday?" Rae suggested.

"I'll pick you up in the morning," Yana volunteered. "I want to get there right when the stores open." She glanced in the rearview mirror. "Hyundai alert." She leaned closer to the mirror, her nose almost touching it. "He's pretty cute, if you like that bad boy look."

Anthony gave an impatient double honk. "Go," Yana told her. "I don't need to meet him. I know the type. And you guys have a mission. See ya later." She lurched toward the exit, tires squealing.

Rae headed over to Anthony's car, but not too fast. That double honk was borderline obnoxious, and she wasn't going to reward him by scurrying over. She opened the door and climbed in.

Weird. She didn't get any thoughts off the door handle. She should have picked up at least one or even the static that came when there was a bunch of old fingerprints.

"I can't start driving until you shut your door," Anthony told her.

Rae slammed it. No thoughts from the inside handle, either. "Did you clean the car before you picked me up?" she asked.

"Does it look clean?" he asked, nodding at the jumble of fast-food wrappers on the floor.

"I meant the handles," she said.

Anthony didn't answer right away. He acted all caught up in maneuvering the car out of the parking lot and heading for the closest freeway entrance.

"Yeah," he finally muttered, sounding embarrassed.

"It's okay," Rae told him. "I have a lot of thoughts I wouldn't want anyone to know."

"You probably *get* a lot of thoughts you don't want to know, too," he answered. "It's not like people walk around thinking about kittens all the time."

Rae shrugged. "A lot of what I get is just routine, you know? Like thoughts about having to study for a test or what to eat for lunch. But yeah, some are . . . some I'd be perfectly happy not to hear." Like the ones about what a freak she was. Her first day back at school she'd gotten a bunch of them. There were fewer now, but she could still be walking around, minding her own business, and—wham—get hit with one. And it wasn't only the ones about her that sucked. Sometimes she got thoughts from total strangers about other total strangers that were so full of rage or jealousy or fear that they made Rae dizzy.

"So, does Mrs. Beven know we're coming?" Rae asked, shifting in the seat.

"I called her yesterday after group. She's up for it. I think she's hoping Jesse will get in touch with me," Anthony answered. He pulled onto the highway entrance and merged into traffic in one smooth motion. *Definitely not a Yana-style driver*, Rae thought.

"So, you're pretty positive that Jesse didn't run away," Rae said.

"Not without saying something to me," Anthony replied.

She'd already known the answer, but she'd felt like she had to keep the conversation going. It was still weird being with Anthony outside of group or the juvenile detention center, where she'd visited him after he was framed for the pipe bomb.

You helped get him out, too, she reminded herself. But she still felt guilt-coated when she thought about it.

"And he didn't even hint or anything?" Rae asked. As soon as the words came out of her mouth, she felt like an idiot. If Jesse had hinted, Anthony would have told her. Now it seemed like she didn't trust him or something. Like she was interrogating him.

"He just acted the way he always does. Didn't even mention a fight with his mom or anything," Anthony answered. Rae glanced at him. He didn't look annoyed. Just tense, his hands gripping the wheel so tightly that the veins were standing out.

They rode in silence until Anthony turned onto a street in a shabby neighborhood full of ragged lawns and houses with flaking paint jobs. "Jesse's is at the end of the block," Anthony said.

"Have they lived here long?" Rae asked.

"About a year. Since they moved to Atlanta," Anthony said as he pulled into the driveway.

"So you guys haven't known each other that long?" Rae was surprised. Jesse treated Anthony like a big brother. And Anthony let him. She figured they'd known each other for years.

"About eight months, I guess." Anthony climbed out of the car and slammed the door. Rae was right behind him, picking up one of her own thoughts off the clean door handle.

/ Yana's right /

Anthony led the way up to the door and rang the bell. Mrs. Beven answered almost before he pulled his finger away. Clearly she'd been watching for them. "Come on into the kitchen," she said, her words coming out too fast, almost running into each other. "I made cinnamon cookies. I hope you like them. About halfway through I realized I should have made chocolate chip."

"I love cinnamon," Rae assured her.

"Sounds great," Anthony added.

"It's right back here," Mrs. Beven told them, heading into the house with jerky little steps.

I never would have pegged her as Jesse's mom, Rae thought as they followed Mrs. Beven. It wasn't just that Mrs. Beven had dirty blond hair while Jesse's was screaming red. Or that she had brown eyes while Jesse's were bright blue. It was more an attitude thing. Jesse was so high-energy, always excited about something or pissed off, willing to talk to anybody. His mom was high-energy, too, but in a totally different way, like she was so nervous, she had to be in motion all the time or she'd start screaming. And Rae got the feeling that Mrs. Beven would rather not talk to anyone if she could help it.

"Sit, sit," Mrs. Beven said when they reached the kitchen. Rae took the chair closest to the window. It had plastic strips for the seat and back, and Rae realized that Jesse and his mom were using patio furniture in the house.

"Go ahead and take the cookies," Mrs. Beven said, hurrying over to the fridge. "And tell me what you want to drink. We have cola, orange juice, milk, and water, of course."

"Milk, please," Anthony said from his seat next to Rae.

"Me, too," Rae added. She took a cookie off the plate in the middle of the table. Anthony grabbed a couple before giving Rae a look that said, *Go ahead and do what you're here to do.*

She'd been planning to wait a few minutes at least, have a cookie, make some chitchat. But whatever. She put her cookie down on the little flowered saucer in front of her. "Um, would you mind if I used the bathroom?" she asked Mrs. Beven.

Mrs. Beven turned around so quickly, she almost spilled the two glasses of milk she was holding. "Of course. I should have offered. You go back past the front door and down the hall. It's the first door on the left."

"Be right back," Rae said. She followed Mrs. Beven's directions, then kept on going. She tried the second door on the left.

/*where is he?*/

Rae felt a lump form in her throat as the thought and static blast behind it hit her. The thought and the salty ball of unshed tears were clearly Mrs. Beven's. And so was the room. Jesse would never stand for a lavender bedspread. There was only one more door in the short hallway, right across from Mrs. Beven's. Rae opened it—

/*maybe I could trade my*/

—and ducked inside. Yep, it was Jesse's. You couldn't even see the paint on the walls. They were covered, top to bottom, with pages from skateboard magazines and comic books.

"Okay, Jesse, what do you have to say for yourself?" Rae

whispered. She turned around and lightly ran her fingers over the inside doorknob.

/can't believe FRINGE/over in Little Five Points/ Mom's sleeping all/that math test/

Emotions flicked through Rae. Irritation, anticipation, worry, anger. But none of it felt intense enough to be a trigger for Jesse running away.

She scanned the handles of Jesse's dresser next. Same deal. Some frustration about his mom. Some hostility about someone Rae thought was a teacher. Some excitement about a new comic book. A fragment of a plan to meet some guys at the skateboard park. But nothing that gave her any reason to think he was planning to take off.

Closet door handle next, she thought. But it was a bust, too. All she really got was the fact that Jesse was not a morning person. Rae opened the closet and peered inside. It was surprisingly neat. Some clothes. A couple of pairs of shoes. A stack of comics, each in a plastic sheath. A baseball bat. She checked the comics—and got thoughts about comics. She checked the bat—and got thoughts about baseball.

Rae closed the closet and scanned the room. She decided to touch the window frame next. If Jesse ran away, maybe he snuck out through the window.

/no air-conditioning/got to ask Mom/set alarm/stupid paper route/

Nothing, Rae thought as the static buzz faded. It wasn't like Jesse would run away because he didn't like his paper route. She wanted to do a few more fingerprint sweeps, but she was worried that Mrs. Beven would come and check on her if she was gone much longer. It seemed like something she would do.

If he was really upset about something, I would have picked it up on one of the places he touches a lot, like the doorknobs, Rae told herself. Because if things were so bad he wanted to take off, he'd be thinking about it practically all the time. She hurried out of the room, letting the thoughts and feelings from the doorknob flow through her again, and returned to the kitchen.

"So there's no place that you can think he might be?" Mrs. Beven was asking Anthony.

"I can ask around. I know some of his friends," Anthony said as Rae sat back down.

"That would be wonderful. I'm so worried about him," Mrs. Beven said. She picked up the glass of water in front of her and took a long swallow. "You know he's run away before. But I thought things were better. Didn't you?" She reached out and covered one of Anthony's hands with her own.

"I did," Anthony told her. He gave Mrs. Beven's hand a squeeze, and Rae was struck again by what a decent guy Anthony was under his bad boy attitude. "Um, I was wondering if Jesse took any stuff with him," Anthony said. "That might say if he was planning to be gone long."

Mrs. Beven took another long swallow, draining her glass. "I checked, but it didn't look like he took anything. I wish he had. He might get cold or . . ." She let her sentence trail off.

Rae believed Mrs. Beven was telling them everything she knew, but just in case—

"Do you have any ideas of places Anthony and I could check?" she asked. "We'll go anywhere you say."

Mrs. Beven picked up her glass again, then realized it was empty and put it down. "You two would know more than I do," she admitted.

Rae jumped up from her chair. "Let me get you some more water," she volunteered. She snatched up the glass before Mrs. Beven could protest.

/oh God / his father / what if / wrong cookies / doesn't know where / his father / what if his father took him /

The glass slipped out of Rae's hand, her fingers suddenly feeling limp and nerveless. Her legs, too. Any second they were going to buckle. Rae stumbled to the counter and braced herself with both hands.

/should have gotten 7-Up / Jesse wouldn't / his father /

"Are you okay?" Anthony demanded.

"I just got a little dizzy for a second," Rae answered. The fear that wasn't her own slowly faded, and the strength returned to her body. She turned around and forced herself to smile at Mrs. Beven. "I guess I need one of your cookies. It will get my blood sugar up."

Rae started for her chair, then paused to pick up the glass she'd dropped. At least it hadn't broken.

"No. Let me, let me," Mrs. Beven exclaimed. Rae obediently

sat down. She could tell Anthony was going insane trying to figure out what had just happened. "Later," she mouthed at him.

Rae took a cookie and choked it down, still feeling a little queasy. God, the fear she'd gotten from touching Mrs. Beven's fingerprints had been almost overwhelming. Rae didn't want to do anything to make Jesse's mom feel even worse. But there was a question she had to ask. She waited until Mrs. Beven was sitting down again.

"Do you think that Jesse's dad might have any idea where he could be?" she blurted out.

Mrs. Beven immediately jumped back up, grabbed a dish towel, and started wiping off the table, her motions abrupt and clumsy. "Jesse hasn't seen his father since we moved here. He wouldn't know how to find Jesse even if he wanted to, which he doesn't."

But she's afraid his father took him. I know it, Rae thought.

"We should probably get going," Anthony said.

"Yeah," Rae agreed. It was clear that they weren't going to get any more info from Mrs. Beven. "We'll let you know if we find out anything."

"What exactly happened in there?" Anthony asked as soon as he and Rae were back in the car. He stuck the key in the ignition but didn't turn it. "You looked like you were about to faint or something."

Rae shoved her curly hair away from her face. "When I touched Mrs. Beven's glass, I got so scared. I knew I was safe, just standing in the kitchen. But I could hardly stand up, I was that terrified."

"You got a thought about Jesse's dad, right?" Anthony asked. "That's why you asked about him."

"Yeah. A bunch of thoughts about him, actually," Rae answered. "The worst one was, 'what if his father took him.' The emotion that came with that one was so strong."

A flicker of motion in the kitchen window caught Anthony's attention. "We should leave. Jesse's mom is probably wondering why we're still here. In another second she'll be making us chocolate chip cookies or something." He reached for the key, then hesitated. "Are you okay to go? I mean, are you still dizzy?" He couldn't shake the image of her in the moment she dropped that glass. It was like she wasn't even Rae anymore. Like all the life got sucked out of her. And he was powerless to do anything about it.

"I'm good. It doesn't last that long. That one was just intense," Rae answered.

Anthony started the car and backed out of the driveway. "I guess you don't know the deal about Jesse's dad," he said. "He beat up Jesse's mom a lot. Sometimes Jesse. This one time he half-killed her, and a nurse at the hospital hooked them up with one of those women's shelters where they help you move and change your name and everything."

"God," Rae said under her breath. Anthony shot a glance at her. She was staring straight ahead, a tiny furrow between her eyebrows. "So Jesse's dad really doesn't know where they are, like Mrs. Beven said?" Rae asked.

"He shouldn't. But who knows? Jesse tracked him down on the Internet. I guess it made him feel better knowing exactly where the guy was. He works at a bar in New Orleans."

"Jesse's never tried to contact him, though?"

"No way. He only wanted to know where the guy was so he could make sure that he and his mom stay far enough away," Anthony answered.

"I can see why Jesse's dad snatching him is the worst thing Mrs. Beven could imagine," Rae said. "But it doesn't seem that likely, does it?" She reached over and popped open the glove box. "Hey, I remember this. We had this workbook in my fourth-grade class. Is it your little sister's?"

Anthony's veins caught fire. Rae's fingers were an inch away from his English workbook. *His.* If she touched it, she'd know he was a total moron.

"What the hell are you doing?" He grabbed the workbook and hurled it into the backseat, then slammed the glove box shut, almost catching one of her fingers.

Rae's eyes widened. "I was just going to look for a piece of gum. Drinking milk always leaves this icky coating in my mouth," she explained, looking at him like he'd grown two heads.

"It's out of line to go rifling through someone's stuff," Anthony snapped, even though he knew he should be apologizing.

"Oh, and it's not out of line to practically chop off my hand," Rae muttered.

They rode for a minute in charged silence.

"It's the fingerprints thing again, right?" Rae finally asked. "You cleaned off the door handles, but you didn't clean inside the glove compartment." She shook her head. "I'm sorry. I'm not trying to . . . to *spy* on you. It's just that it's pretty hard to remember that I can't touch anything."

"It's no biggie. I was an idiot," Anthony said. He opened the glove box, rooted around until he found a box of his mother's Tic Tacs, and tossed them in her lap.

"Thanks." Rae took one and then shook the box at him.

He held out his hand to take one, even though he didn't really like them. "So what were you saying? Before, you know." *Before you almost found out how stupid I am,* he added silently. He'd told Rae once, who the hell knew why, that he was in a slow learner class. But that wasn't the same as her knowing that he was using the same workbook she used in the *fourth grade.*

"Um, I was saying that it didn't seem that likely Jesse's dad took him," Rae answered.

"One way to find out," Anthony answered. "Take out your cell. See if you can get the number for a place called Hurricanes in New Orleans."

"Got it," Rae said a few moments later.

"Call it for me?" Anthony asked.

She punched in some numbers and gave him the phone. A woman answered on the third ring.

"Hey," Anthony said. "I'm a friend of Luke Gilmore's. I wanted to surprise him this weekend. Does he still work there?"

206

"Saturday through Thursday night," the woman said.

"Cool. Thanks." Anthony thrust the cell back at Rae. "We're going on a road trip to New Orleans this weekend," he told her.

Chapter 3

Rae pulled a folded tank top and a pair of cotton shorts out of her dresser, then hesitated before putting it in her gym bag. Should she bring them? Why hadn't she asked Anthony if they were staying over? Wouldn't they have to stay over? It was, like, eight hours to New Orleans, plus time in the bar. They wouldn't try to drive back tonight, would they? Especially because Rae didn't have her license yet and couldn't help with the driving.

She shoved the PJ's in the bag. If she needed them, she'd have them. *Yeah, now you just have one other teeny, tiny little thing to do before you go,* Rae told herself. *Tell Dad . . . something.* Which she should have done Thursday night. Or Friday morning. Or at least Friday night. But she couldn't come up with the right lie. Maybe there was no right lie that would get any dad to give permission for his daughter to go to New Orleans with someone he didn't even know, less than a month after she got out of the nuthouse.

"Okay," she whispered. "Okay. Here goes. Dad, I . . . Dad, I . . ." Hopeless. Totally hopeless. She opened her mouth to try again.

The doorbell rang. "That better not be Anthony," Rae

muttered. He wasn't supposed to be there until eleven. She sprinted for the door. If it was Anthony, she wanted to get to him first. She yanked open the door. "Yana. It's you."

"Got it on the first try," Yana answered. "Ready to shop?"

Rae winced. "Oh God. I totally forgot. I'm losing my mind." She and Yana both cracked up. "My brain," Rae corrected herself. "I'm losing parts of my brain, like the part that remembers stuff. I'm not going insane again."

"But even though you forgot, you still want to go, right?" Yana asked.

Rae frowned. "Wrong. Sorry. The thing is—" She glanced behind her, doing a Dad check. "Remember that kid I told you about? The one who might have run away? Well, there's a chance his father snatched him. Anthony and I are going to go check it out. If I can come up with a good enough story to feed my dad, that is."

"Tell him you're going shopping with me," Yana suggested.

Rae shook her head. "The guy's in New Orleans. I don't think I'll be back until tomorrow."

"Let me handle this," Yana said. She'd been wearing a ripped T-shirt knotted above her stomach, but she quickly undid the knot and smoothed the shirt down over her black skinny jeans, covering up the DNA-strand tattoo that circled her belly button. "Okay, now, where's Dad?"

"He's in his study," Rae answered.

"Take me," Yana instructed, giving her collar-length blond hair a little fluff with her fingers.

Rae wasn't sure this was the best idea. But she had to do

something. Anthony was going to be there in less than an hour. She led the way to the study, gave a quick knock, then stepped inside, Yana right behind her. "Dad, you remember Yana, right? From the hospital?"

A flicker of pain crossed her father's face as he stood up and reached across his desk to shake Yana's hand. "Of course I remember," he said. "I really appreciate what a friend you were to Rae in there," he told Yana.

"Now it's me who needs a friend," Yana said. "See, my father has this business dinner in New Orleans tonight, and he's dragging me along. But I don't want to sit in a hotel all by myself, so I came over here to beg you to let Rae come with us. We'll be back tomorrow."

"I think that sounds wonderful. You'd like to go, wouldn't you, Rae?" her father asked.

Rae blinked. "Um, y-yeah, of course I want to go," she stammered. She couldn't believe he'd given permission so easily.

"Thanks so much, Mr. Voight. We have to get going right away," Yana said.

"I'll just quickly pack some stuff," Rae added. It wouldn't look good if her dad knew she'd packed before Yana asked.

"I'll help you." Yana pulled Rae out of the study, and they rushed down the hall to Rae's room. Rae shut the door behind them. "Oh my God. You were brilliant."

Yana retied her shirt below her chest. "Of course I was." She smiled at Rae. "Do you have any clothes I can borrow?"

"Sure. Like what kind?" Rae asked.

· "New Orleans clothes, baby," Yana answered. "You don't think I'm staying home, do you?"

"Stop here!" Yana ordered, giving Anthony a whack on the shoulder from the backseat. "We need snacks for the road."

He couldn't believe this girl. She shouldn't even be on this trip, and now she was trying to boss him around. "We don't have time," he told her.

"Oh, come on. It'll take two seconds," Yana protested. "You want snacks, don't you, Rae?"

You better not say yes, Anthony thought. *It's your fault I have to deal with her.*

"Sure," Rae answered. "Snacks would be good."

"Fine," Anthony muttered. He pulled into the Quick Stop lot and snagged a space by the door.

"You guys wait here," Yana told them. "I'll go in."

As soon as she'd gotten out of the car and slammed the door behind her, Anthony turned to Rae. "What is she doing here?"

"She's the one who convinced my dad to let me come," Rae answered.

"And?" Anthony said.

"Look, she really helped me out when I was trying to prove your innocence," Rae explained. "It's a good thing she's with us. You'll see."

Anthony snorted. "At least she didn't lie about only taking a minute," he said, spotting Yana getting in line to pay.

"Um, Anthony, she doesn't know about the fingerprint thing, and I don't want her to, okay?" Rae blurted out.

"Oh, you mean it's supposed to be a secret?" Anthony asked sarcastically. Did she think he was an idiot?

"I just thought you might assume she knew," Rae answered. "And, um, I also wanted to tell you that you don't have to worry about me accidentally getting your thoughts anymore. I bought this stuff called Mush. You put it on dogs' paws when it's hot or when it's snowing, and—"

"What are you talking about?" Anthony interrupted.

"It's basically wax," Rae explained. "I put it on my fingers so I wouldn't pick up anything." She waved her fingers in front of his face. They looked a tiny bit shinier than usual, but that was it. "I'll wipe it off when—" Rae stopped abruptly as Yana climbed back in the car.

"Okay, who wants what?" Yana asked as Anthony pulled back out into traffic. "I got your Snowballs. I got your beef jerky. I got your Cheese puffs. I got your M&M's—plain, peanut, and dark."

A road trip with a girl who's in love with the sound of her own voice. Excellent, Anthony thought. From the second he saw her, he'd known Yana would be a pain in the butt. Girls didn't dress the way she did unless they wanted attention—a lot of attention. And girls who wanted a lot of attention were always a pain in the butt. If you gave them some, they wanted more. If you didn't, they got all pouty. He couldn't believe Rae and this Yana chick were friends.

"So, how do you two know each other, anyway?" Anthony asked.

"What, you don't think I go to Sanderson Prep?" Yana replied, running her fingers over her tattoo.

"Well, do you?" She wasn't his idea of a prep school girl. But what did he know? It wasn't like he hung out with hordes of them or anything. Rae was pretty much the only one he'd ever talked to.

"No, Rae and I . . ." Yana hesitated. Anthony glanced in the rearview mirror and caught Yana looking at Rae, as if she was waiting for Rae to tell her what to say. What was the deal there?

"Yana was a volunteer at the hospital where I was, uh, *vacationing* this summer," Rae finished for her. She turned her head and stared out the window.

Nice work, Anthony, he told himself. Now Rae'd probably spend the rest of the trip thinking about how it felt to be institutionalized.

"You should have seen the place," Yana said. Anthony shot her a glare in the rearview mirror. But either she didn't see him, or she didn't care. "The doctors and the nurses, they were as freaky as the patients. Remember the wig lady, Rae?"

Rae laughed. A real laugh, not one of those fake ones people used to show that they weren't bugged by some stupid thing someone just said. "The wig lady was this nurse who had pulled out most of her hair, strand by strand," Rae explained. "She had a different wig for every day of the week. And she really believed that people thought it was her hair."

"It's called trichto something, when you pull out your hair like that. I can't remember exactly," Yana jumped in.

"Yana's the one who found out what the deal was. She was always calling up personnel files on the computer and then telling all of us really personal stuff—like who'd taken a leave of absence to go into rehab for coke addiction," Rae explained. "Did you know there's a rehab place just for medical professional druggies?"

"I only did it because I didn't think it was fair that all the info went one way. Like, why should some doctor get to know everything about Rae's childhood but not have to ever say anything about himself?" Yana asked.

"Oh my God. You should have seen these puppet shows Yana would put on," Rae said, struggling to talk around her giggles. "We had these puppets that we used for therapy sometimes, and Yana would put on soap operas with them, using all the staff people as characters."

"That's cool," Anthony said. And he actually meant it. Maybe it wouldn't totally suck having Yana along on this trip.

Rae glanced over her shoulder. Yana was zonked out, with her head pillowed on Rae's gym bag. "She's asleep," she told Anthony, careful to keep her voice low.

"I figured," he answered, his voice soft, too. "Either that or she fell out of the car. It's been way too quiet back there."

He sounded more amused than annoyed. Rae smiled as

she leaned the seat back and stretched her legs out in front of her. The Yana magic had already started working on Anthony. It was pretty much impossible not to like the girl—unless you were a nurse whose personnel file she happened to have hacked her way into.

Rae rolled the window down a little more, took a deep breath of the warm, moist air, and stared out at the dark highway ahead of them.

"What was it like in there? In the hospital?" Anthony asked. "You don't have to talk about it if you don't want to," he added quickly.

Rae let her eyes drift shut. She saw her hospital room with its two single beds, her roommate pretty much always asleep unless one of the nurses forced her to participate in one of the activities.

"The place was okay," she said. "Except the smell. Way too much disinfectant. But I didn't know about the fingerprints thing. I was sure I was going crazy, and I was so afraid I was going to die in there, like—" She stopped, biting her lip.

"Like," Anthony prompted.

Why shouldn't she tell him? He knew so much already. And he'd been there for her in a way almost no one else had. Rae took in a deep breath. "Like my mother," she said in a rush. "She got put away when I was a baby. She died in the hospital a few months later."

Anthony's head jerked back slightly, but his expression

stayed the same. He cut a sidelong glance at her. "Do you think she had the same thing you did? Maybe she wasn't really, uh, sick, either."

"I didn't tell you everything about her," Rae admitted. "She wasn't just put in an institution because she was *sick*. It was because—" Rae couldn't say it. She'd never told anyone this part. She tried not to allow herself even to think it. "She did something terrible," she finished. "But they found her unfit to stand trial, so she was put in the hospital."

Please don't ask any more questions, Rae silently begged.

"I don't know what to—wow," Anthony mumbled. "That sucks."

She could hardly believe she'd gotten so close to telling him everything. But riding in the car in the dark, it was like a weird kind of slumber party—where the conversations always got really intimate, confessions of fears and crushes and dreams coming out all over the place.

Rae let out a long sigh. "I guess that didn't really answer your question. The answer is, I don't know if my mom had the fingerprints thing. But I hope she didn't. Because if we're alike in that way, maybe—"

"You're not your mother," Anthony cut in. "My mother and me—we're nothing alike."

"You could be like your father," Rae suggested. She knew he'd wondered about that. He'd never told her, but once she had matched her fingerprints up with his and gotten a wave of Anthony thoughts and feelings. Memories of so many experiences, even ones from childhood.

"Maybe," Anthony answered, keeping his eyes on the road now. "Sometimes I hope I am, just because . . ."

"Because why?" Rae asked, still under the spell of the darkness.

"Because I don't really want to be like either of my stepdads, that's for sure," Anthony answered, his voice edged with iron. "Or any of the various almost-stepdads who've lived with us."

"You don't have to be like your dad to *not* be like them," Rae pointed out.

"Yeah. But . . . I don't know. I'd just like to have the chance to find out. If my old man's a loser like Jesse's, I'd want to know. Jesse doesn't sit around hoping his dad will call one day or just walk in—" Anthony stopped abruptly.

"I get it," Rae told him. She had an impulse to reach out and touch his hand as he steered, but she didn't. "Knowing the truth about my mom hurts. But it's better than having some fairy princess mother in my head. Probably."

"Probably," Anthony agreed. He pressed down on the gas, and they flew faster into the night.

$\mathscr{C}hapter$ 4

"Are you sure it's on this street?" Rae asked. She was sincerely hoping Anthony would say no. She'd thought Jesse's neighborhood was kind of run-down, but the houses on his street were palatial compared to these . . . shacks. That was pretty much the only word for them.

"That's what the guy at the gas station said," Anthony answered, inching the car along the narrow street.

"And we should definitely be listening to some loser who pumps gas for a living," Yana said from the backseat. She'd woken up cranky, Rae noticed. Like a little kid.

"We definitely *should*," Anthony told her. "Those guys always know how to hook you up with stuff."

"If that's true, why didn't they give you an actual *address?*" Yana complained. "I don't know why we need fake IDs, anyway. We can all pass for eighteen. And, lucky us, we're in New Orleans. That's all it takes, especially at a place like Hurricanes."

"You can probably pass for eighteen. And I can," Anthony said. "But she—" He jerked his chin toward Rae. "She can't."

"She does have kind of a baby face," Yana agreed.

"Hey," Rae protested. Baby face sounded like code for round, chubby, chipmunk face. And she had cheekbones. Not amazing ones, like Leah's, but they were there.

Yana leaned over and patted her on the head. "A sweet little baby face," she cooed. "I bet all the prep guys fall all over themselves when you walk by."

"You're forgetting that they all think I'm insane," Rae shot back. Yana smacked her on the shoulder. She always got pissed when Rae used words like *insane* about herself.

"Okay, now, that looks like the home of somebody called the chicken man, don't you think?" Anthony asked.

"Oh my God. I didn't think there would be actual *chickens*," Rae said. But there were. About six of them crowded together in the tilting coop on the front porch.

"Oh my God. I didn't think there would be actual *chickens*," Yana repeated, doing a decent Rae imitation. She and Anthony cracked up. They were doing that thing, Rae suspected, where there are three people and two of them don't know each other, so they bond by making fun of the one they both *do* know.

Anthony maneuvered the Hyundai into a small spot between two parked cars. He opened his door and climbed out, Yana right behind him. Rae really didn't want to go inside, but she wasn't going to give the two of them something else to laugh about. She jumped out of the car and headed across the weed-choked lawn and up to the porch. The chickens went crazy as Anthony knocked on the door.

"Why would anyone have chickens?" Rae mumbled. "I

mean, hasn't he heard of a grocery store?"

"They're for his sacrifices," Yana whispered. "Didn't you hear Anthony say he's a voodoo guy?"

Rae had an impulse to reach over and yank open the door of the coop. No animal deserved to be killed for such a ridiculous reason. *Maybe on the way out,* she thought. After *we get the IDs.*

The door swung open, and her plans to free the chickens evaporated. It was all she could do not to stare at the chicken man. He was tall, definitely over six feet, and so thin, he seemed to be made mostly of bones, bones and the masses of matted hair that fell past his shoulders. "Well, don't just stand there on my porch. Come in and tell me what you want."

Anthony, Yana, and Rae obediently followed him inside. Rae's eyes flicked over the room, jumping from the row of crude dolls—voodoo dolls, she realized—to the jars of murky liquids, to a metal bowl with a small fire burning inside it, a fire that gave off the unmistakable smell of singed hair.

"You looking for gris-gris? Something to protect you from the evil spirits?" the chicken man asked.

"We were looking more for something to protect us from evil bouncers," Anthony said, not seeming at all weirded out by the freaky stuff surrounding them.

"Oh, man. I put on the wig for that?" The chicken man pulled off his matted hair, revealing a dark brown crew cut underneath. "Well, come on in the back." He tossed the wig on a rattan chair with a back so high and wide, it could be a throne, then led the way through the door, which was painted a deep rich red and covered with purple symbols.

When Rae stepped through the door, she felt like she'd entered another universe. Or at least another house. The walls were painted bright white, and the small room was empty except for a long table that had photo equipment in one corner and some kind of machine—Rae figured it was a laminating machine—in the center.

"All right," the chicken man said. "Money first. Fifty bucks a pop."

"I heard it was twenty-five," Anthony answered. Rae's eyes widened. He'd said in the car that he didn't know how much the chicken man charged.

"You sure you didn't hear it was thirty?" the guy challenged.

"Yeah. Maybe that was it." Anthony grinned. They all forked over their money, and the chicken man picked up his camera.

He's slick, Rae thought. *If Marcus were here, he'd have just handed the guy the money without saying a word.* Of course, Marcus wouldn't have even been there in the first place. He'd probably have turned around the second he saw the chickens.

"Okay, who's first?" the chicken man asked.

"Anthony, you go," Yana instructed. "Rae and I need to

glam up. I want to put some more makeup on that baby face of hers so she'll look a little older."

"Good idea," Anthony said.

Rae felt herself blush. She never wanted to hear the expression *baby face* again. Yeah, she didn't look as sexy as Yana. But she didn't have chipmunk cheeks, either.

"Is it okay if we use your bathroom?" Yana asked the chicken man.

"Straight through the door," he answered.

Yana grabbed Rae's hand and tugged her across the room. "We'll be back in a minute," she said. Then she pulled Rae into the bathroom and shut the door behind them. The bathroom didn't have anything too freaky in it—except for the porcelain frog toilet brush holder, but that was more cheesy than freaky.

"Should we change into our other clothes first?" Rae asked. "We could go grab them out of the car."

"Uh-uh." Yana shook her head. "It would look weird if our IDs have the same clothes we're wearing. How often would that happen, right?"

"Right," Rae agreed. She never would have thought of that on her own. Even though she *didn't* have a baby face, she felt like she had kind of a baby brain, at least compared to Yana and Anthony. Yeah, she'd made it through a summer at the funny farm and was doing okay being *gifted,* but when it came to fake IDs and the like . . . she was clueless.

Yana yanked open her massive purse and studied the contents for a moment. "I think this is the lip gloss for you. You have a great mouth. And you should make sure everybody sees it."

"I have put on makeup before, you know," Rae snapped, as she took the lip gloss out of Yana's hand, glad her layer of Mush kept her from getting any thoughts. It wasn't cool to peek into someone's head, even if they didn't know she was peeking. At least except when she had to, like to find out if Jesse's dad knew anything about where he was.

"Don't get all bent," Yana said. "I like the makeup you usually wear. It's just kind of quiet for a bar."

"Yeah, which is why I wear it that way for *school*," Rae answered. "You've never seen what I wear when I'm going out."

"Okay, okay," Yana muttered as Rae put on a coat of the dark cherry-colored lipstain. And she didn't say a word as Rae started making up her eyes using her favorite going-out liner, a silver one that went on all cool and slick and made her eyes look even bluer.

She tried to remember the last time she'd worn the liner, the last time she'd even gone out. It was the party at Robert Mandon's, she realized. Leah had come over to her place first, and they'd gotten ready together. Rae'd wanted to look amazing for Marcus, and she'd tried on so many outfits and so many different makeup combos that Leah had finally threatened to leave without her.

But I guess it worked, Rae thought, blending foundation into her forehead, nose, and chin to smooth out her skin tone. That night she and Marcus had gone farther than they ever had before. If they'd been alone—without people banging on the door every few seconds—well, things might have gotten pretty intense.

Thank God that hadn't happened. If she'd gone for it with Marcus and then he'd dumped her for Dori—tears started to sting Rae's eyes just thinking about it.

"Hey, are you all right?" Yana asked as she finished applying a pair of fake eyelashes studded with little rhinestones.

"Yeah," Rae told her. "Just got a little makeup in my eyes." *No more thinking about Marcus,* she ordered herself.

Yana dug around in her purse again and pulled out a container of bronzer and another makeup brush. She dipped the brush in the powder and lightly ran it over Rae's cheekbones. "Now you have a healthy glow," she said, spreading some over her own face. Then she turned to Rae. "You ready?"

Rae nodded, and they headed back into the ID-making room. "Took you long enough," Anthony mumbled. His eyes lingered on her face for a second, and then he quickly glanced away, tinges of red on his cheeks.

"Stand over there in front of that piece of blue curtain," the chicken man told Rae. As soon as she did, he snapped her picture, then motioned for Yana to take her place. "I'll make you both nineteen. No use pressing your luck. You want to use your own names?"

"Sure," Yana answered. "Then we won't mess up."

"Give me some old ID so I have something to work off of," the chicken man said. Yana handed over her driver's license.

Rae gave him an expired gym card. He headed over to the table without another word and started working, his motions sure and economical.

When he handed her and Yana the fake IDs, still warm from the laminating machine, Rae reminded herself to toss her card before they got back to Atlanta. It wasn't something she ever wanted her dad to see. *He'd* end up in the hospital if he did.

"Don't get in any trouble tonight," the chicken man told them. "No drinking and driving. Your spirits would come after me for sure."

"You don't really believe in that crap, do you?" Yana asked.

The chicken man smiled. "Mostly no, sometimes yes."

"And those chickens in front. You don't really—" Rae began.

"Don't worry, baby," the chicken man interrupted. "Just for show."

Baby again. Rae rolled her eyes.

"We've got to get going," Anthony said. "Thanks for the discount," he told the chicken man.

"Just the regular price, dude," he answered, laughing. He led them back through the freaky room and gave them a half salute as they headed out the door.

"So where exactly is this Hurricanes place?" Rae asked when they were all back in the car.

"I found it on the map. It's not that far. Over on Bourbon Street," Anthony answered, concentrating on extricating the

Hyundai from the parking place.

"Come on, Rae. We have to get changed." Yana patted the spot next to her.

Rae wiggled her way into the backseat as Anthony did a Y turn and headed out of the chicken man's neighborhood.

"I borrowed one of your bras, too," Yana told Rae. "With that sheer shirt you lent me, it's all about the bra."

"That's cool," Rae answered. She pulled her arms inside her T-shirt, then pulled her head inside, too. It was like being in a tiny tent. Then she struggled to get into her sequined halter top without giving anybody in another car—or Anthony—a show. Changing from her jeans to her favorite black jeans was easier since the lower half of her body was pretty much hidden. She jammed on her ankle boots, with their skinny high heels, and she was finished.

"Done," Yana said a second later.

"Just in time," Anthony told them. "Hurricanes is right up the street." He inched his way into another barely-there parking spot.

"I love this place," Yana yelled as they crossed the street. There was a different kind of music blasting out of every bar, and they had to weave through a crowd of people—obvious tourists, college students, suits—watching some kids break dancing. Then almost immediately they had to get through another crowd surrounding a guy who was doing some kind of extreme juggling act with hatchets. Finally they managed to get into the short line leading into Hurricanes.

Rae pulled her ID out of her purse, hesitated, then stuffed

it into the front pocket of her pants. She shouldn't have it out, like she was expecting to get carded.

Yana gave her a nudge, and she moved up a step. Then another. Suddenly she was in front of the bouncer, a big, buff guy who looked like he should have his own exercise DVD.

"I need to see some ID," he said. Rae had it out of her pocket and into his hand in a second. The bouncer flicked his gaze over the ID. Then back up at her. "The chicken man does good work. But there's no way you're nineteen."

Anthony slid into the driver's seat and slammed the door. "Crap," he muttered.

Rae got in the shotgun seat, and Yana took her usual place in back, both of them filling up the car with their girlie smells—hair stuff and makeup, some kind of musky perfume from Yana, and that clean, grapefruit scent that Rae always wore. It still seemed strange that someone would choose to smell like a grapefruit, but he had to admit, on Rae it worked. It sort of warmed up when it combined with her skin and got kind of . . . sexy.

"Sorry, guys," Rae mumbled.

"It's not your fault," Anthony said, staring straight ahead at the car parked in front of them. It was too weird looking at Rae in that top, which, whether she knew it or not, was designed to get a guy to stare at her breasts. With her back bare, it was totally obvious she couldn't be wearing a bra, and once you got that info, well . . . that was it.

"So what do we do?" Rae asked.

227

Anthony looked across the street at Hurricanes, which meant looking past Rae. Except his eyes kept getting snagged. And not just on that sparkly top and what was under it. On her lips. On her hair. Her hair drove him crazy—there was so much of it, and it was so curly, that he was always wondering what it would feel like to bury his hands in it.

Knock it off, he ordered himself. How could he sit there obsessing over a girl's hair when Jesse was missing?

"Maybe there's a window in the guys' bathroom I could go through," Anthony said, forcing his mind back to his most immediate problem. Then he shook his head. "But that wouldn't really help."

"The two of us could probably get in with our IDs," Yana told him.

"But we need Rae," he answered without thinking. He shot a glance at Yana in the rearview mirror. She didn't look like she thought it was strange that they needed Rae to ask a bartender a few questions.

They sat in silence for a long moment, until Yana broke it. "I think that bouncer liked me," she said. "I bet I can get us in."

"What, you think you're just going to smile at him and he'll fall on his knees and say yes to anything you want?" Anthony asked.

"Pretty much," Yana said. "Stay here. I'll wave to you when it's okay." And she was out of the car before he or Rae could say another word.

Anthony watched her strut across the street. He had to

admit she was pretty good guy bait. "It's still weird that you two are friends," he said, talking without thinking again. *Okay, here's the order—use brain, then open mouth,* he told himself.

"What are you talking about? Yana's great," Rae protested.

"Yeah," Anthony agreed.

"Yeah, what?" Rae pressed.

Why couldn't she be the kind of girl who let stuff drop? "It's just that you're pretty different," he answered.

"Different how?" Rae asked.

There were the obvious ways—like how they dressed. But the big difference was that even though Yana joked around a lot, Anthony got the feeling that she was hard inside. Kind of like him. And Rae—Rae could come off hard sometimes, but it was like she'd had to learn to be that way to get through the hospital. It was more of a shell—not her center.

"Different how?" Rae repeated, a twinge of that very hardness in her tone. Defense mode.

He didn't think she'd especially like the whole soft-versus-hard thing. "Uh, you know. You're all prep school, and she—"

"That's such crap," Rae interrupted. "Why are you and Yana so hung up on the private school thing? The people who go to my school are just . . . . people."

Yeah, rich people. Smart people, Anthony thought. "Have you ever even been inside a public—" he began. Then he caught sight of Yana waving frantically from across the street. It looked like she'd been waving for a while. "Come on," he told

Rae. "I guess we're getting in after all."

When they got back to Hurricanes, the bouncer waved them in with a bored expression on his face. "I found out from my new best friend that Luke's on a break right now," Yana said as they stepped inside. "He'll be back in about fifteen," she added, her voice rising to compete with the music. "He has red hair and a Simpsons tattoo."

"Great," Anthony said, impressed by her detective skills. Although he wasn't at all impressed by Hurricanes itself. There were chairs and tables attached to the ceiling, which was okay since they were going for the whole hurricane vibe. But the place was not even remotely clean, which took the theme a little too far. The walls seemed almost oil coated. And the crowd . . . the only thing he could say about the crowd was that it looked like it belonged in the bar. Which wasn't exactly good.

"You know what this means? We have time to dance!" Yana cried. She grabbed Rae by one wrist and Anthony by the other and pulled them onto the dance floor.

Anthony was not a dancing kind of guy. Any other physical activity—football, swimming, running, baseball, basketball, even gymnastics—he was fine with. But not dancing. It made him feel like a geek, especially now that Rae and Yana were both towering over him in their stupid high heels. Usually he and Rae were almost exactly the same height, but now he felt like he should be singing, "We Welcome You to Munchkin Land."

"You two go ahead," he muttered. But Yana wouldn't let

go of him. She just started shimmying, still holding on to his wrist. And how much more of a tool would he look like trying to pull away from a hot girl? So he started shuffling his feet a little, trying to blend.

He noticed that he was getting some stares. And not what-a-loser stares. More like what-a-lucky-guy stares. He started getting into the dancing a little more, his hips loosening up. *Yeah, go ahead and look,* he thought. *Look at me here with two hot girls.* Hot girls who were way too tall.

A skeevy-looking guy, who had to be pushing forty, danced his way up to them. "You've got more there than you can handle," he told Anthony. "Why don't I take this one off your hands?" He reached for Rae.

In one second Anthony had his body positioned in front of Rae's. "I don't think so," he said. And the guy assumed the stance that said that he and Anthony weren't going to get out of this without some blood spilled on the floor.

Anthony had no problem with that. Taking this guy out wouldn't be a problem. And it would be fun.

It would also get him booted from the bar.

"Look, man," he said. The guy seemed like someone who'd say "man," and Anthony figured it would be good to sound like the same kind of guy. "You don't just walk up to a beautiful girl and say you'll take her off my hands like you're doing me a favor. It's insulting."

Rae stepped out from behind him. "Totally insulting. You need to work on your approach."

Anthony wished she'd stayed put, but at least she was

following his lead. And Yana was staying out of it, watching the whole thing as if it was a reality TV show that she'd flipped on for entertainment.

The guy ran his fingers through his thinning blond hair. "Okay, you're right," he said, sounding almost pathetic. Anthony realized he was way drunker than he'd seemed at first. "Would you like to dance with me?" he asked Rae.

"No, thanks," she answered. "But that was better."

"You know what would be really great," Anthony leaned in and whispered, hoping he wasn't pushing things too far. "You should go up and ask the band to play a love song. If you do, you might get her in the mood to say yes."

The guy smiled. "Thanks, man," he said. And he turned around and headed toward the band. Rae and Anthony looked at each other for a moment, and then they both started to laugh.

"Pretty smooth, Anthony," Yana said.

"It should give us time to ask our questions and get out of here. Let's head for the bar. Luke should be back any minute," Anthony answered.

"Hey, Yana, why don't you see if you can get any more info from your boyfriend the bouncer?" Rae asked. "Find out if Luke's taken any time off lately, been late more, that kind of stuff. Maybe talk to a couple of the waitresses, too."

"Good idea," Anthony said. It *was* a good idea. It was also a good way to keep Yana out of the way while Rae did her fingerprint thing. Not that Yana would know what she was doing, but clearly Rae didn't want her to see it, anyway.

"I'm on it," Yana answered. She started dancing her way through the crowd. Anthony put his hand on Rae's back, and they started pushing their way off the dance floor and over to the bar.

"Tequila shot?" the woman bartender called over the heads of the people pushed up against the bar. "A dollar apiece for the next minute and a half."

"Okay, we'll take two," Anthony answered. Who knew how much a beer would cost in a place like this. He was just looking for something to hold so he could hang by the bar, and something that cost a buck sounded good to him.

The bartender handed over two shot glasses. Anthony passed one to Rae, who took a tiny sip, and made a face. "Remember, we're not going to actually mention Jesse," Anthony told her. "That will either piss him off or shut him up."

"Right," Rae answered. "Looks like it's show time." She nodded toward a red-haired guy squeezing his way behind the other bartender.

Anthony plunged through the crowd at the bar, Rae right behind him, wanting to reach Luke before he got a ton of orders shouted at him. "We're looking for my little brother," Anthony called, managing to catch Luke's eye. "He disappeared about a week ago. Last seen around here."

"He's thirteen. Red hair. Blue eyes. Talks a lot," Rae added. She grabbed a cocktail napkin off the bar and wiped off her fingers, getting ready to work. "We thought maybe you'd seen him."

Anthony watched Luke's face, searching for any kind of reaction. But he didn't catch a flicker of fear or guilt or anything. "He's really into skateboards. He might have had one with him."

"Sorry," Luke answered, concocting some kind of fruit drink. "You've seen what it's like outside. Madness. Tons of people all the time. If I saw the kid, I don't remember."

Rae leaned over the bar and grabbed the drink as soon as Luke was done. "This looks awesome. I have to have it. You can make another one, can't you?" She slapped down some money, and Luke shrugged, then started mixing another drink.

Anthony turned to Rae as she ran her fingers over the entire glass. She leaned close so she could speak right into his ear. "Nothing that says he's lying so far."

Anthony nodded. She'd just confirmed what his gut had told him while he watched Luke's face.

"You know any places a kid might end up? Shelters or squats or anything?" Anthony asked, not willing to give up just yet.

"We've got to find him. Jerry—that's his name, Jerry—he's not so, you know, mature for his age." Rae's voice caught. "I'm just afraid . . ." She shook her head. "Sorry. I—do you have a Kleenex?" she asked Luke.

"Best I can do," Luke answered, handing her another napkin. "I wish I could help you out. But I'm not a kid kind of person. I don't know where he'd be."

"Thanks," Rae said. She pulled Anthony away from the bar. "That time I got him wondering how old Jesse was the last time he saw him. He was actually kind of sad." Rae squeezed Anthony's arm. "Luke doesn't have him."

Where are you, Jesse? Anthony thought, feeling like his heart had turned to ice. *Where the hell are you?*

Chapter 5

"Ah, the beautiful Gretna Motel Six," Yana said as she flopped down on the closest of the two double beds. Rae sat down next to her and pulled off her ankle boots.

/Anthony handled / hope the place is /

"I don't care where we are as long as there's a shower," she answered. "That bar left me feeling like I've been rolling around in grease."

"But we found out what we needed," Anthony reminded her. He closed the door, locked it, put on the chain, then stretched out on the other bed and closed his eyes.

He looked wiped out—wiped out and worried—with shadows under his eyes and tight jaw muscles.

"We're going to find Jesse," Rae promised. "When we're driving home tomorrow, we'll come up with a plan."

Anthony didn't respond. She opened her mouth to say something else but stopped. He wasn't the kind of guy who let himself be reassured by empty words.

"I don't know about you guys, but I'm starving," Yana announced. "I'm going to check out the vending machines."

"I'll go, too." Anthony sat up with a groan. "But I should call home first."

Rae glanced at the cheap alarm clock on the nightstand. "It's pretty late. Almost midnight. Won't you wake people up?" She'd checked in with her dad when Anthony was hitting up the gas station guys for info on where to get IDs.

"My mom and stepdad are probably still out partying," he answered. "And if they're out, no way are the kids in bed." He pulled out his cell and hit speed dial one.

"Zack, you're getting paid to baby-sit, right?" Anthony asked, without even bothering to say hello first. "So why do I hear Carl crying and Anna and Danny screaming their heads off?"

"He sounds like a dad," Yana whispered to Rae. They exchanged grins. Anthony ignored them, listening to the whiny voice Rae could hear coming through the phone.

"They should all be asleep, anyway, but since they're not, tell Danny that he picked the last show, so Anna gets to pick the next one, and they only get to watch one and that's it," Anthony said. "And did you make Carl take his antibiotics?"

The whiny voice said something, and Anthony shook his head. "It doesn't matter if his ear doesn't hurt anymore. He has to keep taking the pills until they're gone."

"But Dad," Yana mouthed to Rae, and they both got an attack of the giggles. Yana grabbed a pillow off the bed and pressed it lightly against Rae's face. But they both kept laughing.

"Nothing," Anthony said, responding to a question from the whiny voice. "Just a couple of idiots."

"A couple of idiots," Rae repeated, her voice muffled by the pillow. She pulled it away from Yana and tossed it at Anthony's head. He let the pillow bounce off without trying to catch it. "Can't you just do it?" he asked. The whiny voice whined some more. "Fine," Anthony said impatiently. "Put him on." He slid over to the other side of the bed and faced the far wall.

It was clear that he didn't want Rae and Yana to hear him. Yana put her fingers to her lips, and she and Rae leaned forward, determined to catch every word.

"Okay, Carl. But just one time, then you have to go to bed," Anthony said. Then he started to sing. *Sing.* "Froggy went a courtin'; he did ride, uh-huh."

"How sweet is that?" Rae said softly, the desire to giggle drained out of her.

"It's kind of pathetic," Yana answered, and her voice had an edge to it. *She's not kidding,* Rae realized. How could Yana think it was pathetic that tough guy Anthony Fascinelli was willing to sing to his little brother? Especially in front of other people. It was practically turning Rae into butter inside.

She and Yana listened in silence as Anthony finished up the song. "Now, bed," he ordered. "I'll see you tomorrow," he added, then quickly hung up.

"Vending machines?" Yana asked immediately.

Rae glanced around for her purse but didn't see it. "Can I borrow the keys, Anthony? I left my purse in the car."

He pulled them out of his pocket, started to toss them

to her, then hesitated, gave them a fast rub on his shirt, and handed them to her with the tips of his fingers. Rae shot a look at Yana, wondering what she'd thought of that little performance, but she was rooting around for change in the bottom of her bag.

"Get me something, and I'll pay you back," Rae said. She jerked her boots back on, ignoring the blurry repeats of her thoughts, then strode over to the door, unfastened the chain, and opened the lock, touching the metal as little as she could. *I hope he doesn't expect me to turn the doorknob with my teeth,* she thought. She couldn't help feeling annoyed at Anthony, even though she knew she wouldn't want anybody picking up random thoughts from *her.* She reminded herself to put on some more Mush when she got back upstairs.

Rae took another glance at Yana, who was still digging for change, then used the heel of her hand to polish the knob before she opened the door and headed out into the dingy hallway. She pressed the down button of the elevator with her knuckle, and the elevator door slid open immediately. Rae stepped in and knuckled the button for the first floor. When the elevator door opened again, Rae hurried out, made a right by the little pool, and headed to the parking lot.

It felt a lot creepier without Yana and Anthony with her, and she got a prickly feeling in the back of her neck. Like someone was watching her. *Yeah, because muggers always stake out the Motel Six parking lots,* she told herself sarcastically. The people who stay here have *so* much money to spare.

But it wasn't really muggers she was worried about. This

parking lot was like a movie set for a murder. A fast knife between the ribs or a—

Stop, she ordered herself. *Yes, someone tried to kill you. And yes, they could try again. But no one knows you're here. You're safer in this grungy parking lot than you are at home in bed, where everyone expects you to be.*

She half convinced herself, but she was still relieved when she got to the car and unlocked it. She gave the door handle a quick polish, then scrambled inside. *See, Anthony? Even when you're not around, I'm not trying to go poking in your head.*

Her purse wasn't on her seat. It wasn't in the backseat, either. Rae scanned the floor. Nope.

She leaned forward, her forehead pressed against the dashboard, and started groping around under the front passenger seat. Her fingers brushed up against something smooth—

/MORON/BLUEBIRD/DOES RAE/

—and she pulled it free. It was the English workbook, the one she'd thought belonged to Anthony's little sister. But the thoughts she'd gotten off it were all Anthony flavored. And they were so full of self-loathing that it made her stomach cramp.

Rae flipped open the workbook to a page that had already been filled out. There were spots where the answer had been written and erased so many times that the paper had a hole worn through it. And the name printed at the top of the page was Anthony Fascinelli.

No wonder he'd freaked out the day she'd found the

workbook in the glove compartment. Anthony had told her he was in a slow learner class, but clearly he didn't want her to know how much trouble he was really having, and how behind he was.

Gently she pushed the workbook back under the seat, another blast of self-hatred and anger ripping through her. It was like when he thought about himself, all he thought was stupid, stupid, stupid. "He has no idea what a great guy he really is," Rae muttered.

She gave the workbook another push. She didn't want Anthony to get himself in knots wondering if someone had seen it. *Don't worry, Anthony. I'm very good at keeping secrets.*

Anthony studied the row of chips in the vending machine. *Cool Ranch,* he decided, feeding the machine three quarters, then hitting the E3 button.

"So, sounds like you have a big family," Yana said as her diet Dr Pepper shot into the tray of the soda machine with a thunk. "How many brothers and sisters?"

"Three brothers—Danny, Carl, and Zack—and a sister, Anna," Anthony answered. "Zack is step, and Anna, Danny, and Carl are half." He slid some more quarters in the slot and punched the button for a two pack of chocolate chip cookies. He could split it with Rae.

"All younger?" Yana asked.

"Yep. The oldest one, Zack, he's fifteen. Then there's

Danny. He's eleven. Then Anna, nine, and Carl, who's three." Anthony counted up the change he had left. "How about your family?"

"Just me and my dad," Yana answered.

"Like Rae." Anthony decided on another two pack of cookies—all chocolate this time.

Yana snorted. "Yeah, like Rae," she agreed, her voice dripping with sarcasm. "Have you ever met Rae's dad?"

"Huh-uh," Anthony said, turning toward her. "Why? What's the deal?"

"It's just that Rae's his whole life," Yana answered. "You should have seen him when she was in the hospital. He was a wreck. For a while I thought he was going to need to check himself in."

She's jealous, Anthony thought. He knew the feeling. Sometimes he'd see a family at the movies together, and—he didn't let himself finish the thought. "I'm sure your dad would have been the same way if you were in the hospital," he told Yana, jamming some more change into the machine.

"Sure," Yana said, still in full-on sarcastic mode. "You're right. I never, ever thought of that." Another soda shot into the tray, hitting the other one. "You've never even met my dad," she answered.

"Whatever," Anthony muttered. She was right. He should have just kept his mouth shut.

Yana scooped up the sodas, and Anthony gathered up all the crap he'd bought. They headed back to the room together. "My dad . . ." Yana hesitated. "It can be cool. I mean, I get to do pretty much whatever I want." She gave a harsh laugh. "Rae's dad probably still checks her homework and everything. He's a college professor. I'm sure he expects her to go to a great school, too."

Anthony managed to unlock the door without dropping anything. "I guess pretty much everyone who goes to prep school is supposed to go to a great college. That's the point, right?"

"Like I'd know," Yana answered. "But yeah, I guess." She whipped the thin plaid bedspread off the closest bed and spread it out on the floor. "Picnic," she said, pointing to it.

Anthony sat down on the spread and dropped his load of vending machine junk. Yana put down the sodas, then headed into the bathroom. She returned a moment later with three glasses, their little paper tops still on them. "Rae probably doesn't drink directly from the can," Yana said as she took a seat across from Anthony. "Too uncouth," she added, going for a snotty upper-crust accent.

"Yeah," Anthony agreed, even though he'd seen Rae drink out of a can and knew Yana had, too.

"Do you think they teach that stuff in her school? Etiquette stuff?" Yana asked. She didn't wait for him to answer. "I bet they teach them how to walk. When I picked Rae up from school, everyone I saw walked the same way, like they had a stick up their butt."

Anthony laughed. Rae did stand up pretty straight all the time. "You couldn't pay me to go there," he answered. As if he could ever get in. But even if he could, there was no way.

"Me either," Yana answered.

There was a knock on the door. "It's me," Rae called.

Anthony felt a little spurt of guilt for talking about her behind her back. But it wasn't like they were saying anything so awful. She *was* a prep school girl.

Yana flopped onto her back and moaned. "I can't eat another bite."

"Shhh. You'll wake up Anthony," Rae whispered.

"Oh, no! We'll be in big trouble if we wake up Dad," Yana teased.

Rae opened her mouth to respond, but a burp came out instead.

Yana shook her head. "What was that?"

"A burp. Sorry," Rae answered.

"Do they teach you to burp like that in prep school? So dainty?" Yana asked.

Rae snatched up the last soda—the Mush protecting her from getting any thoughts—popped the top, and drained it, ignoring the little stream running down the side of her chin. Then she gave the biggest, longest, loudest burp she could. *Take that, reverse snob,* she thought.

"That's disgusting," Yana told her.

"Disgusting for a prep school girl?" Rae demanded.

"No, just disgusting disgusting," Yana answered.

Rae smiled. "Good." She stretched out on her side and propped her head on her hand, then checked to make sure that Anthony was still sleeping. "So what do you think of our Anthony?" she asked.

"I was wrong when I said I knew the type," Yana answered. "The type I was thinking of would never have sung that frog song."

"I still think it was sweet," Rae told her. She unbuttoned her pants. That last soda had left her feeling ready to burst, and the waistband was digging into her stomach.

"If you like sweet," Yana answered. She picked up a piece of cookie and licked it, then dropped it back on the bedspread.

"You don't like sweet?" Rae could see Yana with a nice guy. She was so supportive and sensitive, really there for people she cared about. Why shouldn't she get some of that back?

Yana shrugged.

"You're not getting away with that," Rae told her. "I want some details. What was the last guy you went out with like?"

"I don't really date that much," Yana answered.

Rae frowned in confusion. Yana seemed like the type who'd have tons of dates, with guys just waiting in line for their chance.

Yana picked the piece of cookie back up and popped it into her mouth. "Actually, if you want to know the truth, I don't date at all. I go out and dance and stuff," she added quickly. "But I've never done the one guy/one girl thing."

"Maybe you're better off," Rae said, thinking about Marcus. "You won't get your heart broken that way."

"I wouldn't mind trying it," Yana admitted. "I just . . . I don't know. Guys go for girls more like you."

"What do you mean—like me?" Rae asked.

"Prettier. Softer. You know," Yana answered.

"Come on. I bet there are tons of guys out there who think you're totally hot," Rae protested. "If no one's approaching, maybe it's because you don't act like you want anyone to. Guys like to have some idea that they're not going to get shot down if they come up to you."

"Maybe," Yana admitted.

"Not maybe. Definitely," Rae insisted. She smoothed the corner of the plaid bedspread, then smiled at Yana. "So, is there anyone in particular you are so sure wouldn't want to go out with you?"

Yana didn't answer. But she blushed. Actually blushed.

Rae sat up. "There is! So who is he?"

"Just a guy," Yana muttered.

"And have you given this just-a-guy any signals?" Rae pressed. "Have you ever even smiled at him?"

"What if he thinks I'm a loser?" Yana asked. "I don't want to be the pathetic girl who goes after some guy who's out of her league."

"Okay, first, if you use the word *loser* about yourself again, I'm going to slap you," Rae threatened. "And second, what guy could possibly be out of your league? You're awesome."

Yana laughed. "Yeah. All males shall bow down and worship me," she said.

For once we're talking about her problems and not mine, Rae

246

thought. It meant that they were real friends. Equals. Yana wasn't just doing her good deed of the day by hanging out with Rae.

Rae closed her eyes for a moment, letting the feeling sink in. Hopefully soon they'd have Jesse back, and then Rae could concentrate on convincing Yana to go after everything she deserved.

Chapter 6

"Where should I drop you?" Anthony asked as he pulled out of Yana's driveway the next evening.

"It's okay to take me home," Rae answered. "My dad meets up with a couple of people in his department every third Sunday to—get ready—play bridge. So he won't be around."

Anthony nodded. The car felt a lot quieter without Yana. Smaller, too. Which was weird. It should have felt bigger with one less person. Except without Yana's musky perfume, all he could smell was Rae's grapefruit scent. Without Yana's yammering, he could hear each breath Rae took. He could almost feel the heat coming off her skin.

Why had she worn that stupid halter top last night? It was like seeing her in it had flipped a switch, and he couldn't quite get back to seeing her in that pre-halter-top way, even though she was back in one of her regular button-down prepster shirts with a bra underneath. A lacy bra. He could kind of see the pattern, just faintly—

I've got one word for you, Anthony told himself. *Cardinal.* No, make that two words. *Cardinal* and *Bluebird.* He and Rae weren't even the same species. Or maybe all birds were the same species. But whatever. Cardinals and Bluebirds didn't hang together. They hung with their own kind.

"We're going to find him," Rae said, giving his arm a fast squeeze.

It took Anthony a second to understand what she meant, then guilt swept through him, strong as battery acid. Rae thought he was all knotted up about Jesse, and Anthony had been thinking about *her*. What a complete jerk.

"I'll pick you up after school tomorrow, and we'll hit some of his usual places," Anthony answered. "You can do your fingerprint thing on anybody we find that knows him or has even seen someone who looks like him."

If he was going to find Jesse, he needed to focus on Jesse. Nothing else. *No one* else.

Usual places. He needed a list. Little Five Points, definitely—the skateboard shop and the comic book store, and the place that sold all the loose candy. Jesse loved the atomic fireballs there. Jesse's school. The 7-Eleven, although Jesse didn't hang there very much without Anthony.

"Any ideas on where to—" Rae began.

"I'm thinking," Anthony interrupted, without looking at her.

"Well, don't let me disturb you," Rae muttered.

He pretended he hadn't heard her. He had to keep focused. Where else? He thought Jesse played b-ball at the park over on Magnolia. He didn't go to the mall that much, but he might have ended up over there. What was the name of that kid with the fully loaded computer? He and Jesse played *World of*

Warcraft over there. Was he even from Jesse's school?

"I know you're *thinking* and everything, but if you're still taking me home, you should have turned left back there," Rae told him.

Anthony made a U at the next light, without bothering to comment. His silence clearly made her somewhat pissed at him, and he kind of thought that was a good thing—focus-wise. He split his attention between the road and coming up with more places to look for Jesse. When he pulled into Rae's driveway, she jumped out like her butt was on fire. "So pick me up after school," she said, then slammed the door and strode toward the house without looking back.

He had this impulse to run after her, and, he didn't know, apologize or something. But it wasn't like he'd actually done anything to her. He couldn't help it if she was so sensitive. Anthony backed out of the driveway and headed for home.

When he walked in the front door, he wished he was still in New Orleans—even in the chicken man's freaky front room. His gaze flicked from Carl, who was eating what looked like Lucky Charms off the living-room carpet, to Anna, who was watching TV at an eardrum-piercing level while trying to keep the remote away from Danny, who was yelling almost as loud as the show. Zack, the so-called baby-sitter, was nowhere to be seen. Neither was his mother.

Anthony strode over to the TV and shut it off, which briefly stopped the fight between Anna and Danny because they both started yelling at him. Zack wandered in from the kitchen, holding a box of Oreos. "I scored lunch," he announced.

"Lunch," Anthony repeated. "Lunch. That's lunch?"

"Luuunnch. What part of it didn't you understand?" Zack shot back as he ripped open the box.

Anthony didn't answer. He just headed into the kitchen. All the cabinet doors were hanging open, and he was starting to see how Oreos could seem like lunch. It wasn't like they could eat a box of baking soda or some vanilla. He slammed the closest cupboard shut. What was his mom thinking? Yeah, she was always sort of a flake, but she usually managed to remember to go grocery shopping.

This was *so* not his problem. But what was he supposed to do? "Everybody in the car," he shouted. "McDonald's run. If you don't know what you want by the time we get there, you're not getting anything." He didn't plan on making a many-houred excursion out of the trip. And Tom and his mother were paying him back.

"Can I get large fries?" Danny asked.

"Yes, you can get large fries," Anthony answered, imitating his little brother's shrill voice. He heard the front door bang shut, and by the time he reached the living room, it had been cleared out. He checked the front pocket of his jeans to make sure he had the keys, then headed out to the car.

When they got to McDonald's, Anthony automatically did a quick scan of the place. It was possible that Jesse could be there. But he wasn't, although Anthony spotted Brian Salerno.

"Yo, fat 'n' smelly," Salerno called from across the room. Zack snickered at Anthony's grade school nickname but only for a second—only until Anthony gave him a fast knuckle to the back of the neck.

"Hey," Anthony answered. He didn't bother to sound at all friendly, but of course Salerno came on over, anyway, joining Anthony's group and cutting in front of the couple who'd gotten into line behind them. Salerno had never figured out that he and Anthony weren't, never had been, and never would be buds.

"So, you ready for English tomorrow?" Salerno asked.

School. Why was the idiot Salerno bringing up school? It was the last thing Anthony wanted to think about. Like he didn't have enough to stress about without imagining sitting in his Bluebird English class with all the other morons, trying to read one sentence out loud without screwing up.

The most important thing is getting Jesse back, he told himself. Screw English. Screw everything else until he and Rae found Jesse. Rae wasn't a quitter—even if she was a little pissed off— and neither was he. They wouldn't give up on Jesse, no matter how long it took.

Rae dutifully copied the definition for *simile* in her note-book—picking up some staticky thoughts, all hers, from the pencil—even though she already knew exactly what a simile was. How could she not, living with her dad? She glanced up and found her English teacher, Mr. Jesperson, looking at her. He did that a lot. Clearly he hadn't gotten over the idea that she needed a special "friend," someone to help her adjust to being back at school. *Forget it, Mr. J.,* she thought, returning her gaze to her notebook. *You and I aren't going to make a heart-warming Lifetime movie together.*

"Okay, all teachers are scum. Is that a simile or a metaphor?" Mr. Jesperson asked.

Anthony's exercise book flashed into Rae's mind. Nothing about similes or metaphors in there. Just things like when you should use an apostrophe. She could still almost feel those spots that had been nearly erased through. Feel the self-disgust that oozed through Anthony, like because he couldn't read that well, he was a total loser in every way.

The bell rang, jerking Rae out of her thoughts. She jammed her notebook into her backpack, grabbed her purse, and rushed out. She wanted to get out of there fast in case Mr. Jesperson decided he wanted a little heart-to-heart before lunch.

Rae's steps slowed as she started down the hallway. She hesitated, then veered to the left, heading away from the cafeteria and toward the library. She wanted to look up some info about learning disorders. Maybe there was something Anthony could do, something his teacher wasn't trying, that would make the English thing easier for him.

And while you're doing this good deed, you can skip going to the caf, which you hate. What a saint. But she didn't turn around. She pushed open the door and stepped into the quiet of the library, then headed to the closest computer and typed in *dyslexia*.

Maybe dyslexia wasn't what Anthony had, but Rae figured it was a good place to start. She jotted the call numbers of a couple of books on the cover of her notebook and tracked them down without a problem, then settled herself in one of the little cubbies at the last table in the back.

"Okay, *The Rewards of Dyslexia*," she mumbled. She flipped open the book and started to read the intro, which basically said that people with dyslexia thought in images, leading them to think a lot faster than people who thought in words. Which was a good thing—there were scientists and artists who probably couldn't have done the stuff they'd done if they hadn't been dyslexic.

Rae wondered what Anthony would think if she told him that. Would he actually get that having a different kind of thought process didn't mean he was a moron?

She kept reading. It turned out that even though people with dyslexia could be really smart, they had trouble reading because if a word didn't call up a picture in their mind—even a really easy word like *the*—it was hard for them to understand it. Pretty soon if there were too many words without images attached, a dyslexic's brain became overloaded so they could even start feeling dizzy or disoriented.

Which would probably totally piss Anthony off. He liked to be in control. And who could blame him? Rae was sort of a control freak herself. Just knowing that Jesse was out there somewhere and they couldn't find him . . .

Rae shuddered. *This is about Anthony,* she reminded herself. Someone she *could* help. She scanned the table of contents and found a chapter that gave some exercises that could help dyslexics with words that didn't bring up images. *Maybe Anthony and I could do some of these together,* Rae thought. She flipped to the chapter and started taking notes. *Make that a very big maybe.* It wasn't like Anthony would be happy that Rae wanted to help him. He didn't like to be helped. They were alike in that way, too. Plus there was the little problem that Rae wasn't supposed to know how badly Anthony needed help.

Rae kept taking notes. She'd deal with how to get Anthony to try the exercises later. For now she'd just get them down.

Someone took the seat in the cubby next to her, but she didn't even glance up.

"Hey, Rae," a low voice said.

Rae scooted back her chair, already knowing who she'd find sitting next to her. Marcus Salkow, looking amazing as always. She didn't say anything, just raised one eyebrow, waiting.

"Hey," Marcus said again. Then he started doing his teeth-clicking thing.

"Hey," Rae muttered. She started to get up from her chair, but Marcus reached out and blocked her with one arm.

"I keep thinking about, you know, the other day in the hall," he admitted. He leaned down and tightened the knot on his sneaker, even though it didn't need tightening.

Rae had a sudden impulse to reach out and rest her hand on his silky blond hair. She twisted her hands together until her nails pressed into her skin. "The day when you were a total moron, you mean?" Rae asked.

"Yeah," Marcus agreed softly, not bothering to defend himself.

Why couldn't he have gotten mad and left? She really

didn't want to listen to him stumble his way through some weak excuse again. Especially not while she was getting these ridiculous urges to touch him.

Marcus clicked his teeth again. He glanced around nervously, as if he wasn't sure exactly where to look. Clearly he was still having trouble looking directly at her.

"Remember the ancient Egypt section?" he asked, nodding toward a row of books a few feet away.

Rae's lips got hot and tingly. Of course she remembered that section. How could she forget? Back in that row of books wasn't the first place Marcus had kissed her, but the times they'd made out back there were . . . molten.

She swiped her hand across her mouth, lip gloss smearing across her palm. "Are you asking me to go hook up with you back there?" Rae asked. "Is that the deal? You think I'm so pathetic that I'll be happy to jump all over you like it's some kind of favor?"

"That's not—" Marcus began to protest.

"I guess you aren't getting everything you want from Dori." God, he was just like Jeff, sniffing around her because he thought she'd be desperate since no one at school would want to be with her. As if she wouldn't rather be alone. Rae stood up and grabbed her notebook, the dyslexia books, her backpack, and her purse, letting her old thoughts wash through her.

"No," Marcus snapped. "You stay. I'm gone. All I was trying to do was explain—" He slung his backpack over his shoulder. "Forget about it." He strode away.

Rae stood there, holding all her junk in her arms. Had she really misinterpreted him? Was he just asking her if she remembered the ancient Egypt section because it was a nice memory for him and he thought it would be for her, too—even now?

She took a step forward. She could still catch him. Then she dropped everything back on the table. Whatever his deal was, it was better to let him go. She had much more important things—and people—to worry about.

$\mathcal{C}$hapter 7

I *wish she'd hurry the hell up,* Anthony thought. He didn't like even sitting in the parking lot of Rae's school. Everyone who passed him had to know he didn't belong here. Even if he wasn't in a Hyundai. But sitting in his car was like taking out an advertisement. He leaned back his head and closed his eyes so at least he wouldn't have to see the people watching him.

A few moments later the passenger door swung open. Anthony opened his eyes and watched Rae slide into the seat and slam the door. "Ready to roll?" she asked. She didn't seem at all pissed off today. Rae clearly wasn't one of those girls who made a guy pay for weeks for one mistake. But then, he and Rae weren't dating, and that was usually when—

He stopped himself and pulled out of the parking lot.

"Yana called me this morning," Rae said. "She wanted to say good luck. Actually, she wanted to come and help us, but she's doing some project for school with a completely militant partner."

"We don't really need her," Anthony answered. Although it wouldn't have been a bad thing. Rae's grapefruit perfume was already filling up the car. And it was . . . distracting. *Cardinal,* he reminded himself. He turned on the radio, cranked it, and drove to Little Five Points faster than he usually drove. He pulled into the parking lot of the strip mall where the comic book store was, then he and Rae headed inside.

The vampire-pale guy behind the counter didn't look up from the comic he was reading until they were standing right in front of him. "You know Jesse Beven, right?" Anthony asked as Rae headed down the closest aisle, running her fingers across a long row of comics.

"Have a Silver Surfer on hold for him," the guy answered. "Not for much longer, though. He was supposed to pick it up two days ago."

He shot a look down at his comic. Anthony reached out and covered it with his hand. "When's the last time he was in?"

The guy let out an exasperated sigh. "A week. About." He used two fingers to try and get Anthony's hand off the comic. Anthony kept his hand where it was. "Sweat damages the pages," the guy informed him.

Anthony realized his palms *were* sweating. The back of his neck, too. And his underarms—a sweat factory. *It's 'cause you don't think this is going to work,* a little voice in the back of his head whispered. *It's 'cause you don't think you're ever going to see Jesse again.*

He pulled his hand off the comic. "If he comes by, would you tell him Anthony's looking for him?" he asked. *Right. Like he's going to just come strolling in,* the little voice commented. Anthony tried to ignore it.

"Uh-huh," the guy muttered, already back to his reading.

"I want to pay for the comic—for Jesse," Rae said as she wandered up to the counter. She slid a twenty in front of the guy. When he gave her the change, Anthony saw that she made sure to touch his fingertips. Anthony studied her expression, but it didn't seem like she was learning anything.

"Nothing," she said as soon as they got back outside. "I mean, nothing useful. I did get a thought of Jesse's off one of the comics I touched, but it was an old one. He was thinking about being late to group therapy."

"It's only our first stop," Anthony answered. "Let's leave the car parked and walk around. There are a bunch of places near here Jesse hits pretty often." *A bunch of places where no one's going to have seen anything,* the doom generating part of his brain commented as Anthony led the way across the parking lot. He wished he could just switch off that part of his brain. Every time it yapped, his body pumped out more sweat. His T-shirt was plastered to his back, and his hair was slicked to his scalp. He pressed his arms close to his sides, hoping he didn't reek.

"I keep thinking about Jesse's mom," Rae said as they headed past the strip mall and down the next block. "She's got to be going crazy. I wish we could at least tell her that Jesse's father doesn't have him."

"It would make her even more nuts to know that we went and talked to Luke," Anthony answered. "She'd never feel safe in Atlanta again. She wouldn't be sure he didn't get some info out of us that he could use to track her down."

"Yeah," Rae agreed, stepping over a buckled section of sidewalk. Anthony caught one of his hands reaching out to steady her and jammed both hands in his pockets. She could take care of herself.

A couple of kids around Jesse's age came speeding around the corner, one on a scooter, the other two on skateboards. "You guys know Jesse Beven?" he called out. One of the kids came to a stop in front of him; the other two swerved around him and Rae and kept on going.

"Is he okay?" The kid used his toe to flip his board on end, then picked it up.

The sweat coating his body turned to ice. "What do you mean, is he okay?" Anthony demanded.

The kid flicked one of the wheels on his board. "I heard that some guy pulled him into a van the other day."

It's not going to do any good to tear his head off, Anthony told himself. *Stay calm.* "Tell me everything," he said. Rae moved closer to him. She grabbed a handful of the back of his T-shirt and held on tight.

"Chris at the skateboard place said he saw Jesse get shoved into a van by this big guy with a purple Mohawk. It was last week sometime. I wasn't sure if Chris was messing with me. He makes stuff up sometimes. But I haven't seen him around." The kid gave the wheel another flick. "So is he okay?"

Anthony didn't answer. He just ran, stumbling over the

uneven sidewalk, Rae right behind him, still holding on to his shirt. At the end of the block he took a right, then cut across the street and into the skateboard shop. "I need to talk to Chris," he announced the second he and Rae were inside.

A tall, thin guy dressed all in spandex headed toward them. "I'm Chris."

"We're looking for Jesse Beven," Rae answered before Anthony could. She gave the cloth of his T-shirt a twist. "We think you're the last person who saw him."

"Yeah," Chris answered. "I saw this guy with a Mohawk pull him into a van."

A kid who'd been studying one of the boards turned toward them. "No way. That lady pulled him out of here, remember?"

"What lady?" Anthony demanded, turning toward the kid.

"I figured it was his mom," the kid answered. "She didn't look happy. Jesse's probably just grounded or something."

"A lady?" Rae repeated.

"What did she look like?" Anthony asked, his words running over hers.

"Short. Kind of chubby. Red hair, like Jesse's," the kid answered. "His mom, I figured. Am I right?"

"Don't listen to him. I'm telling you a guy with a purple Mohawk—" Chris began.

"You're both losing it," the girl behind the counter said. "I saw the whole thing from the window. Jesse headed out, and then he fainted or something. An ambulance came and picked him up."

"Deirdre, you've been watching way, way too much *Grey's Anatomy*," Chris told her. "You're losing your grip on reality."

"Yeah," the kid agreed. "His mom came in and dragged him out. He probably had been slacking on taking out the garbage or he took money from her purse or something like that."

Deirdre shook her head. "I saw what I saw. And since I'm not chemically enhanced most of the time, I think you guys should listen to me," she told Rae and Anthony.

What the hell is going on? Anthony wondered. They'd gotten three stories in three minutes. And Anthony's instinctive lie detector wasn't going off. He couldn't pick up any signs that he and Rae were being fed a line.

Rae reached out and shook Chris's hand. For an instant she got that blank, not-Rae look, then she pulled her hand away. "Thanks for your help," she said. "If Jesse comes by, tell him Rae and Anthony were trying to find him."

She shook Deirdre's hand next, then the kid's, then she led the way out of the place. "What's the deal?" Anthony asked, hoping she'd gotten something that would take them straight to Jesse but almost sure she hadn't.

"The deal is that all three of them were telling the truth," Rae answered. She rubbed her hands together, trying to feel like herself again. All these not-her thoughts and feelings were still swirling around inside her.

"What's that supposed to mean?" Anthony ran his hands through his hair, and Rae saw the deep circles of sweat staining the T-shirt under his arms.

"I don't know what it means," Rae admitted. "But when I touched their fingers, I didn't pick up anything that said any of them was lying."

"That's crap!" Anthony exploded.

"I agree. But that's what I got." Rae gave a helpless shrug. "Do you think—" she hesitated. "Do you think what happened to Jesse could have something to do with me?"

"He's run away before," Anthony said. "But now we're hearing about him getting snatched. And I'm sure he would have gotten in touch with me if he could. I never thought running away was the real story this time."

Anthony looked like he'd really love to punch something. Rae totally understood. But they had to stay focused. "Let's just talk to some more people. Maybe we'll be able to figure out if there's a connection." She scanned the street. "We could start with that homeless lady. She's probably in the neighborhood a lot."

"Okay. Let's go." He spit out the words, and Rae could see his struggle to keep himself under control in the tight muscles of his neck and shoulders. Even the muscles of his arms looked clenched.

I think I'll do the talking, Rae decided as they approached the woman, who sat on a faded piece of carpet in front of a vintage clothing store that had gone under. "Excuse me, my little brother is missing. He comes around here a lot, and I thought you might have seen him."

The woman didn't answer, but she seemed to be listening, so Rae hurried on. "He's thirteen. Red hair. Blue eyes."

"On a skateboard a lot," Anthony added. He pulled out his wallet and slid out a photo of Jesse. The woman nodded when she saw it.

"A couple of skinheads snatched him," the woman said. "Shoved him in the back of a station wagon with the windows painted black."

"Can you describe them more? Or the car?" Anthony asked.

The woman's forehead creased as she thought for a minute. "Not really. You know—skinheads."

Anthony shot Rae a look, and she knew what he wanted her to do. She pulled a ten-dollar bill out of her purse. The woman looked like she could use it. "Thanks for your help," Rae said, pressing the money into the woman's hand, making sure their fingertips touched.

The instant they did, Rae's mind was no longer her own. It was filled with the homeless woman's thoughts, layers and layers of them. Scraps of memory. Fragments of childhood fears. Pieces of dreams. Her stomach cramped with hunger. She felt a dull headache just behind her eyes. Her lips felt the sweetness of a first kiss. A ball of pure pain filled her chest, the pain of a lost child.

Her instinct was to try and block the thoughts and feelings. It was too much. Too personal. Too overwhelming. Too *fast.* She was hit by so much information, so much emotion simultaneously that she felt like she was being pounded into the cement. *Let it come,* Rae told herself. *Let it come.*

A thought about the red-haired boy, about Jesse, joined the cacophony. Skinheads. Station wagon. The thoughts were clean and clear. Rae released the woman's fingers. She'd told them all she knew.

"I hope you find him," the woman answered.

"Thanks," Rae said. She and Anthony headed down the block. "She was telling the truth, just like the others," she told him when they were out of the woman's earshot.

"They can't all be telling the truth," Anthony burst out.

"The thoughts were really clear, clearer than any of the others," Rae said.

"Is that normal?" Anthony asked.

Rae took a deep breath. "I don't know what's normal yet," she replied, shaking her head. "Especially in the fingertip-to-fingertip thing. I mean, normal kind of went bye-bye for me a while ago."

Anthony nodded. "I guess we should ask around at the Chick-fil-A up there." He gave a disgusted snort. "Like it will help."

"You never know," Rae answered, although she had the same bad feeling Anthony did. The Jesse situation had gotten stranger and scarier. It felt a lot more out of control than it had yesterday. "I just need a couple of minutes before I touch fingertips again. My head is feeling kind of gooey. I'm getting the headache everyone else had—right behind the eyes."

"What do you mean, everyone else?" Anthony asked as they headed into the fast-food place.

"All the people I touched to get thoughts from had a headache," Rae answered. "Or maybe I gave them a headache by doing it, which would make more sense than four random people having a headache right in the same spot."

"When you did it to me the other time, it didn't give me a headache," Anthony told her.

"Weird. But you know my motto—Weird 'R' Me," Rae replied.

"I guess." He paused. "Not that you're weird," he added quickly. "That *it's* weird." He got in the shortest line. "Since we're taking a break, I'm getting some waffle fries."

"Me, too. And a massive Coke," Rae said. "Then we'll get back to work." She tried to make herself sound confident and determined. But when she glanced at Anthony, she didn't think he'd even noticed the effort. He'd clearly gotten so caught up in his own thoughts that she could be a hundred miles away.

Maybe while we're eating, I could talk to him about the dyslexia book, she thought. It wasn't exactly the perfect time. But they needed more info before they could come up with a better plan to find Jesse, so . . . she might as well bring it up, right? Her stomach tightened as she tried to figure out exactly what she could say, how to bring it up without being totally offensive.

She still hadn't come up with anything good by the time they'd gotten their food and found a table. Probably because there wasn't any good method. But that didn't mean she shouldn't do it. The info she'd gotten could change Anthony's whole life, the way it had some of the people's in the book.

"Want ketchup?" Anthony asked, holding up some of the little packets.

"I'm not a ketchup person," Rae answered. "I like them plain—so I can really taste all the grease and salt." She popped a waffle fry into her mouth and kept right on talking. Which was gross, but she was nervous. "I had this baby-sitter once who used to put vinegar on her fries. Is that nasty or what? She was from Canada."

"Huh," Anthony grunted.

Whatever that little babble fest was, it was *not* any kind of intro into talking about a learning disorder. Rae took a swallow of her Coke—

/so going to quit/

—then another one, then she tried again. "I was reading this interesting book the other day, about dyslexia."

Not too smooth. But acceptable. At least she thought so until she saw Anthony's face. It was blank, a total mask of a face. Whatever he was thinking or feeling, he wasn't going to let her in. And since he wasn't saying anything, he definitely wasn't going to open the door she'd knocked on.

But too bad for him if he didn't want to hear it. This was too important to just drop.

"Remember when you figured out where I was getting all my psycho not-me thoughts?" she asked.

"Yeah," Anthony said. She was surprised he could get a

word out past his mask face. "So?"

"It totally changed my life. Really," Rae said. "And, um . . ." This was the tricky part. "There's something I want to do for you. A thing like what you did for me."

"Like what?" Anthony asked, with exactly zero amount of interest.

"Like in that book I was telling you about, it gave some exercises for people"—Rae lowered her voice—"people who have trouble reading. I thought maybe you and I could—"

"I never told you I had any problem reading," Anthony interrupted, his voice as low as hers but rough with anger.

"You said you were in a slow learners class, remember?" Rae asked, forcing herself to look him in the eye.

"I never said anything about reading," Anthony repeated. "You got it off my workbook, didn't you?" he demanded. "You touched it when you were going through the glove box, before I got it away."

It would be easier just to say yes. Easier, but not the way to go. The one thing she and Anthony had always been able to do was be honest with each other. "I didn't touch it that day," she answered. "But when we were in the motel and I went down to get my purse out of the car . . . it was an accident. I hadn't put the Mush back on. I was feeling around under the seat and—"

"And now you want to do your good deed and play teacher," Anthony spat out, his eyes flashing with anger. "What, you need some volunteering to beef up your college applications?"

"That's not—" Rae began to protest.

Anthony shoved away his fries. "These things are cold. They're making me want to puke." He stood up. "If you want to talk to more people with me, fine. But that's it. One word out of you about anything but Jesse and you can find your own way home."

"Fine," Rae snapped. "I was trying to do you a favor, but fine. I'll stay and help you out. For Jesse."

Chapter 8

A nthony checked the clock, always a big mistake at school. English still had another twenty minutes to go. And there were hours and hours before gym, the only class that didn't make him want to puke. Wonderful.

He noticed a few people flipping the page in the ancient *People* magazine they were reading—Ms. Goyer, the teacher, had decided that they needed more interesting reading material—so he flipped the page, too. For a couple of minutes he actually listened to Phil Amagast read aloud about the latest Hollywood supercouple breakup. That was about as much as he could take because not only did Amagast read incredibly slowly, like all the Bluebirds, he had allergies that forced him to keep sucking snot back into his nose. Plus, was Anthony actually supposed to care that some B-list actor and his plastic wife had split up a while ago? The magazines were so old, everyone already knew what had happened, anyway.

Amagast paused to pull in what sounded like a truckload of snot, then he went on—word, wet sniffle, word, um, um, word, wipe nose on sleeve, word, uh, um, word. . . .

A craving came over Anthony, like hunger, like thirst, like

the need to piss first thing in the morning. He wanted a joint. He could almost taste it, the thick smoke in his lungs, the world becoming just a little bit nicer.

He glanced at the clock again. Only three minutes had passed. *Get a bathroom pass,* he told himself. Mike or Gregg might be in the bathroom. Or at least somebody who could give him a hit. He didn't need a lot. Just enough to take the edge off . . . so blood wouldn't come gushing out of his ears after his brain imploded, which was what it felt like was happening. Anthony started to raise his hand, then lowered it and gripped the side of his desk until his fingers ached. If he let himself get a little buzz to get through the day today, then he'd be back to getting high all the time. And that was not the best way of getting out of this place for good. He wanted to graduate, and he was barely making it through his Bluebird classes pot free.

In that book Rae was talking about, was there really a way that—

Stop, he told himself. *Remember fourth grade—getting on the moron bus, going to that place where all everyone wanted to do was help little Tony?* Those people couldn't even get his name right. And the crap they made him do—it just made him feel even stupider.

And then there was the seventh grade. Mr. Leary. *Discipline means a disciplined mind.* He couldn't breathe in that guy's room without getting the dictionary treatment—standing in front of the class, arms out, with a massive dictionary balanced on each palm until his muscles quivered, until he had to drop the books no matter what Leary said.

Anthony's skin started to get hot. Hot and itchy. He could feel each spot where a hair connected to his skin. If he didn't get out of here—

Jesse. Think about Jesse, Anthony ordered himself. What could the deal be? He and Rae had talked to a bunch more people in Little Five Points yesterday. Some of them had seen Jesse. But all of them had a different story about what happened, just like the first few people they'd talked to. What could that mean? Some kind of drugs in the local coffee bar? A blast from an alien mind-altering laser after Jesse was abducted? Hypnosis? Mass hysteria?

Anthony knew his theories were getting out of control. But the whole situation was insane. *There has to be an explanation,* he told himself. But he had no idea what. And why? Because he was so stupid. How was he supposed to get Jesse back when he could hardly read two words in a row and basic math problems made his head turn inside out?

Cut it out, Anthony ordered himself. He hated it when he started getting all snively and self-pitying. *Okay. Jesse.* An image of the kid flashed into his mind, followed almost immediately by an image of Rae, her face pale and scared.

Somebody tries to kill Rae, he thought. *Then Jesse disappears.* Could there possibly be a connection? What did Rae and Jesse have in common? They both were in group therapy at Oakvale. What else? They'd both helped clear Anthony of setting the pipe bomb. Which meant they'd both helped put David Wyngard away. So, some kind of revenge thing? But with all those people involved? It made no sense. It—

"Anthony, do you remember?" Ms. Goyer asked, bringing him out of his thoughts. "Without looking at the magazine, can you tell me what the name of their youngest son is?"

"Uh, Booger?" Anthony answered, because he hadn't been listening. It was a totally lame joke, but the Bluebirds laughed anyway. They were probably all bored out of their skulls.

"No," Goyer answered, with her usual poor-learning-disabled-child smile. "Want to try again? I'll give you a hint. It has nothing to do with bodily functions."

"I know," Andi McGee volunteered. She lived to volunteer answers, even though she got them wrong as much as the rest of them did.

"Let's let Anthony try first," Goyer answered.

Then—holy freakin' miracle—the bell rang. Anthony was out of the trailer the class was held in and down the aluminum steps before anyone. His steps slowed as he headed toward his math class. *Just three more until gym,* he told himself.

He gave himself the new score after every class. *Just history and two more until gym. Just drafting and one more until gym. Just freaking tutorial with freaking head-too-big-for-his-spindly-little-body Anderson. Now gym.*

Anthony made it from the tutorial to the locker room in less than thirty seconds. The instant he was inside, he pulled in a deep breath. God, he loved the smell of old sweat and feet and mildew. It was almost as good as weed. It actually gave him a minor buzz.

He headed over to his locker, used the key to open it—he

hated combination locks—and changed into his Kmart brand sweats. Then he strolled into the gym with five minutes to spare. He decided to run the bleachers until everybody else showed up.

A couple of stretches and he was off, running straight up to the top of the bleachers, then back down, across the basketball court, and right up to the top of the opposite bleachers. Back down. Back across. Back up. Back down. Back across. All the hours of bull he'd had to endure that day faded, then disappeared. His body became his whole world.

"Fascinelli," he heard Coach Meyer shout. Anthony spun halfway toward the voice, taking the bleachers sideways. A football came spiraling toward him. Anthony caught it without breaking stride. When he heard Meyer on the bleachers behind him, Anthony swerved right, then left, faked another swerve right—which totally fooled Meyer—and angled up to the top stair, then plunged back down, feet pummeling the wood. When he reached the floor, he turned back and did a little victory dance with the football.

"Not bad," Meyer said casually. But he grinned, and Anthony could tell he was at least a little impressed. "If you'd just apply yourself—"

Anthony's buzz disappeared. He knew what was coming.

"—to your classes the way you do to sports, your GPA would be off the charts. More than high enough to qualify you for a spot on the team," Meyer continued.

"Uh-huh," Anthony muttered. Like it was just laziness keeping him in the moron brigade.

"I need a strong running back on the team," Meyer continued. "You're my first choice. I could talk to your teachers. If they can tell me you're progressing—"

"I'm not a joiner," Anthony interrupted, noticing that about half the class had shown up in the gym and was listening to the exchange.

"What the hell is that supposed to mean?" Meyer demanded.

Anthony tossed him the ball, then turned away.

"I don't understand you, Fascinelli," the coach muttered.

You and Rae both, Anthony thought. If there was a way he could change, didn't they think he'd have done it by now?

Rae headed straight into Oakvale. Usually she waited for Anthony, but she had the feeling he still wasn't done giving her attitude for daring to try to help him, and she didn't see any reason she had to put up with that. She was going to help him with Jesse, but that was it. Unless he managed to pull his head out of his butt.

She hesitated in the main hall, then decided to go upstairs. She had to pee, and the downstairs bathroom gave her the creeps. She knew it was ridiculous. She knew that the odds of someone planting a second pipe bomb in there were billions to one. But she'd still rather not use it.

Not that it's totally creepy free up here, she thought. The second floor was deserted. But at the same time Rae kept getting the prickly-back-of-the-neck feeling that somebody was watching her, through a crack in one of the doors or on some kind of hidden camera. It was a feeling she got a lot lately. Not just at Oakvale. Everywhere. It's like she was a character in one of the *Halloween* movies.

"Get a grip. You're imagining it," she muttered as she stepped into the bathroom, using her elbow to open the door. She peed, washed her hands, did minor makeup repairs, put on a little more perfume, made a mental note that she needed to visit Sephora because the bottle was almost empty, basically stalling, ignoring the old thoughts touching her stuff brought into her mind, then headed back down to the group therapy room with about four seconds to spare. The only seat that was empty was next to Anthony. Figured. Rae took it. Anthony grunted something that might have been a greeting. Rae resisted the urge to grunt back. "Hey," she mumbled, lacing her hands together to eliminate any accidental touching of stuff. She was glad that Ms. Abramson didn't waste any time getting started.

"Hopes and dreams," Ms. Abramson said, beginning to pace around the inside of the circle of metal chairs. "Nothing is more important. Without hopes and dreams, there are no goals. No accomplishments. No new visions in the world. No heroes. No stars. Today I want you to pair up and help each other discover what your hopes and dreams are. Ask each other questions. Really listen to what is said. Then ask some more. When you're done, each of you will tell the group about what your partners aspire to do and become."

Rae turned away from Anthony toward Shawn Miller. But Shawn had already turned toward Kim Feldon. Reluctantly

Rae turned back to face Anthony, just as he was reluctantly turning back to face her.

"So. You first. Dreams," Rae said quickly. She planned on controlling this little session.

"Don't have any," Anthony answered. "What about you?"

"Don't have any, either," Rae shot back. They stared at each other for a long moment. "I don't buy it, anyway," Rae finally said, breaking the silence. "You have to have something you want to do. I know—*American Idol.*"

"*I* have to have something, but *you* don't." Anthony shook his head. "How does that make any sense?"

"Look, it's different for me, okay?" Rae answered. "I just want to be normal. Not have people think I'm a freak anymore."

Anthony raised one eyebrow. "You're lying," he announced. "You don't want to be normal. You want things to be the way they used to be, before, you know." He wiggled his fingers at her. "And I'm one hundred percent positive you weren't happy just being normal then. I've seen girls like you."

"Girls like me," Rae repeated. She didn't ask him what that meant. She knew it was just going to piss her off.

"Yeah, girls like you," Anthony went on, uninvited. "You have to have the perfect clothes. The perfect boyfriend. The perfect everything. You have to be the girl that all the other girls want to be. Which isn't being normal. Normal's not nearly good enough for a girl like you. If you thought you were normal—at least before the whole meltdown thing— you probably would have wanted to slit your wrists."

So much for me being in control. A few questions and Anthony had already drawn blood. Rae drew in a long, slow breath. Then she tried to answer calmly. "Maybe I was like that. Maybe that is what I wanted." Actually, there was no maybe about it. From the time she'd hit junior high, Rae had been completely focused on making it into the school elite.

"But even if I wanted that now, it's a ridiculous thing to have as a dream. It's never going to happen. Not unless I develop the ability to turn back time." She was talking to herself as much as Anthony. Laying out the logic, trying to make herself believe it deep down where she still kind of didn't.

"Abramson didn't say the hopes and dreams had to be possible," Anthony answered.

"Only complete losers have dreams that don't have any chance of coming true," Rae told him. She might be a freak. She might be a social pariah. But she wasn't going to be a loser.

"So you're saying there's nothing else you want. If you can't be Little Miss Popular Prep School Girl, you're just going to lie down and die because that's the best thing that could happen to you in life," Anthony said.

"Look, you said you didn't have any dreams at all, so it's not like you're—" Rae began.

"We're talking about you right now," Anthony interrupted. "We're talking about what a shallow, spoiled little rich prep school—"

"I know your dream," Rae said triumphantly. "*You* want to be a rich prep school guy. That's why you're always ragging on me. It's because you want it, and you can't have it." His expression barely changed, but his eyes narrowed the tiniest bit, and she thought the rate of his breathing picked up a little. *Direct hit*, she thought. But the burst of triumph faded. It didn't make her feel that much better that Anthony had something he wanted but couldn't have.

"The only reason I'd want to go to your school is that they have the best football team in the state," Anthony answered. "That's it."

"Would you say that's a dream of yours?" Rae answered. "To play on the Sanderson Prep team?" She hoped Anthony could tell it was an attitude-free question. She really wanted to know the answer.

Anthony played with the hole in the knee of his jeans. "Maybe," he finally admitted, a flush climbing up his throat.

"I can see you doing that. I mean, you're not—" Rae stopped herself from finishing the sentence. She hoped Anthony wouldn't realize she'd been about to say, "You're not that tall." "You've definitely got the build, all muscley and everything," she said, starting over. "I bet you're good. And it's not like everyone who goes to Sanderson is rich. They have scholarships."

"Are you forgetting who you're talking to?" Anthony burst out. He yanked on the hole in his jeans, and the denim ripped further. "Or is there some special scholarship for morons that I don't know about?"

Rae reached out and pulled his hand away from the hole in his jeans, careful to keep her fingertips away from his. "Did you listen to anything I said yesterday?" She kept her voice so low, there wasn't a chance anyone else could hear it. "Being dyslexic, which you definitely could be, doesn't mean you're a moron. It just means your brain works differently than most people's. Like I told you, people with dyslexia have made all these advances in tons of areas because they *do* think differently." She tightened her grip on his hand. "The book had a bunch of different techniques to help dyslexics adapt. Why won't you at least let me tell you about them? Why won't you let me help you?"

Anthony eased his hand out of hers. "Okay," he muttered.

"Okay?" Rae repeated. She could hardly believe she'd heard him say the word.

He nodded, not quite looking at her. "Okay."

Chapter 9

"So, none of you have seen Jesse in at least a week?" Anthony asked, searching the faces of the kids who had been playing basketball in the park.

Rae gave him a nudge, then jerked her chin toward a kid who was way too involved in positioning his water bottle in his backpack. Looking at him gave her a tingling sensation all down her spine. He clearly didn't want to talk to them. And maybe whatever he was keeping secret could lead them to Jesse.

Anthony tossed the ball he'd been holding to the closest boy, then strode over to the kid kneeling next to his backpack. Rae followed right behind him.

"I guess you heard we're trying to find Jesse Beven," Anthony said.

"Haven't seen him," the kid muttered, fiddling with the zipper on his backpack. It was obvious he hoped if he just kept working the zipper that she and Anthony would go away.

"Let me help you with that." Rae knelt down and jerked the zipper closed.

/can't tell/tattoo/come kill me/

The fear that came with the thoughts made Rae gasp. Yeah, this kid had information. But he wasn't going to give it up, at least not willingly.

"Okay, well, thanks for answering the question," Rae said. She stuck out her hand. For a second she didn't think the kid was going to take it, but then he gave it a hard, fast shake.

It was enough. Rae got her fingertips into position and used her free hand to keep the connection. She was sucked up into a tornado of thoughts and feelings. An old fear of the two strange lights that appeared on his bedroom wall every night. Embarrassment over some stupid nickname his friends had given him. The secret fact that he liked to pretend he was Harry Potter even though he was way too old.

Jesse, Rae thought. She needed anything he knew about Jesse, and time was running out. "Tattoo." She forced the word out, even though it was hard to speak during the fingertip-to-fingertip contact, and she tightened her grip on the kid's hand.

New thoughts exploded in her brain. He was remembering a dark-haired man with the tattoo of a scorpion on his hand, grabbing Jesse. The man seeing the kid watching. Telling him to keep his mouth shut or the man would be coming after him next. The kid running until he felt like his lungs would burst.

The kid jerked his hand away from Rae's and leaped to his feet. "I've gotta go," he told them as he rushed off. Then he paused and looked over his shoulder. "Good luck finding Jesse." He ran off before either Rae or Anthony could answer.

"I didn't get a lot of details," Rae told Anthony as they headed out of the park. "But that kid was the real deal. I'm sure of it. I didn't think about it before, but those other people I touched when we were asking about Jesse—their thoughts didn't have emotions attached to them. The kid's did. He saw Jesse get snatched, and he's terrified the guy will come after him if he talks about it."

"Did you get any thoughts about the guy? What he looked like?" Anthony asked. He sounded ready to tear the guy's head off.

"The kid didn't have a great memory of his face. But he remembered that he had dark hair. And a tattoo of a scorpion on his hand," Rae answered.

"A scorpion," Anthony repeated. "I feel like I've seen that tattoo. But I can't remember where. I've got that itchy feeling in my head, you know? But it's not coming."

"Maybe if we touched fingertips, I could find the memory," Rae suggested. "But if it's not something you're able to access, I'm not sure how easy—"

"No, you're right. It wouldn't work. If I just stop trying to think of it, it will pop into my head," Anthony said quickly.

He doesn't want to let me in, Rae realized.

"Now I just have to figure out how to think of something else. Because right now all I can think about is Jesse." Anthony rubbed his forehead with the heels of his hands, as if that would help his brain work the way he wanted it to.

"Well, um, I know one other thing you could think about," Rae answered. She cut a glance at him, sure he wasn't going to want to hear what she had to say. "You said you'd be up for trying out some stuff from that book after we hit the park. It's at my house. Would you want to come by for a while? Maybe you'll think of where you've seen the tattoo while we work."

Anthony had been praying that she'd forgotten about the whole reading thing. Which was pretty delusional because it hadn't been that long since that hopes-and-dreams group therapy exercise. "Okay," he muttered. What else could he say? That he had changed his mind? That he was a total wuss?

"So, I was thinking," he said as they started walking back to the car. "Maybe you were right about this stuff with Jesse having something to do with you."

"It's a bizarre coincidence if it doesn't," Rae agreed.

"All these people with all these different thoughts in their heads about Jesse," he said, kicking at the gravel on the path as they walked. "That's pretty weird. And right after someone hired David to set that pipe bomb to ki—to, you know." He cringed, realizing Rae probably didn't need to be reminded about the attempt on her life.

"Those thoughts I got really didn't feel like the ones I usually get," Rae told him. "This isn't *Supernatural*. Weird things don't happen once a week. Two strange psychic phenomena should be connected."

She fastened her seat belt, and Anthony pulled out into traffic. "But unfortunately, even if we're right, it's not going to help us any. We're as clueless about who went after me as we are about what actually happened to Jesse."

"How are you doing, anyway? With knowing someone is . . ."

"Is probably looking for another chance to kill me?" Rae finished for him.

Anthony nodded, feeling like an idiot for not asking more often. Rae wasn't the kind of girl who'd blab on and on about how scared she was. She could be half out of her mind with fear and never bother saying anything to him about it.

"I'm, you know, as well as can be expected," Rae answered. "Except, and this is probably total paranoia talking, a lot of the time I feel like someone is watching me, following me, even."

Anthony's eyes automatically went to the rearview mirror. He saw cars back there, but on this street that was normal. "Have you seen anything?"

He caught Rae doing a rearview mirror check, too. "No. Like I said, it's just a feeling, an eyeballs-on-my-back kind of thing."

All Anthony wanted was to have whoever was after Rae and whoever had snatched Jesse in front of him. He would pummel them until his hands bled and love every second of it. If he could just remember where he'd seen that scorpion tattoo—

"Let me tell you some of what the book said. That way we can get down to work as soon as we get to my house," Rae suggested, pulling him out of his thoughts.

Her house. They were getting way too close to her house. The lawns were getting bigger. The houses were getting bigger, too. Bigger and cleaner looking. Like someone spent all day buffing up every inch with a toothbrush.

"You know what? I think we've got more important stuff to spend time on," Anthony said. "After Jesse's back and after we get whoever's after you put away, then we can—"

"Forget it, Fascinelli," Rae interrupted. "You're not weaseling out of this."

She meant it. And she wasn't going to budge. Sweat started popping out all over his body. He could hardly read. He could hardly do a simple math problem. But when it came to sweat—he was A-plus all the way.

Anthony turned onto Rae's street, then pulled into her driveway next to the Chevette already sitting there. Great. Her dad was home. And he was some kind of college professor or something. He was going to take one look at Anthony and realize—

"I know. I feel the same way about the Chevette," Rae said, obviously misreading the pained look on his face. "But my dad thinks it's cool. He specializes in Arthurian stuff, so he doesn't have the greatest grip on reality."

Arthurian stuff. Anthony had no idea what that was. He hadn't even met the guy, and already Rae's father was making him feel stupid.

Rae gave the door handle a quick rub with her sleeve—she hadn't put her waxy stuff back on yet—then got out of the car. Anthony got out, too—what choice was there?—and followed her into the house.

"Are you hungry or thirsty or anything?" Rae asked.

"No," Anthony answered quickly.

"Then let's just go back to my room," Rae said, starting down the hall, which had been painted with fluffy clouds. "Dad," she called over her shoulder. "I'm home. And I brought one of my friends from group."

"That's nice," a male voice called back.

"He's relieved that anyone will even come over," Rae whispered. "Other than you, Yana's the only person who has since The Incident." Rae opened one of the doors and ushered him into her room. It was . . . *sophisticated*. That was the word that came—slowly—into Anthony's mind. The walls had been painted to look like green and black marble, and there was a black leather chair in front of the black desk. Total Cardinal room. Just standing in it ramped up the sweat production.

"So, um, sit down and let's get started," Rae said. Anthony glanced at the chair. If he sat in that thing, he was afraid he'd leave a wet streak across the back. But it was the only chair in the room. Anthony cautiously sat down on the edge of the bed, and was immediately ten times more uncomfortable.

Rae grabbed a binder off her desk and a magazine off her bedside table, then she sat down next to Anthony. He'd been thinking she'd take the chair, but now he'd have to contend with the grapefruit smell of hers on top of everything else.

"Okay, I want you to read a page of one of the articles in here out loud." She passed the magazine over to him. "Sorry it's *Glamour*. I meant to buy something more manly, but I forgot."

"Whatever," Anthony mumbled. The choice of the magazine

was way low on the list of his problems right now. He flipped past the pages and pages of glossy ads, trying not to look too closely at the babes, especially the ones in their underwear. He stopped on the horoscope page, figuring it was as good as anything.

He opened his mouth, then closed it. He couldn't do this. Couldn't. Even if he wanted to—which he didn't—he couldn't. There was no way he would even be able to force out a sound. It was like even his teeth were sweating now.

"It's just me," Rae said, her voice gentle and understanding.

Just her. Yeah, like that made it easier. She'd seen his workbook. She'd gotten some of his thoughts. But that wasn't the same as actually hearing him attempt to read in his completely pathetic way.

He shot a glance over at her. She was waiting. And knowing Rae, she'd just keep on waiting and waiting and waiting. She was as stubborn as . . . as stubborn as he was.

He stared at the first word in the first paragraph. "Libra," he said, getting an image of a scale. He moved his eyes to the next word. His finger itched to underline it because that helped him focus, but he kept both hands wrapped around the magazine. "Don't"—he got an image of one of those circles with a slash through it—"bet"—a picture of a pile of poker chips flashed into his head. Then he hesitated. He knew the next word was an easy one. It was only two freakin' letters long. *Focus*, he told himself. *Focus*. "On," he said. Out of the corner of his eye he caught sight of Rae making a note in her binder.

Great. He really needed a permanent record of his humiliation. Anthony swallowed. Or tried to. His throat felt about as wide as a piece of wire. Then he moved on to the next word. Crap. Another little one that everyone in the entire world would know with no problem. Everyone except him. He moved his finger over until it was positioned under the word. He didn't care if it made him look stupid. Not being able to come up with the word at all would make him seem a lot stupider.

"An," he managed to get out. He looked at the next word. An image of a blond in a thong filled his head—"easy." A picture of a clock replaced the blond—"time."

He had to stop and think again. Another one of those baby words. And he didn't know what it was. He felt like a giant hand had just clamped down on his head, pressing through the bones of his skull, squeezing his gray matter.

"Screw it." Anthony thrust the magazine back at Rae and leaped to his feet. With two long strides he was at the door. "We shouldn't be wasting time with this, anyway," he said, turning to face her. "Maybe the tattoo parlors in town keep records of who gets what kind of tattoos."

"It's worth a shot," Rae answered calmly. "We can work on the reading more later." She stood up and took one step toward him.

"Frank," Anthony burst out.

"What?" Rae asked.

"Frank. That's the name of the guy with the scorpion tattoo

on his hand. I met him at a keg party I went to with my friend Gregg," Anthony explained.

"Just Frank. No last name?" Rae said.

"Gregg will know how to find him. Can I use your phone?" He didn't wait for her to answer. He rushed over to her bedside table, snatched up the sleek black phone, and punched in Gregg's number. He let out a low curse when an answering machine picked up. "Gregg, it's Fascinelli. I need to ask you something right away. Call me at—" He looked at Rae. She told him her number, and he repeated it into the phone. "First thing, Gregg, all right?" Anthony hung up, hoping Gregg wouldn't be too high to focus on the message.

"So, I guess we don't have to hit the tattoo parlors," Rae said. She sat back down on the bed and picked up her notebook.

"Yeah, but I can't concentrate on anything else now. I don't know how you can, either. With Jesse missing and everything," Anthony said.

"Don't you want to know what the words you had trouble with have in common?" Rae asked, ignoring him.

"They're all just baby words," Anthony answered, flopping down next to her.

"They're all words that don't have images associated with them," Rae countered. "They're all words the book said a lot of people with dyslexia would have trouble with."

Anthony looked over at her, but he didn't say anything. He was afraid of what would come out if he tried.

"Just stick with it for ten more minutes. Less than that if

Gregg calls first," Rae urged. "We'll take one word that was a problem for you—" She flipped open the magazine and found the spot where he'd had his little meltdown. "We'll take *and* and come up with a visual for you. That's it. It won't even be ten minutes. Just try it, okay?"

Anthony knew when somebody was bullshitting him. And Rae wasn't. More than that, she really seemed to care. "One word," he finally agreed.

Rae jumped up and darted over to her closet. She pulled out a big plastic box and an old sheet. She spread the sheet on the floor, then sat down with the box in front of her. "We'll use clay," she said as she opened the box.

"Clay, yeah," Anthony repeated, as if he actually had some idea what she was talking about. He walked over to the sheet and sat down across from Rae. She gave him a lump of yellow modeling clay and took a lump of blue clay for herself. "Make a hand," she instructed. "Doesn't matter how good it is."

You can do that, Anthony told himself. About a minute later he had something that looked pretty much like a hand. Close enough, anyway. He wanted this whole deal over with. "Now what?" he asked Rae.

She quickly finished up the last two clay fingers she'd been working on. "Now you take your hand and my hand—" She passed him the blue clay hand she'd made. It had wrinkles and knuckles and everything, even a ring on one finger. "And you link them together so they're hand *and* hand. Keep the word *and* in your head as you connect them."

292

Anthony obediently joined the hands by smushing the clay fingers together. *And,* he thought. *And, and, and, and, and.*

"So hopefully, next time you see the word *and,* you'll get an image of the clay hands, and that—"

Rae was interrupted by the phone ringing. Anthony snatched it up. "Gregg?" he burst out, then he nodded at Rae to let her know it was Gregg. "Remember that guy we met at that party a couple of months ago, Frank something? Brown hair. Tattoo of a scorpion on his hand."

"With the girl in the short skirt?" Gregg asked.

"Yeah! Yeah! Him," Anthony exclaimed. "Do you know where he lives?"

Gregg hesitated for so long, Anthony wanted to reach through the phone and strangle him.

"Dude, he lives right next door to the house where the party was. That's why he was there," Gregg finally said.

"Thanks." Anthony hung up without saying good-bye. "Ready to roll?" he asked Rae.

"Always," she said, snagging her jacket off her desk chair. "Dad, we decided to go out and grab some food at Red Robin," Rae called as she led the way back to the front door.

"Bring your BlackBerry," he called back.

"He likes to be able to be in touch all the time since I got out of the hospital," Rae explained as they headed to the car.

"That's cool," Anthony answered. He could almost feel his blood slamming through his veins as he got behind the wheel and pulled back onto the street. They were getting close now.

Very close. Maybe they'd even have Jesse back by the end of the night.

Even though I'm not good at reading, I'm good with directions, Anthony thought. He'd only been to the house where the party was one time, but he remembered exactly where it was. He didn't even have to think about how to get there. He just drove. Fifteen minutes later he was pulling into a parking spot about a block away from the place. He figured he shouldn't have his car exposed, just in case.

"What do you think?" he asked as they got out. "The one on the left or the one on the right? All Gregg said was next door."

"Let's go right. Right for Rae," she answered. It was her usual confident tone, but he could hear a slight shake in her voice. "So, do we have a plan here? Or are we just going to say, 'Hi, we know you have Jesse. Give him back'?" she asked.

"First we're going to make sure the guy even lives in one of these houses," Anthony answered. "Gregg isn't always that clear about stuff. If Frank's home, I'll say I heard there was a party at his place. That should get us inside. You can do your fingerprint thing. If we find out Jesse's there, we can call in an anonymous tip to the police. Jesse's mom's already filed a missing persons, so they'll know they should be looking for him."

"Okay. A plan. Good," Rae said as they cut across the front yard, maneuvering around the toys lying all over the place. When they reached the front porch, Anthony tilted his head from side to side, cracking his neck, then rang the doorbell.

This is it, he thought when a twenty-something woman answered the door, only opening it halfway. She was wearing an old terry cloth robe with big stars on it, but she'd definitely been the one in the short skirt at the party.

"Hey, I heard you and Frank were having a blowout over here. But it looks like I got the wrong night," Anthony said.

"Yeah," the woman answered. That was it. Just yeah. *Thanks for being so friendly,* Anthony thought. She was clutching the edge of the door as if he and Rae were about to storm the place.

"Is Frank around? Since we're here, might as well say hi," Anthony continued.

"No, he's working late," she said. "Look, my little boy has a fever. I have to go check on him. Call first next time, okay?" She shut the door, and Anthony heard it lock.

"Well, that was informative," he muttered.

"Let me try," Rae said. She ran her fingers over the side of the door, biting her lip in concentration. "She was lying," Rae said. "She has no idea where Frank is. He's been gone for more than a week, hasn't called or anything. She's afraid he's gotten himself into some kind of trouble again."

"So he's been gone for pretty much the same amount of time Jesse has," Anthony commented.

Rae ran her fingers over the doorknob and grimaced. "What?" Anthony demanded.

"Sticky," she answered. She sniffed her fingers. "Grape jelly. From the little boy, I guess. Blocked out any thoughts I might have gotten." She dug around in her purse, found a tissue, and wiped her fingers. Anthony would have just used the side of his jeans. "If I'm going to get any more, we'd have to get inside."

"That's not going to happen. At least not tonight," Anthony said. "If we stay out here on the porch too long, she's probably going to call the cops. Come on."

"I guess I can put the Mush back on my fingers," Rae said as they headed to the car. When she got there, she gave the door handle a quick wipe with her sleeve, then pulled it open. "Oh God," she whispered.

Anthony was back around to her side of the car in half a second. He had to pull her away so he could see what she was staring at. When he saw it, his body went cold.

A knife. A knife plunged deep into the back of the passenger seat. None of the blade was visible, only the shiny red handle.

The sour taste of bile crept up Anthony's throat. "I think I recognize that knife," he managed to get out. "It's Jesse's Swiss Army. It was a birthday present."

"So . . . so whoever has Jesse . . . must have put it there. As a message to stay away," Rae said.

They'd been up at the house for only a few minutes. That meant whoever did this was probably still very close. Anthony scanned the street. It was empty. At least it looked empty. But that didn't mean someone wasn't watching them right now. "Let's get out of here." He wanted Rae somewhere safe, somewhere where he had a better chance of protecting her.

"One second," Rae said. She reached out, fingers trembling,

and touched the hilt of the knife.

In the dim glow of the closest streetlight Anthony could see her face turn pale. Even her lips lost their color. A shudder rippled through her body, then she slowly pulled her hand away.

"The thoughts are all from Jesse," she told Anthony, her voice trembling. "He's being held in some kind of warehouse. He thinks it's about a half an hour from the skateboard place in Little Five Points. He can hear the trains from where he is. And sometimes—" Her voice caught. "Sometimes there's a smell of tar." She swallowed hard. "Anthony, he has three guards on him. And they have guns."

Chapter 10

Rae sat at the kitchen table, a mug of hot chocolate cradled in her hands. She didn't really feel like drinking it, but the warmth was comforting. She glanced at the clock on the microwave. After eleven. But Rae couldn't even imagine falling asleep.

Yana had called before, and Rae'd told her some of what was going on. Yana, being Yana, had immediately volunteered to help them look for the warehouse the next day. And it had helped. It had helped a lot. But Rae still couldn't sleep. Her mind was whirling with questions.

I bet Anthony's still awake, too, she thought. She grabbed the phone and called Anthony's cell. It was the first time she'd called him.

"I just keep thinking about the knife," Rae blurted out when he answered. "I know I'm the one that said it was a warning for us to mind our own business. But now—I don't know. I just don't know. Maybe someone else knows what I can do. Maybe the info from the knife is going to lead us into some kind of trap." Rae drew in a deep, shuddering breath.

"Can I talk now?" Anthony asked.

The sound of his voice was better than the hot chocolate. Much more calming. Rae sat back down. "Please. Talk."

"I've been thinking all the same stuff," Anthony admitted. "And I'm as confused as you are. One thing's for sure—that feeling you've had of being followed is on target. We were only away from the car for a few minutes. Somebody had to have the knife on them. And they had to have been waiting for the chance to leave it for us."

"Frank?" Rae asked.

"Maybe," Anthony answered.

Neither of them said anything for a long moment. "When you said you'd been thinking the same stuff I've been thinking," Rae finally said, "did you mean the part about someone knowing about my fingerprint thing?" She stood back up and started pacing around the kitchen.

"Yeah," Anthony said. "I did think about it. Because all those stories we got in Little Five Points . . . that's too random just to be—"

"People's bad memories or—I can't even think of anything else," Rae interrupted. She crossed over to the kitchen door and made sure it was locked. She'd checked it so often, she was wearing the Mush off her fingers.

"I can't think of anything else, either," Anthony admitted. "Even though it seems impossible, somebody had to have done something to those people. Which I guess means they have some kind of, uh, ability, too."

"And that someone, that someone who has powers, they know the truth about me," Rae said. She checked the lock on the kitchen window.

Anthony let out a sigh. "Seems that way. Or maybe they just did it to confuse anyone who would be asking about Jesse. Even if you hadn't been able to check out what they were really thinking, it would have gotten us—or anyone else—totally off track."

"Oh God, I'm so confused." Rae groaned. She felt like her skull was too small for her brain, like the bone was pushing down so hard, it was causing thought malfunctions. "If someone knows the truth about me—then they'd know I'd get info from the knife. So why leave it unless they wanted to . . . to lure us someplace?"

"It's the best reason I can think of," Anthony said. "*If* they know about you."

"And . . . and the best reason I can think of to try and get us to some deserted warehouse is because it would be a great place for someone to try to kill me again," Rae blurted out.

Anthony was silent for a moment. "I think it would be better—safer—if I look for the warehouse myself," he began. Rae winced. He wasn't telling her she was wrong. "Tomorrow I'll—"

"I'm going," Rae interrupted. "Trap. Warning. Assassination plot. Whatever the deal is, I'm going. We're getting Jesse back, together."

Anthony cruised slowly down the dark, empty street. "Any-place around here would fit what we got from Jesse," he said.

He and Rae had told Yana Jesse managed to call him but could only risk staying on the phone for a minute.

"We're close enough to the tracks to hear trains. We're about a half hour from the skateboard place. And they've been doing repairs a few streets over, so Jesse could have smelled tar."

"Thanks for the recap," Yana teased. "I think I missed something when—oh, wait. I've been here the whole time."

Anthony shot her a dirty look, but Rae didn't mind having someone around who was attempting to lighten the mood a little. It wasn't that Rae didn't care what happened to Jesse or that she'd magically forgotten that she could be walking into a trap. All the nerves in her body felt like they'd had a curling iron used on them until they were singed. Having Yana around just made the stress almost bearable.

Anthony turned right. "Why this way?" Rae asked. So far Anthony'd been completely methodical, going down each street until they were two miles away from the skateboard shop, then turning down the next street and going all the way back to the street the shop was on. Now he'd suddenly changed his pattern.

"I just remembered there's an old fire station a couple of blocks over," he answered. "When I was around seven, one of my mom's boyfriends used to work there. She has a fireman thing. Anyway, he brought me there a couple of times. It's big enough that it might seem like a warehouse to Jesse, and it closed down more than six years ago when they built a new station on Meridian."

"Definitely sounds worth checking out," Rae said.

"A thing for firemen, huh? Your mom sounds cool," Yana added.

Anthony just snorted in response. He made a left and parked the car. It wasn't hard for him to find a spot. They were almost the only ones around. There were a couple of teenage guys drinking beers out of paper bags on the corner, and that was it.

"So what now? Do we try and look inside?" Yana asked.

"We wait. We watch," Anthony answered. "If this is the right place, there are guys with guns in there."

"I don't get how Jesse was even able to call you guys with that many guards," Yana said.

"Maybe they locked him in a room that somebody had accidentally left a cell phone in or something," Rae answered quickly, wanting the lie she'd told Yana to make some kind of sense. More and more, she thought Yana would be able to deal with the truth without freaking out. But Rae just wasn't ready to risk it. Yana was the only real girlfriend she had. And how could she exist without one solid girlfriend to cover her back and talk bad about the guy who broke up with her?

"Probably," Anthony agreed, his eyes locked on the abandoned fire station. Rae focused her gaze on it, too, searching for a flicker of light or a fast movement in front of one of the dark windows.

"Do you think they're planning to send a ransom request

to Jesse's mom?" Yana leaned her elbows on top of the front seat and propped her chin in one hand.

"Jesse's mom doesn't have any money," Anthony answered.

"So why the guys with guns?" Yana asked slowly, clearly thinking out loud. "I mean, there are lots of reasons for a kid to get snatched. But not that many for being held under an armed guard. Do you think that *whoever* could think Jesse is somebody else? Some rich kid?"

"Maybe," Rae said. "Except then wouldn't they have already contacted the rich parents—and found out their kid was still all safe and sound at home?"

"Yeah. You're right." Yana slumped all the way back into her seat.

Rae shot a quick look over at Anthony. She was surprised he hadn't joined in the conversation. But it was like every part of his attention was on the fire station, like he didn't even realize she and Yana were in the car anymore.

"Yana, I appreciate you being here. But you're not forgetting the guns part, are you? I mean, this could end up being really dangerous," Rae said, feeling a spurt of guilt for agreeing to let Yana come with them. "If you want to go, it's—"

"Oh, shut up," Yana said.

Rae turned around and smiled at her. "Okay," she answered. She rolled the window down a little farther, keeping the end of her sweater over her fingers since she'd decided not to wear her Mush tonight. The cool night air would help keep her awake. And maybe she'd hear something that told her someone was inside the station.

Yana followed Rae's lead, going completely silent. They all watched. They all listened. An hour went by. But they got nothing. No hint of what was going on inside. No hint if they were at all close to finding Jesse.

When another half an hour had passed, Anthony let out a growl of frustration. The sound made Rae ache inside, as if she was absorbing his pain and anger into her bones.

"What if I—" Rae began. "What if we; I mean," she corrected herself. "What if we get a little closer? Try to see in a window?"

"I say we go for it," Yana agreed. "If the guards were keeping tabs on the street, I think we'd have seen *something.*"

Anthony hesitated, then he opened his door, got out, and closed it with a soft click. He started toward the station. A second later Rae and Yana were right behind him.

"I'll take those," Rae whispered, nodding toward the windows set in the huge sliding doors. She didn't care that much about looking in. She wanted to get her fingers working. But when she touched the metal door handles, all she got was static. The fingerprints were so old and coated with grime that she couldn't even pick out a word. *There has to be a smaller door,* she thought.

She started around the building, keeping her shoulder close to the wall so she'd be harder to see. No use making herself an easy target if someone was waiting here to try and kill her.

Yes. There was another door on the other side of the

station, a door that looked like it went to an office or something. *Please, please, please,* Rae thought as she reached for the doorknob. *Give me something here.* But all she got was more static.

"Anything?" Anthony asked softly from behind her.

Rae's heart slammed into her ribs. She hadn't even realized he was there. "Nothing," she answered. "From what I've gotten so far, no one's been in here for a long time."

"Hey, guys. There's a door that's been busted open in the back," Yana said breathlessly as she hurried up to them.

"Show us," Anthony ordered.

Rae positioned every foot carefully as they crept to the back of the station. She got to the door first and did a fingerprint sweep.

/ COLD / why didn't I / no one knows /

The thoughts came through sort of fuzzy with a layer of static underneath. Rae didn't think it was very likely that the people who left them were still inside. Although if whoever took Jesse knew Rae's powers, they would know not to leave any fresh prints.

She pushed open the door. What choice did she have? Anthony managed to beat her through it. Then he just stood there, blocking it.

"What? What do you see?" Rae whispered. She gave him a hard poke in the back when he didn't answer immediately.

"Nothing," Anthony answered. "It's empty." He stepped the rest of the way inside, then led them on a top-to-bottom

305

search. It was useless. The whole place was empty, empty and coated with an even layer of dust. No one had been inside for a very long time. They weren't going to get Jesse back that night.

Chapter 11

"**D**own to the final five, Anthony told himself. He forced his eyes away from the clock. He'd managed to make it almost all the way through English without getting called on, but if Goyer caught him clock watching, she'd definitely shoot him a question. He tilted his head toward Kelly Middleton, as if he didn't want to miss even one word of what she was reading.

Anthony thought he was putting on a good show. But as soon as Kelly managed to get out the last word on the page, Goyer called on him. *At least it won't be like reading in front of Rae,* Anthony thought. *It's not like anyone in here is even listening, except Goyer, and she's completely used to Bluebirds.* He turned the page and put his finger under the first word of the sentence at the top. Nothing came into his head. He narrowed his eyes, trying to block out everything but the page in front of him. "Wh—" He sucked in a breath, tried again. "When."

"Yes," Goyer said softly.

"When," Anthony repeated. He moved his finger under the next word. He got blank head again. Crap. *Come on,* he thought. *You know this one. It's one of the easy, little ones.* A rushing sound filled his ears as he stared at the tiny word. "The," he burst out. He shoved his finger over to the next word. An image of Noah's ark filled his brain—"animal." An image of Carl, Danny, Anna, his mom, and his stepdad appeared—"family." An image of a pair of linked clay hands, appeared—"and."

Suddenly Anthony felt like he'd been sucking on helium or something, like any second his body would start floating toward the ceiling. The word *and* had just popped out of his mouth. That had never happened before. He always got stuck on that one. Always.

I owe Rae another one, he thought. *Maybe with that book of hers . . . maybe with her helping me . . . maybe I won't be a total moron for the rest of my life.*

Rae hurried toward the back exit of the school. She knew Anthony was probably already out in the parking lot, waiting for her, getting more annoyed by the second. It was like even breathing the air around Sanderson Prep gave him mad cow disease. Just as she started to elbow open the closest half of the big double doors, Rae felt someone give her a quick tap on the shoulder. She glanced back—and saw the person she least wanted to see. Okay, maybe there were one or two people lower on her list, but Dori Hernandez was right up there.

"What?" Rae snapped, then immediately felt a pang of guilt. Snapping at Dori was like telling Bambi he was a bad,

bad little deer. She was pretty much the nicest, sweetest girl in school.

"I just wanted to ask you . . ." Dori's words trailed off, and she gave Rae a helpless look. Like she wished Rae would take over and just read her mind. Ha. If she only knew.

"What, Dori?" Rae asked, managing to keep all but a tinge of snappishness out of her tone this time. "I'm kind of in a hurry." *And I kind of wish you were dead,* she added silently. Not that she wanted Marcus back, after the way he'd treated her. But it still wasn't easy trying to be polite to the angelic and way too beautiful girl that had taken Rae's place.

"I don't know how to say this," Dori confessed, giving Rae the pleading face again. "But I have to ask you. I need to know . . . really, I want the truth—"

"You're going to have to give me a little more to go on here," Rae told her. She glanced at her chainwrap watch. Anthony was probably already at the mooing stage.

"Okay, you're right. Here's the thing. Last night Marcus and I were, you know, hooking up," Dori began, hesitating between practically every word.

I do not want to be hearing this, Rae thought. *Isn't it enough that Jesse's gone? Isn't it enough that I could be walking into a death trap in a couple of hours?*

"When we were right in the middle of it, he . . ." Dori gave her a sad look. Rae felt like shaking her. "Marcus called me your name," Dori continued in a rush. "And I really, really need to know if anything is going on between the two of you.

I won't be mad at you if there is. But I need to know. Or I'm going to go crazy." Dori gave a horrified little gasp, and a blush colored her cheeks. "I'm sorry. I'm really sorry. I didn't mean it."

"It's okay to use the word *crazy* in front of me," Rae mumbled, on complete autopilot. Marcus had called Dori by *her* name. Rae flashed on their encounter in the library, the one where she'd thought Marcus wanted a fast makeout in the stacks. Had he been thinking of more than that? Could he possibly be hoping to get back together with her?

"You haven't answered the question," Dori said, her eyes getting wet. "Which I guess is kind of an answer."

"I've hardly even talked to Marcus since I got back from the—since school started," Rae told Dori. "Next time he does that—if there even is a next time—just, I don't know, hit him over the head with a pillow."

Dori gave a choked laugh, then reached out and squeezed Rae's arm. "Thanks. Thanks so much. I've been wanting to talk to you for a long time, to tell you that I didn't go after Marcus or anything. I mean, he told me that you two were about to break up before you went . . . before school ended last year."

That was a big, fat lie. But Rae didn't bother to set Dori straight. Why? It wasn't her fault that Marcus was scum. "Look, I really have to go," Rae said. "And I don't think you stole Marcus from me or anything. He has a mind of his own."

Rae turned and rushed out the door. She spotted Anthony's car almost immediately and bolted toward it. "Get me away from here," she said as she climbed in, the Mush keeping her from getting thoughts off the door handle.

"Bad day, dear?" Anthony asked sarcastically. "What happened? Was someone wearing the same outfit?"

"I knew you'd be in a pissy mood," Rae shot back. "Come on. Let's go." Anthony was backing up before the words left her mouth. He maneuvered the car out of the parking lot and then headed in the direction of Little Five Points.

"I asked around at school, and one of the guys said there's an empty warehouse a couple of blocks behind that strip mall with the really bad pizza place. You know the one—GGs?"

"Is that a half hour away from the skateboard place?" Rae asked.

Anthony shook his head. "Not quite. But I figured maybe they didn't take Jesse straight there. Maybe they drove around a while to confuse him." He rolled his window halfway down. "Was something wrong before?" He rolled the window a little lower. "You actually did look kind of upset."

"My old boyfriend's new girlfriend just wanted to know if I was still fooling around with him. And that just puts a cherry on top of any day, don't ya think?" Rae answered.

"So, are you?" Anthony asked, eyes locked on the road in front of them.

How could he even ask her that? "Are you serious?" she exclaimed.

He glanced over at her, one eyebrow raised. "I guess that's a no."

"The guy dumped me when I was in a mental hospital,"

Rae reminded him. "And he didn't even bother to tell me. He just let me find out on my first day back at school."

"People get back together sometimes," Anthony answered. "You don't have to act like I'm an idiot."

For one instant Rae flashed on what it would be like to be with Marcus again. She'd get to feel Marcus's hands on her again, feel his mouth—

She refused to let her imagination take the picture of her and Marcus farther. It was pointless. Ridiculous. Hopeless.

It was also a lot more fun than thinking about what was really going on in her life, about what could happen if she and Anthony did find the right warehouse. But that was where she needed to keep her focus. She needed to stay sharp. Alert. Her life could depend on it. So could Jesse's.

Rae pulled a Kleenex out of her purse and wiped the Mush off her fingers. This was a situation where she was going to need all the help she could get.

"I wonder how Yana's doing with the history partner from the pits of hell today. Yana said the girl was going to chain her to a library chair until—"

"Does that car look familiar to you?" Anthony interrupted. "The blue Dodge that's two cars back?"

Rae turned around and peered at the car. "I don't know. I'm not a car person. One blue car is pretty much like another blue car."

"You've got to start paying more attention," Anthony snapped. "I think I saw that car when I was driving you home yesterday." He abruptly pulled over to the curb. "Yeah, that's it," he said when the car passed them. "I remember the orange bumper sticker."

"So do you think it's—following me?" Rae asked, watching the car until it was out of sight.

"I don't know," Anthony answered. "But we can't ignore stuff like this. We both have to really look at what's going on around us. So let's not talk, all right? Let's just keep our eyes open."

Rae nodded. It had been stupid of her to get so caught up in the Marcus-and-Dori sitch. As Anthony drove, Rae made a point of studying the cars and people around them. She hardly allowed herself to blink.

Her eyes were burning from the effort of keeping watch when Anthony parked about half a block down from a beat-looking warehouse about twice as big as the fire station. "That's it," he announced.

Rae scooted down in her seat, settling in for a bunch of hours of staring at a building. About forty-five minutes into the stakeout Anthony broke the silence.

"That thing we did, with the clay, it worked," he admitted.

"No way!" Rae exclaimed. "Why didn't you tell me? That's so great."

"I read the word *and*. It's not that exciting," Anthony muttered.

Rae slapped him on the side of the head. "It *is* exciting," she told him. Then she gave him another slap. "Admit it."

"Okay, okay. It's sort of cool," Anthony said, a wide smile—a little shy, a little proud, and a little embarrassed all at once—breaking across his face.

"So, we're going to keep working on it, right?" Rae asked.

"Right," Anthony answered. "And thanks. Thanks for not letting me get out of it."

"You know what? There's something we could do right now," Rae told him. "This other book I found said that it helps if you use other senses when you're having trouble with words. So lean forward a little. Actually, it would probably be better if you rested your head on the steering wheel." Rae pulled a couple of books and a binder out of her canvas bag.

/ got to reread the / tell Dad / / what's Marcus /

Then she rolled it up, letting more of her old thoughts run through her head without really paying attention to them, and handed the backpack to Anthony. "You can use this as a pillow. Don't worry. I can watch the warehouse and do my part at the same time."

"Your part," Anthony repeated. He gave her a wary glance, then pressed the bag against the steering wheel and lowered his head down to it.

"Close your eyes. Breathe deeply. Try and relax as much as possible," Rae instructed, noticing the way Anthony's hair curled against his collar.

"It would be easier if I knew what we were doing," Anthony said.

"I'm just going to use my finger to write some words

314

on your back. You don't have to do anything except repeat the words in your head as I write them," Rae explained. She checked the warehouse. Still no sign of any activity. "Okay, we'll start with *on*." As she spoke, she traced the word in big letters, pressing firmly. His back was warmer than she expected, even through his T-shirt, and hard with muscle. She traced the word over and over, starting right below his neck and working her way down until she could feel the waistband of his jeans under her finger. When she realized she'd somehow started staring at the wide T-shirt-covered expanse, she jerked her eyes back to the warehouse. Still nothing.

"Okay, I'm going to switch to *at* now," Rae announced. She began tracing the word in rows that went from one side of Anthony's back to the other. The chains that made up her watch band jangled softly. Anthony didn't answer. "You're not asleep, are you?" she asked.

"No," he said, his voice coming out all husky. "But maybe we should stop for a while."

"Don't worry about it. I'm watching the warehouse," Rae assured him, still writing on his back. "You just keep thinking the word *at* while I do this." She filled his back with *at*'s three times, eyes on the warehouse. No sign of life yet. Pretty soon they should probably risk getting close enough for her to do a fingerprint sweep.

"I wish I'd thought to bring some sandpaper," Rae said. "The book said different textures help, so if you used your finger to write words on a piece of sandpaper, it might make them easier to recognize when you read them. I guess having a bunch of different sensations connected to the words is good."

"Since you don't have any, maybe we should stop," Anthony said.

"Just using my finger will still—" Rae caught a flash of movement at the side of the warehouse. "Get down," she ordered. "Someone's coming."

Anthony scrunched down in his seat as Rae did the same. She watched as a man—maybe six feet with a bear build—headed away from the warehouse and over to a beige Toyota parked about a block from Anthony and Rae.

Anthony started the car. "What are we going to do?" Rae asked.

"Follow him," Anthony answered. "We get this guy and trade him for Jesse. Or at least make him tell us everything he knows about the setup inside. Where the guards are. If this whole thing is part of a plan to get you."

Anthony let the man get a little head start, then pulled out onto the street and began following him. "Do we have any kind of plan going here?" Rae asked, gripping the dashboard with both hands—

/got to get to *Margarita Madness night*/NEED TO MAKE ANNA/Barbie's hair/

—even though Anthony wasn't speeding.

"I've got no plan until we see where he stops," Anthony

answered. "I'm not going to try and run him off the road or anything."

"Probably a good decision," Rae muttered as Anthony kept on the man's tail without getting too close, heading through Little Five Points.

"He's turning left up here," Rae said, pointing toward the blinking signal.

"Yeah, I got that," Anthony answered sarcastically. He got into the left lane. "I wish there was at least a car between us here," he commented as the man's Toyota pulled out into the intersection.

"Wait. He's doing a U-y," Rae cried. But Anthony was already making a smooth U behind the Toyota.

"Good. He's stopping at that gas station," Anthony said. "That means we'll have at least a minute." He pulled into the gas station, too, and parked by the air hose, then got out and studied the tires like he was trying to decide if they needed air.

Rae watched as the man went into the minimart, then came back out with a key attached to a large piece of wood. A second later he disappeared into the men's room.

Anthony waited until the door shut behind him, then started to follow. Rae reached out and grabbed his arm, holding him tight. "You can't just go walking in there. He probably has a gun."

Anthony pulled his arm away. "Which is why the bathroom's the perfect place to go after him. He's not going to be holding his gun in there." He headed straight for the bathroom.

"Anthony, I think you should wait," Rae called after him. He didn't even glance back at her.

Chapter 12

A nthony forced himself to wait for a fifteen count before he stepped into the bathroom. Luckily the guy hadn't let the door close all the way, so the lock hadn't caught. Immediately he spotted the guy in front of the last urinal in the row. He'd just about finished zipping himself up. Perfect. Anthony lunged at him and tackled him low, slamming him to the floor. He planted one knee in the man's chest, pinning him.

"Tell me everything you know about Jesse Beven," Anthony ordered. The man didn't answer—at least not fast enough. Anthony ground his knee harder into his chest. "Talk," he ordered.

"I don't know . . . what are you talking about?" the man choked out, sounding sort of dazed.

Very smart, Fascinelli, Anthony thought as he frisked the guy, finding nothing. *Yeah, cut off his air,* then *ask him a question.* He lowered his knee a little and dug it into the man's soft gut. The little jab of pain might clear his head. "The kid you snatched. Jesse. I want to hear everything from the beginning."

"You got the wrong guy," the man wheezed, a string of

saliva dripping out of the corner of his mouth.

"I got all night, buddy," Anthony told him, staring the man in the eye. He heard the bathroom door open wider and jerked his head toward the sound. Rae stood in the doorway. "I don't want you in here. Leave!" Anthony barked.

Of course, Rae didn't listen. "There are easier ways to get information," she told Anthony as she made straight for the man and knelt beside him. Anthony's stomach seized up as Rae pressed her fingertips against the man's. Her face went blank for an instant, then a series of expressions crossed her face so quickly, he could hardly identify them. Fear, greed, malice, joy.

And then horror, horror as Rae ripped her fingers away. "Tie him up," she ordered. "I don't want him to be able to move."

Anthony didn't have to be asked twice. He yanked off his belt, then straddled the man and used the belt to tie his feet together. The man gave a weak buck, but he didn't have a chance of getting Anthony off him.

"Hurry," Rae urged, sounding seriously freaked out.

"What's the deal? Where's Jesse?" Anthony asked her.

"He doesn't have anything to do with Jesse. Just get him restrained and let's get out of here. Then I'll tell you everything," Rae answered.

Anthony jerked the man over onto his side, then pushed him onto his stomach and pulled his wrists together behind his back. The man started trying to fight again, so Anthony had to give his head a light rap against the cement. That kept the man quiet until Anthony had used the guy's belt to get his hands tied together as tightly as his feet.

"Let's go, let's go," Rae cried.

Anthony climbed off the man, leaped to his feet, and rushed out of the bathroom, Rae right behind him. He slammed the bathroom door shut, then spun to face her. "Okay, what?"

"The guy is part of a group using the warehouse as a crystal meth kitchen," Rae burst out. "One screwup and they could demolish half the neighborhood."

"I'll call the cops. Tell them where to find our friend and the kitchen," Anthony said, pulling out his cell. This problem at least he could deal with. But the Jesse situation . . . the Rae situation . . . Anthony wasn't going to lie to himself. He was in way over his head.

When he'd finished the call, he pocketed his cell and headed back over to Rae. "I guess we need to find another warehouse. You up for more driving around, or—"

"Let's go," Rae answered. They both climbed into the car.

"We covered most of the area to the west of Little Five Points, so I figured we'd just start driving up and down the streets to the east," Anthony said.

"I'll keep doing car watch," Rae answered.

Anthony settled into a slow, methodical search. Up one street for half an hour, back down the next one. Up and down. Up and down.

"You're not going to believe this," Rae burst out. "Our friend in the blue Dodge just drove by."

•   •   •

Rae jerked straight up in bed, her breath coming in harsh pants. She stared wildly around her room, half expecting to see . . . she wasn't even sure what. The dream had been horrendous, but it had faded so fast that all she was left with was the sensation of someone—or something—coming after her. "You're okay," she muttered. But there was no way she was lying back down and closing her eyes. Not when that dream could be lurking.

She climbed out of bed and pulled on her robe, then glanced at the clock. Quarter to one. She'd hardly been asleep any time at all, even though the dream had felt endless.

Rae pushed a few curly strands of hair away from her face and sat down in front of her computer. She needed some kind of mindless game to distract her. All she could think about was that blue Dodge—who was in it? Who was following her and Anthony? They'd tried to go after the car when she'd spotted it, but Anthony had lost it after a few blocks of heavy traffic. So if the driver really was tracking her, he or she was still out there somewhere. . . .

Rae shook her head, then clicked on the icon for solitaire. But before she could start playing, the phone rang. She snatched it up. "Hello?"

"It's Anthony."

His tone made the little hairs on her arms stand straight up.

"What? What happened?" she demanded.

"It's not that big of a deal," he answered. "It's just—I took my car over to this place after I dropped you at home, where

I've done some work for extra cash. I wanted my friend to check things out, see if he could get a handle on how that blue Dodge kept finding us." He paused, and Rae pressed her lips together, afraid of what was coming. "He found a bug in the car," Anthony finished.

"And that's no big deal?" Rae exclaimed.

"We already knew we were being followed," Anthony said. "We just didn't know high-tech equipment was involved. Anyway, I got rid of it. And now I'll be looking for more, so that will make it a little harder on the Dodge guy."

"Whoever that is," Rae said.

"Yeah. Well, I just thought you should know, it's under control. I've gotta go. See you tomorrow, okay?" Anthony hung up without saying good-bye. But a second later the phone rang again.

"Anthony?" Rae said as soon as she picked it up.

There was no answer. Only a low male laugh. "Who is this?" Rae said, trying not to sound as scared as she was.

"I get it now," a voice replied. Rae instantly recognized Marcus Salkow's arrogant tone. A mixture of relief and a new kind of dread washed over her. "Rae's got herself another guy."

"Marcus, why are you calling?" Rae asked. He sounded buzzed—not off-his-butt drunk, but like he'd had a couple of beers.

"I was making out with Dori the other night, and I called her Rae," Marcus said. "I called her Rae," he repeated, as if she might have missed it the first time.

Rae opened her curtains halfway and cracked the window.

She needed some air. "Why are you telling me this? This is something between you and Dori."

"Because . . ." The pause went on so long, Rae wanted to scream. "Because . . . I think I called her that because I miss you," Marcus admitted.

The confession was like a body blow. Rae didn't think she'd be able to say anything, even if she knew what she wanted to say.

"I know I really hurt you. I totally screwed up," Marcus continued. "And no matter what happens, I want you to know that I'm sorry. What I did to you . . . that's the worst thing I've ever done to anybody."

"Thanks," Rae murmured, surprised to feel tears welling up in her eyes. It was just that this was too familiar, talking to Marcus on the phone late at night. When they'd been together, they'd talked like this all the time.

"I want . . . would you want . . ." Marcus let out a frustrated sigh. "I thought maybe we could try getting back together. Whenever I see you at school . . ." He let his words fade away again.

"I don't know. I don't know if that could even be possible," Rae said in a rush. But God, it would feel so incredible to be part of Rae and Marcus again. So good. So safe.

But would he be able to take the stares? Because people would definitely stare if they got back together. Yeah, they'd be more subtle about it. And yeah, Marcus's friends would be cool because whatever Marcus did was okay with them.

But he still might not be able to handle going out with the school freak. He might just dump her again, and that . . . she might not recover from that.

"Rae?" Marcus finally said.

"I don't . . . this isn't something I can say yes or no to right now," Rae answered. "I have to go."

"Wait. Wait. I just want to play you this one song first," Marcus said. The song that was on the radio the first time Marcus kissed her began to play. It took her right back to that moment. They were sitting in his car, parked outside her house. She'd known he was going to kiss her, and as each minute ticked by that he *didn't*, it was like the air got more and more charged with electricity. When his lips finally touched hers, the kiss swept through her entire body.

And he put the song on his iPod. *I can't listen to this,* Rae thought. *I can't deal with this right now. Not with everything else that's going on in my life. After we get Jesse back, then I'll think about Marcus.*

Anthony felt someone poke his arm. He slitted open his eyes. There was no light outside his window. The sky hadn't even lightened to gray yet. He rolled onto his side. "Way too early," he mumbled. He got another poke on the arm. Reluctantly he opened his eyes all the way and sat up. Anna stood next to him.

"I wet the bed," she said, staring down at the floor.

"Why are you telling me about it?" Anthony asked, still

half asleep. "You have a mother."

Anna backed up a couple of steps. "Tom might wake up, too."

"All right, all right," Anthony muttered. He climbed out of bed. It wasn't that Tom was some kind of wicked stepfather. But the guy did have a mouth on him sometimes, and he knew exactly what to say to make any of them feel about an inch and a half tall. And as he got a good look at Anna's face, he realized that she was already feeling like a total loser. She kept biting her lip, probably to avoid bawling, and her eyes were darting around like she was scared somebody was going to see her.

Anthony grabbed a pair of sweatpants off the floor and pulled them on over his boxers. "Okay, this is no big deal. I'm going to show you what to do, and next time you won't have to wake anybody up," he said as he led her back to the room she shared with Carl.

He crossed over to her dresser and fished out a new pair of pajamas—Dora the Explorer ones. "First, get cleaned up and put these on," he told her. He checked on Carl while Anna ran to the bathroom. The kid probably wouldn't wake up if someone set off an air horn next to his head. Anthony reached out and ran one finger down Carl's cheek. It was so soft, it was hard to believe it was skin. *Wonder what it feels like to be three?* he thought.

"Okay, I'm done," Anna whispered as she slipped back into the room.

"Okay. Next step, take the sheets off your bed, and put on

new ones." Anthony grabbed a pair of worn sheets off the shelf inside her closet. He and Anna each took one side of the bed and got the new sheets on—about twice as slowly as it would have taken him to do it himself. But he knew if Anna was going to stop feeling like a screwup, she needed to learn how to deal with the wet bed situation on her own.

"Now what?" Anna asked. Anthony noticed she'd stopped biting her lip.

"Now we put the old sheets and pajamas in the washer. Come on. I'll show you." He took her little hand in his and led her down to the kitchen. "You turn this knob to small," he explained. "Then you put this one on hot/hot, open the lid, and stick the stuff in."

He waited while Anna followed his instructions, wonder-ing what his sister would think if she knew how long it had taken him to memorize the stupid words for each setting on the machine. "Now put in the detergent. One capful." Anna measured the soap out like it was some kind of explosive.

"Good job," Anthony said. "Now shut the lid. Then move this big knob to regular"—he pointed to the spot on the dial—"and pull it out." He nodded as Anna got the load started. "Now first thing in the morning, you take the stuff out and put it in the dryer. All you have to do is move the knob to the thirty or forty mark, then close the dryer."

"But what if somebody gets up before me? They'll know," Anna said. Her voice had a little quiver in it.

"Look, I'm pretty wide awake, so tonight I'll stay up and put the stuff in the dryer. When it's done, I'll stick it back in your closet," Anthony told her. What else was he supposed to say? "Next time—'cause you know, it happens sometimes, which is no big thing—you can stay awake if you want. But you know how it is here in the morning. It's not like anyone's going to be checking out the dryer to see if someone was doing wash in the middle of the night."

Anna hurled herself at him, wrapping her arms tight around his waist. "Thanks." Before he could answer, she was out of the kitchen. Anthony sat down at the kitchen table. Already his eyes felt droopy. But he couldn't fall asleep. He'd told Anna the sheets and pj's would be in her room in the morning, and that was going to happen.

He glanced at the kitchen clock—one of those cat ones with the swinging tail and the eyes that rolled back and forth. Not even midnight.

By now the Dodge guy has to know his tracking device has been flushed, Anthony thought. Crap. He should have put it in another car. That would have kept the guy off their tail for— for what? Another few hours? Another day? It wouldn't take a genius to realize that he and Rae weren't in whatever car Anthony would have stuck the bug in.

And by now whoever was following them knew the basics. They had to know where Anthony lived. Where Rae lived. Where the group therapy was held. Where he went to school. Where Rae went to school.

He had a bad feeling that Jesse wasn't the only one in danger. And there was nothing he could do to keep any of them safe.

• • •

Rae sat cross-legged in the center of her bed. There was no way she could sleep now. Not after Marcus's call, and especially not after Anthony's news about the bug. Plus fear for Jesse. Fear for herself. God. She might never sleep again.

Rae leaned over and grabbed her sketch pad and a piece of charcoal off her nightstand. The charcoal instantly started moving across the paper. She was in the zone, that place where her hand felt like it had a will of its own. Her art teacher, Ms. O'Banyon, always said that Rae's best work came when she trusted the hand. Rae agreed, but it was still kind of a freaky sensation.

Figures quickly began to appear on the paper. Marcus smiling. Anthony, ready to fight. Jesse curled up in the bottom corner, half off the page. And over all of them, taking up most of the top half of the sketch, a face. Almost featureless. Except for the eyes. The eyes that seemed to see everything.

She ripped the page off the pad and crumpled it up. This was not helping. She turned off her light and crawled back under the covers, deciding to at least attempt sleep. Then she realized she'd left the curtains open.

Great. She couldn't sleep like this. She never could. She felt way too exposed. With a sigh she climbed back out of bed and started toward the window. Her heart turned to stone in her chest. Somebody was out there. She could make out a dark figure right across the street from her house. Staring at her window. They probably couldn't see her now that her light was off. But how long had they been there? What had they seen?

Rae jammed on her Paul Frank monkey slippers and pulled

on a jacket. Then, without giving herself a chance to change her mind, she darted out of her room and through the house. She crept out the front door, opening it just enough to squeeze through. The person—she couldn't tell if it was a man or woman—was still there. Now what was she supposed to do?

You're supposed to find out who they are, she answered herself as she crossed the damp lawn, keeping her body low. She moved up to a parked car and crouched behind it, leaning out just enough to spy on the person who'd been spying on her. They were glancing around as if they had a feeling they were being watched. *Don't leave,* Rae silently begged. *Not until I get a good look at you.*

But the person was already starting down the street away from Rae's house, first walking, then jogging. Rae did the only thing she could think to do—she started after them, slippers flopping. When the person broke into a sprint, Rae did, too. She ran until her chest burned and she had to gasp for every breath. God, why hadn't she ever actually tried in gym?

The person ahead of her was almost out of sight. They stumbled, fell, but quickly regained their footing and kept running until they were lost in the darkness. Rae couldn't make herself take one more step. If she did, her lungs would explode. She sank down on the cold sidewalk, feeling her frantically pounding heart slow down. This might have been her only chance to find out who was following her, and she'd blown it.

Rae pushed herself to her feet. Something white halfway down the block caught her eye. Had the person following her dropped it? Still breathing hard, Rae walked down the sidewalk. As she got closer to it, she realized the white thing was a large envelope. She picked it up, moved under the closest streetlight, and opened it.

"Oh God," she whispered. The envelope was full of pictures—pictures of Rae. In her bedroom. In her kitchen. In her living room. At school. At the institute. In Little Five Points with Anthony. All the nightmares she'd been having were more real than she could have imagined. Someone really *had* been watching her—everywhere.

Chapter 13

"Okay, everyone, that's it for today's session," Ms. Abramson announced. *Today's group session at least,* Rae thought. She still had to have a private chat with Ms. Abramson. Rae was a newbie in the group, and she hadn't been out of the hospital all that long, so she was still on the list of people needing some . . . special attention.

"I'll meet you out in the parking lot," she told Anthony. "Abramson said it wouldn't take that long."

Anthony leaned close, a section of his brown hair brushing against her cheek. "The faster you give it up, the faster you get done," he advised.

"Ready, Rae?" Ms. Abramson asked.

Rae nodded, and Ms. Abramson led the way down to her office. *Anthony's right,* she thought as she took a seat in front of Ms. Abramson's desk. Rae was going to have to dredge up some of the ugly stuff, some of the feelings she didn't want to feel. No way was Ms. Abramson going to let her get away with saying everything was fine, fine, all fine.

"So how's life been treating you?" Ms. Abramson asked as she sat down. She reached for a cold cup of coffee, and Rae noticed there was a long, raw-looking strip that ran almost from her wrist to her elbow.

"I fell playing tennis," Ms. Abramson said, noticing the direction of Rae's gaze. "I admit it. I'm a klutz. But we're not here to talk about me."

"Stuff with my dad is going pretty well," Rae began, wanting to get this over with as quickly as possible. Every second that she and Anthony weren't out there searching for Jesse was longer that he was in danger. That they all were. "I don't think he's as worried about me," she continued, twisting her hands together in her lap. "So that makes it less tense. Before, I was always kind of stressing about him stressing about me, you know?"

Ms. Abramson nodded. "I think a lot of times parents forget that their kids worry about them almost as much as they worry about their kids," she answered. She took a sip of the coffee, grimaced, and put the cup back down. "How about school? How does it feel to be back there? I know you've talked about it some in group, but I'd like to hear more."

"Classes are good. Especially art. My teachers are still watching me pretty closely. It's like there are eyes on me everywhere," Rae said. She definitely wasn't going to tell Ms. Abramson that she was being followed. Talk about a one-way ticket to the hospital.

"School is more than classes. What about friends? Do you feel like they're watching you, too?" Ms. Abramson asked.

"Pretty much everyone is still weird around me, but I'm getting through," Rae said. She glanced at Ms. Abramson, and it was clear that she was going to have to get more detailed if she was going to satisfy the woman and get out of there. She couldn't talk about the really huge stuff in her life. Her fingerprint power. That there was someone who wanted her dead—someone who might have even kidnapped Jesse to get to her.

But there was one thing that kept creeping into her mind. And it was probably big enough to satisfy Ms. Abramson, who was just sitting there, watching Rae, waiting, obviously willing to wait all afternoon. "Um, my old boyfriend, Marcus . . . he says he wants to get back together with me."

"That's big," Ms. Abramson said, fiddling with the handle of her "World's Best Aunt" coffee cup. "Is it something you want?"

Rae shrugged. "I don't know. I mean, I was so happy with him, totally, completely happy. But then when I was in the hospital, he moved on to another girl in, like, three seconds. Does he actually think I can trust him again after that?"

"Do you see any set of circumstances in which you *could* trust him again?" Ms. Abramson asked. She took another sip of her coffee, grimaced again, then put the cup on the bookshelf behind her.

"Maybe if he was wearing one of those ankle bracelets—the ones cops put on people when they're confined to their house or whatever," Rae joked nervously. "It's like Marcus ripped a chunk out of my body and now he's saying he's sorry, like he forgot to call me when he said he would."

"Have you ever considered saying any of this to him?" Ms.

Abramson asked. "It sounds like something that needs to be addressed before you can even think about whether or not you want a relationship with him again."

"I've talked to him a little," Rae said. She sighed, a sigh so deep, it hurt coming out of her lungs. "But I don't think he really gets it."

Ms. Abramson leaned across her desk toward Rae. "I don't want to be dismissive of your feelings about Marcus, but is anything else bothering you? It doesn't look to me like you've been sleeping well. There are dark smudges under your eyes, and in group you seemed to have some trouble concentrating." Ms. Abramson pinned Rae with a gaze so intense, it got Rae squirming in her chair. "Is something else going on, Rae?" Ms. Abramson pressed.

"Jesse," Rae blurted out. "I'm worried about Jesse. He's been gone so long. I keep thinking about what could have happened to him."

"Jesse," Ms. Abramson repeated. Her gaze grew even more intense, like she'd switched on the high beams or something. "That is a disturbing situation. Tell me more about how you feel when you think of Jesse."

"The idea that someone's holding him prisoner just makes me insane," Rae burst out. Immediately she realized she'd made a big mistake.

And of course, Ms. Abramson picked right up on it. "Why would you think someone's holding Jesse prisoner?" she asked, her voice coming out the slightest bit strained.

"I guess I just . . . lately I kind of imagine the worst. I don't know why. Maybe it's because I was in the hospital and saw all these people who had ended up so badly. I—I don't know," Rae stammered.

"You've gone through a lot in the past months. It's not uncommon for people in your situation to become more pessimistic." She flipped open her date book. "I only scheduled time for us to have a quick chat today, but I'm concerned that you've begun to see the world in a negative way, and I'd like to work with you on it. How about if we meet for an hour after the next group meeting?"

It was one of those adult questions that weren't really questions at all. "Sure. Okay. That would be good." Rae jumped up from her chair. "So can I go now? Someone's waiting for me."

"You can go," Ms. Abramson said. "I'm glad we'll have some more time to spend one-on-one. You have so many gifts, Rae. I want to help you to realize all the potential inside you."

"Um, thanks," Rae answered. Then she hurried out to the parking lot and climbed into Anthony's car.

"How'd it go?" Anthony asked.

"You know . . . she wants me to be the best me I can be and blah, blah, blah." Rae opened her backpack, pulled out her binder, and flipped it open, allowing her old thoughts to rush through her head. She'd decided not to wear the Mush for a while. If she hadn't been wearing it so much, she might have touched a print that would have told her Anthony's car was bugged. She couldn't afford to miss any information right now.

"So I went online at lunch and found a couple more

buildings that fit the info we got from Jesse. I made a little map." Rae tilted the binder toward Anthony. "I think the old meatpacking place is the best bet. The other ones are farther away from where they're repairing the streets, and I'm not sure if the tar smell would reach them, although it might."

Anthony nodded, and he pulled out of Oakvale's parking lot. "Are we picking up Yana first?"

"She can't come. She said either she and her partner are finishing their project tonight or Yana's going to strangle the girl."

Anthony punched on the radio, and pounding techno filled the car. The beat of the music filled her body, revving her up. *We're going to find him today,* she thought. *No matter what it takes. If we have to stake out every warehouse in Atlanta, we're finding Jesse before we go home.* She tried not to let herself think about the fact that finding Jesse could mean finding the person who wanted to kill her.

"We're finding him tonight," Anthony half shouted over the music, echoing Rae's thoughts. When they were about a block away from the meatpacking factory, he killed the music, then parked as close as he could to the factory without being totally obvious. The building was set about fifty feet back from the street and surrounded by a high metal fence.

"You want to do a little work while we wait?" Rae asked. "I brought some clay."

"Okay," Anthony answered. He was actually giving it a

real try. But that was Anthony. He didn't back down once he said he'd do something.

Rae pulled a Ziploc bag out of her purse—

/Anthony will / want to try another / maybe felt /

—and took out a couple of balls of colored clay. "What word do you want to do this time?" she asked.

"How about *on*?" Anthony asked as she handed him some of the clay.

"You could make a skateboard, and I could make Jesse. Then we could put Jesse on the skateboard," Rae suggested. Anthony gave one of his signature grunts, and they both started to work. Rae made sure to glance at the factory every few seconds. So far, it looked deserted.

After they finished the clay representation of *on*, they did one for *after*—a baby elephant holding a big elephant's tail; one for *even*—a perfectly balanced scale; and one for *what*—a girl with a question mark for a head.

"Let's stop for a while," Rae said, doing another factory check. Still nothing going on. Anthony handed her the clay, and she stuck it in the Ziploc along with hers, then jammed it back in her purse. As she pulled her hand back out, her chunky silver ring hit on something hard. She felt around and realized that there was something in the inside pocket.

What would I have put in there? she wondered. She never used that pocket. She unzipped it and slid in two fingers. Almost immediately they brushed against something cool and smooth.

/never felt like I do about Rae / hope she knows /

Oh God. Rae recognized the flavor of that thought. It came from Marcus. She pulled the hard, smooth object free. It was the locket Marcus had given her on their two-month anniversary. The chain had broken a few days before The Incident. Rae'd put the locket in the little pocket for safekeeping. Then with everything that had happened, she'd forgotten about it. Gently she ran her fingers over it.

/ want to be with her all the time /can't stop thinking /think I love him /

That last thought, the think-I-love-him one, was Rae's. It brought with it a burst of old emotion, of love so new and wonderful, it made her giddy, and of a passion that burned until she thought she'd go crazy.

Tears stung her eyes. Would she ever feel that way again? Would anyone ever feel that way about *her*? Could Marcus still actually feel that way after everything that had happened? He was so freaked out by her being hospitalized. How could he even want to look at her again?

"What's that?" Anthony asked, glancing over at her, then returning his gaze to the factory.

"Nothing," Rae said quickly.

Anthony paused, then shrugged. "We've been here a couple of hours and haven't seen anything," he said. "I think it's safe to go a little closer. At least up to the fence."

Rae climbed out of the car—

/ today has to be /

—and she and Anthony walked across the street and down the sidewalk to the fence. There was a gate held closed by a thick chain and a padlock. Rae took a deep breath, then ran her fingers lightly down one of the metal bars. A blast of pure terror slammed into her, knocking her heart back against her spine.

/don't make me go in there/don't/what if gun/

"What?" Anthony took Rae by the shoulders and pulled her away from the fence.

"Jesse's in there," Rae answered, rubbing her fingers against the front of her pleated pants. "At least he was. And Anthony, he's terrified."

Anthony wrapped his arm around Rae's shoulders and walked her back to the car, trying to look casual in case anybody in the factory was watching. He opened the passenger door and helped her inside. Her whole body was trembling, and it made him want to punch something. Instead he slammed the door as hard as he could, then strode around the car and got in his side. He slammed his door, too. It didn't make him feel any better.

He ran his hands through his hair. He couldn't just sit here. "Wait here," he ordered Rae. "I'm going in."

Rae grabbed his arm with both hands. He could feel her nails, even through his sweatshirt. "Are you insane? There are guys with guns guarding Jesse. This whole thing could be a trap. You can't just go strolling in."

Anthony jerked away. "I'm going." He studied the factory. "It looks like there's a skylight up there. I can climb onto that Dumpster over on the side, and from there I can make it up the fire escape to the roof. No one'll be expecting me to come in that way."

He opened his door. Rae grabbed his arm again. "If you're going, I'm going with you."

"You don't look like you could even do one pull-up. You're not going to be able to haul yourself up from the Dumpster to the fire escape." He could give her a boost, but he wasn't going to tell her that. He wanted her in the car. Safe.

Before Rae could protest, Anthony pulled away from her again and scrambled out of the car. He headed back to the gate, not going too fast. If someone was watching, he wanted them to catch him while he was still outside. He'd have a lot better chance of staying alive that way. But no one stopped him when he approached the gate again. He waited a few more seconds, then climbed over. Keeping low, glad that it was dark, he ran to the Dumpster and swung himself on top of it. One half was open, and he could see that it was empty. Whoever was inside the factory was being careful not to leave any traces.

Anthony looked up at the fire escape. The bottom rung of the ladder was almost in reach. He stood on his toes and stretched one arm up until it felt like it was about to pop out of its socket. He reached for the rung, missed it, tried again, and snagged it with two fingers. *Yes!* He gave the ladder a yank, and it came down with a rusty screech. Anthony froze, sure someone would come running to check out the sound. But the only sound was his heart pounding in his ears. No footsteps running toward him. No gunshots.

Go. Just go, he thought, hauling himself up the ladder. It swayed under his weight, but Anthony concentrated on moving up one rung at a time. When he reached the roof, he muttered a quick prayer, then crept over to the skylight. He stretched out on his stomach and pressed his face against the grimy glass. But he couldn't see anything. Too dark.

Anthony reached out and started to scrub one section of the glass with the sleeve of his jacket. He heard a faint cracking sound and saw a hairline fracture run through the glass. *Okay, okay, don't panic,* he told himself. He slowly began to slide backward. If he could just get off the skylight—

But it was too late. The glass shattered, and Anthony was falling. He hit the floor with a bone-crushing thud, then everything went black.

Chapter 14

"Oh my God," Rae gasped. She wasn't completely sure; it was almost too dark to tell, but it looked like . . . it looked like Anthony had just fallen through the skylight. She scrambled out of the car and ran down to the gate. There was no way she could climb it. Why was she such a weakling?

Rae's eyes darted along the fence. Maybe there was a place she could squeeze through, or . . .

Her gaze fell on the large padlock holding the gate together. When people opened combination locks, they usually thought about the numbers as they did it. "Let this work. Let this work," Rae muttered as she ran her fingers over the lock's dial.

/thirteen/twenty-seven/five/

With shaking fingers Rae dialed in the numbers she'd gotten from the fingerprints. The lock didn't open. And Anthony and Jesse were inside with who knew what happening to them. *Panicking isn't going to help,* she told herself. *Focus. Maybe you got the numbers right but the order wrong.* She shook out her hand, then tried again. Twenty-seven. Five. Thirteen.

Rae yanked down on the lock. It didn't open.

Five. Thirteen. Twenty-seven. "Please, please, please."
Yank. And the lock opened with a well-oiled click. Rae pulled
it off the chain, dropped it on the ground, and shoved open the
gates. She didn't care who saw her. She hoped somebody did.
Maybe it would create enough of a diversion to give Anthony
a chance to do . . . something.

Rae raced toward the factory. She grabbed the long metal
handle of the front door with both hands and tugged with all
her strength.

/no one's ever gonna find me/

But it was locked. Of course it was locked. "Don't worry,
Jesse," she said as she ran to the closest window. "Somebody's
gonna find you right now."

There was no point in trying to be quiet anymore, so Rae
jerked off her Theory cashmere sweater, wrapped it tightly
around her fist, then slammed her fist through the window.
One of her fingers started to bleed, but she ignored it. She used
her sweater-wrapped hand to knock away as much glass from
the frame as she could.

Then she climbed into the factory.

Anthony slowly sat up, clenching his teeth so he wouldn't cry
out. It felt like someone was stomping across his back in baseball cleats.

He did a quick scan of the dark room, ignoring the little
explosions of light in front of his eyes. The room was huge,
clearly running the length of the building. It was also empty.

But I had to make a hell of a lot of noise falling down here,

Anthony thought. He wondered how long he'd been knocked out. It could have been less than a minute. But a minute was long enough for somebody to be practically on top of him. He pushed himself to his feet and listened hard. Yeah, someone was coming up the stairs. They were trying to be quiet, but he could hear the creak of the treads.

Weapon. He needed some kind of weapon. There wasn't going to be a spare gun lying around, but there had to be something he could use. Anthony spotted a pile of construction materials against the back wall. He crept over. A bunch of boards. And some bricks. He grabbed a couple of bricks as quickly as he thought he could without alerting whoever was coming for him, then he tiptoed back across the room and positioned himself just inside the doorway. He raised the bricks over his head.

Come and get me. You're going to be the one who goes down, he thought.

Rae crept up the last flight of stairs. Her footsteps echoed as if she was the only one in the factory. But she knew that there had to be others in here.

She took another step. Hesitated. She held her breath, hoping to hear the tiny sound again. But the factory stayed silent. *You've got to keep going,* she told herself. The hair on her arms began to prickle, and she got that familiar feeling, the feeling of being watched.

Oh God. Who was in here? Did they have a gun pointed at her right now? Were they waiting for her to move into the right position so they could shoot her through the head?

Rae's heart pounded so hard that the sound filled her ears.

She had only two choices. Up or down. She chose up. Took a step. Hesitated. Tried to listen. But all she could hear was the thud of her heartbeat.

Rae took another step. She peered at the open doorway at the top of the stairs. It was too dark up there to see anything. She hurled herself up the last few steps. If someone was there with a gun, at least she'd be harder to hit, she thought as she plunged through the open doorway.

Something moved in the darkness to her left. A man. She dropped to the floor and rolled. But he was too quick for her. A second later he had her shoulders pinned to the floor.

"I told you to wait in the car," he whispered furiously. Rae opened her eyes and saw it was Anthony kneeling over her. The rush of relief made her dizzy.

"I almost bashed you with one of these things," Anthony said, holding up a brick. "What is the matter with you?"

"I would have waited in the car if you hadn't fallen through the roof," Rae shot back. "And you don't have to whisper. The place is deserted."

Anthony dropped both bricks. "Crap," he exploded. "They must have moved him."

Rae hadn't even thought of that. She'd been so relieved to find Anthony alive—without getting killed herself—that she'd forgotten all about Jesse for a second.

"Now we have nothing to go on. All the info you got from the knife was about this place. It's useless to us now," Anthony burst out. He slammed his fist into the wall.

Rae winced, imagining the pain. She wanted to say something reassuring, something comforting. But he was right. They were back to square one. And the more time that passed . . . she didn't let herself complete the thought.

"Come on. Let's get out of here." She wrapped her fingers around the sleeve of his jacket, not wanting to accidentally invade his thoughts by touching his fingers, and led him down the first flight of stairs, through the next level of the factory, also empty, and down to the main level, which still had rows of meat hooks hanging from the ceiling. "Quite the decor, huh?" she muttered.

"Yeah. I—" Anthony was interrupted by a faint, rhythmic knocking. "It's coming from over there." Anthony spun to the left and ran between a row of the hooks, Rae still clinging to him. The knocking grew louder and louder. Anthony veered toward a door and yanked it open to find a small supply closet. Jesse was huddled in the back, a sponge duct taped into his mouth, wrists and ankles bound.

Rae let out a horrified cry. Anthony reached Jesse in two long strides and had him free in seconds. Then his arms were around Jesse, his cheek pressed against Jesse's head. Rae hung back, her heart aching with a mix of joy and relief and leftover fear.

Anthony and Jesse broke apart. Rae didn't know if Jesse'd want her hugging him. But she couldn't help herself. It was too good to see him. Jesse hugged her back hard, for a second, then gave her a little push away.

"What happened?" Anthony asked him. "Just start at the beginning, and don't leave anything out."

Jesse's wide grin faded. He started to sway on his feet, and Anthony reached out and steadied him. "I don't remember," Jesse said. His voice was husky, and for the first time Rae noticed how large his pupils were. *What did they do to him?* she wondered.

Rae knelt and picked up a piece of the duct tape, ran her fingers down it, and got—nothing. She checked the other pieces—nothing. "They must have been wearing gloves," she murmured. She checked the skin of Jesse's arms, the doorknob of the closet, the roll of duct tape she spotted on a shelf. "I'm not getting anything at all."

"Then let's get out of here," Anthony said.

Jesse took a step toward the door, and his knees buckled. "My legs are kind of numb."

Anthony didn't say anything. He just looped one arm around Jesse's shoulders. Rae positioned herself on Jesse's other side and wrapped one arm around his waist. Together she and Anthony half carried Jesse out of the warehouse and down to the car. They eased him into the backseat, and Rae climbed in beside him. "There's some soda in my backpack," she told Anthony.

He pulled out a can, popped the top, and handed it to Jesse. Jesse drank deeply, then started to choke. "Easy, easy," Rae said.

"It was a test. A test for you," Jesse blurted out.

"Who told you that?" Anthony asked, and Rae could tell he

was struggling to keep his voice calm.

"I don't remember," Jesse answered. He rubbed his forehead with both hands. "My head feels like it's getting stabbed with ice picks."

Anthony started the car. "We're going to get you home to your mom. Then we'll call a doctor."

"Can I touch your fingertips?" Rae asked. "I know you're still shaky, but maybe you still have some memories there that I can reach, and we can find out who did this to you."

Jesse held out his hands, and Rae took them in her own, carefully matching up their fingertips. The emotions and memories hit her like a punch. Fury over a woman—Jesse's mother—being beaten. Exhilaration at making an impossible skateboard jump. An oily mix of pleasure and guilt as a fire spread out of control. Faster and faster the memories came. Thoughts and emotions almost too quick to connect to each other, overlapping as they sped through her brain. Then clear as an announcement over a loudspeaker, she got a thought all by itself—*a test for Rae.*

She dropped Jesse's hands. "He's right," she whispered. "It was a test for me. But I don't know what kind of test, or why, or who was doing the testing." She shook her head. "At least it wasn't a trap. Or not the kind we thought."

"This is screwed up," Anthony exploded. "I don't understand it."

"It was all about me," Rae told them. "That much is very clear. It had nothing to do with Jesse. Whoever did this was just using him to find out something about me." She swallowed hard and felt her throat burn.

"It's okay," Jesse said.

"No, it's not okay!" Rae burst out. "You both have to stay away from me. Somebody was willing to risk Jesse's life to find out something about me. Somebody else—or maybe the same person—tried to kill me. This has nothing to do with the two of you. Just drop me off. I'll find my own way home."

"You didn't have any problem putting yourself at risk to get Jesse back," Anthony snapped, glaring at her in the rearview mirror. "We wouldn't do any less for you. If you think we would, you're the moron."

"Yeah," Jesse agreed. "This isn't over until we find the creeps who did it. All three of us."

"All three of us," Anthony repeated.

Rae looked from Anthony to Jesse. They meant it. She nodded. "All three of us," she agreed.

Epilogue

Kidnapping Jesse gave me some interesting information about you, Rae Voight. I finally know what you are capable of—what your power is. But it might be useful to wait and watch a little longer. Especially because now I know someone else is watching you, watching you almost as closely as I do. I can't stop wondering why. Is their reason anything like mine? Do they dream of seeing you dead, too? If I let you stay alive—just a little longer—I know I'll be able to find out the answers. And once I have them, you'll be useless to me. Then comes the fun part. Then comes my revenge. Then, Rae, you die.

Trust

$\mathcal{C}hapter\ 1$

Rae Voight hurried down the long hallway leading to Oakvale Institute's group therapy room on Wednesday afternoon. She tried to breathe mostly through her mouth because the smell of the industrial cleaner they used on the linoleum floor brought back memories of being in the mental hospital. Not even memories, exactly. It was more like the harsh smell transported her right back to the hospital, to her room with her silent roommate, to taking pills from little white accordion-pleated cups, and to feeling like she was free falling into insanity.

But now you know you're not insane, she told herself. Now Rae knew she was a fingerprint reader—whenever she touched a print, she got a thought from the person who left it. Weird. Spooky. But not insane. She pulled in another breath, the chemicals sour on her tongue. *Next time I'm bringing gum,* she thought.

Footsteps pounded down the hall behind her, coming right in her direction. Rae whirled around, her heart rate already doubling. At any moment the person who'd tried to kill her in this very building could decide to try again. She was stupid to let her guard down for even a second. She stiffened, ready to run—or just scream really loudly—but then she saw Anthony Fascinelli, and her pulse immediately slowed back down.

"Charging after a girl who's already had one assassination attempt on her isn't the smartest . . ." Rae's words trailed off as she took in Anthony's expression. His mouth was tight, and his dark eyes were practically crazed with fear. Anthony wasn't a guy who looked scared very often.

"What?" Rae demanded, wrapping her arms tightly around her waist.

"I just got a call from Anna, my little sister," Anthony said. His voice came out husky, and he cleared his throat. Then cleared it again.

Rae wanted to grab him and shake the words out of him. Instead she pulled in a deep breath and waited.

"She said that Zack ran away," Anthony finally continued. "He left a note. But what if he—"

"What if he got snatched, the way Jesse did?" Rae finished for him. *Oh God.* This couldn't be happening again. She and Anthony had managed to rescue Jesse Beven—a kid in their group therapy who was pretty much Anthony's honorary little brother. But it had been a close call. If it had taken them a few more days to find out where he was being held . . . even thinking about it made Rae feel sick to her stomach.

"Yeah. What if he did," Anthony answered. "I need you." He shoved his hands through his sandy brown hair. "I need you to try and read the prints," he added quickly.

"Of course." Rae was already heading back out of the

institute, Anthony right behind her. She wanted to run, just tear down the hall, but that was the best way to get stopped and asked a bunch of questions. She forced herself to keep her pace to a fast walk. *Maybe Zack did just run away,* she thought frantically. She tried to remember how old Anthony's brother was. About fifteen. Kids that age ran away all the time. *And if he ran, we'll have him back today,* she promised herself.

But if he was snatched . . .

"Why doesn't whoever the hell is doing this just take me?" Rae exploded as she climbed into Anthony's mom's Hyundai and slammed the door. "Whoever took Jesse did it just to test me. If they still want to know more, why won't they just take me? Why go after Zack or anybody else?" She swallowed, feeling a mixture of fear and guilt rise up inside her. "It's not like they don't know where to find me," she added, tugging her jacket tighter around her. "I mean, they bugged your car, they're taking photos of me wherever I go—"

Rae shot a glance at Anthony as he pulled out of the parking lot, noticing his lethal grip on the steering wheel. Even through his T-shirt she could see how bunched the muscles in his shoulders were. She was just making things worse.

"But we don't know that anyone took him," she added lamely. Anthony gave a grunt in response. It was clear he had no interest in talking, so Rae clamped her teeth together to prevent any nervous chattering and stared out the window as he drove.

Her teeth squeaked against each other as she tightened her

jaw until the muscles ached. *This is all my fault,* she thought. *Anytime anyone gets close to me, something bad happens to them.* Not even that close. She'd never even met Anthony's brother, and now because of her—

You don't know that, she told herself. But in her gut she didn't believe it.

"This is my street," Anthony announced as he made a left turn onto a block filled with small houses crammed together. It wasn't hard to figure out which of the houses was Anthony's. A girl and two boys stood on the small front lawn. They ran to the curb when they saw Anthony driving toward them.

The second Anthony stepped out of the car, the girl— Anna, who was nine, if Rae remembered right—rushed over to him, towing the littler boy, Carl, behind her. She pulled a folded piece of paper out of the pocket of her denim jacket. "I found this in his room," Anna announced, thrusting the paper at him. "You've got to do something. Tom's going to lose it."

Tom was Anthony's stepfather. Rae knew he was Carl's natural father, and she thought Anna's, too, although she hadn't quite mastered the intricacies of Anthony's family.

"No one's going to lose it," Anthony answered. He unfolded the letter and read it slowly, his jaw muscles tightening. Rae realized how much his trouble with reading must be getting to him right now, when he needed the information fast.

Anthony finally finished and passed the note to her, and she saw his fingers were trembling. So were hers. She ignored the questions the kids were hurling at Anthony and quickly scanned the page. It was short, with the usual words—the *expected* words. Zack couldn't handle it anymore, so he was leaving. They shouldn't look for him. It sounded like a kid who was running away. *Or like someone wants us to think he ran away,* Rae couldn't help adding in her head. There was nothing personal, nothing specific. Anyone could have made up this note.

She shook her head. It was time to let her fingertips do their work.

/what if he never comes back?/

Rae's throat went dry with fear. Anna's fear. She moved her fingers a little lower.

/Nothing I need here/can all piss off/

The back of Rae's neck flushed as Zack's anger jolted through her. Followed by her own relief. This was definitely Zack's letter. No one else was involved.

Okay, Zack, tell me where you are, Rae thought, letting out a deep breath. She ran her fingers lightly down the page. She picked up some more fear from Anna, a mix of fear and anger from Anthony, then she got another blast of pungent Zack.

/can't stand/Tom is such a/can crash in Todd's shed/

Got you, she thought. She handed the note back to Anthony. "Why don't we drive around a little?" she asked, unable to blurt the truth out in front of Anthony's siblings. "I bet you know a bunch of his usual spots."

"I'm coming with you," the older of the two boys—Danny—announced. Rae's lips twitched. Danny didn't look anything like Anthony—he had longish curly blond hair and blue eyes—but his attitude was clearly something he'd picked up from his big brother. Even his tough-guy stance, feet planted apart, reminded her of Anthony.

"You are staying here," Anthony shot back. "All of you," he added before Anna or Carl could start to plead. "If Zack gets back before I do, you three sit on him, okay?"

He didn't wait for an answer. He climbed back in the car and slammed the door. Rae scrambled into the passenger side, shut the door, and fastened her seat belt.

"He really did run away," she told him. "He's all right." She watched as Anthony's whole face relaxed, the terror easing out of his expression.

"So where is he?" he asked.

"You know a friend of his named Todd?" she replied.

Anthony nodded, already pulling back onto the street.

"Did you get any idea why?" Anthony asked Rae after they'd gotten some distance from his house. He hadn't trusted himself to speak for a little while there, afraid he'd get all mushy on her for letting him know his brother wasn't in danger.

"Not much," she answered. "A little burst of anger at Tom."

Anthony snorted. "Big surprise."

"Did they have a fight recently?" Out of the corner of his eye Anthony saw Rae tuck her wavy reddish brown hair behind her ear, a habit of hers he'd picked up on.

"Recently?" Anthony repeated. "Would you call breakfast recently? Or last night? Or last weekend?"

"That bad, huh?" Rae let out a long sigh.

"Tom's a jerk. End of story," Anthony said. At least it was the end of the story he would be telling Rae. He cut a glance over at her. How much had she noticed about his house? Had she been too caught up in the minidrama to take it in? He hoped so, because compared to where he lived, she and her dad resided in a mansion.

"This is Todd's place," he told her, pulling into the driveway of a house that didn't look too much different from his own. "Wait here, okay? I need to talk to Zack alone."

Rae nodded, and he hoped she wouldn't touch anything in the car while he was gone. She wasn't wearing the waxy stuff that blocked out the thoughts she got from fingerprints. He knew she wouldn't go rooting through his head on purpose, but it was easy to touch something—the radio, the dashboard—without actually deciding to. *As if she'd find out something that she doesn't already know,* Anthony thought as he headed up the front walk. He punched the doorbell. After almost a full minute's wait Todd answered. One look and Anthony knew Todd was going to give him some line of crap.

"I know he's here," Anthony said before Todd could get a word out. "I want to talk to him. Now."

Todd was almost as tall as Anthony, but he was a featherweight, with pretty much no muscle of any kind. It had to be clear to him that Anthony could destroy him in a second. Todd backed away from the door and pointed to the living room. Then he disappeared into the kitchen.

Anthony moved quickly to the living room, releasing a short breath when he spotted Zack in front of the television.

"What do you want?" Zack muttered, not taking his eyes off the screen as Anthony plopped down on the couch next to him.

Anthony didn't answer. He pretended he was just as interested in watching Comedy Central as Zack was, even though they'd both seen this Chris Rock wanna-be's act at least five times.

"So are you supposed to drag me home?" Zack finally asked, eyes still glued to the TV even though a commercial had come on.

Anthony stretched out his legs. "Nah. I was thinking of moving in here myself," he answered. There were only two ways to get Zack out of this house—an explosion or making him think it was what he wanted to do.

They watched the TV in silence. Todd poked his head into the living room for a second, then scurried away.

Finally Zack turned and actually looked at Anthony. "Tom is such a freakin' idiot."

"You're not gonna get any argument from me," Anthony answered. "Maybe Mom will finally realize that herself and trade up. She's got to be getting itchy by now." His mother and Tom had been together for about four years, and living together for over eight months—almost a record for her. She usually treated guys like Kleenex. Or maybe it was more like they treated her that way. It was hard to tell.

"So, what, I'm just supposed to be a good little boy? Be *respectful* until he gets the boot—if he ever does?" Zack demanded.

"I do it," Anthony answered. "I keep my head down so I can live there until I finish high school, because there's no way I could do that if I was working enough to pay rent and buy groceries. Next year I graduate, and I'm out of there. And you're right behind me."

Anthony couldn't believe he was sitting here, giving the rah-rah speech. But he was telling Zack the truth, even if he didn't like it any more than Zack did.

Todd stepped back into the living room. "My mom's gonna be back soon. You should head out to the shed. And make sure she doesn't know you're out there."

"Screw it." Zack stood up. "See you later," he told Todd. Then he headed for the door. Anthony followed him. That hadn't been nearly as hard as he thought it would. Although Zack liked his electronics. It was hard to picture him as shed boy.

"This is Rae," Anthony told his brother when they got in the car. He turned to her. "I've just got to drop him off, then I can take you home." He didn't really want to give Rae another look at his house, but there wasn't really a way around it.

"Sure," Rae answered. She twisted her fingers together in her lap.

Anthony flipped on the radio. It seemed like the best way

to fill the silence. Almost too quickly, he was turning back onto his street.

"Crap," Zack burst out. "Mom and Tom are home."

Not just home, but standing in the driveway.

"Anna must have called them when she called me," he said.

"Little snitch," Zack muttered.

Anthony reached back with one hand and flicked Zack on the forehead. "She was worried about you, moron." He parked along the curb. Rae climbed out before he could say anything to her, as if there was anything he could say to prepare her for his mom and Tom. They were nothing like her college professor dad. Probably nothing like any adult in her little prep school life.

"No point in sitting here," he told Zack. Then he climbed out of the car and slammed the door. Zack got out a second later. And their mom was all over him. "Honey, what were you thinking?" she cried, her voice too loud as usual. None of the neighbors would have to strain their ears to hear the latest Fascinelli drama.

"He wasn't thinking, period," Tom cut in, hitching up his pants before they could fall off his bony hips. "He's just like his father. If things get tough, just leave."

Oh, crap. Tom would have to play the father card two seconds after Anthony managed to get Zack home. He shot a glance at Zack. A dark red flush was creeping up his neck. Anthony knew exactly how he was feeling. Whenever Tom started going off about Anthony's father, Anthony felt like any second he'd go volcanic.

"Although I don't know what's so tough about your life," Tom continued. "Free food. No rent. All those video games your mother keeps buying you. What's your complaint, Zack? That you have to take out the trash once in a while?"

"Take out the trash? How many times do you two leave him to watch the kids while you're out partying?" Anthony demanded. If Tom wanted a fight, Anthony would be the one to give it to him.

"Yeah, watching a couple of kids once in a while is way too much work for Sam Plett's boy to take on," Tom shot back.

"My dad—" Zack cried.

"What do you do that's so hard?" Anthony asked Tom, interrupting Zack. He squared off with Tom, keeping Tom and Zack apart. "You paint a house once in awhile if anyone is dumb enough to hire you and your buddies. You fill in at the hardware store if good old Bob is feeling sorry for you. And what else? Oh, yeah. You spend a lot of time on your ass."

"Anthony! You apologize!" his mother exclaimed. She tried to squeeze between him and Tom, half falling out of her low-cut top in the process. Her nauseatingly sweet floral perfume filled his nose.

Anthony caught Zack's eye and jerked his chin toward the house. Zack disappeared inside, then joined Danny, Anna, and Carl at the living-room window.

365

"I'll be happy to apologize. If he apologizes to Zack," Anthony shot back.

"The last thing that little punk needs is an apology. Do you know how worried your mother was—" Tom began.

"And Anthony got Zack back," Anthony's mother cut in. "Happy ending. Let's just say that everyone has apologized to everyone." She gave Tom a little push with one hand, and Anthony a harder push with the other. Reluctantly they both backed a step away from each other.

"Good boys. Now, Anthony, I see you brought a friend home! That's wonderful. I'm always telling you to bring friends home," his mother said as she headed over to Rae, adjusting her shirt.

Rae stepped forward awkwardly. "Hi, I'm Rae," she introduced herself.

"Well, Rae, you come on in. We can't stand out in the front yard all day." Anthony's mother led the way inside.

"Welcome to Springerville," Anthony muttered to Rae as he fell in step beside her.

"You guys would never make it onto *Springer*," Rae whispered back. "You wouldn't even make it onto *Dr. Phil*."

The girl was cool. He had to give her that. If anybody had to see his family, it might as well be Rae.

"Everybody sit down," Anthony's mother said as she threw a stuffed Dora the Explorer off the sofa and picked a bowl of crusty Cocoa Puffs off the coffee table.

"Rae can't really stay that long—" Anthony began.

"She has to stay a little while," his mother protested. "I

don't know any of your friends anymore." She winked at Rae. "Anthony hasn't brought a girl home since the second grade."

"Rae goes to Sanderson Prep," Anthony volunteered, just to shut his mother up. If he let her go on another minute, she might start hauling out a photo album.

"Great football team," Tom said as he sank down on the couch. "A lot of those kids go on to play college ball."

"That's true. Football is a huge deal at Sanderson," Rae answered. She touched Anthony's arm. "Anthony plays, right?"

"He messes around sometimes, yeah," Tom answered. "He's actually not bad. Maybe even good enough to play for your school."

Okay, where's the punch line? Anthony wondered.

"Except that you have to be smart to go to one of those prep schools. And Anthony inherited his brains from his old man," Tom added.

Shake it off, Anthony ordered himself. He didn't need to get into round two with Tom. Not with Rae watching.

"You never even met my dad," Anthony said quietly.

"Yeah, well, I've heard plenty from your mom," Tom answered. "She never runs out of stories about what a loser Tony Fascinelli was."

Even though Rae wasn't touching one of Anthony's finger-prints, it was like his feelings were her own. Anger, shame, hatred, and the desire to slam a fist into the closest wall jangled through her body.

"Rae, come help me get some drinks for everyone." Anthony's mom interrupted Tom, just as he was about to launch into another stream of insults, she imagined.

Rae didn't want to go. She wanted to stay with Anthony. But he'd hate that.

"Sure," Rae said. She followed Anthony's mother into the kitchen, where Zack was doling out peanut butter sandwiches to the other kids.

"Thanks, baby," Anthony's mom said. She reached out— maybe to kiss him on the forehead—but Zack dodged her. Anthony's mother pretended not to notice as she pulled a can of powdered iced tea mix from the cupboard. "I think I'll mix us up a pitcher," she told Rae. "You want to get some glasses?" She nodded at the dish drainer.

Rae grabbed four of the clean glasses and set them on the table while Anthony's mom dumped a scoopful of the tea powder into a plastic pitcher and added water. "Don't take Anthony and Tom too seriously," she said as she stirred the mix. "They're like bulls, you know? Fighting for dominance. Snorting and charging at each other."

"Uh-huh," Rae murmured. But she knew it was much more than that. At least to Anthony. The one time they'd made fingertip-to-fingertip contact, she'd been almost over-come with his longing to know his father, to find out if he was anything like his dad.

He should know the truth, Rae thought. Not the garbage Tom kept spewing at him. But how was that supposed to happen?

Rae gave a jolt. Maybe there was a way she could use her

gift to help Anthony find his dad.

"Do Anthony and his father ever see each other?" Rae asked, even though she knew the answer.

"Not since Anthony was a baby," Anthony's mom answered. She plunked the long spoon into the sink. Rae wandered over, trying to look casual, and picked it up—

/ Tony / Tom shouldn't / Why won't Anthony /

"Oh, you don't have to bother washing that," Anthony's mother said. She plucked the spoon out of Rae's hand and dropped it back into the sink.

Well, that didn't get me anything useful, Rae thought.

She tried to shake off the mix of fear and annoyance and protectiveness that the thoughts had brought up inside her. Anthony's mother was filling the glasses with the tea. Rae didn't have much time. She was going to have to go fingertip to fingertip.

Rae reached out and grabbed Anthony's mother's free hand. "I want to thank you for making me feel so at home," she said. It was corny, but it worked okay. Anthony's mom gave Rae's hand a little squeeze, and Rae positioned her fingertips over hers.

Immediately a hard knot formed deep in her stomach— the fear of getting older, of ending up alone. A craving for the burn of alcohol streaked down her throat. And the powerful, primal love for her children overwhelmed everything else.

Tony, Rae thought. *What about Tony?* She tried to go deeper into Anthony's mother's thoughts, even the thoughts she didn't know she had. Slimy guilt for words spoken that couldn't be taken back. Weariness. An iron spike of anger. And the sweetness of a first kiss. Back in Fillmore High—Anthony's school. At a dance with crepe paper streamers. With one of Tony Fascinelli's hands inching toward her butt.

Anthony's mother pulled away, giving Rae a forced smile. "Let's get these drinks in to the bulls," she said. Rae grabbed two of the glasses, getting nothing off the clean surfaces. *At least I found out that Tony and Anthony's mom went to high school together,* she thought. It was a place to start.

She followed Anthony's mother back into the living room. As Rae handed one of the glasses to Anthony, she realized there was a streak of numbness running up her right arm, from her wrist almost to her shoulder. She rubbed it, but it didn't go away.

"Are you cold, honey?" Anthony's mother asked.

"No, I'm fine," Rae answered. She pressed one of her fingernails deep into her skin along the numb streak. And felt nothing. *Maybe it's just some holdover from going so deep with Anthony's mom,* she thought. But she'd never felt anything like it before.

She took a sip of tea. She was probably just stressed or something.

"We've got to go," Anthony said abruptly. He put his untouched glass on the coffee table.

"Aren't you even going to let Rae finish her—" Anthony's mother began.

"We should see if we can still catch the last part of group," he interrupted. Then he took Rae by the wrist and hurried her out of the house.

"Group will definitely be over by the time we get there," Rae told him after they got in the car.

Anthony raised an eyebrow. "You're telling me you wanted to stay?"

"Well, you know, I just wanted more quality time with Tom," Rae answered, going for a cheap laugh. He didn't get it. "You know what he was saying about you and the Sanderson football team?" she plunged on. "I bet he was right. I bet you are good enough to be a Sabertooth. And isn't that what you said you wanted in that hopes and dreams exercise we did in group?"

"Did you forget what else he said?" Anthony shot back. "About how I'm just too stupid?"

"But he doesn't know how much you've been working," Rae protested. "God, Anthony, do you have any clue how much better your reading is? You told me your teacher even mentioned it."

"Whatever," Anthony said. "Why are we talking about me? You're the one who never coughed up a real answer during that hopes-and-dreams crap."

Rae felt like asking him why he was bringing it up if it was such crap. But it was obvious why. He was looking for a subject change, and any subject would do.

"Okay, a dream." Rae thought for a moment. "Since the fingerprint thing started up, I really like taking baths. It's one place where I don't pick up anything. Every thought is mine.

So, a dream would be that I could swim. I bet that would feel amazing."

"You can't swim? I thought all girls like you took swimming and ballet," Anthony answered.

"I had a bad experience when I was little, okay?" Rae responded. "The idea of being in water where my feet can't touch the ground freaks me out."

"You're meeting me at the Y tomorrow," Anthony said. "I'll teach you how to swim. I owe you, anyway." He paused. "You know, for helping me with my reading."

I say I want something, and just like that, he tries to get it for me, Rae thought.

I'm definitely finding his dad for him. And maybe, just maybe, there's something else I can do for him, too.

Chapter 2

Rae took another sip of water from the drinking fountain outside the cafeteria on Thursday, even though she was already sloshing inside. It gave her something to do while she waited for Marcus Salkow. She felt weird just standing in the hall. Exposed. *Get over yourself, Rae,* she thought. *Your little psychotic episode was last spring. People aren't whispering about it anymore. They don't walk around all day thinking about you.*

She pulled her curly auburn hair away from her face and took another sip of water, anyway, the wax on her fingertips preventing her from picking up anyone else's thoughts.

When she straightened up and turned back around, she spotted Marcus turning the corner and heading for the caf. Rae noticed a lot of girls appraising him not so discreetly. And why not? He was gorgeous—blond, green eyes, broad shoulders. Your basic high school god.

"Marcus," she called. A few waterlogged butterflies began circling her stomach when he looked at her and smiled. *But that doesn't mean anything,* she told herself. *It's just a leftover response from when we were together.*

"Rae, hey, hi," Marcus said as he hurried up to her.

Maybe he thinks I want to talk to him about that phone call, she realized, *when he said he wanted to get back together.* She felt like blurting out, "It's okay, Marcus. I know you'd knocked back some beers that night." But she didn't. If he mentioned it, then she'd deal with it. If he didn't . . . it was probably a good thing. The idea of being with Marcus again brought up so many feelings—bad and good—that her brain froze up whenever she thought about it.

"Um, how's it going?" Marcus asked, standing too close to her, so close, she could smell that Marcus smell—a mix of soap, sweat, and wintergreen Life Savers.

Just ask what you want to ask and get away from him, Rae told herself. "How are the Sabertooths going to get through the season now that Vince is out of commission?" she blurted out.

Marcus's eyebrows shot up, but he answered as if it was normal for them to stand around chatting about football. "It's going to be tough," he said. "Without Vince, getting into the state play-offs isn't a done deal anymore. None of the second-string guys come close."

Rae nodded. It was exactly what she wanted to hear. "I should go," she said. "I'm in the middle of a painting. I'm going to eat in the art room." She knew she should talk for a few more minutes, but she didn't want him to bring up the phone call, and she didn't want to breathe in any more of him. It was making her dizzy. "See you," she said, and she started away from him.

"Rae." He caught her by the elbow, and she reluctantly turned to face him. "I wanted to tell you . . . I thought you should know . . ." He tightened his grip a little. "I broke up with Dori this morning."

Rae stiffened, her heart doing an involuntary extra beat in her chest. Marcus and Dori were split up? So Marcus was . . . single?

What are you thinking? she immediately chided herself. It didn't matter if Marcus was with Dori or not—he and Rae were over. For good.

Rae blinked, realizing that Marcus was still standing there, still too close, waiting for a response. *So am I just supposed to fall into his arms?* she wondered. Getting together with Dori two seconds after Rae was tucked away in her hospital bed didn't exactly call for an easy I-forgive-you.

But Marcus was looking at her with such intensity, Rae knew she had to say something.

"Um, well, I hope you're both doing okay," she finally mumbled. Then she turned and rushed away without giving him a chance to say anything else.

She headed straight for the gym. *This isn't the time to think about Marcus,* she told herself. *You're on a mission for Anthony.* She pushed open the double doors and stepped inside. The football coach was sitting on the bleachers, eating his lunch.

"Mr. Mosier, hi," Rae said as she approached him. He took a minute before he looked up from the sports section in front of him. "I . . . I . . ." *Why didn't I rehearse this?* she thought. "I know this great football player who goes to Fillmore. Playing on our—your—team is, it's pretty much all he ever talks about."

"Great, huh?" Mr. Mosier asked. He took the last bite of his PowerBar. "How great?"

Stats. He's looking for stats. Which I don't have, Rae thought. "So great. Tearing-up-the-field great. State-champion great," she added, inspired.

Mr. Mosier narrowed his eyes. "He your boyfriend or something?"

"No," Rae said quickly. She sat down next to Mr. Mosier. "He's just someone I thought you should know about—with Vince out for the rest of the season and everything. Marcus was telling me Vince left a big hole in the team."

The magic word, Rae realized. Mr. Mosier had forgotten all about the sports page, and all it took was invoking the name of Marcus.

"It's not impossible to get a scholarship for the right public school kid," Mr. Mosier told her. "His academics okay?"

Damn. She'd wanted him to see Anthony play before the school situation came up. "Here's the deal," she answered. "Anthony has dyslexia. It was just recently diagnosed." She didn't mention that the diagnosis had come from her. "He's working really hard on it, and it's starting to come together for him. But his academic records are going to say that he is a poor student—at least until he gets this semester's grades. Then I'm sure there will be big improvement."

Mr. Mosier folded his PowerBar wrapper into a little triangle. He used his thumb and forefinger to flick it down the long bleacher. "Touchdown!" He turned back to Rae. "If the kid's willing to come to tomorrow's practice, I'm willing to watch. That's all I'll say."

Rae jumped up. "He'll be there," she promised. "His name is Anthony Fascinelli. And he'll definitely be there." She headed for the doors.

"If I like what I see, he'll have to take some academic placement tests," Mr. Mosier called after her. "But if he's that good, I can probably make it work for him."

"He is. He is," Rae called back. She'd never seen him play, but she was certain of it.

She couldn't feel her feet hitting the ground as she headed to her locker. Anthony was going to be so psyched, she thought as she dialed in her locker combination. And going to Sanderson could change his whole life. She snapped the lock open and pulled open the metal door. A large, deep purple envelope was jammed in front of her books.

Rae swallowed, staring at the envelope without moving. Her first impulse was to just slam the locker shut and run. She didn't want to know what was inside that thing.

Everything unexpected doesn't have to equal bad, she told herself. She took a deep breath, then grabbed the envelope and ripped it open, revealing the top of a photograph. "See, someone left you a picture. Maybe Marcus. Nothing scary," she whispered, then glanced down the hall to make sure no one had caught her talking to herself.

She pulled the photo all the way out. As soon as she saw the rest of the image, her breath caught in her throat. Marcus had nothing to do with this. She stared down at the picture, unable to move her eyes away although she wanted to more than anything. But her gaze remained locked on the woman in the photograph. She was beautiful, standing in the surf with a big beach ball tucked under one arm, and a huge grin on her face.

But on her forehead . . . someone had used red nail polish to paint a bullet hole and drops of blood. A coffin drawn in thick black enclosed her body.

"And you'd never seen the woman in the photo before? She didn't look at all familiar?" Anthony asked.

Rae shook her head. She wrapped her towel tightly around her shoulders, even though she hadn't even stuck her feet in the pool yet.

"Did you get anything off the picture? Or the envelope?" he pressed.

"The first thing I did was get the wax off my fingers so I could do a sweep. And nothing," Rae answered.

Anthony felt like someone had just run a finger down his spine. "That means—"

"It means that whoever left me my little present probably knew I can read prints," Rae interrupted, her voice low and strained. "It means yet again there's someone out there messing with me. And I don't know who or why—except that whoever it is had no problem finding my locker."

"Crap," Anthony muttered.

"Yeah," Rae said.

"I guess we have to assume that it was the work of the

same person who was behind the pipe bomb and kidnapping Jesse," Anthony said.

"And bugging your car, and taking all those pictures of me, and who knows what else," Rae answered. "Yeah, let's hope it's all the same person; otherwise . . ." She didn't finish the thought.

Anthony wanted to pummel someone. He hated feeling so *helpless*.

"But you know, there was one good thing that happened today," Rae told him. And she smiled, her eyes crinkling.

"Cool. Tell me. But make it quick," Anthony added. "We've got to get some pool time in." He knew swimming scared her, but it would be a distraction from all the other crap that was happening. And she really did need to learn.

"Okay, so Vince, he's a running back on the Sanderson team, he broke his leg," Rae said in a rush. "The team needs a killer replacement; otherwise they're not going to make it to state. And I told the coach about you."

"About me?" Anthony repeated. His head filled with static.

"Yes, about you. And how great you are. And how you could be the savior of the Sabertooths," Rae said. She gave a small bounce on her toes like a little girl. "The coach says you should show up for practice tomorrow. If he likes what he sees—"

"I'm supposed to go to a practice?" Was she really saying what he thought she was saying? Playing on the Sabertooths, maybe getting to state—Anthony suddenly got a picture of Tom in the stands, watching him. That would finally shut him up. Maybe his dad would even—he shook his head and forced himself to listen to what Rae was saying.

"—need to be on the field at three. The coach, Mr. Mosier, said that a scholarship is a possibility if you're as good as I said you were, which I know you'll be. You'd just have to take some academic tests—"

Rae kept talking, but Anthony didn't hear a single word after "academic tests."

"What is wrong with you?" he demanded. "You know better than anybody that I have zero chance of passing any kind of test."

"That's not true." Rae's blue eyes were almost shooting sparks at him. "You've been working really hard, and you've improved a ton. Even your English teacher mentioned it."

"Yeah, I've been doing really good—for a complete idiot," Anthony snapped.

"Don't say that," Rae ordered.

"I'll say whatever I want," Anthony replied. "Now stop stalling and get in the pool."

Rae whipped her towel off her shoulders and threw it over against the wall, then she strode over to the shallow end and marched down the steps without a second of hesitation. Anthony followed her more slowly, trying not to focus on just how much of her skin was exposed right now.

"Okay, first thing you have to learn is how to float on your back. Try it," he instructed. He noticed that she was trembling, just a little. He didn't know if it was because she was cold, or scared, or if she was just furious at him. He didn't care. She had no idea what she'd just done to him. She'd held out the thing she knew he would die to have, then snatched it away. Why had she even brought it up when she knew there were tests involved? He was stupid to begin with. But on tests—forget about it.

"Why are you just standing there?" he barked at Rae. "You're supposed to be practicing floating."

"I told you I don't know how to swim. At all," Rae shot back.

Anthony reached over, wrapped one arm around Rae's shoulders and one around her knees, and maneuvered her into position on her back. "Just keep your head back and your chest out, and you'll float," he told her. "I'll hold on to you until you've got it," he added.

Rae pulled in a long, shuddering breath and squeezed her eyes shut. She looked like she was about to face a firing squad.

"You don't have to try so hard," Anthony said. "Think about something else. Like those clouds you painted on your hallway. Just forget you're in the water and imagine yourself floating on those clouds."

Rae's body stayed tight. He could feel her muscles clench as he held her. "I've got you. I've got you." He kept repeating the words until he could see her begin to relax. Then he just shut up and waited until she started to float on her own.

"You're doing it," he finally announced, keeping his voice soft so he wouldn't startle her.

Rae opened one eye and looked up at him. "I am?"

"You are," he answered. He slowly pulled his hands away from her and held them up. "See? It's all you."

She floated for half a second more, then she tilted her head too far back and pulled in a snootful of chlorinated water. And it was over. She went down kicking and flailing.

Anthony reached out, grabbed her hand, and pulled her back to her feet, sputtering and coughing. A stream of water was running out of her nose. "You look—"

He stopped abruptly when his fingers began to tingle. It felt like an electric charge was running from Rae to him, up his fingers, up his arm, all the way up to his brain. He glanced at her face, nearly jerking backward when he saw the expression in her eyes as she stared at him. It was almost like she was staring *inside* him.

She's getting a mind dump from me, he realized. He pulled his hands from hers, breaking the fingertip-to-fingertip contact.

"Sorry," she muttered. "I wasn't trying to—"

"I know," Anthony answered. He didn't even want to think about what she'd yanked out of his head. Not like she didn't know pretty much everything about him from the last time they went fingertip to fingertip.

"So, you ready to try again?" He knew she was still shaky from going under, but if she called it quits for the day, it was going to make it a lot harder the next time.

"There's this spot on my leg that got numb," Rae answered. She ran her fingers down her left calf.

"Like a cramp?" he asked.

"Like a dead place. I can't even feel it." She jabbed her calf with one finger. "I need to get out for a minute." She started for the steps, but before she was halfway there, her left leg buckled.

Anthony caught her around the waist before she went under again and helped her out of the pool. He led her over to their towels and grabbed hers without letting go of her. She was really shaking now. "You okay?" Anthony asked as he wrapped the towel around her.

"Uh-huh. Fine," Rae answered, her teeth chattering. Anthony used a corner of the towel to dry off her face. "Thanks," Rae mumbled.

Anthony kept smoothing the towel down her cheek, even though it was dry. She was so beautiful. Why did she have to be so beautiful?

His eyes drifted down to her lips. They were full, lush, like they were filled with something sweet. And all he wanted was to kiss them, and pull her close to him.

Rae moved a fraction of an inch toward him. Did she know what he was thinking? Did she *want* him to kiss her?

Anthony let go of the towel and stepped back. "Maybe you should sit down for a while," he said. "I'm going to swim a couple of laps." Then he got himself into the cool water before he could do something stupid. Because kissing her would be very stupid. Nothing could happen between him and Rae. They were friends, yeah. But they were way too different to be anything more than that.

* * *

Rae put her book down on the bedside table and ran her fingernail lightly down her calf. Even though the nail was barely touching the skin, she felt it. The numbness was gone. It had been gone by the time she got home from the pool almost an hour ago, but she was compelled to keep checking. Because what if—

Don't, Rae ordered herself. She picked up her copy of *The Scarlet Letter* again, found her place, read a sentence, read it again, then firmly closed the book and flung it across the room. She had zero concentration.

What if . . . she squeezed her eyes shut as if that would keep the thought from coming. It didn't. *What if what's happening to me is what happened to Mom?*

It wasn't a new thought. Rae had been wondering for a while if her mother ended up in the mental institution because she had a power like Rae's, a power she hadn't understood the way Rae did. Getting random thoughts all the time was enough to make anyone think they were crazy. Rae knew that from personal experience.

She tapped her leg. Still fine.

The thing was, until today she hadn't thought that maybe the way her mother died had been connected to the fingerprint ability, too. Did the power do something to the body? Was that why her mother's body had deteriorated so quickly? Rae's dad had told her the doctors never figured out exactly what caused the deterioration to start. And obviously they'd never figured out how to stop it.

A couple of brief numb spots don't equal deterioration, Rae told herself, tapping the spot on her arm that got numb at Anthony's house.

Maybe I should have used Tom as a motivator to make Anthony get his butt to practice tomorrow, Rae thought, remembering the fight Tom and Anthony had had yesterday. She looked over at her phone. She could call him. Give it another shot.

No, he'd been way too pissed off. If she could just make him see how much he'd really improved—Rae sighed. She guessed that was something he'd have to figure out for himself. Big, stubborn . . . Anthony.

Everything had gone wrong with him today. First the crash and burn of the football surprise. Then he'd freaked out when she accidentally touched his fingertips. They'd broken contact quickly, but she still got a rush of thoughts, fears, desires.

The longing to know his father had been so strong, and Rae had the feeling it was something Anthony carried around all the time. She wished there had been more about his dad, something that would help her track him down. But the only other father-related info she'd just gotten was a tiny piece of memory from when Anthony was really little, a toddler, probably.

Anthony was sitting on his dad's lap, and his dad was playing peekaboo with him. Each time he uncovered his face, his dad would give a different name. "Now I'm Joe Malone."

"Now I'm Andy Hall." "Now I'm Rick Ramos."

That was it. A sweet little memory. But nothing she could use.

The phone rang, interrupting her thoughts. Rae snatched it up eagerly. "Hello?"

"Hey, it's Yana."

Rae smiled, relieved to have an interlude of "normalcy." "Hey," she replied. "What's up?"

"Tomorrow we're going shopping," Yana announced in her typical blunt manner. "I'm picking you up at your school."

Rae pressed her lips together. "Actually, tomorrow's not that good for me," she said. She was planning to go over to Anthony's school and see if she could dig up *something* about his father.

"No. You don't understand," Yana said. "It's either that or you're going to have to kill me. I just had a huge blowout with my dad—again. If I don't have some kind of fun, soon, well, you might not even have to kill me. I'll probably just sponta-neously combust."

"Does it have to be right after school?" Rae asked, feeling a twinge of guilt. "Could we meet up at, like, five?" That would give her enough time to go by Fillmore.

"Nooo," Yana wailed. "Just whatever you're doing, let me go with you. If you're going to the dentist, I'll sit in the office and read magazines. I don't care. I just can't be by myself."

"Okay, fine. Pick me up," Rae answered. Having Yana there would make the errand more fun, anyway. "Do you want to tell me about the ugliness—"

"Damn it! I was doing my toenails, and I spilled the matte navy polish I just got all over the rug. I'll call you back." Yana hung up before Rae could answer.

Rae set down the phone, then pushed herself up from the bed. *I'll just read until Yana calls me back,* she thought as she walked over to the book. She leaned down to pick it up—and froze.

Someone was outside her window. She could hear them rustling around in the bushes. *This time I'm going to find out who you are,* Rae thought.

Staying low, she crept toward the window. The spot on her leg that had been numb started to prickle, but she ignored it. When she was close enough, she grabbed the windowsill, and staying in a crouch, peered out the window. She didn't see anything. But she could still hear the rustling sound.

Rae cautiously raised herself a couple of inches to get a better view. "Pemberly!" she exclaimed. It was just the neighbor's calico cat, stalking a bird. "God, you scared me," she said as she straightened up.

Rae didn't know which was worse—the fact that someone probably really was after her or the way it was turning her into a paranoid nutcase. A *real* nutcase this time.

Chapter 3

---

*S*omeone's chewing that grape gum again, Anthony thought. How was he supposed to think with that smell gagging him? He shifted in his seat. Whose idea was it to put a ridge down the middle of the chair? And it was way too hot in here. Having class in an aluminum trailer in a place that got as hot as Atlanta was moronic.

Face it, Fascinelli. If they held Bluebird English in the Waldorf-Astoria Hotel, where your butt was cradled by some four-thousand-dollar cushion and the AC was fully cranked, you wouldn't like it any better.

He glanced down at his reading book and found the sentence Brian Salerno was trying to hammer his way through. He wanted to be ready when Ms. Goyer called on him. And he knew she would. She kept giving him her special encouraging smiles.

Salerno finished the sentence. Goyer made some good-boy noises, and then—as Anthony predicted—she called on him. Suddenly he became aware of his shoelaces pressing down on his feet through his Payless sneakers, and his T-shirt felt like it now weighed about twenty pounds. He took a deep breath and pretended he was sitting in Rae's bedroom. No pressure. Just the two of them.

Okay. Okay. He put his finger under the first word of the sentence—and he could almost feel Rae tracing the word on his back. "A," he said. The image of Jesse flashed into his mind—"friend." He hesitated when he moved to the next word. It was one of those short ones, the ones he always felt like he should know, that anyone should know. *Just focus,* he told himself. "Of," he managed to get out a second later. Then the image of all the junk in his closet popped into his head—"mine," followed by the image of a chain saw—"saw." He could almost feel Rae's finger pressing on his skin through his T-shirt again—"a." He got a mental picture of Big Bird— "bird's," then a nest in a tree—"nest." And he was done with the sentence.

Anthony pulled in a deep breath and moved his finger to the first word of the next one. He got the picture of the clay sculpture he and Rae had made together—a little elephant holding on to the tail of a big elephant. "After." The word just popped out of his mouth. Instantly a new image appeared— the stick figure on a men's-room door—"he."

The bell rang. Every Bluebird in the room scrambled up. For the first time ever, Anthony wished the class had lasted just a little longer, long enough for him to finish the second sentence. He gave a snort as he pulled on his jacket. He was really losing it.

"Anthony," Ms. Goyer called as he started for the door. Okay, he'd wanted class to go on a minute longer, but that didn't mean he was hoping the teacher would ask him to stay. Reluctantly he turned around.

"Great job again today," she told him. "You're obviously doing some work at home."

"I got a tutor," he muttered.

Goyer smiled like it was the best news she'd ever heard. Which was kind of pathetic. Anthony smiled back at her—just to be decent.

"Good for you," she answered.

Anthony swung his backpack over his shoulder. He didn't know what he was supposed to say, so he gave a little half wave and hurried out the door. As he headed to the main building for math, a couple of pom-pom girls passed him, the plastic of the pom-poms making a whispering sound.

Wonder how it would feel to be out on the field and have girls like that cheering for me. The thought came into his head like a scene from a movie. Except in the movie, the girls all looked like Rae. And Anthony was in a Sanderson Prep football uniform.

He shook his head, trying to make the vision disappear, but it stayed with him. Maybe Rae was right. Maybe he actually did have a shot at making the Sanderson team.

If he wasn't too much of a wuss to show up at their practice after school.

"Anthony's a really private kind of guy," Rae told Yana as she drove out of the Sanderson parking lot on Friday afternoon. "So don't tell him you went on this little fact-finding mission with me, okay? *I'm* not planning to tell him anything at all unless I actually manage to track down his father."

"Got it," Yana answered. She pulled her collar-length bleached blond hair into a stubby ponytail with one hand and drove with the other. The way Yana drove, Rae thought it would be better if she had *three* hands to control the wheel, but she kept the thought to herself.

"How're things with your dad?" Rae asked instead.

"You wouldn't ask if you'd ever met him." Yana made a screeching left turn. "Just picture your father." She shot a glance at Rae. "You got it?"

"Uh-huh," Rae said.

"Now all you have to do is imagine the exact opposite, and you'll have mine," Yana explained.

"You mean he has all his hair?" Rae teased. Her dad could definitely use some Rogaine, not that it would ever occur to him.

"I mean my dad is dumb as dirt," Yana replied, without taking her eyes off the road. "I mean he'll throw a fit over anything. *Anything.* Like that there is hardened ketchup on the inside of the ketchup bottle."

"Wow. That—"

"Sucks," Yana interrupted. "Yeah, I know. But in two years I graduate, then I'm gone for good. No forwarding address."

Rae just nodded. It didn't take a genius to get the message that Yana was done talking about her dad. "We need to make a right at the corner," she reminded Yana, who immediately cut across two lanes of traffic, ignoring the blaring horns. Rae took a peek in the rearview mirror to see how close the car behind them had come to their bumper—and she saw a tan SUV making an equally fast lane change about half a block back. When Yana made the right, Rae kept her eyes on the rearview mirror. Her stomach turned inside out when she saw the SUV make the same turn a few seconds later.

"Um, everything okay over there?" Yana asked. "Is there some hot guy behind us or something?"

Rae quickly jerked her gaze from the mirror. "No," she said. She paused. "It's just—okay, I might be being totally paranoid, but there's an SUV that's kind of following us."

Yana laughed. "Following *us?*" she echoed. "Doubtful. Want me to try to lose it?" she joked.

"No!" Rae said quickly. "I'd rather live." *And if we took off too quickly, it would be pretty obvious that we knew we were being followed,* she added silently.

Rae continued sneaking quick glances in the rearview mirror as Yana drove. The SUV stayed a few cars away from them until they were about a block away from Anthony's school, then it made a left and disappeared. Rae let out a deep sigh.

"So, you're really serious, aren't you?" Yana asked.

Rae bit her lip. "Yeah, I am," she admitted. "Remember I told you someone was following me and Anthony when we were looking for Jesse? I think whoever it is knows where Anthony goes to school. Maybe it was them, and they turned because they figured out where we were going." Rae sighed again. "Or maybe the SUV wasn't following us at all. Who knows?"

Yana pulled into the parking lot of Anthony's school.

"Just to be sure, I want this friend of Anthony's, Dan, to check out your car," Rae said. "He's the one who found that bug in Anthony's mom's Hyundai."

"If it will make you happy," Yana answered as she pulled into a parking place.

"It definitely—" Rae began. Then she grabbed Yana by the arm. "Get down!" she ordered. Yana obediently slid as far down in her seat as she could while Rae struggled into a half crouch.

"What did you see?" Yana whispered.

"Anthony was heading this way. I don't want him to know we're here," Rae whispered back. Her neck was already cramping. An old VW Bug wasn't designed with hiding room. Silently she counted to ten. Then counted to ten again. "We should be okay now." Rae wiped the door handle with her sleeve and climbed out.

"Ginny, the girl I talked to on the yearbook committee, said she'd meet me outside the main doors," Rae told Yana. She shut the car door with her hip, then led the way across the parking lot.

"This isn't exactly a *Charlie's Angels*–type assignment, is it?" Yana complained. "I seriously doubt I'm going to get the chance to kick anyone in the head or even flash some cleavage."

"You never know the kind of danger you can find while

going through old yearbooks," Rae answered. There were two girls hanging out near the entrance. "Ginny?" Rae said to the closest one.

"No, that would be me," the other girl answered. She closed the book she'd been reading and smiled. "And you're Rae?"

Rae nodded. "I brought a friend along to help. This is Yana."

"Hey, nice to meet you," Ginny said. "All the old yearbooks are in the supply closet." She pushed open the nearest door. Rae noticed there were tiny wires running through the glass. Did that mean it was bulletproof?

"I keep telling the principal that they need to be stored someplace with better temperature control, but since half our classes are held in trailers out behind the baseball field, it's not exactly a priority," Ginny continued. She led them down the hall and around the corner, then pulled open the supply closet door and waved them inside. "All yours. Just don't take anything, or I *will* find you," she warned with a laugh, then left them alone.

"I really believe that girl would hunt us down," Yana said. "Clearly the yearbook is her life, and that's a sad, sad thing."

"I don't think Anthony's mom is over thirty-five, so—" Rae did some quick subtraction. "We should start with these." She grabbed three old yearbooks off the highest shelf and handed two to Yana. "Look for Fascinelli. I don't know Anthony's mother's maiden name."

Rae sat down on the floor and flipped open the top book in her pile. She'd wiped the wax off her fingers, but all she picked up was a bunch of static. There was too much dust on the books to get any clear thoughts. She flipped past all the club photos until she got to the individual pictures. Before she could turn to the Fs, Yana gave a little whoop of triumph.

"Got it in one," she announced. She turned her open yearbook to Rae and pointed to a picture of a guy who looked a lot like Anthony, except with longer hair. "Meet Tony Fascinelli—football team and possum club, whatever that was."

Rae grabbed the book and paged through until she found a big picture of the team. "There's our boy," she told Yana. "I'm going to write down the names of everyone else on the team. Some of these guys must still live in town. Maybe one of them will know where Anthony's dad ended up."

She pulled a notebook out of her tote, letting her old thoughts run through her without paying attention to them. She found a blank page and wrote the words *football team*.

Anthony's going to like that part, she thought happily. *He and his dad already have one thing in common.*

"You Fascinelli?" a stocky forty-something guy yelled. Sweats. Clipboard. Whistle around the neck. He had to be the coach.

"Yeah," Anthony called back, starting toward the coach. He wished he hadn't been spotted so fast. He'd still been trying to decide if he wanted to stay or go. But now that decision had been pretty much made for him.

"The locker room's through there," the coach said when Anthony reached him. "Ask one of the guys to show you the gear, then get back out here and let's see what you can do."

Anthony nodded and trotted toward the gym. What else could he do—except run in the opposite direction? He didn't allow himself a second of hesitation when he reached the metal door, just walked on through. *At least the locker room smells like a regular locker room,* he thought, breathing in the smell of sweat, sour tennis shoes, and moldy towels. He followed the sound of voices until he reached a row of lockers with someone standing in front of practically every one.

The locker room might smell normal, but the guys, there was just something different about them. *Money,* Anthony thought. *That's what it is.* Money for perfect teeth and top-of-the-line shoes. *Yeah, and probably private home gyms and steroids,* he added. These guys had clearly put in the hours building up their muscles.

"Did you want something? Or are you just window shopping?" a hulk of a guy at least a foot taller than Anthony asked.

Nice start, Fascinelli, he thought. *Guys always like it when you just stand there checking them out.*

"The coach sent me in," he answered, feeling like a little kid—"I'm supposed to be at the practice today."

"Oh, you're the guy," someone said from the next row of lockers.

"I'm supposed to get suited up," Anthony went on, feeling shorter by the second. A helmet came flying over the lockers and hit him on the side of the head. It was followed by a jock-strap, shoulder pads, knee pads, and a sanitary napkin.

So they look a little . . . polished up, Anthony thought. *They're just a bunch of idiots, like half the guys at my school. And it's going to be just as much fun to knock them down.* Anthony put the gear on over his sweats, making sure not to hurry, then he headed back out to the field.

"We're doing a scrimmage game," the coach announced as soon as everyone was on the field. "Usual teams. Fascinelli, you're with Salkow." He pointed to a blond *über*-prep. Anthony nodded.

"I'll hand off to you," Salkow said when Anthony joined the huddle.

Of course you will, Anthony thought. *That way every guy on the other side will get a shot at crunching me.* He adjusted his helmet. Well, they could bring it on.

He got into position. One of the guys hiked the ball to Salkow, and in seconds it was in Anthony's hands. He took off for the goalposts, and, just like he thought, every guy on the other team was gunning for him. No one was even attempting to block anyone else.

Fine. Anthony feinted right, then went left, managing to fake out a couple of the guys. He hip-checked the closest guy, who gave a satisfying grunt of pain, and looked for an opening. There wasn't one. He aimed himself at the biggest guy, since a lot of times big meant slow, and charged.

The guy moved in for a tackle. Anthony straight-armed him, one hand shoved against the guy's helmet. Then he gave a shove and spun to the left. Another guy was waiting—number 33. They all wanted a turn. Anthony let out a roar. He wasn't going around this one. He was going straight over.

Anthony hit 33 low. He staggered but remained upright. Anthony just kept on going, legs pumping as hard as they could. Number 33 was down.

But number 48 was ready to take his place. Anthony bobbed his head left. The guy bought the fake out. He went left, and Anthony went right. And the field opened up in front of him. A long, beautiful stretch of green.

Now see how the little guy can run, Anthony thought as he powered forward. He knew he'd never make it to the goal. He could already hear at least two guys moving up on him. But he was going to make them work for it.

Anthony gave it all he had, but his teammates had clearly decided to let him handle things on his own. Not even one of his guys was bothering to block for him.

He felt a shoulder hit his leg. Pain exploded in his thigh, but he kept running. Until a second guy hit him from the side. He went down hard. And at least three guys managed to land on top of him.

Through his ringing ears, he heard a whistle blow. The pressure on his back eased up as the guys climbed off him. Then a hand was thrust down in front of his face.

Anthony stood up without assistance. He found Salkow, the quarterback for his team, in front of him. Salkow grinned. "Not bad," he said. "Think you could do it again?"

"Not a problem," Anthony answered.

The movie started up in his head again. The one with all the preppy pom-pom girls cheering for him, one of the Sanderson Sabertooth running backs.

It's not impossible. At least, not quite, Anthony thought.

Chapter 4

"I just have to stop at home for one sec," Yana told Rae. "Then it's on to Al Schumacher's Big and Tall."

"Can you believe Al Schumacher was ever even in high school? Never mind friends with Anthony's dad," Rae said. "I mean, you've seen him in those commercials, right?"

"I have nightmares about those commercials," Yana answered. "Big Al's coming after me, trying to sell me a prom dress." She gave a snort. "As if I'd go to the prom."

"Oh, come on." Rae protested as Yana made a hard right, tires squealing. "I thought we agreed that the reason guys don't approach is because you give off a stay-away vibe."

"I didn't mean I wouldn't go to the prom because no one would ask—I mean I wouldn't go to the prom because it's the *prom,*" Yana answered. "That's your kind of deal, not mine."

Rae groaned. "Is this the start of another rant about prep school girls?"

"Nope," Yana answered. "No time. We're here." She pulled into the driveway of a green house and brought the Bug to a jerky stop. "Wait in the car. I'm just going to run in and right back out."

Before Rae could answer, Yana was slamming the door behind her and trotting up the front walk. *I've never been inside her house,* Rae realized. Although it wasn't that strange. It felt like she and Yana had been friends forever, but they'd only known each other about six months, and half that time Rae was in the hospital.

Yana's dad must be into gardening, Rae thought. There was a row of flowers running along both sides of the walkway. Somehow Rae couldn't picture Yana enjoying playing Martha Stewart.

The front door swung open, and Yana reappeared. She locked the door, then rushed back to the car and climbed inside. "I had to take out some meat to defrost," she explained.

"You cook?" Rae asked, surprised.

"Yeah. Someone has to. What, does your dad cook all the time?" Yana asked. She backed out of the driveway without checking the rearview mirror.

"We order in a lot," Rae admitted. "And Alice, she's the woman who cleans our house, she leaves stuff in the freezer for us."

"Ah. The woman who cleans your house," Yana repeated. She gave a laugh that didn't sound at all amused.

Very nice, Rae thought. *Shove it in Yana's face that you and your dad have more money.*

"So your dad likes gardening, huh?" Rae asked, wanting

badly to change the subject. "I was noticing the flowers."

"Oh, our gardener does that," Yana answered. She shot a fast look at Rae. "That would be me."

Rae tried not to register her surprise. Yana gardening? Somehow that really didn't fit.

"I wonder if Al Schumacher even remembers Anthony's dad," Rae said, attempting the subject-change maneuver again.

Yana shrugged. "We'll soon see." She took a left and pressed on the gas. A few moments later Rae spotted Al Schumacher's Big and Tall sign.

"I guarantee we have your size in stock. Double-G guarantee," Yana said, imitating Al in one of his commercials. She pulled into the strip mall and found a parking space outside Big and Tall. "You ready to do this, Nancy Drew?"

"Yep." Rae gave the door handle a quick polish with her sleeve, then jumped out of the car and led the way inside the store. Al Schumacher immediately descended on them.

"Girls, girls, girls, what can I do for you today?" he asked, the flesh of his double chin wiggling as he talked. "A present for dad? Or a boyfriend? I'm sure girls as pretty as you have boyfriends."

"Actually, we're here to talk to you," Rae told Al.

He let his eyes trail slowly from Rae's face down to her black Frye boots. She felt like turning around and running straight to the closest shower, but she smiled instead.

"I'm flattered," Al answered.

"You're delusional," Yana muttered.

Not helping, Rae thought when Al's eyes narrowed in annoyance. But she was glad Yana was there. It definitely reduced the creep-out factor a little.

"I was looking at an old Fillmore High yearbook today, and I saw the football team photo," Rae said. "I recognized you right away from your commercials. And I thought maybe you could tell me where Tony Fascinelli ended up."

"Fascinelli? Well, there's a name I haven't heard in a while." Al shook his head, leaning back against the wall. "Last I heard, he was living in Selma," he continued. "But I'm a lot more fun than Tony." He started to give Rae the look again.

"Okay, thanks," Rae said, ignoring his last comment. She stuck out her hand and gave his a hard pump, then slid her fingers back, matching her fingertips to his. The first thing she got was a semipornographic thought about her. Then an ache in her knee that she knew was from an old football injury of Al's. A shot of regret that he'd never told his mother he loved her before she died. And the thought that Tony Fascinelli was a first-degree SOB.

Rae released Al's hand and stepped away. "Well, that's all I needed. I don't want to waste any more of your time." She grabbed Yana by the arm and tugged her out the door, even though Al was still talking.

"Guys like that make me wish I was like those fembots in *Austin Powers,*" Yana said as they hurried over to the car. "I would have loved to shoot bullets out of my boobs right when our friend Al was taking a look."

Rae laughed as she gave the door handle a quick rub. She climbed into the passenger seat. "There'd be dead guys lying all over the place," she said when Yana slid behind the wheel.

"Fine by me." Yana gave a tight smile. "So when are we going to Selma?"

Rae loved that *we*.

"Monday after group—if I can find an address for a Tony Fascinelli there," she answered.

Yana nodded and cranked the radio. She punched the channel buttons until she found some good classic rock. Rae let the music thrum through her body until the feeling of having been slimed by Al washed away.

"You want to stay and have dinner?" Rae asked as Yana pulled onto Rae's street.

"Can't. I'm cooking, remember?" Yana said. She came to a stop in front of Rae's driveway.

"I know you hate to be thanked—but thanks," Rae told her as she scrambled out of the car.

"Later," Yana replied, then she was burning rubber.

Rae shook her head as she watched the little yellow car disappear. As she headed inside, she reminded herself to make sure Anthony's friend got Yana's VW checked out for bugs ASAP.

"Dad, I'm home," she called out. Her father popped out of his office a second later, a big grin on his face. "What?" Rae asked.

"You've got a secret admirer," he told her. "There was a

package waiting for you on the front porch when I got home. It's on your dresser."

A lump formed in Rae's throat. What if it was from whoever left that picture in her locker at school? Now they were leaving things at her *house,* too? Rae rushed down the hall and burst into her room, stopping to stare at the object waiting on her dresser, the perfectly folded violet paper covering the small box.

Just pick it up, she ordered herself. Why was she so sure it was from the same person who left the picture? Maybe it was even from Marcus. She shook her head, then strode over and took the box in her hands.

/things are getting back/Rae will be/those papers are/

All the thought echoes she got were from her dad. She did a more thorough search, lightly running her fingers over every inch of the paper. The three dad thought fragments were all she picked up.

A cold chill traced the ladder of her spine, and she felt her skin break out in gooseflesh. There should be other fingerprints on that package unless . . .

Unless someone didn't want their identity revealed.

Whoever sent this knows the truth about me, Rae realized. And that meant it probably *was* the same person who'd left that gruesome photograph in her locker. She took in a long breath, then pulled off the four pieces of tape and let the violet paper flutter to the floor. Slowly, carefully, she pulled the top off the plain white box.

It was halfway full of gray powder. Rae tilted the box a

little and used her fingers to brush the powder over to one side. Underneath was a photo of a woman, the same woman who had been in the picture Rae had found in her locker. The words *ashes to ashes* were written across the woman's face in black pen.

"Ashes to ashes," Rae whispered, her pulse racing. She shook the box, staring at the powder. Could it be? She spotted a sliver of something white and carefully fished it out.

Her stomach dropped as she realized she was holding a tiny piece of bone.

"Yo, Anthony." Anthony turned around just as he was about to go into the Oakvale Institute on Monday afternoon.

"Hey," he said as Jesse Beven caught up to him. It was good to see Jesse running around. For a while there he'd doubted he'd ever see Jesse again.

"I've been trying to come up with our next step," Jesse announced. "You know, to find the guy who snatched me, the one who's after Rae."

"I don't think there is one. Not right now, anyway," Anthony told him, even though he hated to say the words out loud. "Frank hasn't been back home since he grabbed you. If he hasn't left town, he's an idiot. I'm sure his girlfriend told him Rae and I came around looking for him when you were missing." Anthony ran his hands through his hair. "Besides, the guy we really want is whoever hired Frank."

"It has to be the same guy who hired David to plant the pipe bomb and off Rae," Jesse answered.

Anthony nodded. "And what do we know about that guy? A whole lot of nothing," he reminded Jesse. "Rae touched everything in David's room and said even David didn't know anything about the guy."

"So we just stand around waiting until something happens again?" Jesse demanded. He sounded pissed. But he couldn't be as pissed as Anthony felt.

"For now," Anthony answered. He checked his watch. "Group's about to start." He reached for the door handle. Jesse grabbed his shoulder.

"Wait. I've got to tell you something. Out here," Jesse said. He glanced over his shoulder, then returned his gaze to Anthony. "You know Sean McGee, that friend of Nunan's?" He rushed on without leaving a space for Anthony to answer. "Well, he got ahold of a bunch of security codes. For houses. He's—" Jesse checked over his shoulder again. "He's looking for a couple of guys to help him clean the places out. I was thinking we—"

"I'll kick your ass if you even talk to McGee," Anthony told him, his voice coming out rougher than he meant it to.

Jesse's chin came up. "What? You afraid? You think it might hurt your chances of getting into that snotty prep school?"

Anthony felt like he'd been sucker punched. "How the hell did you—"

"Nunan was over there making a delivery. He saw you at football practice," Jesse answered. "I thought you hated those prep school—"

"This has nothing to do with prep school," Anthony

interrupted. "I've been trying to get my crap together since school started. Have you seen me anywhere near weed?"

Jesse shook his head.

"That's why," Anthony answered. "It took me a while, but it finally sank in that if I wanted to get out of school, I had to get my head out of my butt."

"Sean's paying—" Jesse started to protest.

"Money's not going to do much good if you're locked away in juvie," Anthony told him. He wanted to shake Jesse, but that would be acting way too much like Jesse's old man. "You're smarter than me, Jesse," he continued. "Just put in the time, then you can graduate and get a real job that pays decent money." He locked eyes with Jesse. "I want you to promise me you won't go in on this house deal."

Jesse hesitated. Anthony waited. "Okay," Jesse finally muttered.

"Okay." Anthony shoved open the door. "We have about a minute to make it to group on time."

"Race you," Jesse said, taking off down the hall. Anthony took off after him. Jesse gave a triumphant smile as he headed into the room.

"I let you win," Anthony muttered as they took seats in the cold metal chairs. Automatically he searched the room for Rae. She wasn't there, but a moment later she rushed into the room and took the only empty chair. Which happened to be directly across from Anthony.

Did her skirt have to be so short? Because it made him think about things he shouldn't be thinking. At least things that he shouldn't think about Rae. She was Miss Prep School, and he—

And he might end up at that same prep school with her. The realization made Anthony's brain itch. If they were both at Sanderson, would it be so weird if—

He refused to let himself finish the thought. No matter where he went to school, he was still going to be a Bluebird. And Rae was still going to be a Cardinal. End of story.

The second Ms. Abramson announced their group session was over, Rae stood up, smoothing her pleated skirt. She couldn't wait to get out of there so she and Yana could continue their search.

"Hey." Rae turned and saw Anthony standing beside her. "I had Dan check out Yana's car on Saturday," he told her, his voice low. "You were right. He found something. He stuck it on somebody else's car, but that's—"

"Only a temporary solution," Rae finished for him.

"Yeah." Anthony shifted his weight from one foot to the other. "So, there's something else I wanted to tell you. I ended up going to that practice Friday."

"You did?" Rae yelped. She grabbed him and gave him a fast hug before she could think about it, his muscles hard and tight under her arms. "That's so great," she said.

"Don't get too excited," Anthony warned her. "There's still those academic tests I have to pass. I thought maybe when you tutor me tonight, we could—"

"Oh God," Rae exclaimed. "I'm sorry. I completely

spaced. I promised Yana I'd—"

"No problem," Anthony cut in. He started to turn away. Rae grabbed him by the sleeve and pulled him back to face her.

"Don't get all testy," she told him. "How about after we do my swimming thing tomorrow—if you still want to do it—"

"We're doing it," Anthony interrupted.

"Okay, so after that, we can do a marathon tutoring session. And tonight you should make some clay models on your own for words you still need visuals on. I might have the list with me." Rae opened her purse, ignoring the fuzzy old thoughts she picked up.

"I don't need the list," Anthony told her. "I know what I always screw up on."

Rae didn't bother to chide him for saying he screwed up. He never listened. "So, I'll see you at the Y tomorrow."

Anthony grunted something, and Rae hurried out to the parking lot. Yana was already waiting, the motor in her Bug running. Rae ran over and climbed in after doing a door handle polish.

"I brought us a map." Rae gingerly buckled her seat belt, using minimal finger-to-metal contact. "I already found the street."

"Lucky Tony Fascinelli was listed," Yana said as she pulled out of the parking lot at her usual Indy 500 speed.

"Actually he wasn't," Rae answered. "But Anthony told me about this game that he and his dad used to play," she lied. "His dad would call himself all these different names. One of them was Andy Hall. When I did a search online, I found an Andy Hall in Selma."

"Kind of a long shot, isn't it?" Yana asked.

"Yeah. But I really want to do this for Anthony," Rae answered.

"Are you sure Anthony even wants to find his father?" Yana asked. "If it was me and my dad was MIA, I'd be dancing with joy."

"I've talked to Anthony about it," Rae answered. "Not about me looking for Tony," she explained. "But about Anthony wanting to know him. He's always wondered if he's like his dad, since he's nothing like his mom."

Yana shrugged. "There's a snack food bag in the backseat. Get me one of those Sno Balls, okay? It's not a road trip without Sno Balls." She turned on the radio as Rae rooted through the bag, easily spotted the bright pink coconut of the Sno Balls, and handed a package of them to Yana. She chose a bag of jalapeño chips for herself and became hypnotized by the white lines of the freeway flying past.

She was almost sorry when, a while later, they took the Selma exit, but she sat up, unfolded the map—

/*Anthony's going to*/ pumping gas sucks/
and found the circle she'd made that pinpointed Tony Fascinelli's house. At least what she hoped was Tony Fascinelli's house.

Yana got them there in less than fifteen minutes. "Now what?" she asked Rae.

Rae unbuckled her seat belt. "Now we go see if Andy Hall

has a son named Anthony," she answered. She pulled her sleeve over her fingers and climbed out of the car. "Here goes nothing," she muttered as she headed up to the front door, Yana right behind her, and gave a hard double knock.

The door swung open a moment later. *Yeah, this is the place,* Rae thought as she looked up at the guy standing in front of her. There was no doubt he was Anthony's half brother. She hadn't even thought that Anthony's dad might have another family, but why wouldn't he?

"Hi," she said, realizing she'd been staring at the young Anthony like an idiot. "I was wondering if I could talk to your father for a minute."

Young Anthony gave a bark of laughter. "If you want to talk to my dad, you're in the wrong place. He's in Scott State."

"Scott State," Rae repeated. The name sounded sort of familiar, but—

"As in Scott State Prison."

$\mathscr{C}hapter\ 5$

"Can I have the number for Scott State Prison?" Rae said into her cell phone after dialing information. She glanced around the quad to make sure no one was close enough to overhear her. Her reputation wasn't ready for speculation on who she was calling in prison. But the quad was still mostly empty. Most people at Sanderson ate in the cafeteria.

An actual person told Rae to hold for the number, then the automated voice recited it. Rae pressed one to have the number dialed for her. She was too impatient to wait.

Rae got the prison's automated answering system, and pressed three to get information on visiting hours. She'd spent half the night trying to figure out if she should tell Anthony what she'd discovered about his dad. Finally she'd decided that she had to see Anthony's father first and find out what the deal was—what he was in prison for, what his attitude was toward Anthony—before she made up her mind whether to tell Anthony the truth or try to forget everything she'd learned.

"Good," Rae muttered when the recording told her there

were visiting hours that afternoon and evening. She went back to the main menu and pressed five to get directions to Scott State by bus. It wasn't too far outside Atlanta, so she should be able to round-trip it and get home early enough to make her dad happy.

Rae hung up the cell, a little of the wax on her fingers crumbling away. She considered wiping all of it off. With everything that had been going on, it was smart to be on guard. *I'll leave it until after school, at least,* she decided. She needed a break from the constant murmur of thoughts that weren't her own.

She turned around, took two steps toward the main building, then pulled out her phone again, pretending she needed to make another call. Mr. Jesperson, her English teacher, had the entrance staked out. One look at him and Rae knew he wanted to have one of their little talks. The guy was obsessed with helping her through her "tough time." Maybe it was a new-teacher thing. Whatever it was, Rae wasn't interested. Group sessions at Oakvale three times a week was more than enough *talking.*

I'll give him a few minutes, then if he's still standing there, I'll just rush by him and say I have to pee or something, Rae thought. She tilted her wrist and waited while the second hand made a full circle and started another.

"Rae," a voice called from the direction of Mr. Jesperson. Rae rolled her eyes, reluctantly turned toward the voice— and saw Marcus Salkow jogging toward her. *Much better than*

Jesperson, Rae thought, suddenly feeling nervous.

"I'm heading over to Sliders," Marcus said as he stopped in front of her. "I've been thinking about those little burgers they have all morning. Do you want to come? I know you love those veggie ones with the pickles."

"Um . . ." Was he going to try to talk about getting back together again? Because she really wasn't ready for that. She—

"Come on, Rae. You'll have to be with me for less than an hour. And you'll get veggie burgers," Marcus coaxed.

Rae glanced at the school. Jesperson was still waiting. "Okay, sure, why not?"

Marcus grinned, and deep lines appeared in his cheeks, long dimples, that's what Rae called them. "The Range Rover's in the parking lot." He took a step in that direction, then hesitated and looked at Rae like she might have already changed her mind.

"Hurry it up. I'm starving," she told him.

"Me, too. I'm going to get a dozen of the little guys," Marcus said as they headed to the parking lot. "That's probably what—a triple-decker Big Mac? Two Whoppers?"

"Mmmm. Maybe even more," Rae answered.

They managed to talk about little versus big burgers until they'd reached Sliders, gotten their food, and found a table. Rae was glad they had. It was a ridiculous conversation, yeah, but it wasn't awkward silence. And it wasn't a heart-wrenching discussion about how Marcus wanted her back and how Rae was uncertain—and *scared*—to ever trust him again.

"Gooood," Marcus groaned as he ate half of his first miniburger in one bite.

Rae laughed. "You sound like Frankenstein," she told him.

"Gooood," Marcus repeated, going into an all-out Frankenstein impression. He tilted his head toward the side and stared at Rae. "Preeeety," he said, drawing out the word.

The busboy cleaning the table next to them gave Marcus a you're-losing-it look, but Marcus didn't seem to notice. He kept going with his Frankenstein routine. "Rae frrriennnd."

Rae laughed again—she couldn't help herself—and it felt like half the tension and anxiety built up in her body escaped with the sound.

"Frrr—iennnd?" Marcus repeated, his green eyes intense. Rae realized he was asking her a real question.

Should she trust him? If she let him back into her life even a tiny bit, would she end up a walking pile of pain?

Marcus stuffed the other half of his miniburger into his mouth. "Frrr—iennnd?" he asked again, more insistently, letting pieces of burger fall back onto his tray.

It was disgusting. And Rae laughed until she snorted. This was how it used to be with Marcus—he'd always been able to crack her up, especially when they were alone together.

Marcus isn't Jeff, she told herself. *You have no reason to think he just wants to get into your pants because he thinks that you're a pathetic crazy girl and easy.*

Marcus pounded on the table with both fists. "Frrr-ieeennnnnnd?" he howled, getting the attention of everyone in the place.

Rae didn't want to go back into a boyfriend-girlfriend thing with Marcus. She wasn't at all ready for that. But—she looked at him, and for a second it was as if she'd stepped back in time, back into the skin of her old self. It felt good.

She picked up her veggie burger and crammed the whole thing in her mouth. "Frrr-ieeennnnnnd," she groaned back at Marcus. Bits of bread and a chunk of burger sprang out. People were staring, but for the first time in months, Rae didn't care.

Anthony absentmindedly rubbed the bruise on his thigh. It had gone from black to the yellow-green stage. *I bet some of the Sabertooth guys are nursing a few bruises themselves,* he thought. He'd definitely given his all during the scrimmage. He tried not to let himself feel too psyched about that. It didn't change the fact that he still had to face the academic tests.

He glanced at the clock positioned over the diving board of the Y pool. He'd been a few minutes early. But now Rae was a few minutes late. If she wimped out—Anthony shook his head. Rae just wasn't the kind of girl who wimped. No matter how scared she was last time, he knew she'd get back in the pool, pretending it was nothing.

When she gets here, keep your eyes on her face, he reminded himself. *Don't let them go wandering all over the bathing suit. And avoid the hair.* For some reason Rae's hair made his imagination X-rated, and he was always fighting off the urge to touch it and see if it was as soft as it looked.

Out of the corner of his eye he caught the motion of the girls'-locker-room door swinging open. He turned toward the door to see Rae coming out. But she was still in her regular clothes. "What's going on?" Anthony asked as she rushed over to him.

"Sorry, sorry," Rae said breathlessly. "My dad is having this cocktail-party thing at our house tonight. I told him I'd help out, so I—I can't do the swimming today."

"A cocktail party," Anthony repeated. That didn't sound like a last minute kind of deal.

"Yeah, for the people in his department," Rae answered. Her eyes skittered around his face, never quite meeting his gaze. *She's lying,* Anthony thought. But he still didn't think she'd wimp on the swimming, so something else had to be going on.

"What time will it be over?" Anthony asked.

Rae bunched her hair into a ponytail with her hand, then immediately let go, her hair spilling back over her shoulders. "Pretty late, probably," she answered. "I've really got to go. I need to, uh, help with hors d'œuvres."

She didn't wait for him to answer. She just gave a little wave and disappeared into the locker room. Anthony's gut was telling him that something was wrong, and his gut was usually dead-on.

Rae's stomach started doing origami when the bus pulled up at the Scott State stop. Was she insane for doing this?

It's too late to be thinking about that now, she told herself as she stepped into the aisle. A lot of other people were getting off at the stop, too.

See? It's just a normal thing. A thing people do. she thought. But her stomach upped the speed of the origami production as she stepped off the bus. She followed the little clusters of people moving toward the prison. A straggling line formed in front of a security station.

As she waited her turn to check in, Rae pulled a tissue out of her purse and wiped the Mush off her fingers, noting that the numb spot on her right index finger was only the size of a pinprick now.

"Um, I don't have to say why I'm visiting or anything, do I?" Rae asked the woman behind her as the line moved forward a few feet.

"None of their business," the woman answered. She shifted the toddler she carried to her right hip. "All they want to know is who you're here to see. Then they check your bag and ID, and that's it—you're cleared to go into the waiting room."

"Thanks," Rae murmured. The line moved forward again—and Rae was one person away from the guard taking names. How did that happen? This was going too fast. She wasn't ready, hadn't even figured out what to say to Anthony's dad. She'd had the whole bus ride to figure it out, but nothing sounded right to her.

"Name?" the guard asked. Rae stepped up in front of him. "Rae Voight. I'm here to see Tony Fascinelli." The guard

419

gestured for her purse, and Rae handed it over. *I'm sure the guy's seen tampons before,* she told herself, but her face got hot when she saw the guy push one of them aside so he could look deeper into her purse.

"You're good. Go on in," the guard said after a quick look at her student ID. He handed the purse back to Rae, and she followed the couple who'd been ahead of her into a low building. It smelled like industrial cleaner, just like the hospital, just like the institute. Rae pulled a little bottle of Clinique Happy moisturizer out of her purse and worked some into her neck, hoping its fresh scent would block out the cleaner, but instead it mixed with it, making the smell all the more disgusting.

Rae sat down in one of the molded plastic chairs, breathing only through her mouth. A moment later the woman with the toddler sat down beside her. "You want a magazine?" she asked. "It's going to be a while before they start calling people in."

"No, thanks," Rae answered. She really needed to figure out what to say to Mr. Fascinelli. What she wanted to ask—or yell—was, "Why haven't you seen your son in so many years?" But she knew that wasn't the way to go.

So what is the right way? she considered. But her brain kept going dead when she tried to come up with the answer.

A different guard stepped into the waiting room and started calling out names. Rae's muscles tensed when she heard hers. *This is what you came here for,* she reminded

420

herself. *You'll just have to wing it.*

Rae got in yet another line—this one to go through a metal detector. "Table four," the guard manning the detector told her as she stepped through. Rae nodded and stepped through the door to the visitation room. The first thing she saw was a man and a woman practically doing it, their bodies pressed together in the tiny sliver of space between the water cooler and the wall. Whoa. That couldn't be allowed, could it? She glanced over at the two guards strolling between the rows of tables. They didn't appear to have noticed.

Rae scanned the room, looking for table four. She saw Tony Fascinelli before she saw the number. Just like Anthony's half brother in Selma, Tony looked way too much like Anthony not to be related. His hair was shorter—a crew cut—and darker and he was more beefy than muscley. But he was definitely Anthony's dad.

Rae slowly approached him, her throat getting drier with every step. "Mr. Fascinelli?" she managed to squeak out when she reached the table.

"Yeah, that's me," he answered. His voice even sounded sort of like Anthony's. "You got money for the vending machines?"

"Uh, I think so," Rae answered, startled. She started digging through her purse, pulling out every coin she could find and making a little pile on the table.

"It takes singles, too," Mr. Fascinelli told her. He stood there, his eyes unblinking as he stared at her.

"Oh. Okay." Rae pulled out her wallet and plopped the four singles she found next to the change.

Mr. Fascinelli scooped up the money. "Okay, when I get back, I'll give you twenty minutes to read me the Bible or witness to me. Whatever gets your little teenage Christian self going."

He was striding toward the vending machine before Rae could answer. She slowly sat down and rested her hands flat on the table.

*/ He looks so / shouldn't have come / **OH GOD** / want to be /*

The thoughts came through fuzzy. The emotions—the anger, the sadness, the hopelessness, the happiness—came through fuzzy, too. So many fingerprints on the table. So many people going through so much. How many of them—

Mr. Fascinelli, loaded down with vending machine snacks, sat back down in front of Rae, pulling her away from her thoughts. "Go for it. You're on the clock."

Rae clasped her hands, not wanting to be distracted by any thoughts but her own. "Okay, first, I'm not from a religious group."

"Then who are you?" Mr. Fascinelli asked, his fingers frozen on the soda can he'd been about to open.

"I'm a friend of your son's," Rae answered. "Anthony," she added quickly, remembering Mr. Fascinelli had at least one other son.

Mr. Fascinelli jerked to his feet. "I'm ready to go back in," he called to the closest guard.

Rae stood up, too. "I just want to talk to you for a minute," she pleaded. "Anthony's been wanting to find you for a long—"

"Don't bring him here. If you do, I won't see him," Mr. Fascinelli interrupted. He scooped up the bags of chips and nuts and the cans of soda as the guard stepped up to the table.

"You sure you're ready—" the guard began.

"Get me away from her," Mr. Fascinelli answered.

$\mathcal{C}$hapter 6

$\int$ o I called your house last night. You weren't there. And I didn't hear any kind of cocktail party going on.

That's exactly what Anthony was going to say to Rae. If he didn't just grab her and scream, "Why the hell are you lying to me?" Not that he was going to be able to do either if she didn't get her butt to group. The session was supposed to start in less than five minutes, and Rae was still a no-show.

Anthony leaned against the front wall of the institute. *Has something happened to her?* he wondered. *Has* whatever *it is she's been hiding gotten out of control?*

Hadn't the girl figured out how dangerous it was to try to handle a bad situation with no backup?

"Anthony," a voice called. He whipped his head toward the sound and saw Ms. Abramson, the group leader, heading toward him. "Come on. Time to get inside," she told him. He pushed himself away from the wall and followed her into the building. What else could he do? When they reached the therapy room, he took a seat in the metal chairs in the circle like a good boy, nodded to Jesse, then locked his eyes on the door. *Come on, Rae,* he thought.

As if he had willed it, the door swung open and Rae hurried inside. She had on another one of her short skirts, short but classy somehow—with two little zippered pockets. She slid into the closest chair, and Anthony realized she looked terrible—sweaty and gray faced. All Anthony wanted to do was rush over to her and just . . . he wasn't even sure what he wanted to do. Accuse her of lying. Put his arm around her. Ask her if she was all right. Call her an idiot.

"Okay, gang, time to start," Abramson announced. Which meant for now, Anthony wasn't going to do anything at all.

"Let's begin by going around the circle and hearing updates," Abramson continued. "Matt, why don't you go first this time?"

Anthony reluctantly turned his gaze toward Matt, and only half listened as Abramson pried out a response from him one word at a time. The other half of his head was totally occupied by Rae. He cut a quick glance at her. She was blotting the sweat off her forehead with a Kleenex, but it wasn't helping. New droplets kept popping up. She looked like any second she could puke.

"Ms. Abramson," Rae called out, interrupting one of Matt's long silences. "I'm not feeling well. My dad's in the parking lot. Can I—?"

"Of course. Go on," Abramson answered, making little shoo-shoo motions with her hands. "Give me a call if there is anything you want to talk about before our next group."

"Thanks," Rae mumbled. Then she stood up and rushed out of the room.

She's lying again, Anthony thought. She looked sick, but there was something . . . off. Something false.

"I just, uh, want to make sure she gets to the car okay. She looked kind of shaky." Anthony didn't wait for Abramson to reply. He just strode out of the room, slowing down when he hit the hallway. All he wanted to do was make sure she actually ended up in her father's car. There was no reason Rae had to see him checking up on her.

When he reached the main doors, he gave a five count, then pushed them open. With three long steps he was in a position that allowed him to see the entire parking lot—including Rae climbing into Yana's car.

He'd known something was going on. If he'd thought it was some girlie thing—like a covert trip to the mall—then hey, no problem. But Rae'd lied to him. She'd forgotten about two of their tutoring sessions. She'd cut out on a swimming lesson.

Anthony knew whatever was going on with her was big. And he was going to find out what it was before the day was out.

"Did you actually buy this stuff so you could play sick?" Rae asked as she wiped the foundation off her face.

Yana laughed. "No. The first time I put it on, I realized it made my face look gray. I was going to return it, but I was too lazy. Then I realized it could actually be useful."

"And dabbing your face with a damp tissue—sheer brilliance," Rae said.

Yana pulled onto the freeway entrance ramp and pressed down on the accelerator. "Yeah, I should write a book, huh? *How to Fake Your Way Out of Anything.*"

"Into or out of," Rae added. "That is, if you really do get me as close to Tony Fascinelli as you say you can."

"You never should have tried to see him without me," Yana told her. "When are you going to realize that you need me for these little missions?"

Yana smiled, but her smile looked a little tight. *I think I actually hurt her feelings*, Rae realized. Yana always acted like she didn't care about anything. But clearly at least a little part of her attitude was forced.

"You're right," Rae answered. "I wasted a trip because I didn't bring you in right away. I just thought Anthony wouldn't want—"

"And I'm going to say something to him?" Yana demanded.

"No. Of course not. No," Rae said quickly.

Yana nodded, then punched on the radio. Rae was glad to have the music fill the car. It made it almost impossible to talk, and even though she was dying to ask Yana exactly how she planned to get them into Scott State, the mood Yana was in told her it was better just to wait and see.

Rae kept her mouth closed when they pulled in the Scott State parking lot. She didn't ask one question as they headed over to the security booth.

"We have an appointment to see the warden. Yana Savari

and Rae Voight," Yana told the guard.

An appointment? Rae wondered. This would be interesting.

The guard spoke into his walkie-talkie, and a few minutes later another guard appeared. "I'm Jon Powning," the new guard said. "You can call me Jon. I'll take you inside." He had a nice face—long dimples like Marcus's and hazel eyes that seemed to say, I'm a friendly guy. Rae told herself she shouldn't be surprised. She had to get over her prejudice that everyone who worked in a prison was some kind of monster.

All Rae's rational thinking didn't stop her knees from shaking as the guard led her and Yana inside the prison, through the metal detector, past the drug-sniffing dogs, then into an elevator and up to the warden's office. It was like the prison itself was sending waves of fear directly into her bones.

Rae rubbed her hands together, her fingertips feeling vulnerable without their coat of Mush. The last thing she wanted to do was touch anything in here, but she knew she was going to have to if Yana managed to get her close enough to Tony Fascinelli for Rae to take another shot at him.

Jon pressed down the intercom button. "Powning here. I have the girls," he said. He released the button, and a second later there was a long buzz and the click of the lock releasing. Jon shoved open the door and gestured the girls in ahead of him.

"Just one second," the man behind the desk said. He held up one finger and did hunt-and-peck on his computer keyboard with a finger on his other hand, then looked up and smiled at Yana. "Welcome back. I've got everything set up for you." He turned toward Rae and stuck out his hand. She shook it, managing to avoid fingertip-to-fingertip contact.

"I'm Jason Driver, the warden," he told Rae. "You're pretty much guaranteed an A on your paper, thanks to your persuasive friend here." He winked at Yana. Yana winked right back. "After we're through with you, you're going to know exactly what it feels like to be a prisoner at Scott State," the warden continued.

Rae wrapped her arms around herself, hoping the little shiver that had skittered through her at his words hadn't been visible to anyone. "Great," she answered. "That sounds great."

"Yeah," Yana added. "I told the warden that you and I had already toured a women's prison but that we wanted to do a compare and contrast with a men's prison."

"Great," Rae repeated.

"Our tour is going to be a little different," the warden told them. "We want you to see the place through the eyes of a prisoner. So the first step is to get you into your prison clothes."

Anthony stared at the prison through the windshield of the Hyundai. What could Rae and Yana possibly be doing in there? It didn't even seem to be visiting hours—at least, Anthony hadn't seen anyone else going in.

He twisted in his seat, trying to get more comfortable, but

his muscles were too tight. *There could be a completely normal reason for them to be here,* he told himself. Except if the reason was so normal, why had Rae been sneaking around?

Anthony glanced over at Yana's beat-up yellow Bug. It was parked in the row ahead of him, in plain sight. Rae wasn't going to get out of the lot without an explanation.

How long have I been in here? Rae wondered, her heart beating so fast, it felt like a flutter in her chest.

It can't have been even half an hour, she told herself. *Jon the guard is having a cigarette. In a minute he's going to come and let you out.*

Rae pulled her knees tighter to her chest and tried to scoot even farther away from the open toilet. It was pointless. Her solitary cell was so tiny that no matter where she moved, she was way too close. Jon had told her and Yana that the toilets in the hole were flushed automatically by the guards every few hours. It smelled more like it was every few weeks. But maybe some of that smell came from the other prisoners. Part of the punishment for the men kept in the isolation area was no personal hygiene. No showers— not even splashing birdbaths in a sink—no toothbrush, no deodorant, no hairbrush. Just you. Your little patch of cement. And the toilet.

"It has to have been at least five minutes," Rae whispered. It felt like hours, but time didn't work the same way when you were sitting alone in the dark. That was why she needed her watch, which Jon had taken away from her. So she wouldn't be able to see that time was actually passing. So she couldn't be sure she wasn't going to die down here.

Her fluttering heart picked up speed, and she felt a hot spot form at the back of her neck and slowly move up her skull. *Okay, okay. You're just having some kind of panic attack,* Rae thought. *Just hang on. Jon will be here soon.*

The heat moved up inch by inch, passing over the top of her head, then starting down her face. Her heart felt like it was trying to pull free from her chest.

"I can't . . ." Rae wheezed out. She took as deep a breath as she could, ignoring the stench, then she screamed.

A shrill voice screamed back at her. "Yelling won't help, baby girl," a man added, his voice low and rough, as if he hadn't used it in a long time.

Rae hadn't realized that anyone was close enough to hear her—anyone but the guards monitoring the hole from somewhere where there was light and clean air. The knowledge calmed her down a tiny bit. "Yana, can you hear me?" she called.

"Yana, can you hear me?" someone echoed in a mocking singsong. There was no response from Yana.

"I'll be your friend," a voice whispered. The leering tone was like a hand running down her body. "I'll be your good, good friend."

"Put me down for seconds," somebody else chimed in.

Rae's panic turned to anger, her heart slowing to a hard,

steady beat. What scum these guys were. But she'd be walking out of here today, going home. And they'd still be sitting here.

God, what did you have to do to be sent to the hole? Had Anthony's father ever—

The door clicked, then slid open. "You're out of there, Voight," Jon told her. "On your feet."

Rae leaped up and bolted out of the cell. Yana stood next to Jon. It was all Rae could do not to grab her and hug her. She would have except she didn't want to give the scum an extra thrill.

Jon led the way out of solitary and back into one of the long, puke-green hallways. "You two were in the hole for twenty minutes. Try to imagine how it would feel to be in there for a couple of days."

Rae's stomach turned over.

"I'd have one sore butt," Yana answered. She sounded actually . . . cheerful. Rae shot her a glance. Yana didn't seem like she was putting on an act. She looked like they were on a school field trip to a bakery or a paint factory.

"The men call it elephant hide," Jon answered as they walked down the hall. "Spend a lot of time in the hole and you get patches of thick skin. Like giant calluses." He paused next to a set of double doors. "The showers are in there. Open room. Guards watching. I can't take you inside, obviously."

Thank God, Rae thought.

"And the worst thing—no hair conditioner." Jon winked

at Yana. "Unless the family sends money. Guys that don't get any money from the outside have to really stretch what we give them. And we don't give them much—toothpaste, soap, the basics. You always hear taxpayers complain about paying for prisoners to sit around pumping weights and watching TV, but the families end up picking up a lot of the cost."

They reached the end of the hallway, where there was another set of double doors. "Okay, now I'm going to take you out in the yard. The inmates who have behaved themselves get to come out here for a little air and exercise. There are plenty of guards on duty, but I want you two to stick close to me," Jon told them. He signaled toward the security camera mounted in the corner, and a moment later the door lock clicked open.

Jon ushered them outside, and Rae pulled in a deep breath of the clean, sun-warmed air. So good. She wished she could stand there and just breathe until she felt purified. But she was on a mission. Rae scanned the yard, looking for Anthony's father. It was a long shot that he'd be out here at the same time she was, but it wasn't impossible.

Her eyes moved from face to face. She tried to ignore the blown kisses and catcalls from the men and focus on what she needed to do. Tony Fascinelli wasn't in the group playing basketball, or hanging out with the smokers, or jogging around the perimeter of the high fence. She turned to the left and started checking out the bodybuilders, who all went into strut mode when they noticed her staring.

An injection of adrenaline hit her system when she spotted a dark-haired guy doing bench presses. She stood on tiptoe to get a clearer look. "That's him," she whispered to Yana. "Second bench press in the row back there." He didn't appear to have noticed her. Good.

"Hey, Jon," Yana said. "We were hoping we could interview a couple of guys for our paper. At the women's prison we talked to some women who used weight lifting and exercise to keep themselves sane. For the compare and contrast, it would really help if we could talk to some of the men who are into bodybuilding."

Jon rubbed his forehead with the heel of his hand. "I don't see why not," he answered. "Let's go over and talk to the guards posted in the weight area. See what we can work out."

Rae took a step forward, and a basketball hit her on the calf. The men playing laughed, and she had a feeling it hadn't been an accident. They were all staring over at her. It was like being slimed by Al Schumacher—times fifteen. *Stay calm,* she told herself. *Yana's going to get you what you came here for, and then you're gone.* She bent down and grabbed the ball.

/perky breasts / SCHOOLGIRLS / NOT A FOUL /girl /Melissa's daughter? /

The thoughts were staticky because of all the old prints underneath them, but Rae'd been able to make them out. Her fingers began to shake, and she tightened her grip on the ball. Melissa was her mom's name. Why would someone in *prison* know her mother?

Melissa's a common name, she thought. *Don't be paranoid.* But the other thoughts—the fresh ones she could get—were from right now, about her and Yana. And there weren't any other girls around. So it had to be her, didn't it?

"You coming or what?" Yana asked.

"Yeah," Rae answered. "Just let me give the ball back." She moved toward the men.

"Look, she's holding my ball," one of them yelled, starting a fresh round of comments about Rae's body and what they'd like her to do to them. *Dogs barking,* she lectured herself. *They're just dogs barking.*

"I wish I could play with you guys," she called, getting a big laugh that made her feel scuzzy all over. "I'm not a bad player." Rae threw the ball at the closest guy. "My mom must have known I would be decent. She called me Rae—not a girlie name like hers, Melissa."

There. Maybe she'd sounded like a weirdo, but now whoever had had that thought would know that she *was* Melissa's daughter. *That should bring up some more thoughts about me—if the first thought was even about me. Later I just need to touch the ball again,* she thought, glancing back at Yana and Jon.

"Hey, Voight. I told you to stay close," Jon barked. Rae happily hurried back over to him and Yana, and they all started toward the weight-lifting area. Rae kept herself behind Jon so Tony wouldn't see her. She didn't want to give him a heads up.

"Can you tell us anything about any of the weight lifter guys?" Yana asked. "It would be perfect if we could talk to a couple who had the same kind of background as the women we—"

Jon stopped so abruptly, Rae walked right into him. "Weapon!" he shouted. He reached behind him, grabbed Rae by the arm, and pulled her up next to him, catching Yana with his free hand.

"Fight, fight, fight," the prisoners began to chant. A cluster of men had formed around the weight area. Two guards each armed with a drawn Taser pushed their way through.

"It'll be over in a second," Jon said. "We drill for situations like this all the time."

Rae nodded, even though she could hear the tension in his voice, feel it in his grip on her arm. Tony Fascinelli was in that group somewhere. Was he in the fight or—

An alarm bell began to shriek. Almost instantaneously the men fell into ragged lines. The guards began marching them back inside. Within moments the yard was empty—except for four guards and two prisoners, now restrained. One of them was Anthony's father. His eyes flicked to Rae as he was escorted off the yard. Flicked to her, then away, fast. She didn't have time to read his expression.

"We'll wait here for another minute. Just until the men are secured in their cells again," Jon said. "You two will have to get your interviews another time."

"That's okay," Rae answered. "I think we have enough."

"Are you sure?" Yana asked, her blue eyes concerned.

Rae nodded. All she was collecting was negative info about

Anthony's father. What was the point of trying to find out more? Clearly she wouldn't be doing Anthony any favors.

The alarm bell abruptly cut off. Jon released Rae and Yana. "Come on. Tour's over. I'll take you back to the warden's office."

Just get us out of here, Rae thought as they headed back across the yard. Then out of the corner of her eye she caught a spot of orange. "I'll grab the basketball," she said. She trotted over and scooped it up without waiting for Jon's response.

/Aaron's going down /heart-shaped butt on blondie / SCORE / Melissa in group /

Rae moved her fingers back to the last thought. She did a gentle sweep, hoping for more.

/Rae born while Melissa in group? /

Rae froze. The Melissa *was* her mother. Rae *was* the girl.

Cold little mouse feet ran up and down her back as she touched the spot on the ball. The fear was partly her own but partly the man who'd left the thoughts, too. What had he been afraid of? Afraid of Rae's mother? The group—whatever it was?

"You can leave it there," Jon called.

Rae rolled the ball between her fingertips, searching for anything more, but there was nothing else about Melissa. Or Rae. She let go of the ball and watched it bounce across the basketball court.

"Come on. I want to get you two out of here," Jon said. "The place always gets a little more intense after an incident."

"Is that what that was—an incident?" Yana asked as Rae rejoined her and Jon.

"A minor incident," Jon answered as he led them inside. "But I'm sorry you were there when it happened." He brought them down another puke-green corridor to an elevator, swiped his ID card in the scanner, and waved them inside when the door opened. "I'm sure the warden will be, too," he added as the elevator climbed the floors, smoothly and quickly.

"It was no big thing," Rae muttered. The elevator door opened, and she saw that the warden had come out to meet them.

"I saw what happened on the security cameras. You two okay? Shaken up, I bet," he answered for them. He turned to Jon. "Take them to the changing rooms so they can get back into their own clothes, then bring them down to my office."

"Will do," Jon said. "This way, Voight and Savari." He gave a smile that showed his long dimples as they started down the hall. "Or I guess I can start calling you Rae and Yana again since your time as prisoners of Scott State is over."

Another guard rounded the corner and headed their way. "You should see what I took off Fascinelli," he said to Jon.

"Could I see it?" Rae blurted out. "I, uh, we have a section on prison weapons in our paper."

Jon and the other guard exchanged a look. Jon paused, narrowing his eyes. "I don't know if I should—"

"You can hold on to it," Yana cut in. "Can we just get a glimpse?"

Jon frowned, then finally shrugged. "I guess it's okay."

The guard pulled a knife out of his belt. It was obviously homemade. The handle was several layers of thick cardboard, and the blade looked like a piece of scrap metal that had been banged into a point.

"We do searches all the time to make sure everyone's clean, but we find stuff like this all the time," Jon admitted.

Rae stepped closer, then reached out and traced the cardboard handle with her finger. Her stomach began pumping out acid as a burst of fury roared through her.

/hate the /not going to take /jab it in /jab it in/

"What—" Rae cleared her throat. "The man who had this—what was he in prison for?"

"He killed a woman during an armed robbery," the guard holding the knife answered.

Rae's whole body turned to ice. Anthony's father was a murderer.

Chapter 7

A nthony ran his fingers over the dashboard of the car. *If I was Rae, I might be able to get some clue about what's going on here by touching stuff,* he thought. But he wasn't Rae. And all he could do was wait. He'd already been waiting more than two hours.

He knew he should probably be working on his list of problem words, as Rae called them. If he was going to take those academic tests at Sanderson, then he needed all the prep time he could get. But all he could think about right now was Rae. "Would you please just get your butt out here?" he muttered. "Please?"

He changed radio stations, listened for half a minute, and then changed stations again. The music felt like it was scraping the inside of his ears. Didn't matter what kind it was—it all irritated him almost to the point of pain. He clicked the radio off. The silence in the car was only marginally better.

"Crap," he muttered. He slammed his fist into the dashboard, and he could feel the force of the impact all the way up his arm. "Good job, Fascinelli. Real intelligent. Helped a lot." He got the urge to punch the dash again, but he didn't give in to it. Anger Management 101—*Punching stuff is not the answer to any problem.* And it messed up your hand. Besides, Rae was probably safer in there than most places, with all those guards and security systems.

Maybe it has something to do with Yana, Anthony suddenly thought. He tilted his head from side to side, letting the muscles crack, the desire to punch something fading. It took him a while, but he'd finally figured out the Rae situation. She was lying to protect a friend. Total Rae. He stretched out his neck muscles again, then twisted his torso from side to side, working out the tension in his back. When he leaned back in his seat and looked out the windshield, he saw Rae and Yana walking toward Yana's Bug.

Should I just go? he wondered. *If this is about Yana, I—*

Too late. Rae had spotted him. Her mouth went slack. Anthony shot a look at Yana. She looked concerned—concerned for *Rae.* She had one hand on Rae's shoulder in a protective way.

So he was wrong. Big-time wrong. Whatever was going on here had nothing to do with Yana. Anthony climbed out of the car, slammed the door, and strode over to Yana and Rae. "What's going on?"

"Hello to you, too," Yana said. Anthony didn't bother to glance at her.

"What's going on?" Anthony repeated, trying to make his words come out a little softer but not having much success.

Rae pulled in a shaky breath. "I'm working on a paper comparing and contrasting the treatment of men and women prisoners. The warden let me and Yana take a tour," she answered, her words crashing into each other because she was talking so fast. "It was pretty intense."

Liar, Anthony thought. Rae's expression had changed when she'd seen *him.* It was like someone pulled the plug on her.

"They made us stay in the hole for a while," Yana added. "It would give even you the creeps, Anthony. And you know our Rae. She's a lot more sensitive than she preten—"

"Get in my car, Rae. I want to talk to you. Alone," Anthony said, biting out the words.

"Rae and I already decided we were going to stop and eat on the way home," Yana told him. "Why don't you follow us and—"

"Get in the damn car, Rae," Anthony ordered, ignoring Yana's narrow-eyed glare. He knew he was being a bully. But he didn't care. He'd been right about there being something going on with Rae. And now he knew it involved him. He wasn't waiting one more minute to find out what it was.

"It's okay, Yana," Rae said. "Just wait for me?"

"I'll be right over there." Yana jerked her thumb at her Bug.

Anthony turned on his heel and headed back to his car. He heard Rae trailing a few steps behind him. They both got inside without a word, then shut their doors.

"What right do you have to be sneaking around following me?" Rae asked before he could say a word. But she didn't sound angry. She sounded kind of scared.

"I was afraid you were putting yourself in danger, all

right?" Anthony shot back. "You've been lying to me for days, and I thought you were trying to deal with something too big for you to handle alone."

Rae shook her head. "No. Just a paper, like I told you."

"Will you stop lying!" Anthony burst out. His hands balled into fists, and he had to concentrate to get them to uncurl. "If you were just working on a paper, why'd you tell me your dad needed your help at a cocktail party?"

"That night he did," Rae protested. "I was just working on the paper today."

"There was no party, Rae. I called your house," Anthony told her.

"Oh," Rae whispered. She pulled the sleeves of her deep blue sweater down over her hands and rubbed them together.

Anthony felt like someone was playing cat's cradle with his intestines. He hated seeing Rae like this, like a frightened little girl. He reached over and ran one finger down her cheek. "I pretty much know what's going on, anyway. I just need you to tell me the details."

Rae looked over at him, her blue eyes shimmering with unshed tears. "You do?"

"Yeah. Our guy—the one who tried to kill you, the one who kidnapped Jesse—has decided to make a play for me. You, for God knows what reason, figured it would be safer for me if you and Yana tried to deal with the guy alone. Am I right?"

Rae hesitated.

"I know it has something to do with me," Anthony pressed.

"I saw your face when you saw me. You didn't look pissed off that I'd followed you. You looked . . . horrified. If someone's coming after me, you've got to tell me everything."

"No one's coming after you." She gave a harsh laugh. "Not that I know of, anyway. Get too close to me and pretty much anything can happen, right?" She rolled her window down halfway and stared out as if there was a circus going by.

Uh-uh. If she thought he was just going to drop it now, she was dreaming. "Okay, so no one's coming after me. Great. But I still need to know what the hell is going on."

"That time we touched fingertips, back when you were in the detention center, I—well, I found out some stuff about you," Rae answered, still looking out the window.

Anthony gave a noncommittal grunt, even though his guts were stretched so tight, they felt like they could start snapping any second.

"One thing—the big thing—I got was how much you longed to know your father," Rae continued.

"Longed? *Longed?*" The word tasted repulsive on his tongue. "The guy was a sperm donor, nothing else," Anthony insisted.

Rae turned to look at him. "We both know that's not true. I know how many times you've wondered if you were like him."

"So what if I have," Anthony muttered.

"So I decided . . . I decided that I would find him for you, you know, by using my fingerprint thing," Rae confessed, her expression a mixture of hope and apprehension.

Anthony's eyes locked on the Scott State buildings. "And this—" His mouth went dry as sandpaper, and he had to swallow a couple of times before he could get out another word. "This is where you found him?"

A tear spilled out of one eye and rolled down Rae's cheek. "Yeah." She reached out and put her hand on his arm, twisting her finger in the cloth of his jacket. "I wasn't going to tell you. I swear."

Anthony jerked away from her. "You weren't going to tell me? You were going to protect poor little Anthony from the truth about his father? Because my father's nothing like yours, is he, Rae?"

Rae didn't answer. Another tear slid down her face. She didn't bother to wipe it away.

"What did he do?" Anthony asked.

"Can't we just pretend this never hap—"

"What did he do?" Anthony repeated.

Rae met his gaze directly. "He took part in an armed robbery." She stopped, but he could tell there was more.

"And," he prompted, his voice hard.

Rae winced. "I'm sorry, Anthony, but he—he killed someone. I'm so sorry."

"Get out of the car," Anthony ordered. He couldn't stand to look at her, to see the pity in her expression.

When she didn't move fast enough, Anthony reached across her and opened her door. "Get out. Right now."

She left without another word, without a glance back.

Why would she want to look at him? His father was a murderer.

Anthony is never going to want to talk to me again, Rae thought. She lay on the antique French sofa in the living room staring up at the ceiling. She wished her dad was home. The place was too quiet. There was nothing to drown out her thoughts.

The stereo remote was on the table next to the overstuffed armchair, about three steps away. But Rae's blood had been replaced with cement, slowly hardening cement.

Her cell phone was in her purse, which was on the floor. She could probably snag it without even sitting up. But who was she supposed to call? Not Anthony. The image of his face when he ordered her out of the car sprang up in her mind. She squeezed her eyes shut, trying to block out the pain and anger she saw there. But of course closing her eyes didn't help. The memory of Anthony's expression in that moment had been burned into her brain. She was never going to be able to forget it.

She could call Yana. Yana would listen or fill up the silence with chatter if that's what Rae wanted. But God, Yana deserved a few hours of peace. She'd had to listen to Rae blubber all the way home—and she hadn't even said, "I told you so." Not even once.

Yana knew it was a bad idea from the start, Rae thought. *But did I? No.* It had been so egotistical to just think she could go poof!—and give Anthony the thing he'd wanted all his life.

Rae sighed, dropped her hand into her purse, extracted her BlackBerry with two fingers, then used her shirt to polish it off. The last thing she wanted to hear right now was more of her own thoughts. She held it up in front of her face and stared at it. She really needed to hear a human voice, preferably the voice of someone who didn't think she was scum.

"Just stop it," she said out loud. The main reason she wanted to talk to someone was that *she* couldn't stand herself. If she had to spend one more second alone with herself, she'd start screaming until she got put in a padded cell somewhere.

I could call Dad, she thought. But she never called him for no reason, and she couldn't think of a passable reason right now.

Marcus. The name popped into her head from nowhere. Just the thought of talking to Marcus made her feel less cold and hard inside. She dialed his number before she had a chance to talk herself out of it.

He answered on the second ring. "Hello."

Rae's tongue tied itself into a knot. This was the first time she'd called Marcus since before The Incident, since before the hospital, before their nonbreakup breakup, before Dori. "It's Rae," she managed to get out.

"Rae, hi," Marcus said, sounding one hundred percent happy to hear from her.

"Hi," Rae repeated.

Marcus laughed. "Hiiiii," he groaned in his Frankenstein voice.

Rae smiled, her lips trembling. She promised herself

she wasn't going to lose it on the phone with Marcus. "So, what's up?"

"Well, I'm sorta trying to get back with my old girlfriend, but I did a lot of stupid stuff, and I'm not sure I'm going to be able to get her to forgive me," Marcus answered.

Oh God. She wasn't expecting him to go *there*. She'd thought he'd keep it light, the way he had at Sliders. "Um, hmmm, tough one," Rae said. "Maybe you need to just give her some time."

"I know. I know. But it's making me crazy." Rae could almost see the long dimples appearing in his cheeks.

"Well, suck it up. You said you did a lot of stupid stuff," Rae answered, surprising herself. When she was with Marcus, she would never have said something like that. "So, you still been watching *Lost*?"

"Who wants to know?" Marcus asked.

Rae *almost* laughed. "Just tell me what's been going on," she said. "Do a good deed for a poor girl whose father thinks television rots the brain. He *still* limits my viewing hours. Start with Jack and Kate," she urged.

"How far back?" he asked.

"Since the last time you told me, if you can remember," Rae answered. She rolled onto her side. This was perfect. She didn't have to say anything. She could just let his words wash through her, turning her from stone back to flesh.

Marcus talked on and on, and Rae's breathing grew deeper. "Hey, I need a massive Dr Pepper if I'm going to keep talking," he finally said. "How about if I pick you up and we hit the food court?"

Rae knew if she stood up from this couch, it was all going to hit her again, all the guilt over what she'd done to Anthony. Just the thought brought up the image of his face. The pain, the anger.

"Rae? Did you fall asleep on me?" Marcus asked.

"No. No, it was great. Thanks. But I need to go," Rae said in a rush.

"Okay," Marcus answered. "Do you think . . . would it be okay if I asked you again sometime? I had fun at Sliders."

Rae squeezed her eyes shut against the image of Anthony's face. Of course, it didn't help this time, either. "I had fun, too. But I have to go. Bye." She hung up without answering his question.

Anthony saw the pothole, but he didn't slow down. He pushed down on the accelerator and went over it with a bone-jarring thump-thump. The thumps seemed to say *murder.*

I should have asked Rae how he did it. Did he use a knife? Or was it a semiautomatic?

It doesn't matter. I don't even know the guy, Anthony thought. *He was in my life a total of what? A couple hundred minutes out of seventeen years. He means nothing to me. He—*

He's my father. The answer came clear and strong. And true. *He's in my blood. He's part of me, a part I can't rip out even if I slash a chunk out of my heart or my brain.*

449

Anthony came up to the street he needed to take to his house and passed it by again. He wasn't ready to go home. He wasn't ready to do anything except drive. That at least took a fragment of his attention. If he stopped, all he'd be thinking about was his father, and that would make his head explode like a volcano. He hit the accelerator and made it most of the way across the street before the yellow light went red. He didn't want to stop. He couldn't stop.

The next light was a solid red when he reached it, so Anthony took a right without lifting his foot off the gas. He got a honk from the guy he ended up tailgating. "Screw you," he muttered.

He heard a little cough from the Hyundai's engine and shot a glance at the gas gauge. The red line was riding below the E. "Screw you, too." The 7-Eleven where Nunan worked was only a couple of blocks away. If he could just get there, he could pump in enough gas to—

The engine coughed again. Anthony jerked the wheel from side to side, weaving the car back and forth in his lane. Sometimes that would slosh enough gas from the sides of the tank over the hole to get a car at least a little farther down the road.

But not this time. The engine died. Right there in the middle of the street. Anthony switched on the flashers, put the car in neutral, got out, and—steering with one hand—managed to shove the Hyundai over to the side of the road. He yanked the keys out of the ignition, then slammed the door so hard, the frame shimmied.

All you have to do is get over to Nunan's. He'll have a gas can he can loan you, Anthony told himself. He kicked the closest tire as he passed the car. "Piece of crap. Mom should have traded it in a long time ago. She—"

My father is a murderer.

The thought shoved everything else out of his brain. Questions pounded through him as he started walking, questions hard as stones thrown at his head. Knife? Gun? Up close? Man? Woman? With a family? Planned or did the robbery get out of hand? Did his father . . . did he *like* it? Did it give him some kind of rush? Had he killed before but not gotten caught?

Anthony started to run. If he could just get to the 7-Eleven, there'd be someone to talk to. Maybe that would stop the questions or at least turn down the volume on them. He turned the corner, spotted the big red-and-green sign, and kept his eyes locked on it.

He swung into the parking lot and forced himself to slow down. Then he shoved his hands through his hair, pulled in a couple of deep breaths, and sauntered through the door.

Nunan looked up when he heard the electronic doorbell. "Fascinelli. What's up? Haven't seen you in a while."

"Been busy," Anthony answered. Although the truth was, he'd been avoiding the place. Avoiding temptation. "I ran out of gas a couple of blocks away."

"I can hook you up with a gas can," Nunan answered. He ran his fingers over his shaved head and giggled, a sure sign that he was high. "Is there anything else I can get you— smoked almonds, some other kind of smoke?" He laughed until he snorted. The guy actually thought he was Craig Ferguson.

Anthony started to shake his head. He hadn't bought any weed since the first day of school, when it finally sank in that if he was ever going to graduate, it wasn't going to happen if he spent all his time sharing joints in the bathroom.

But somehow right now he was finding it hard to remember why that even mattered. "Actually, yeah. I could be up for some herb," he answered.

Tonight it was just what he needed. He loved the way he felt when he got high. The world slowed down, and nothing seemed all that important anymore.

Nunan gave him an I-knew-you'd-be-back-buying smirk and pulled a paper bag out from under the counter. Anthony knew Nunan already had the stuff in the bag—and that Nunan would be selling him the smallest amount possible. Even when Anthony was a regular, he'd always bought a little at a time since he never had much cash on him. "Okay, you got a Slim Jim and a pack of gum," Nunan said, adding them to the bag and ringing them up with a flourish directed at the nearest security camera. "You want the gas now, too?"

Anthony shook his head. "I'm going out back for a while. I'll get it later." He handed over a twenty-dollar bill and got back a lot less change than he would have for a Slim Jim and some gum. Nunan gave him a big grin as Anthony headed out. He found a seat in back of the place where a Dumpster hid him from view. Usually there were a couple of guys back there, but tonight it was empty. He pulled the little bag of weed out of the plastic sack and realized he didn't have any rolling papers.

He could feel the questions starting to build in his head again, getting ready to stone him. He needed this. Fast. That would at least dull the questions out, make them feel like they were being asked from far away.

If he went back in the store, Nunan might be in a talkative mood and keep him in there for half an hour before coughing up the papers. There was no way Anthony could wait that long. He scanned the ground. Yeah. Halfway under the Dumpster was a bong someone had made out of a beer can. He grabbed it, turned it over in his hands. Still usable. Less than a minute later he was inhaling deeply. Yeah. Exactly what he needed.

"You wasted yet?" a voice asked in the darkness.

"No. Sadly," Anthony answered. He wished whoever it was would just go away, but Sean McGee appeared from around the Dumpster and sat down next to him.

"Good. Because I have a business proposition for you," McGee told him.

"I heard about the security codes," Anthony replied.

McGee scowled. "Somebody talks too much."

"It's not like I heard it all over the place," Anthony answered, not mentioning that he'd gotten the info from Jesse. He held out the bong to McGee, but Sean shook his head.

"Got to stay focused," he said. He reached down and adjusted himself. Not something Anthony needed to see. "So I need one more guy. Getting in the houses is going to be no

453

problem—I've got all the security codes, which is probably what you heard."

Anthony nodded.

"I just need help moving stuff out. We've got to be fast. Organized. And I don't want anyone who panics. You interested?" McGee asked.

Anthony took another breath and held it in. He'd always wondered if he was like his dad. Maybe he should find out if he was, especially since Rae went to all the *trouble* of tracking the guy down.

"I need a decision now," McGee said. "I'm picking the last guy tonight."

"I'm in," Anthony told him.

Chapter 8

"I brought Chinese food," Rae's father called as he came through the front door.

Rae started and almost fell off the couch. *I must have dozed off after I hung up with Marcus,* she realized. God, what an awful dream. Anthony had been in the electric chair, and Marcus was pulling the switch. Rae was watching through a sheet of glass so thick that Anthony couldn't hear her screaming that she was sorry, that she was so, so sorry. Then it had switched, and Rae'd been about to get a lethal injection. She'd been strapped down; the needle had—

Rae's father leaned over the back of the couch and shook a large brown paper bag in front of her face. Her stomach curled up into a squishy little ball when the odor of the food hit her. The last thing she wanted to do was eat. But she needed to talk to her dad, and she didn't want to wait. She pushed herself up. "I'll heat up some water for tea," she said.

"I'm always bragging to the other professors about how

domestic we are," her father teased as he followed her to the kitchen.

Rae forced a laugh as she grabbed two mugs out of the cabinet.

Okay, I need an intro, she thought as she began filling the first mug with water. Yeah, she and her dad had talked about her mother a few times. But almost all those times Rae had ended up getting furious and slamming into her room or making up some excuse to get out of the house.

She put the mugs of water into the microwave and hit the beverage button, then shot a glance at her father. He was humming to himself as he set the table with the paper plates and plastic utensils from the takeout bag.

How can he be so smart and so delusional? she asked herself. She knew that as soon as she mentioned her mother, he'd be all goo-goo romantic and start telling Rae what a wonderful person her mother had been. Even though they both knew what she'd done.

The microwave beeped, and Rae pulled out the mugs and plunked a teabag into each one. *Tonight you can't get pissed off,* she told herself. *You have to let him talk. You've got to find out about "the group" and why someone in prison knew about you and your mom.*

Rae sat down at the kitchen table and plopped a couple of vegetable dumplings on her plate. "Those are all for you," her dad told her as he took a seat across from her. "I was in the mood for pork ones."

"Dad, did you and Mom name me while she was pregnant?"

Rae blurted out. "Or did you wait until I was born to see, you know, what kind of name went with me?" There had to be a smoother way to bring up the Mom subject, but Rae was interested in the time frame when her mother was pregnant with her. At least the question got them there.

Her father rubbed the bump on the bridge of his nose, the one that matched the bump on Rae's. "We started talking about names almost the moment your mother found out she was pregnant," he answered, not even reacting to the random factor of her question. "Boys and girls, since we wanted to be surprised. I think your mom bought every baby name book ever published. She'd read them to me every night before we fell asleep. It took us a while, but we finally narrowed it down to Rachel Morgan Voight for a girl." He smiled at her. "I think it suits you."

"I like it," Rae answered. She took a tiny bite of her vegetable dumpling, hoping her stomach wouldn't revolt. "So did Mom have any strange cravings when she was pregnant?"

Her father laughed. "She craved meat. I don't know how you became a vegetarian."

"Hmmm," Rae said, trying to act interested. "What else? Like, what did she spend time doing? You know, some people knit or wallpaper the baby's room. Or they join some kind of mommies-to-be group. Was Mom in a group like that?"

Rae's father lowered his eyes to his plate and busied himself spooning out some lo mein. "She *was* in a group," he finally acknowledged. Rae's heart rate increased as she waited for him to continue. "It was a bit of a New Agey thing. But she joined it before she got pregnant. It wasn't for people expecting kids." He frowned. "It was funny, though. Quite a few of the women members did get pregnant around the same time. They always joked there was something in the coffee."

"Did you ever go to the meetings?" Rae asked.

Her father shook his head. "I teach medieval literature, remember? New Age is just too . . . modern for me. But your mother seemed to enjoy it."

He's holding back, Rae thought. But why? There was one easy way to find out. *Sorry, Dad,* she thought as she reached for the lo mein carton, sliding her fingers over the surface.

/changed her/pork smells great/nice to eat with Rae/secretive/ changed her/didn't talk to me about/

Rae focused on the thoughts that were about her mother— *changed her, secretive, didn't talk to me.* From those thoughts she picked up a mix of guilt and betrayal and anger from her father. Like thinking anything negative about his dead wife shouldn't be allowed, even though he was angry with her for keeping secrets. The hair on the backs of Rae's arms stood on end, and she realized she'd gotten another emotion from her father—a ripple of fear.

Whoever left the print on the basketball was afraid, too. Not just of the group or my mom, but afraid of me, too.

"So what'd they do in the group?" Rae asked.

Rae's father took off his wire-rim glasses, polished them on his sleeve, then put them back on. One of his favorite stalling techniques. "Your mom didn't tell me much about them.

It's good for people in a couple to have a few things that are completely their own." He took a big bite of lo mein and spent more time than necessary chewing it. Then he smiled at Rae. "You know what she used to do? She used to put the headphones of her Walkman against her stomach and play you music. Mostly stuff from her high school days—Supertramp, Styx, ELO. I told her she absolutely couldn't play you ABBA, but I know she sneaked it in." He laughed. "I used to play you Gregorian chants when she was sleeping. And some country-western."

"No wonder I'm such a freak," Rae joked.

Her dad's expression turned serious. *Oops*, Rae thought. *I guess we're not far enough away from my hospital days for me to be joking about not being quite normal.*

"She would read to you, too. All kinds of things. Even the back of cereal boxes," he added.

Rae tried to smile. But it was hard. Because she knew he was talking about a woman with a violent streak. Her dad seemed to be able to forget that part so easily.

She pushed herself away from the table and stood up. "I'm not really that hungry tonight. I think I'll go hit the books for a while." It was clear she wasn't going to find out any more about the group from him. And she couldn't take any more anecdotes about Saint Mom.

"The leftovers will be in the fridge if you get hungry later," her dad called after her. He sounded a little worried. But not as worried as Rae felt. She had to find out the truth about the group, and why whoever left the print on the basketball was unnerved by the idea that she'd been born while her mother was a part of it.

"That place across the street, the one with the green shutters, is the first one we're going to hit. We're going in Friday night," McGee told Anthony.

"Big," Anthony muttered. One of those places that could hold three or four of Anthony's family—and give each kid a separate room.

"That's why we need the extra muscle," Aaron Kolsen said from the backseat.

Anthony didn't know Kolsen very well, but he'd seen him and McGee's other guy, Chris Buchanan, around. They were a couple of years older than Anthony, and seemed decent enough.

"We've been watching the place in shifts," Buchanan said. "It's just a couple who lives there. Fifty something."

"There's a gardener and a cleaning person, but they're never around at night," McGee added. "And you won't even believe this—the wife left this afternoon with enough suitcases to crash a plane."

"So we just have the guy to worry about," Anthony said.

Buchanan tapped Anthony on the shoulder and held up a joint. Anthony shook his head. He hadn't had a buzz before McGee found him out by the Dumpster, and he didn't want to get one now. If he was doing this thing, he was going to be on his toes. Trying to plan a robbery while high was a Bluebird move.

"Yeah, just the guy," McGee agreed. "He isn't home yet. Usually doesn't make it in until about nine."

"Workaholic," Kolsen added. "Maybe that's why she left."

"I'm going with alcoholic," Buchanan said. "Our bud doesn't always look so steady on his feet."

"Are we doing this before he gets home, then?" Anthony asked. Going in there at seven or even eight seemed dicey. There'd still be lots of people around the neighborhood. He felt the back of his neck break out in droplets of sweat.

"We're going in at about seven. That gives the gardener and the maid time to leave and us some space before our guy gets home," McGee explained. "I borrowed my cousin's van. We—"

"We painted it with the Salvation Army logo," Kolsen cut in. "So it'll look like we're just doing a regular pickup for them."

McGee shot him an irritated look, clearly not happy to have been interrupted. Anthony reminded himself to stay on McGee's good side. At least until the job was over.

"I got some Salvation Army uniforms," McGee continued. "We'll go in wearing those. Since it's early and the alarm won't go off, nobody should get suspicious. Those guys pick up donations from people at all kinds of weird times."

"What about when they see us carrying out the big stuff?" Anthony asked. "The Salvation Army doesn't usually pick up stereos." He wasn't going to get caught loading a wide-screen TV into a Salvation Army van.

"We'll put the van in the garage and load the stuff through

the garage door," McGee answered. He sounded the way some of Anthony's special-ed teachers had—like he couldn't believe how much of a moron Anthony was being.

"Sounds good," Anthony said quickly. He wasn't going to mess this one up.

Rae slipped out of bed that night, carefully pulling her covers back up to her pillow. There was no way she was going to be able to sleep until she got answers to at least some of the questions jangling inside her head. What was the group—and what was so scary about it? That was question number one. But there were other questions about her mother that she could never quite stop thinking about—had her mother had the fingerprint ability Rae did? Did she know she had it, or had she thought she was losing her mind? Did the disease, the degenerative disease, have anything to do with the power? And if it did, was Rae going to die, too?

She'd been trying to pretend that she didn't even have most of these questions, to shove them so deep into her brain that they wouldn't resurface. But if Anthony could take learning the truth about his dad, then she could take learning the truth about her mom. And herself.

And there was one obvious place to start—the box with her mom's stuff in it. Rae tiptoed out of her room, down the hall, and into her dad's room. Luckily he was a heavy sleeper—and from the sound of his snoring, he was in deep by now. She made her way over to the closet and eased open the sliding door. The cardboard box was in the same place as always. Rae pulled it down from the shelf—

/love you, Melissa /*why am I doing this* /*sweet*/

—above the clothes rod and hurried back to her room with it. Her heart felt like it had moved from her chest to her throat. The throbbing lump made it impossible to take a deep breath.

There's nothing to be scared of, she told herself as she set the box down on the bed. But she opened the box gingerly, using only her fingernails, as if something deep inside was going to spring out and attack her. Her eyes immediately lit on an old-fashioned glass perfume bottle, the only thing inside the box that she'd ever touched.

"Can't deal with that right now," she whispered. The last time the blast of pure mother love she'd gotten off the bottle had almost annihilated her. If her mother had been a different person, it probably would have been the best sensation ever. But an overpowering rush of love from a mother who was capable of the kind of violence and rage Rae's mother had been—it was almost like it wasn't love at all, but just the opposite because the person who felt it was so twisted inside.

Next to the bottle lay a pink-and-white doll. It was shaped sort of like a snowman—snowbaby—with three fuzzy orbs for a body, and it had a little plastic face with two straggly pieces of yellow yarn hair drooping over its forehead. Rae gently picked it up. She got mostly static off the body, static and a feeling of deep contentment and affection. This freaky little dolly had been held a lot by someone who adored it. "Had to have been Mom's," Rae muttered.

She swallowed hard, then ran one finger slowly over the doll's face. Static, static.

/for Rachel / little baby Bonnie /

Rachel's name radiated pride and love and joy. She quickly put the doll aside. That wasn't what she came here for. That wasn't what she wanted.

Just keep going, she told herself. She hooked a plastic mug by the handle and pulled it out. On the front was a joke photo of her parents as Tarzan and Jane. She'd never seen her father smile like that. The way he looked at her mother . . . God. She did a fingerprint sweep.

/ can't believe I got him to do this / best day / I'm changing / we should go back / coffee /

Rae's hands began to tremble, and she almost lost her grip on the cup. It suddenly felt much too heavy. She took a deep breath and let the emotions finish sweeping through her, the love, the amusement, the fatigue, and the sweaty-sweet mix of apprehension and excitement. Rae moved her finger back to the spot where she'd felt that thrill of danger.

/ I'm changing /

"Yeah, you were changing the way I've changed, weren't you, Mom?" Rae asked. When Anthony finally figured out what was going on with Rae, that she was a fingerprint reader, there had been exhilaration mixed with the fear. Her feelings had been a lot like what she'd just picked up.

Rae shook out her hands, then pulled out a small velvet

purse. It was empty, and the thoughts were ordinary. She tried to let them go right through her without registering them. If she was going to touch everything in the box, she had to stay a little numb. Yeah. That was easy.

Rae set the purse on the bed and picked up a silver hairbrush. Nothing. God, nothing but more love for the baby growing inside her.

She started moving through the items more quickly. Yearbook. Nothing. Framed sonogram printout. Nothing. Nothing she needed. Jewelry box. Nothing on the outside, but there was something rattling around inside.

Rae opened the box and saw a small glass bottle with a rubber stopper. The stopper was attached to the bottle. It couldn't be pulled off. Rae'd seen a bottle like that before, but where?

Leah's cat. Leah's cat, Smoochie, had diabetes. The insulin came in a bottle like that, and you stuck the needle right through the stopper to get the insulin out. The little bottle resting in the jewelry box didn't have a label, but Rae's fingers started tingling just as she looked at it. She used two fingers to pick it up.

/ hurt the baby? /

The bottle slipped from Rae's fingers and fell to the floor. It didn't break. Rae stared down at it. She had to pick it up, had to see what other thoughts were on it. But her knees wouldn't bend. That thought—*hurt the baby?* had been laced with so much terror, it had paralyzed her.

"Move your butt, Rachel Morgan," she ordered herself. Slowly she managed to sit down next to the bottle. A shudder went through her as she reached for it, but she didn't pull back.

/left group/hurt the baby?/ask Amanda Reese why/did she leave because/I'm changing/hurt the baby?/

Rae gently placed the bottle back on the floor, then wrapped her arms against her knees and put her head down, waiting for the emotions to pass.

At least I have a place to start, she thought. *Someone I can ask questions. I just have to find Amanda Reese.*

Chapter 9

Anthony sucked on the little piece that was left of his joint. Man, he couldn't believe he'd already used all the pot he'd gotten off Nunan. And he still felt edgy.

He glanced at the dashboard clock. Group therapy started up in ten minutes. The last thing he needed. But he had to go. He didn't want to do anything the slightest bit suspicious before the robbery tonight. He took one last pull, inhaling as much smoke as possible, then tossed the last eighth of an inch out the window.

He left the window down as he drove the block and a half from his nice suburban street parking space to the institute, figuring it would blow the smell of the pot off him. When he pulled into one of the spots in the institute lot, he caught sight of Jesse in his rearview mirror. Crap. Anthony really didn't want to talk about the new skateboard park or whatever it was Jesse was going to be yammering about today.

Maybe if I pretend I don't see him, Jesse will—

"Anthony," Jesse called. He reached Anthony's car door before Anthony even had it open.

"Hey," Anthony mumbled as he climbed out.

"I heard about you and McGee," Jesse said, his voice high and shrill. It took Anthony a moment to realize that Jesse was pissed off.

"What? Were you afraid you wouldn't be able to get a big enough piece if I was in on it, too?" Jesse demanded, his blue eyes bright with anger.

Anthony glanced around the parking lot, squinting against the sun. No one was close enough to hear them—right now. "You mind keeping it down?"

"Oh, right, yeah, I'm supposed to care if I blow it for the rest of you guys," Jesse shot back. He shoved his hands through his hair, making it stand on end. "Maybe you should have thought about that before you gave me the big speech about how it wasn't anything either of us should be involved in. Either of us!"

Jesse's words were like mosquitoes biting his face. "I was right, okay?" Anthony answered. "It's nothing you should be a part of. You should keep your head down, go—"

"Go to school," Jesse interrupted. "Blah, blah, blah. If you didn't want me hanging out, you should have just told me."

"I'm telling you now," Anthony bit out. "And if I catch you anywhere near McGee and the rest of us—"

Jesse didn't wait to hear the rest. He turned and ran toward the institute.

Anthony sighed, then slowly headed toward the institute himself, feeling like he'd spent the day eating boulders. Well, at least Jesse'd stay away. He might hate Anthony for the rest of his life, but he'd stay away. That was the most important thing.

"Hey, Jesse, how're—"

Jesse shoved through the main doors of the institute without a glance at Rae. *Oh God, Anthony's already told him what happened Wednesday,* Rae thought. *Now he hates me.*

Maybe she shouldn't even wait for Anthony. Maybe it was way too soon to try to—

There he was, coming toward her. She could just hurry inside, pretend she hadn't seen him. But it was way too clear she had. Rae forced a smile and took a few steps toward him. "Anthony, could we talk for a minute. . . ."

Her words trailed off as she got a good look at him. Bloodshot eyes. Blank expression. Clothes that looked like he'd slept in them. She took another step closer. And caught a whiff of the thick, sweet smell of pot. There was no way Anthony could go into group like this. Abramson would nail him in a heartbeat.

Rae grabbed Anthony by the arm. "You're coming with me." She gave him a jerk, and he didn't move an inch.

"I'm not going anywhere except away from you," Anthony told her, his eyes straight ahead, as if she were invisible.

"Anthony, you're clearly stoned," Rae said, speaking slowly and distinctly. "You can't go into group like this. You could end up back in the juvenile detention center. Now, let me help you get cleaned up." She tugged on his arm again, and this time he let her lead him. Rae hurried him to the upstairs ladies' room, took a quick peek inside, then shoved him in.

"This is the girls' room," Anthony said.

"Hey, yeah, you're right," Rae shot back. She opened her purse and started rooting through it. "Eyes first," she muttered, pulling out a bottle of Visine. "Tilt back your head," she ordered Anthony.

"Why should I do anything you—"

"Detention center," Rae snapped. Anthony gave her the kind of look he'd give a worm under his boot, then he tilted back his head. *Good thing we're about the same height,* Rae thought as she gave him a hit of Visine in each eye. "Stay that way for a second," she told him. She dug around in her purse again and brought out a travel toothbrush and a little tube of toothpaste. "Okay, you can put your head back up." She shoved the toothbrush and paste into Anthony's hands. He dropped them both. Rae grabbed them and put them into his hands more carefully, not letting go until his fingers curved around them. "Brush," she told him.

"You just love this," he accused her. "You think I'm some big doll for you to play with. Oh, look, what a sweet troubled boy. I know! I'll fix him up. It's way more fun than being on the . . ." He paused, staring into space. "The prom decorating committee. In just a few weeks I'll have all his problems solved. Then I'll get a dog from the pound and fix it up. Give it a—"

"We're running out of time here," Rae interrupted. "I'm

sorry about looking for your dad. I shouldn't have done it, not without talking to you first. And if you want me to, I'll spend the rest of my life apologizing, but first we have to get you to group. So brush!"

"Oh, she's sorry. Well, that makes everything okay." Anthony's words dripped with sarcasm. Rae tried not to let him see how much they hurt. God, she deserved everything he said and worse—much, much worse.

Finally, Anthony started to brush. Rae pulled a bottle of her Clinique Happy perfume out of her purse and spritzed him down. "Hey!" Anthony protested, spitting toothpaste foam.

"It's not that girlie. It basically smells like grapefruit," Rae told him. "And it's not as if you can go into group wearing eau de marijuana." She gave him a couple more good sprays, then wet down one of the thick brown paper towels from the dispenser and went to work on the big spot on the front of Anthony's flannel shirt.

He leaned over the sink and spit, barely missing her arm. "I'm done."

"Your hair—" Rae began.

"I'm done," Anthony said. "Let's just consider this your last day on the Anthony Fascinelli project. I'll write you a letter for your college application." He stepped toward the door. Without thinking, Rae blocked him.

"Anthony, it's totally understandable that you got wasted after what you found out about your father, but—"

471

"Understandable. Oh, I'm so glad you find it understandable," Anthony told her.

Rae cringed but didn't move out of his way. "But you can't start getting high every day," she continued. "The Sanderson Prep tests are coming up, and you need to—"

Anthony let out a harsh laugh. "Screw the tests. I'm not taking them," he said. "I told you, I'm done being your project."

Rae wrapped her arms around herself, suddenly chilled to the bone. "Anthony, please, no matter how you feel about me, don't throw away this chance."

"Screw you, Rae." He stepped around her and left her standing there.

She should never have told him the truth. He was already thinking he was going to turn out like his dad. Why try to get into Sanderson Prep?

Rae knew that's what he was thinking because a lot of the time she was thinking the same kinds of things about her mom. She was so scared she was going to end up just like her mother. And she wasn't sure there was any way for her to stop it from happening.

"I'm always happy to be your chauffeur," Rae's dad said when she climbed into the car. "But what happened to Yana and Anthony? Between the two of them I'm hardly ever on duty anymore."

Rae understood the subtext—she'd just started having friends again and was there some reason these new friends weren't around? Some reason that her dad should know about?

"Yana's working on a big project for school," Rae answered. "And Anthony . . ." She'd meant to spit out some lie, but Anthony's name was like broken glass in her mouth, and her eyes welled up despite herself. *I'm not going to cry*, she told herself. *I am not going to cry*. She blinked rapidly and rushed on. "Anthony had to pick his mom up from work. He drives his mom's car, you know. Part of the deal is he has to pick her up and do errands for her and stuff."

"Well, I guess that's fair since it's her car," her father answered. His voice sounded completely normal, but he shot her a concerned glance.

"Completely fair," Rae answered. She gave him a smile that she hoped looked well-adjusted and happy and not like some hideous grimace. "How were your classes?"

Her father laughed. "My classes are good. A few of my students actually stay awake during my lectures."

Rae nodded. "That's important." She couldn't think of another question to ask, and her dad seemed to get that she'd rather not talk. They rode the rest of the way home in silence, but it was a good kind of silence. She guessed she'd managed to reassure her father enough.

"So what do you think?" he asked as he pulled into their driveway. "Pizza? Or heat up something Alice left us?"

"You pick," Rae answered, unbuckling her seat belt. The thought of any kind of food was repulsive to her right now, although she figured she'd have to choke something down to convince her dad she was OK.

"Well, dig out your sombrero," her father said as he led the way to the house. "I'm pulling out the tamale pie."

Rae's stomach did a flip-flop. "Good choice. I'm going to go start on my homework before we eat." She hurried down the hall, past the fluffy white clouds painted on the blue background, and into her room. She went straight for the phone books in the bottom drawer of her dresser and pulled out the white pages. She'd been dying to do this ever since she'd found Amanda Reese's name, and now she finally had time. "Amanda Reese," she muttered as she paged through. "Here we go. Only three of them. Good."

She sat down in her black leather desk chair, grabbed a pen, and circled the numbers. Then she sat there. *You've got to know the truth,* she thought. *It might even save your life.* She snatched up the phone before she had time to change her mind and punched in the number of the first Amanda Reese.

"Hello?" a woman answered.

Guess I should have planned what to say first, Rae thought. "Hi. My name's Rae Voight. I'm trying to track down some old friends of my mother's. I found your name in a box of her stuff, but I'm not sure if you're the right Amanda Reese. My mom's name was Melissa. You would have known her about sixteen years ago."

The woman laughed. "Sixteen years ago I was in grade school," she said.

"Oh." Rae let out a deep breath. "Well, I guess you're not

the Amanda I'm looking for," she said.

"Did you say her name *was* Melissa?" the wrong Amanda asked.

"Yeah. Um, she died when I was a baby," Rae explained.

"Oh, I'm sorry. I didn't mean to laugh. I just didn't make the connection at first," the woman said. She sounded like she wanted to rush over and make Rae cookies or something.

"It's okay. It was, you know, it was a long time ago," Rae managed to get out. "But thanks for your help." She hung up quickly.

"Time for Amanda Reese number two," Rae muttered, punching in the numbers. She was going to get through the calls as fast as possible. It was the only way she'd get through them at all.

Rae heard someone pick up the phone on the other end, but no one said anything. "Hello. I'm trying to reach Amanda Reese."

"No, I'm not interested in changing my long-distance service," a woman snapped. Rae could hear a little boy asking for juice in the background.

"That's not why I'm calling," Rae began.

"I'm not interested in donating any money to anything," the woman said.

"I'm not selling anything. I just—" Rae heard the phone hit the floor with a clatter. There was a scuffling sound, then the woman came back on the line. "Dropped you. Sorry. I was trying to pour juice and hold the phone. So what is it you do want?"

Rae gave the woman the same speech she'd given Amanda number one. Only this time she made sure not to imply her mother was dead. She didn't want to go into that until she was sure she'd found the right Amanda.

"Melissa Voight," Amanda number two repeated. "Doesn't sound familiar."

"You would have known each other in some kind of New Age group," Rae prompted.

"Then I'm definitely not the person you're looking for. I've got five kids. Even back then, when I only had the twins, I didn't have time for anything like that," Amanda number two told her. "Sorry. Look, I have to go." She hung up.

One Amanda Reese left to go. At least one Amanda Reese in Atlanta. *My Amanda Reese could be anywhere by now.* Rae reached for the phone, but it rang before she could touch it.

"Hello," Rae said into the receiver.

"I'd like to speak to Erika Keaton," a muffled voice said.

"Erika Keaton," Rae repeated, unsure whether she'd heard the name correctly.

"Yes, Er-i-ka Kea-ton," the voice—Rae wasn't sure if it belonged to a man or a woman—answered. Then Rae heard a long laugh, a laugh that soared into a screech. "What am I thinking? Of course Erika Keaton isn't there. Erika Keaton is dead!"

The receiver clicked down, and the dial tone filled Rae's ear. She didn't put down the phone. She was too stunned.

Prank call, she told herself. But how strange that someone made a call like that right when Rae was trying to find out info about her dead mother?

"Let's just see who that was," Rae said. She hit star sixty-nine. But it didn't go through.

Just go on with what you were doing, Rae told herself. She dialed the number for Amanda Reese number three. A girl picked up who didn't sound any older than Rae.

"Um, I think I have the wrong number. I was trying to track down a friend of my mother's named Amanda Reese. They were in a group together about sixteen years ago. But I don't think you could be her," Rae said.

"I'm Amanda. But I'm only sixteen now, so . . ."

"Yeah. Well, thanks," Rae answered.

"Wait," Amanda said. "It could be my mom. I was named after her."

"Is she home? Could I talk to her?" Someone who had a daughter the same age as Rae had at least a chance of being the right Amanda.

"I . . . my mom." Amanda number three cleared her throat, but her voice continued to sound clogged. "My mom died last year."

"Oh God. I'm so sorry," Rae said.

There was something more she wanted to ask. Needed to ask. But how could she?

Rae heard the sound of soft crying. "I hate when I do this," the girl said. "It's been a year. I should at least be able to talk about her for two seconds without . . ."

"It's okay. I understand." Rae hesitated a moment longer. "I . . . I was wondering," she said carefully. "Could you tell me how your mother died?"

There was silence for a moment, and Rae wondered if Amanda was even still there.

"She was murdered," Amanda finally choked out. Then she hung up.

Chapter 10

"Anthony?"

Anthony whipped his head around. His little sister, Anna, stood in his doorway. As soon as he saw her, she came in and made herself comfortable next to him on the bed. "Can we order pizza?" she asked.

"I didn't say come in," Anthony muttered.

"I didn't knock," Anna answered, giving him her aren't-I-cute smile.

"Leave." Anthony rolled over onto his side so he wouldn't have to look at her. In less than three hours he was going to be robbing a house. He needed to have his game head by then. He needed to be calm and sharp. He couldn't do that dealing with the rug rats.

"But there's nothing to eat," Anna whined. "No one ever goes shopping."

"Fine. Call Domino's Pizza. There's money on my dresser," he answered without turning back toward her.

"What kind should I get?" Anna asked.

"I don't care," Anthony told her, his voice coming out

harsher than he meant it to. "Get what you want and stay out of here, okay?"

"Fine." He heard Anna pawing through the stuff on his dresser, then she left with a door slam.

Give her money for pizza and she gets angry. Great, Anthony thought. He jerked a piece of the comforter over his shoulders. If he really wanted it to cover him, he'd have to get up and climb under it, but he didn't want to move that much. He just wanted to lie there, maybe even fall asleep for a little while. Yeah. That would make his nerves stop twitching. Right now it was like he could feel each of them vibrating in his body. He pushed his head deeper into the pillow and closed his eyes.

The bedroom door opened with a bang. "Anthony, the phone's not working," Anna announced.

"I'm asleep," Anthony mumbled, keeping his body absolutely still.

"He's not asleep," another voice said. Carl. And his gleeful tone made it clear that the three-year-old thought Anthony had just invented a new game. Anthony heard a scuffling sound, then Carl landed on top of him.

"Damn it, Carl." Anthony sat up so fast that he dumped Carl onto the floor. Carl started to cry, those high, gulping sobs that were like ice picks in Anthony's ears. He took a look at his little brother, trying to ignore the sounds coming out of him. No blood. No knots forming on his head. No limbs at strange angles. "You're fine," he said. Carl's wailing went up a notch. "You're fine," Anthony repeated, shouting to be heard over Carl.

"You hurt him," Anna accused, hands on hips.

"I did not," Anthony shot back. "And he shouldn't have jumped on me." He glared down at Carl. "You shouldn't have jumped on me." Carl howled louder. "You want something to cry about, I'll give you something to cry about," Anthony warned.

The words echoed in his head. It was probably something his dad would have said.

I'm like him, Anthony thought. *I really am just like him.* He sprang off the bed. "I'm outta here." Anna stared up at him as he stalked by her, looking like she was going to start bawling next. Not his problem. He rushed over to the couch and snatched up his jacket.

Danny looked up from the TV. "I thought we were getting pizza," he said, unfazed by the stereo crying of Anna and Carl.

There probably wasn't any food in the house, and who knew what time his mother and Tom would come home. Anthony scanned the room for the phone, spotted it halfway under a chair, and pulled it out. It took him about two seconds to realize that somebody had forgotten to pay the bill again. His mother and Tom could never agree on who the somebody was who was supposed to do it, so a lot of the time nobody did.

He grabbed his cell. Dead battery. "No phone," he told Danny.

"Micky D. run!" Danny cried.

"No. I'm going out. Alone," Anthony added before Danny could start begging to come.

"But what are we supposed to eat?" Danny complained.

"Not my problem," Anthony answered, ignoring the twinges of guilt flaring up inside him. He took one step toward the front door. Zack appeared from the hall bathroom.

"I poured a whole bottle of Liquid Plumr down the john, and it's still clogged," he said.

"I told you, you have to use the plunger," Anthony snapped.

"That's gross," Zack answered.

"Yeah, well, it's that or start peeing in the backyard," Anthony said. Zack started to argue, and Danny joined in. Anna and Carl were still crying. "Not my problem," Anthony muttered as he left, slamming the door behind him.

Man, was this how his dad felt when he took off—like if he stayed inside that house one more second, he'd either suffocate or try to kill everyone in sight?

Anthony cut across the lawn, then hesitated. He could go back. He knew how to deal with the kids. He could calm them down, even deal with the food and toilet situation and still have some time to himself before he had to meet up with McGee.

Screw it. They had parents. It wasn't his job. And all he should be thinking about right now was what he had to do tonight.

At least it's not the same hospital I was in, Rae thought as she climbed on the bus. That would be a nightmare. She could just see it. *Hi, I'm the lunatic girl who was here during the summer, and I was wondering if there was a doctor or a nurse who might remember my lunatic mother who was here about sixteen years ago.*

Rae found two empty seats together and took one. *I can't believe I'm doing this,* she thought. For pretty much her whole life, she'd avoided finding out anything about her mother, avoided even thinking about her as much as she possibly could. But now information about her mom could be a life-or-death matter. And since she'd run out of leads on this mysterious "group," the hospital was the only place she could think to try.

As the bus approached the hospital, Rae's blood felt colder and colder, chilling her body instead of warming it. She zipped her jacket all the way up to her chin, even though the bus's heater was blasting out hot, stale air.

The bus stopped and a plump twentyish guy with shaggy brown hair climbed on. There were lots of empty seats, but his eyes immediately locked on the one next to Rae. She sent out a mental message—*Leave me alone.* Either he didn't get it or he ignored it because he plopped down next to her.

"Want one of my cookies?" he asked. He pulled a box of them out of his backpack. "They're chocolate. The only kind worth eating, in my opinion." He tapped one heel against the floor as he ripped open the box and slid out a cookie. He waved it in front of Rae's face.

"No, thanks," she said, making sure there wasn't a trace

of friendliness in her voice.

"You're going to Fair Haven, aren't you?" the cookie guy asked.

"What?" Rae exclaimed, her eyebrows shooting up.

"You have the look. The tense look. I'm going there, too. I'm Paul." He wiggled chocolate-stained fingers at her in a half wave. "My brother's in there. My twin. Identical twin. Not fraternal. So whenever I see him, I keep thinking, when is it gonna happen to me?" Paul grabbed a bunch of cookies and managed to fit most of them in his mouth.

"That has to be pretty scary," Rae said. She didn't want to talk, but God, if she was that guy, she'd be freaking out, too.

You are that guy, said a little voice in her head. *You're afraid of exactly the same thing.*

Rae gave her head a little shake. Paul covered his mouth. "Sorry. This has to be pretty disgusting to look at. I just . . . when I get nervous, I have to eat something." He swallowed and wiped his mouth with the back of his hand. Then he took another bite.

"Does it help?" Rae asked.

Paul laughed. "Not really. And since I know that, you'd think I'd stop doing it, but—" He shrugged. "Who are you going to see?"

"My mom," Rae said. It was the easiest answer. "Look, I don't want to be rude, but could we not talk? I just—"

"It's okay. Don't worry about it. Pretend I'm not even here," Paul answered. He started on another couple of cookies. He ate steadily until the bus pulled up in front of Fair Haven.

"Well, good luck," he told Rae.

"You, too," she said. Impulsively she reached out and touched his sleeve. "You seem—you seem okay. I mean, everyone likes chocolate cookies."

"You seem okay, too," Paul replied. He crossed his fingers, then headed off the bus.

Rae waited until everyone else had exited. The driver gave her a questioning look. She looped her hobo bag over her shoulder and walked purposefully down the narrow aisle and then down the steps. The door wheezed shut behind her. Without allowing a moment's pause, Rae strode to the main entrance, stepped inside, and headed over to the reception desk.

"Hi," she said, her voice coming out shaky. "Hi," she repeated.

"Hi," the nurse behind the desk said, giving her an encouraging smile.

"I have this whole little speech rehearsed," Rae confessed.

The nurse's smile widened. "Well, let's hear it since you've rehearsed."

Rae nodded. "Okay. I'm Rae Voight. My mother, Melissa Voight, was a patient here about sixteen years ago. I have some questions about her, her condition, and I wanted to find out if there is a doctor or nurse working here who might remember her." She took a deep breath. She didn't think she'd breathed during her whole speech.

"All right. That wasn't so hard, was it?" the nurse asked. She started punching keys on the computer. "It might have helped if you'd called first, though."

"I know. I just couldn't wait anymore," Rae answered, listening to the clicking of the computer keys, praying that the name of someone she could talk to would come up.

"It's your lucky day," the nurse said. "We just recently upgraded the computer system here to contain all our files. Here we go." She stopped typing and glanced up from the computer. "Your mother's physician was Dr. Tugend. He's here today, and he's a real sweetheart. I bet he'll make time to talk to you. Have a seat over there." She gestured to a row of plastic chairs. "It might take a while."

"Thanks. Thanks so much." Rae hurried over to the chairs.

A few minutes later a man Rae assumed was her mother's doctor showed up at the desk. He spoke to the nurse while they both kept shooting looks at her. Rae sat up a little straighter and tried to look like someone who would be easy to deal with.

The doctor turned around and walked over to her. "Rae Voight? I'm Doctor Tugend. Why don't we go down to my office."

"Great, thanks," Rae said, almost tripping over the chair as she stood up.

"Have you ever been to Fair Haven before?" Dr. Tugend asked as he led the way to a double-glass door.

"No. I don't think so. I was just a baby when my mom was here. But maybe my dad brought me," Rae answered.

There was a short buzzing sound, and the doctor pushed open the doors. *Just like the prison,* Rae thought wildly.

"Is there any reason you decided to try to find more about her at this time?" he asked after they'd stepped through the doors. *He has eyes like Anthony's,* Rae realized. Like melted Hershey's Kisses.

"I . . . I wasn't going to tell anyone this, but this summer I was in a hospital for a while. I had what my doctor called paranoid delusions. I was wondering if that's what my mom had, and . . ." Rae couldn't get out the rest.

"You're wondering if there are similarities between what happened to you and her case," Dr. Tugend said.

"Yes," Rae admitted, a tiny shiver ripping through her. She was still so cold.

"Makes sense to me. Here we are." He pulled out a key and unlocked one of the doors that ran along both sides of the hallway. "My office. Take a seat."

Rae glanced from the overstuffed sofa to the two armchairs. She chose a chair. To her surprise, Dr. Tugend sat on the sofa instead of sitting behind his desk. "It's been many years, but I remember your mother quite well," he said. He studied Rae for a moment. "You know, the resemblance between you two is quite striking."

Rae tried not to cringe. "Tell me everything," she said, bracing herself for the worst.

"Everything. Hmmm." Dr. Tugend crossed his legs, showing off a pair of psychedelic socks. "Well, I remember how much your mother looked forward to your father's visits. He—"

"Please. I know I said everything. But that's not what

487

I want to know," Rae interrupted. She could tell he was getting ready to sugarcoat what he said. "I—my father said that she was delusional, that she thought she had psychic powers or something." Her father hadn't told her anything like that, but she needed to start steering the conversation. "Is it true?"

Dr. Tugend frowned, his eyebrows coming together in a deep furrow. "Yes, it is," he finally responded. "I suppose your father told you your mother had a hearing to decide whether or not she was fit to stand trial. Her belief that she had the ability to implant thoughts into other people's heads was one of the key facts in the hearing," Dr. Tugend said.

Implant thoughts? Rae struggled to keep her expression blank. "Was it true?" she asked.

Dr. Tugend's eyes widened.

"I don't mean was it true that she could implant thoughts in people's heads," Rae added quickly. "But did she actually believe she could do it? Or did she make it up to stay out of jail?"

"It's my opinion that she believed it wholeheartedly," Dr. Tugend answered.

Because it *was* true. All this time Rae had been wondering if her mother's "insanity" was really some kind of paranormal ability. Her poor mother—she must have been so scared.

Remember what poor Mom did, Rae told herself.

Implanting thoughts. That wasn't so different from reading thoughts.

How many other ways am I like her?

488

"It's a lot to take in, I know," Dr. Tugend said gently. "Let me pull out her file so I can give you more specifics. I'm a pack rat. Most other doctors send files as old as your mother's to storage, but I like to have them here. I never know when an old case will help me with a new one." He stood up and crossed the room to the long row of tall wooden file cabinets. In moments he'd retrieved a thick file. He returned to the sofa with it. "I'm a pack rat, but an organized pack rat."

Rae managed a smile. *Even my teeth feel cold,* she realized.

"Is there another question you have? Or should I just summarize our findings?" Dr. Tugend asked.

"The violence," Rae managed. "How violent was she? Was she dangerous?"

Rae knew the answer, but she'd had to ask the question, anyway.

Dr. Tugend didn't reply at first. His left eye twitched slightly. "Rae, I want you to know that there isn't any reason for you to assume that what happened to your mother will happen to you," he said. "I don't know the details of your case, but I'm sure your doctor was made aware of your family history and would have talked to your father—"

"I know, I know," Rae told him. "But could you please just tell me?"

Dr. Tugend looked at her for a long moment. "Your mother was placed in a ward with the highest level of security. That is because we believed she could be a danger to herself or others." He flipped through a few pages of the file. "There weren't any violent incidents during her time with us, but we had to accept that they were possible at any time."

Rae bit the inside of her cheek. The little spot of pain helped her keep a grip on herself. "Those were two of my big questions," she said. "The other one is about how she died. My dad said her body just . . . just started to deteriorate."

Dr. Tugend scrubbed his face with his fingertips. "Even now, with all the advances in medicine over the past decade and a half, I can't explain it. The symptoms were similar to some viruses we've seen, but no evidence of a virus was found. The disease progressed so quickly that we had almost no time to determine the cause. Even afterward . . ." He shook his head. "I'm sorry not to be able to tell you more."

"No, you've been great. Really," Rae answered. Should she try to shake his hand? See if he was holding back? He didn't seem to be, and she'd started thinking making fingertip-to-fingertip contact had something to do with her numb spots.

"What else can I tell you?" Dr. Tugend asked.

"Could you tell me more about the delusions? Or did she ever mention anything about a group she was in? I—"

Dr. Tugend's pager went off. He glanced at it. "I have to go, but I shouldn't be long. Would you like to wait for me?"

"I don't want to take up too much time, but there are—"

"Don't worry about it. If for some reason I can't get back as fast as I think I'll be able to, I'll send someone to tell you." With a grunt he shoved himself up from the deep cushions of the sofa and left the office.

As soon as he'd left, Rae's eyes went right to her mom's file, which he'd left sitting on his desk. Rae didn't need an invitation. She jumped out of her chair and snatched up the file.

/ poor girl / that woman was / buy coffee /

She flipped it open and started skimming. Lots of stuff about medications. Observation notes that seemed to say that her mother basically just sat and stared at nothing except during visits. Rae turned the page.

/ repulsive /

Rae felt her lips twist into a sneer, as if she was the one feeling repulsed. *It had to be one of the nurses or doctors making observations,* she thought. It wasn't Dr. Tugend. She'd gotten his flavor from the cover of the file, and this was different. Rae turned the page again and ran her fingers over each line as if she were reading Braille.

/ *what she did* / can't stand to touch her / belongs in prison /

Rae's teeth began to chatter as she felt the fear and hatred that had been directed at her mother. Her mother.

This isn't news, she told herself. *You've always known what she was. You've never had the kind of fantasies about her that Dad does.*

Rae turned to the next page, using her fingernails. She wanted as much information as possible, but she didn't have to get slammed with all of the thoughts. More lists of medications. Notations of blood pressure. Of urine output. Of fluid intake.

Next page. More of the same. Except descriptions of sores—much too extreme to be bedsores, one notation said. Rae kept reading. It sounded like her mother's body had been devoured from the inside.

Next page. Rae flicked her eyes down the notations as quickly as possible. *There isn't going to be anything that will help you in here,* she thought. *The doctor said they never figured out what was happening to her. That means you're not going to find any miracle cure.*

But she couldn't stop flipping the pages, reading snatches here and there. Descriptions of sores in her mother's mouth and nose. Next page. No notations. Nothing about medications or diet or activity level. This page was a clipping from a newspaper.

She read the headline, and the air went out of her lungs as if two fists had squeezed them flat. She slowly sat down on the floor and began to read, to read every single word.

With each sentence she got colder. Her heart and stomach felt like lumps of ice, heavy and lifeless. And cold. So cold.

You knew this is what happened. You knew what she did. Dad told you. This is nothing new.

But it was. Because there were pictures. And details her father never would have wanted her to know.

"Okay, let's do this," McGee said as he backed the van into the driveway of the large house they'd been staking out. "I'll use the code to get inside, then I'll open the garage."

Anthony gave a grunt of acknowledgment. Kolsen and Buchanan nodded. *Are those two guys half as wired as I am?* Anthony wondered. They didn't seem to be. And McGee. The guy was like an android. Anthony ran his hands over his shirt to wipe off the excess sweat and peered out the window as McGee strolled up to the front door. He'd bought one of those picks over the Internet that could open any door. They were supposed to be for people who got locked out of their houses. Yeah, right.

The pick was worth whatever McGee paid for it. He was inside the house in under ten seconds. Anthony's breath hitched in his chest. If McGee had the wrong code—if he punched in the numbers wrong—

McGee's hand appeared from inside the doorway and gave a little wave. Anthony was able to breathe again. *We're just going to be in and out,* he told himself. *Think of it as a moving job. Load the van and leave before anybody gets home.*

The garage door opened in a smooth motion. Kolsen backed the van inside and parked it right next to a bright red '68 Mustang convertible. "Midlife crisis car," Buchanan joked. Anthony couldn't manage to squeeze out a laugh. He climbed out of the van, feeling a little calmer as the garage door slowly lowered behind them.

"Okay, like we said, Anthony goes for the big stuff. He's got the muscles." McGee looked at Anthony. "All the major electronics. Don't forget the kitchen. With this house, they probably have an espresso machine."

"Got it," Anthony said. He figured it was best to talk as little as possible. He just didn't trust the way his voice would come out of his mouth. He could end up squeaking like Mickey Mouse.

"Kolsen, you're looking for the small stuff," McGee continued. "Stuff they think they've gotten really smart and hidden. Check inside Tampax boxes. Inside the freezer. Inside canisters in the kitchen. Any small place someone could stash cash or jewelry."

How many times has he done this before? Anthony wondered.

"Buchanan, you've been bragging about you've been practicing opening safes. Now's the chance to prove it," McGee said.

"And what are you going to be doing?" Kolsen asked.

"Supervising and troubleshooting," McGee answered, getting right in Kolsen's face. "You have a problem with that?"

"Nope. No problem, boss," Kolsen said quickly.

"Okay, let's do it." McGee led the way through the garage door and into the house.

It even smells rich, Anthony thought. *Extra clean.* He found the living room without too much problem and went right for the Aperion minitower speakers. He crouched down, unhooked one of them, and hoisted it. He'd only taken three steps when he heard McGee's voice ring out in the silent house.

"Car in the driveway."

Anthony dropped the speaker and bolted toward the sound of McGee's voice. He found him in the kitchen. Buchanan and Kolsen were already there.

"Let's just get the hell out of here," Buchanan said. He ran for the garage door.

"He's right," McGee said. He, Kolsen, and Anthony took off after Buchanan. They flew down the hall and through the open door leading to the garage.

Anthony froze when he saw that the big garage door was up. A middle-aged guy was standing just outside it, holding a remote in his hand.

Before Anthony had finished processing the situation, McGee was on the guy. He tackled him and dragged him a few feet into the garage. "The door," McGee barked.

A jolt went through Anthony's body at the command. He spun around and pushed the button that would lower the door again. It started down. The thing moved like it was snail powered.

McGee crouched on top of the man, one hand pressed over the man's mouth, one covering his eyes. "I need rope or duct tape or something," he commanded.

Again Anthony moved without thinking. He grabbed a roll of duct tape off the Peg-Board over the workbench. Kolsen tossed McGee some clothesline.

And it was as if Anthony had left his body. It was his hands covering the man's mouth with the duct tape. It was his knee pinning the man to the ground. But it was like the rest of him was floating somewhere around the ceiling.

"Now get him in the house," McGee ordered.

495

Anthony's hands grabbed the man by the shoulders. Buchanan got the man's feet. They lugged him into the kitchen and set him on the floor. McGee pointed at Kolsen. "You watch him. Don't talk." He turned to Anthony and Buchanan. "You two come with me."

"What are we going to do?" Buchanan burst out as soon as they were out of hearing range.

"The guy saw us. There's only one thing we can do," McGee answered.

Anthony knew what McGee was going to say. It was what Anthony's father would say.

"We're going to have to kill him," McGee told them.

Chapter 11

R ae shot up in bed at the loud noise outside, her heart pounding. She'd been drifting asleep while trying to read, but the sound of someone outside had jolted her awake. She sat still, listening. She could hear rustling through the bushes outside her window.

Rae held her breath, wondering what she should do. The rustling sound grew louder. *It's probably just the cat again,* she thought. It had scared her more because she'd been half asleep. Trying to read *The Scarlet Letter* when all she could think about was the details of that horrible article she'd seen earlier wasn't working too well, so she hadn't tried to fight it when the drowsiness began to overcome her.

But she was wide awake now and terrified. At least that was one thing she could do something about. With a sigh Rae tossed her book aside and got up from her bed, then hurried over to the window. She pulled back the drapes—and gasped. Someone was staring back at her.

It took her a moment to realize it was Jesse. She jerked open the window. "What's going on?" she hissed.

Jesse was breathing so hard, he couldn't answer at first.

"Anthony's in trouble," he finally managed to get out between pants.

"Wait right there. I'm coming out," Rae told him. She shut the drapes again, jerked on her boots, grabbed her jacket, and left her room.

What about Dad? she realized. She couldn't let him know what was going on. She slowed down, stepping carefully and quietly down the hall. She paused by his door, but the light was out. He was probably still in his study, working. How was she going to get out of here?

She'd just have to figure it out. She moved slowly down the hall. Every second longer it took to find out what had happened to Anthony made her want to scream, but she had to do this right. She let out her breath in relief when she spotted her dad in the living room. He was out cold on the couch, snoring away, his textbook on the floor next to him.

Quickly Rae rushed outside, relieved to see Jesse waiting for her on the front porch.

"Anthony and these other guys were robbing a house tonight," he burst out before she had a chance to say anything.

"What?" Rae exclaimed. She grabbed Jesse by the arms.

"They've been planning it for a couple of days. I knew it was happening tonight, so I went over there. I saw a car in the driveway—and the guys were driving a van." Jesse pulled in a deep, shuddering breath. "I think maybe the owner might have caught them. Because he wasn't supposed to be home that early. I went up to the garage—it has three little windows in the front—and looked inside. The guys' van is in there. I don't know if the owner called the cops or if they're holding him or what."

"We've got to get over there," Rae said. She didn't know what they'd do when they arrived, but she needed to be at that house. With the mood Anthony was in, he could do something really stupid. Or worse. Something that could ruin his whole life. And it would be her fault. Because whether Anthony knew it or not, this was all about his dad. "Is it far?" she demanded, squeezing Jesse's arms tighter.

"About five miles," Jesse answered, pulling free of her grip. "I was on my bike, but I got a flat about half a mile from here. I ran the rest of the way."

"I'll get my dad's car keys," Rae said. She darted back in the house and snatched the keys off the hall table. The last thing she wanted to think about right now was her father. He'd kill her if he knew she was going to take his car. She'd only had a couple of driver's ed classes, and those hadn't gone incredibly well.

Five miles is nothing. I can do it, she thought as she rushed back outside and over to her dad's Chevette. She scrambled inside, and Jesse grabbed the shotgun seat. "Where?" she asked as she shoved the key in the ignition.

"Go out to Blackburn Road and turn right," Jesse answered.

Rae gunned the engine, wincing at the loud sound. Hopefully her dad wouldn't hear. He was a snorer. She pressed down on the gas—and the car didn't move. "What the hell is wrong with this thing?" She floored the gas, and the engine whined.

"It's in park," Jesse yelled at her. "What is your problem?"

Rae put her foot on the brake. "I'm just nervous, okay?" She jerked the car into drive.

"Don't put on the gas!" Jesse cried. "We'll go crashing through the garage." He pushed her hand away and put the car in reverse. "All right. Now it's okay." He spoke softly, the way you'd talk to a dog that looked rabid.

"Okay, backing out," Rae whispered. She took her foot off the brake and gave the gas a tap. The car jerked back a foot. She gave the gas a harder tap. The car lurched down to the sidewalk. One more tap and they were in the street.

"You should turn the wheel," Jesse said, in the same calm voice.

"Oh! Right!" Rae turned the wheel and managed to get the car heading down the street without scraping any of the parked cars. "Okay, doing good," she muttered to herself. She thought she heard Jesse give a muffled snort, but she didn't look at him. She didn't even want to blink right now. She needed all her attention on the road.

Once she'd maneuvered them onto Blackburn Road, she had a couple of other cars to contend with. "They're going too fast. Aren't they?"

Jesse buckled his seat belt. "They're going the speed limit. You should, too, if you don't want to get rear-ended."

She jammed her foot down on the gas.

"Whoa!" Jesse shouted. "Whoa," he repeated more softly as she pulled her foot off the gas completely. "Just somewhere between those two speeds," he instructed. "Actually maybe we should take Margot. Main streets aren't the best idea for you. You're going to get pulled over any second, and—"

"Shut up, please," Rae begged.

"I just want to get us there," Jesse said.

"Me, too. Me, too," Rae answered. *Just hold on, Anthony,* she thought. *And don't do anything to make the situation worse than it already is.*

"This isn't a democracy, Fascinelli," McGee said. "I've listened to you go on and on about how killing the guy isn't the smart thing to do—but it's my decision."

The more I say, the more he digs in, Anthony thought. *What am I gonna do?* He'd been stalling McGee for a while now, but it couldn't last much longer. He turned to Buchanan. He wished he could remember the guy's first name, but it wouldn't come to him. "So you're okay with McGee offing the guy? That makes you an accessory to murder."

Buchanan's gray eyes were blank. He was in lockdown mode. Anthony wondered if Buchanan could even hear what Anthony'd just said.

"The guy saw us. Buchanan knows there's no option," McGee answered.

"And Kolsen? He doesn't get a vote?" Anthony shot back.

He'd already tried this argument once, but he had to keep talking until he had some kind of a plan to stop McGee. Maybe he could say he had to use the john and then call the cops. Yeah, he'd get caught, too, but no one was going to die tonight. He wasn't letting that happen.

If I can't figure out another way, that's my backup, Anthony decided. He'd definitely end up in—Anthony didn't let himself complete the thought. If he had to turn them all in, then he'd do it. No matter what happened to any of them.

"Buchanan, go get Kolsen, and you watch the guy for a while. Make sure his blindfold's still on," McGee ordered.

Anthony felt a tiny spark of hope. If McGee was worried about the blindfold, maybe he wasn't as sure as he sounded that he had to kill the guy.

"Has the guy been trying to get loose?" McGee asked when Kolsen came into the living room.

"No. He knows somebody's there," Kolsen answered. "He's being a very good boy." Anthony noticed the deep circles of sweat staining Kolsen's shirt under his arms.

I'm not the only one who sweats when I'm nervous. He's trying to look all cool, but he's as freaked out as I am, Anthony thought.

"So, Kolsen, McGee thinks our only way out of this is to kill the guy," Anthony said. "What—"

A loud knock on the door interrupted him.

"Who the hell is that?" McGee asked.

"If we don't answer, they'll probably leave," Anthony

answered. The last thing this situation needed was more people.

"Unless it's the cops," Kolsen said, rubbing his hands on the sides of his jeans.

The knock came again. Insistent.

"Kolsen, try and get a look at whoever it is without them seeing you," McGee said. Kolsen nodded and headed toward the front of the house.

McGee and Anthony stared at each other. Anthony didn't say anything. He could see the tension in McGee's body. The muscles in his neck were standing out, and his jaw looked locked into place. Anthony's gut told him if he said the wrong thing right now, McGee could totally lose it.

Kolsen rushed back into the living room. "It's that kid, that redheaded kid."

"Jesse Beven?" McGee asked.

No, Anthony thought. *No, Jesse, you didn't.*

"Yeah, that's him," Kolsen answered. "And he has some girl with him."

Anthony felt like acid was pumping through his veins instead of blood. Rae. Now he had to worry about getting them out alive, too.

"The girl—she have long curly hair, blue eyes?" Anthony asked.

"Couldn't see the eyes, but yeah, her hair's like that," Kolsen said.

"Crap," Anthony burst out. "It's my girlfriend." He figured

503

that might do a slight bit of damage control.

"You told her about tonight?" McGee demanded.

"Whipped," Kolsen muttered.

Another knock came on the door.

"Let them in," McGee said. "They're causing way too much attention out there."

"I could send them home," Anthony volunteered.

"No," McGee shot back. "I don't want anyone who knows anything about what's going on out of my sight. Bring them in. Kolsen, you go with him."

Kolsen led the way to the front door. Anthony jerked it open.

Rae took an involuntary step back when she saw the expression on Anthony's face. He looked ready to strangle her. Instead he reached out and took her hand, sliding his fingertips until they were right over hers.

Rae realized he had something to tell her that he couldn't say aloud. She put all her energy into catching the thoughts and feelings pouring into her from him.

McGee has a gun. Going to kill owner. Those two thoughts repeated over and over, clear and strong. Underneath was anger at Rae and Jesse. Fear for all of them. Thoughts about his family. Scraps of memories about his father. The sensation of duct tape pulling off a roll. But the other two thoughts—*McGee has a gun. Going to kill owner*—dominated all the rest.

Rae looked up at Anthony and nodded. Message received.

He instantly released her hand. "Just because you're my girlfriend, it doesn't give you the right to come barging over here," he snapped.

"I was worried about you," Rae answered. It was the truth, and it sounded girlfriendlike, which was clearly what Anthony wanted.

"We're bringing you two into the living room, and you're not moving from there," the guy with Anthony—blond and scrawny—said. He locked the door behind them, then led the way to the living room. Another guy waited there.

He's McGee, Rae thought. She couldn't be sure, but he looked like the guy in charge.

"What in the hell are you doing here, Beven? And why did you bring her along?" McGee asked.

"I came by—we did—because I—we—just wanted to make sure everything, you know, went okay," Jesse stammered. "We saw the guy's car in the driveway, and we figured there might be trouble, that you might need backup. So we came."

"And what did you two think you were going to be able to do?" McGee demanded.

"Yeah, what were you going to do?" the scrawny blond guy asked.

"Shut up, Kolsen," McGee ordered.

Rae glanced at Anthony. His face was blank. *He doesn't have a plan yet,* she thought. *If he had, he would have gotten that in when we touched fingerprints.*

"Tell us what happened, and maybe we can help," Rae said.

"Oh, the little girl thinks she can help," McGee answered.

"Well, we got caught. And we have the guy tied up. You want to go into the kitchen and kill him for us? Because that's the only way we're getting out of here without landing in prison. No matter what your boyfriend thinks."

"Hey, I found some brews in the fridge," a guy with scruffy brown hair announced as he headed into the room.

"Buchanan, you moron, you left the guy alone?" McGee asked.

"He's not going anywhere," Buchanan answered. "We have him taped so tight, it would take him hours to break free." He took a beer and held the six-pack out to Kolsen, who grabbed a can, popped the top, and drained it in record time.

"Put that down," McGee ordered Buchanan as he was about to take the first gulp. "We start drinking, and we're going to screw up." Buchanan obediently put his beer on the coffee table. Kolsen set his empty can beside it, avoiding looking at McGee.

Time to get some info, Rae thought. She sat down on the couch and casually moved Kolsen's can away from the edge of the table.

/so screwed/wanted some easy cash/McGee's crazy/pictures of grandkids on fridge/

Not the thoughts of a trigger-happy idiot. *Good,* Rae thought.

"Who is this guy, anyway?" she asked. "This place looks like it could belong to some old grandma and grandpa. Check out the goofy golf trophy on the mantel."

"I think he does have grandkids," Kolsen said. "I saw some pictures on the fridge."

"Me, too," Buchanan added.

Rae ran her fingers around Buchanan's can.

/get me outta here/Dad's going to kill me/supposed to be in and out/in and out/and now guns/gotta get out/

So, okay, they weren't dealing with wanna-be gangsters here. Kolsen and Buchanan were just looking for a way out.

If I can give them an alternate to McGee's plan, they'll leap at it. Rae's hand tightened on the beer can, denting it. *But what is your plan B, Rae?* she asked herself.

"The longer we stay here, the more dangerous it is." McGee pulled a gun free from the back waistband of his jeans. Rae knew he had it, but the sight of it made her dizzy. "I'm taking care of this right now. We'll need to put some trash bags or something down to get most of the blood, and we'll need to wipe down everything we could have possibly touched. Then we gotta figure out where we can dump him. Maybe we can take his car and leave it at some dive bar or something."

He has this way too planned out. It could happen any second, Rae thought. "Are you even sure the guy saw you?" she burst out. "I mean, it was dark, right?"

"And you took him down really fast," Anthony told McGee.

Kolsen sat down on the couch next to Rae. It was as if suddenly he'd realized he no longer had the strength to stand. "Anthony's right. He might not have seen us. We could just lea—"

"Maybe he can ID us, maybe he can't," McGee answered. "But since we have no way of knowing, we have to assume that he did."

"There is a way of being sure," Rae said.

"Like what?" McGee challenged.

"I. . . . I was kind of messed up this summer. I had to stay in this mental hospital, and my therapist taught me how to hypnotize myself as part of my treatment. It helped me remember stuff I didn't even know I knew." Rae took a deep breath, thinking frantically. "I can do it to other people, too. I could hypnotize the guy, find out what he knows."

It was a ridiculous suggestion. But of the five other people in the room, four were looking to get out of there without any violence.

"Rae hypnotized me once," Anthony volunteered. "She made me remember how I used to suck two of my fingers when I was a little kid. I'd make this sound when I did it, too—kind of a goi-ng goi-ng."

Rae flashed Anthony an approving glance. He'd been right to go with something embarrassing. It made it seem more likely to be true.

"You really think you could do it?" Buchanan asked eagerly.

"Yeah," Rae answered. "And if Grandpa didn't see anything, why not leave him be?"

"Yeah," Kolsen agreed.

Rae looked at McGee. He met her gaze directly, staring at her as if he could read her soul through her eyes. Finally he nodded, then he stuck his gun back in his waistband. "You can try it. I'll give you fifteen minutes. That's it."

"Okay. Anthony, you want to help me?" Rae asked as she stood up.

"Yeah," Anthony said at once, moving to her side.

"I'm coming, too," McGee stated.

"You can't," Rae said. "You can't because if there are too many distractions, he's not going to feel comfortable going under."

"I won't say anything," McGee answered, eyes narrowing in suspicion.

"It doesn't matter. He'll be able to sense the presence of too many people in the room. I'm sure he's already completely terrified. It's going to be hard enough to get him to enter the hypnotic state as it is."

Rae didn't know where all this bull was coming from, but she was glad it kept spilling out of her mouth.

McGee gave a reluctant nod. "Kolsen, go get the phone out of the kitchen." Kolsen jumped to his feet and left the room. He turned to Rae. "You leave your purse in here. You leave your cell, Fascinelli. And we'll keep an eye on Jesse for the two of you, in case you decide to leave."

"We're not going to leave," Rae answered, speaking directly to Jesse.

Kolsen came back with the phone. "Okay, go ahead. But I'm timing you," McGee told Rae and Anthony.

Anthony wrapped his arm around Rae's shoulders, the heavy weight warm and comforting, and led her out of the living room and down the hallway. "I cannot believe you're here. You are an even bigger idiot than I thought," he whispered. But he didn't drop his arm.

"You're the idiot," Rae whispered back. "I wouldn't be here if you weren't here first." But she didn't pull away. Anthony shoved open a swinging door and guided her into the room. Her eyes went immediately to the man strapped into a chair with duct tape and clothesline. He was blindfolded and gagged. He looked dead already.

Rae's stomach began to heave, and her mouth went dry. She closed her eyes and concentrated on not throwing up. After a moment the sensation subsided, and she was able to open her eyes again. She stepped away from Anthony and moved up next to the man. "I'll see what he knows," she said softly. She reached for his hand and touched his fingertips.

The amount of fear she was already feeling tripled as she took in the man's. He was sure he was going to die.

"It's—it's going to be okay," she nearly whispered, feeling like she had to give him some kind of reassurance. "I'll get you out of this alive. I promise."

Forming the words was a struggle as she tried to speak through everything that was pushing from his mind into hers. All kinds of memories swirled around while he tried to picture his wife's smile. Remember what their baby girl smelled like when he first held her. She caught a fantasy of revenge, where the man broke free like Superman and annihilated the people who had done this to him.

"Garage," Rae said quietly. "Guys."

The man remembered a garage door opening. Figures inside. A flash of blue rushing toward him. Then the pain of his head hitting the cement. A sweaty hand on his eyes. Over his mouth. Hard to breathe. What? Who?

Rae released his fingers. "Well?" Anthony asked, voice tight with strain.

She opened her mouth to answer, but her throat was too dry. She stumbled over to the sink and took a long drink directly from the faucet, then turned to Anthony. "He doesn't remember anything important. He can't call up a face or even a build on any of you guys."

"Let's go tell them," Anthony said.

It felt like years later that Anthony pulled Rae's father's Chevette into the driveway. Convincing McGee that the owner of the house couldn't ID them wasn't nearly as hard as Rae feared it would be, especially with Kolsen, Buchanan, and Anthony urging him that the best thing to do was wipe down everything they could have touched and just get the hell out of there.

The cleanup had taken longer. Then she and Anthony had picked up Jesse's bike and gotten him back home. Finally they'd made an anonymous call to the cops, telling them that they thought a robbery was in progress. They figured the cops would find the owner of the house and free him.

"You must be wrecked," Anthony said, staring straight

ahead even though the car was parked. She knew he was telling her to get her butt inside and leave him alone. But she wasn't ready to do that.

"Anthony, I wanted to say—I need to say how sorry I am that I went looking for your father without asking you if that was even what you wanted," Rae told him.

"Look, it's late. I have to find a bus and get home." Anthony raked his fingers through his hair, pushing it off his forehead. "There's no point in talking about this. You did it. You're sorry. What else is there to say?"

"What else is there to say?" Rae repeated. "How about that you almost screwed up your whole life because of what I told you? Is this going to be a regular thing with you or what?"

"You're pissed off at *me*?" Anthony asked, his eyebrows shooting up in surprise.

"Yeah, I'm pissed off at you," Rae shot back. Now that he was safe, she was getting angrier by the second. "I know what I did was wrong. I know it had to hurt like hell to find out the truth about your father. But that's no excuse—"

"You have no idea what you're talking about," Anthony said, whipping his head toward her. "What's the worst thing your dad ever did—got a parking ticket? Or, ooh, had to pay an overdue fine at the library? I'm the kid of a *murderer.*" He opened the car door and started to climb out. Rae pulled him back, using both hands.

"So am I," she told him.

His eyes locked on hers. "So are you what?"

"You don't know everything about me, okay?" Rae hardly

512

recognized the sound of her own voice. "You're not the only one who has to live with being the kid of a killer." She let go of his arm, but he didn't move.

"What are you talking about?" he demanded, his jaw tight.

Rae shut her eyes, then opened them again. "Anthony, my mom—my mom killed someone. Shot her right in the fore-head. Close range." Tears filled Rae's eyes, and she roughly wiped them away with the back of her hands.

Slowly Anthony sank back into the car next to her. He leaned his head back against the seat, then turned to face her again. "And you've known this—" Anthony began.

"Since I was about twelve," Rae answered, looking at him out of the corner of her eye. "Not all of it. But that she killed someone. My dad always said it was an accident. And mom died in a mental hospital a few months after it happened, so it's not like she was around to tell me any different." Rae stopped as the words from the article she'd seen today flashed through her brain. "But I found out more," she said, her voice catching. She turned to meet his gaze, swallowing hard. "Anthony, it was her best friend. Not just some random stranger like with your dad. She killed her *best friend.*"

"Rae . . ." Anthony's voice was so soft, softer than she'd ever heard him speak.

She took in a deep breath. "I just—I wanted you to know that I understand how you feel," she said, trying to keep her voice even. "I do. And I hate that I'm the one who told you about your dad. I should have lied. I shouldn't have looked for him in the first place, but after I found out the truth, I should have lied."

Anthony shook his head. "You knew how much I wanted to find him. It's not like you had to ask to know that," he said. Rae struggled to read his expression in the dark car, but she couldn't see enough to know what he was feeling.

"Yeah, but I also knew how you'd feel when I told you about him," Rae argued. "Now you're thinking you're going to turn out like him."

"You can't keep telling me how I feel," Anthony protested.

"That's crap. It's exactly how you feel," Rae said. "If it wasn't, you wouldn't have ended up in that house tonight. You wouldn't be blowing off your chance to get into Sanderson." Rae squeezed her hands together so tightly, the bones ached. "I'm afraid, too. I'm afraid I'm becoming more like her every day. But I don't go and seek it out. I try. I try to hold it back."

Anthony reached out awkwardly and covered her hands with one of his own. The warmth of his touch shot through her whole body. "You could never do anything like your mother did," he told her. "You can't seriously think you could kill someone. You just saved someone's life tonight, remember?"

"You'd have found a way to do it if I hadn't," Rae answered. "You were already working on it. The way you feel about me and my mom—that's how I feel about you and your dad."

They looked at each other for a long moment, and the air in the car felt charged, the way it was outside right before a storm. Finally Anthony glanced away.

"Um, I guess there's one other thing I should tell you," Rae said. "Since I know you hate it when I—"

"What?" Anthony cut in.

"Someone's been sending me pictures of Erika Keaton," she admitted. "Erika's the woman my mom, you know." A shudder went through Rae. "I never knew the details—I mean, I didn't know who it was, what her name was. But I found this article about what happened, and now I know. . . . Anyway, whoever's out there even sent me some of her ashes and called my house asking for her. So maybe that's why all this stuff has been happening—the pipe bomb, Jesse's kidnapping. Someone wants revenge."

Anthony tilted back his head and let out a long sigh. "You're right." He glanced at her, not quite meeting her eye. "But until it's over, you've got me at your back." He climbed out of the car, and this time Rae didn't try to stop him. She got out, too, and closed the door with a soft click.

"Thanks," she said as he started heading toward the street. He stopped, turning back to face her. "I mean, for covering my back," she added.

Anthony nodded. "Well, you got mine tonight. It's only fair." He stood there a second, staring at her. She stared back, not making a move toward her house. Then he was striding toward her, and a moment later his arms were around her, holding her tightly against him. Rae wrapped her arms around his back.

Let me stay like this forever, she thought. She could feel

Anthony's heart beating against her chest, almost like it was her own. She pulled him even closer, burrowing her face into his shoulder.

That was when she realized that her neck had a numb spot on it the size of a child's fist. *It's from holding on so tight,* she told herself. But even the security of Anthony's arms couldn't keep the next thought from coming.

Or I'm dying. Like my mother.

Epilogue

R ae Voight has finally discovered the truth about her mother. That knowledge is like a sweet taste in my mouth, a taste I want to savor. If only I could kill her right now, right this second—but someone else has been watching my Rae. And if I kill her now, the way I'm burning to do, I may never find out who it is. That could be dangerous for me. It's clear that, like me, this person wants Rae dead. But Rae and I are connected, in one of the deepest ways possible. And if that connection has something to do with why this other person is after Rae, then I could be the next target.

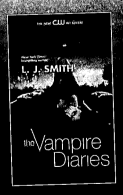
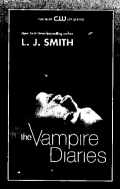
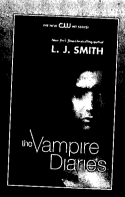